Why was everyone so convinced that she wasn't human?

"But why would they bother stopping anyone getting access to my files? I'm not so special."

"Aren't you?" He leaned back in the chair, and studied her for a moment. "You sensed the kites. You sensed the fact that Jack's clone was a vampire. And despite the psychic deadeners we have in place, you knew the shifter was in here."

The intensity of his gaze cut right through her, stirring something deep in her soul. Suddenly uneasy, she cleared her throat, and looked back at the screen. "I was tested for psychic ability when I entered the academy. I came up with a big fat zero."

"Most talents come on with full maturity."

She shot him a quick look. His gaze was calculating, thoughtful. *He knows.* That's what the second set of biological tests had been about. They'd obviously discovered what she'd known since she was fifteen. That she'd never fully mature as a woman. Never have children of her own. Not unless she had a complete uterus and ovary transplant. And even then, the children would never *really* be hers.

"You obviously know that can't be the case here. I'm twenty-nine. A little past puberty, I think."

He shrugged. "Shapechangers tend to mature a lot later than humans. My two sisters were well into their thirties before they actually started menstruating."

That was really a little more info than she needed about his sisters. "But I'm human, not a shapechanger."

"But maybe that unknown chromosome we found has delayed your development in much the same manner."

She shook her head. "They ran all manner of tests on me when I was fifteen. They all came up with the same answer. This was it, this was all I was going to get."

He raised an eyebrow. "You resent it, don't you?"

She snorted softly. Of course she resented it. Having a family of her own had been the one dream she could remember clearly through the fog that was her childhood. "You don't know how lucky you are, having sisters and a family. I have nothing. Not even memories."

Memory Zero

***

Keri Arthur

ImaJinn Books

Memory Zero
Published by ImaJinn Books, a division of ImaJinn

ISBN: 1-893896-35-8

10 9 8 7 6 5 4 3 2 1

PUBLISHER'S NOTE:
This book is a work of fiction. Names, characters, places and incidents are products
of the author's imagination or are used fictitiously. Any resemblance to actual events
or locales or persons, living or dead, is entirely coincidental.

Books are available at quantity discounts when used to promote products or services.
For information please write to: Marketing Division, ImaJinn Books, P.O. Box 545,
Canon City, CO 81215-0545, or call toll free 1-877-625-3592.

Cover design by Patricia Lazarus

ImaJinn Books, a division of ImaJinn
P.O. Box 545, Canon City, CO 81215-0545
Toll Free: 1-877-625-3592
http://www.imajinnbooks.com

One

It was the type of night only the dead could enjoy—as dark as hell, and as warm as the Antarctic. Add to that the bonus of rain that bucketed down, and it was no wonder the streets were deserted.

Well, almost deserted, Sam amended, glancing at the alleyway across the street. An old man in a threadbare coat rummaged through the garbage bins that were lined up behind the Chinese restaurant, filling a plastic bag with God-knows what. And not five minutes ago, two prostitutes had come knocking on her car's window, their faces almost blue with cold as they'd tried to convince her to take them for a ride. Their expressions, when she'd flashed her badge, were almost relieved. But then, a warm cell block was certainly more enticing than trying to ply their trade on a night like this. Had she not been waiting for her partner to turn up, she might have taken them downtown and charged them with soliciting, just to get them off the street and warm again. Prostitution might be legal these days, but it was restricted to certain areas, and this particular street in old Footscray wasn't one of them.

But she'd had no choice except to let them go with a warning. To say they weren't happy with this stroke of fortune was an understatement. Obviously, they'd been looking forward to being locked up in a warm cell and cuddling up with a blanket or two. And right now, she knew exactly how they felt. Even a cup of the shocking coffee they served at the station house would be heaven right now.

She glanced down at the onboard computer and noted it was already after three. If her goddamn partner didn't turn up soon, she was heading home. Why the hell he'd insisted on meeting in this ratty section of the city in the first place was beyond her. It wasn't even close to their patrol zone.

Sighing, she crossed her arms, and glanced out the car's side window again. A plastic bag tumbled down the road, ghostlike in the darkness. Unease pricked across her skin, though she wasn't sure why. Maybe it was just nerves. After all, it wasn't every night she got an urgent call from a man who'd been missing for weeks. And it certainly wasn't every night she went against department policy and agreed to a secret meeting.

She glanced back to the alley. The old man had disappeared.

6

Keri Arthur

While she knew he'd probably just moved beyond her line of sight, that vague sense of unease increased. She stared through the rain-washed darkness, watching for some form of movement that would indicate the old man was still there.

Nothing.

And instinct was insisting something was very wrong in that alley.

She rubbed a hand across her eyes and silently cursed her partner's tardiness. She didn't need this, not after a fifteen-hour shift, and especially not in a patrol zone that wasn't hers. Just thinking about the extra paperwork made her head ache.

Still . . .

She leaned forward and pressed the locater switch. The onboard computer hummed to life, producing a map of the immediate vicinity. The only way out of the alley, besides the entrance she could see, was via a fire escape on the building that hosted the Chinese restaurant. She stabbed a finger at the screen, and the computer immediately listed other occupants. The top two floors were empty, but the second floor was rented to an R. C. Clarke.

She frowned again. The name rang a bell, though she didn't know why. She pressed the screen a second time, but the computer had no additional information. For several seconds, she blindly watched the rain race down the glass. It was very wet out there. But the sooner she got out and investigated, the sooner she could get back to the relative warmth of this icebox they had the cheek to call a squad car.

With a slight grimace, she opened the glove compartment and retrieved her wristcom. In reality, it wasn't just a communications unit, more a two-inch wide minicomputer capable of doing just about everything but make coffee. She wasn't supposed to be using it after hours, but there was no way she going into that alley without it. Not when unease sat like a lead weight in her belly. If things went wrong, she wanted an electronic record of everything that happened.

After fastening the unit onto her wrist, she flicked the record button, checked that it was working, then collected her gun and climbed out of the car. As the door automatically locked behind her, she zipped up her jacket and eyed the dark alley. It was quite possible that this was some sort of setup. In the last few weeks, five detectives had disappeared, one of them Jack, her partner. And while he'd finally contacted her earlier this evening, it was extremely odd that he'd called neither headquarters nor Suzy, his wife. She knew, because she'd checked.

It worried her.

And it was what held her still, even as the drenching rain sluiced off her coat and soaked through her boots. Jack loved Suzy more than life itself, and there was no way he'd contact her before he contacted his wife.

The wind lifted her hair and wrapped icy fingers around her neck. She shivered, but it had nothing to do with the cold. Suddenly, the night felt very wrong.

Which was crazy. It was probably just the cold, the rain, and her severe need for sleep. If Jack hadn't made an appearance by the time she checked the alley, she was going home. She didn't need to be involved in another of his stupid games, in the dead of the night, after a very long shift. If he wanted to talk to her, he could do so in the heat of day. He knew were she lived—knew he was welcome there anytime. She clipped the gun to her belt. Its familiar weight offered a sense of comfort to the uneasiness that still stirred through her as she walked across the road.

The rain eased a little as she entered the alley, but the wind danced through the darkness, a forlorn moan that made the hairs on the back of her neck stand on end. She hesitated, her gaze skating across the shadows. The old man's possessions were strewn across the ground near the garbage bins. They amounted to little more than a few old books, a couple of credit cards and the scraps of food he'd ferreted out of the bin.

She bent and picked up the cards. The names on them were all different—Joseph Ryan, Tom King, Jake George. Obviously, the old guy had not been above a little credit fraud. She dropped the cards, then stepped across the books and cautiously walked deeper into the alley. The darkness was blanket heavy, but her eyes slowly adjusted. Shapes loomed through the ink of night. On the right hand side of the alley, a dozen or so large boxes were stacked haphazardly against a graffiti decorated wall, and to her left was the fire escape that zigzagged up the restaurant wall.

She walked past the rusted metal ladder, then stopped. With the full force of the wind blocked by the buildings on either side, the smells that haunted the alley came into their own. Rotting rubbish, puddles of stale water, and the faintest hint of human excrement all combined into one stomach-churning stench. She shuddered and tried breathing through her mouth rather than her nose. It didn't help much.

Twenty feet away the alley came to a dead end, blocked by a wall at least fifteen feet tall. Unless the old guy had springs for legs, or wings hidden under his threadbare coat—both of which were certainly possible in this day and age—there was no way on Earth he could have gotten over it. She glanced across to the boxes. It didn't make any sense for him to be hiding there, either, especially when he'd abandoned his belongings to do so. Most street people clung to their few possessions with a ferocity only death could shatter. Besides, the rain had made the boxes a sodden mass that would have collapsed with the slightest touch.

Which left only the fire escape.

She glanced up. Moisture dripped from above, splattering across her face. She wiped it away with her palm, then frowned and glanced down. Why did the rain suddenly feel warm?

In her heart, she knew the answer to that question even as it crossed her mind. Grimly, she pressed a small switch on her wristcom. Light flared from the unit, a pale yellow glow that jostled uneasily against the darkness. She raised her arm and shined the light on the metal walkway above her.

As she thought, it wasn't rain dripping down from the fire escape, but blood. But there wasn't a body—or, at least, not one that she could see from where she stood.

For a moment, she considered contacting headquarters about a possible homicide. But Jack had asked her to come here alone. Had specifically asked her not to contact them. She didn't understand why and, in the end, didn't really care. He'd been her partner for close to five years, and she trusted him more than she trusted the boneheads and politicians back at headquarters.

Wiping her palm down her thigh, she reached back for her gun. Then slowly, cautiously, she began to climb.

Three flights up she found the old man. He'd been thrown against the far edge of the landing, his body a broken and bloody mass that barely resembled anything human. She closed her eyes, and took a deep breath. Death was never an easy find. In her ten years on the force, she'd come across many of its masks, yet it still had the power to shock her.

Especially when it was as gruesome as this.

The old man's eyes were wide with fear, his mouth locked in a scream that would never be heard. His flesh had been stripped from his face, leaving a bloody mass of raw veins and muscle. No vampire had done this. In fact, none of the nonhuman species currently on record were capable of an act like this.

She took another deep breath, knelt by the old man's side and felt his neck. No pulse, as expected, but his skin was still very warm. The murderer had to be close.

Real close.

Metal creaked above her. Her pulse rate zooming, she grabbed her gun and twisted around, sights aimed at the landing above her. Nothing moved. No one came down the stairs. The wind moaned loudly, but nothing else could be heard beyond the harsh note of her breathing.

Cautiously, she rose and walked back to the ladder. One more flight and she'd reach the roof. Whoever, or whatever, had done that to the old man might still be up there.

She had to call for backup. There was no other choice, not in a situation like this. Pressing the communication switch, she waited for a response and quickly asked for help. The closest unit was seven minutes away.

Her gaze went back to the landing above her, and she bit her lip. Was there anyone up there? Was Jack up there? Or was this all some sort of weird set up that somehow involved Jack? No, she thought. He wouldn't do that to her. And it had been him on the comlink. Her security system had identified his voice. That the old man was murdered at the same time she was supposed to have met her partner had to be random chance.

So where was Jack?

She glanced down at her wristcom. Twenty-nine minutes past three. It wasn't unusual for him to be late. In the five years she'd known him, he'd only managed to be on time for his wedding.

Maybe he was here. Maybe he was a victim of the creature who'd destroyed the old man.

Panic surged at the thought. God, she couldn't risk the wait for backup. Not when Jack's life might be at stake. She had to go on. Had to try and find him. If the department decided to discipline her for leaving a crime scene, then so be it. As long as she found her partner safe and sound, she didn't really give a damn.

As she reached the top landing, the full force of the wind hit her, thrusting her back a step before she regained her balance. Shivering, she dragged her coat zipper all the way up her neck, but it didn't stop the rain from getting past the collar and trickling down her back.

"This is great, just great," she muttered, wiping the water from her eyes—a totally useless gesture, given the conditions.

Visibility was practically zero. If there was someone up here with her, all they had to do was remain still and she'd never even see them. With a final, regretful glance back to the fire escape, she moved forward. After a dozen steps, a dark, boxlike shape loomed out of the grayness. Stairs to the rooms below, presumably.

She found a door, and tested it cautiously. The handle turned. With her back to the wall, gun raised, she pushed the door open and listened for any sign of movement. Still nothing.

Yet instinct told her the murderer had to be inside. There was nowhere else he could be, nowhere else he really could have come from. Unless, of course, he could fly. But if he could fly, why would he have used the fire escape? Why wouldn't he have just dragged the old man's body down to the end of the alley rather than up the stairs, then flown away?

He was here, down those stairs, somewhere.

She switched the com-unit's light back on, and then crossed her wrists, holding the gun and light to one side of her body as she edged forward.

The light gleamed off the metal stairs and puddled against the deeper darkness of the room. Three steps down, she halted again, listening. The silence was so intense it felt as if she could reach out and touch it. Unease growing like a weight in her stomach, she frowned and edged down the remaining steps.

In the small circle of light she could see several stacks of chairs lined up against the wall. Beyond that, the vague shapes of upturned tables. Obviously, someone was using the empty floor as a storage facility. She moved across to the first stack of chairs and stopped again.

Something hit her, an invisible force that came out of the darkness to slam her back against the wall. Her breath left in a whoosh of air, and for several heartbeats, she saw stars. Then her senses seemed to explode outwards. Just for an instant, the darkness became something that was real, something that had flavors and taste and body. And then she realized it did have bodies, that she was sensing its inhabitants through every pore and fiber of her being. As if, in that one moment, she inhabited the skins of the beings out there in the shadows, learning their secrets, feeling their thoughts.

One of those who hid in the shadows was a vampire.

The other wasn't human, wasn't vampire, wasn't anything she actually recognized. But it was filled with an evil so complete it seemed to seep into her very bones and made her soul shake.

The sensation disappeared with a snap that left her weak and shaking. She collapsed onto her knees and took a deep, shuddering breath. What the hell had happened? Never in her life had she experienced anything so weird . . . or so frightening. For a brief moment, she'd become one with those others. Had felt the uneven pounding of their hearts, the rush of blood through their veins. Had felt their desire to kill seep through her being and become her own.

She wiped a trembling hand across her brow. The sooner backup got here, the better. A vampire intent on grievous bodily harm she could handle. That other thing, whatever it was, tipped the odds way too far in favor of the bad guys.

She forced herself upright, pressing her back against the wall as she listened to the silence. Still no sound or movement. Warily, she took a step towards the stairs and then stopped. A light prickling sensation ran across her skin, a faint wave that again tasted of the secrets of the night.

Someone approached.

Not understanding what was happening she nevertheless clicked the safety off her gun and held it at the ready. "Police! Come out with your hands up."

Laughter ran across the stillness, soft and warm. Laughter she'd heard before. Laughter she knew.

"I never could sneak up on you, Ryan."

Jack stepped into the small circle of light and stopped. She lowered her weapon, but she didn't relax or reapply the safety. Not until she knew what the hell her partner was up to. Not until she knew whether he was with those other two she'd sensed. Trust was one thing. Complete stupidity another. "What the hell is going on? And why haven't you phoned Suzy or the department?"

He smiled, and there was something decidedly odd about it. "I didn't come here to talk about Suzy. Or the department."

There was a chill in his green eyes she'd never noticed before, an edge to his voice that spoke of violence. This was the Jack she knew—and yet, in many ways, it wasn't. "Why not? What are you up to?"

He smiled and lowered his gaze, silently studying the floor. She had an odd notion that time was running out, that this man, her partner, had come here to kill her. It was a ridiculous thought, it really was, but it was one she just couldn't shake. Licking dry lips, she raised her gun a little.

Just in case.

"There's a war about to begin, Ryan."

The abrupt sound of his voice made her jump slightly. She met his gaze squarely and saw in the green depths only death and determination. And felt no safer about his intentions.

"What sort of war?"

He shrugged. "A war in which man will play no part, and yet ultimately be the loser. The wise will choose sides."

She frowned. Since when had Jack begun speaking in weird riddles? "And that's what you've done? Chosen a side?" She shifted her feet a little, strengthening her stance. If Jack came one step closer, she'd fire, partner or not.

So much for trusting this man beyond all others.

He smiled his strange smile. "Yes. And now it's your turn."

She stared at him, wondering what was really going on. Surely he hadn't called her down here just to pick a side in some upcoming mythical war. "We're cops, Jack. We're supposed to be impartial and all that."

He snorted heavily. "Yeah, right. Tell that to someone who doesn't know the truth."

The cynical edge to his voice made her feel no easier. If there was one thing Jack had always been proud of, it had been his badge. "So why do I have to choose?"

"Because for you, there can be no standing in the middle. It's one side or the other."

She wondered if pinching herself would wake her from this weird dream, or make sense of what Jack was saying. "That doesn't actually answer the question of why me. I mean, why not the thousands of others who work for the department?"

"Most of them haven't your intuitive nature, or your determination to act on a hunch." He shrugged. "And we need more people who can move around in the daylight."

Right now, her so-called intuitive nature was telling her he was lying through his back teeth—at least when it came to the reasons for wanting her to join them. "Who are you actually working for, if not the department?"

She might not have spoken, for all the notice he took. "We could continue as partners," he added softly.

God, how deep did he think their partnership had become? "Sorry. Still doesn't appeal to me."

"That's unfortunate. Already, too many good men and women

have gone missing."

A chill ran down her spine. He knew about the disappearances. Had somehow been involved in them. "I really think you should come back to headquarters with me—"

She hesitated. The odd, prickling sensation ran across her skin again, whispering dark secrets to her mind. She stared at Jack, her gaze widening. Her partner, and friend of five years, was the vampire she'd sensed earlier.

And that thing out there in the darkness, the creature she could not name, was with him.

He studied her for a moment, and then he sighed, almost sadly. "So, you know."

Her finger curled around the trigger, and it took every ounce of strength she had to resist the urge to shoot him. Not all vampires were evil—how often had he told her that? Certainly she had no evidence that Jack himself had crossed the line between good and evil, when he'd taken the step from life to death.

Only instinct, and the oddly ferocious look in his eyes, said that he had.

"But I don't know why."

"Why does one normally undertake the ceremony?" Amusement touched his green eyes. "I have no wish to die, Ryan. With the eve of the war at hand, I had no option but to cross over. Humans have no place in what is coming."

The sensation of danger was becoming so strong her muscles were twitching under the force of it. She took a deep breath, trying to calm down. Yet if Jack were a vampire, he would know her fear, her uncertainty. Would hear it in the thunderous pounding of her heart. "So why call me here?"

"Because, as I said earlier, it's your time to choose."

"I made my choice long ago." And her badge was all she really had. She wasn't about to walk away from it, even for her best friend. "I intend to stick to that choice."

Sadness briefly touched his eyes. "I'm asking you, as a friend, to join me."

Her finger tightened reflexively on the trigger, and it was all she could do not to press it a tiny bit more and actually fire the weapon. "No."

"One last chance." He took a slight step forward. The touch of sadness in his eyes was quickly giving way to the certainty of death.

"One more step, and I'll shoot."

He smiled. "I don't think so."

Sweat trickled down the side of her face. "I mean it. Stay where you are."

He took another step forward. "We're friends, Ryan. Partners. You can't shoot me."

There was no humanity in his eyes now, only that certainty of death. She'd seen that look in vampires before and knew it precluded an attack. "Please, Jack. Don't make me shoot you."

He raised an eyebrow. "You won't. You can't," he said, and took another step.

She aimed low and pulled the trigger.

Through the booming retort of the gun, she heard his curse, heard him stagger away. She lowered her weapon, hit the panic button on her wristcom and ran for the stairs.

Heat flowed over her, whispering secrets. The thing with Jack was after her, running swiftly and silently through the darkness. If it caught her, she would die, as the old man had died. Quickly, but horribly.

She grabbed the railing with her free hand and took the stairs two at a time. At the top she hesitated and glanced down. A shadow flowed across the bottom step, then stopped and looked up. For just a second she found herself staring into eyes that were milky white and as bright as the stars. In them was a hunger unlike any she'd ever seen before.

Get out, she thought. *Just get the hell out of here.*

She scrambled through the door and slammed it shut behind her. An inhuman roar followed her into the wildness of the night. She ran for the fire escape stairs, but the wind hit her with the force of a gale, thrusting her sideways. Somehow, she managed to stay on her feet and keep running. Behind her, the door slammed open, the sound like a gunshot ricocheting across the force of the storm. Swearing, she leapt onto the fire escape and scrambled down the slick metal stairs.

One flight gone. The old man stared up at her, a grim reminder of her fate if she wasn't fast enough. Onto the second flight. Was that a footfall? She didn't dare look up, just kept on running.

She hit the lower landing, then grabbed the rail and leapt over it. She landed awkwardly, and pain curled like fire up her leg. She ignored it and ran for her car.

A sighing sound carried across the howl of the wind. She caught a hint of movement out of the corner of her eye, but before she could react, something hit her hard and flung her sideways.

She struck the ground with a grunt of pain, her weapon flying from her hand. She twisted, throwing punches at the heavy weight that had landed on top of her. His curses stung the night, and then he caught her hands, his grip like iron as he held her still. She found herself staring into eyes that were an odd, green-flecked hazel, and not entirely human.

Not Jack or the creature. Someone else entirely. Someone she hadn't sensed.

"If you want to live, remain still and be quiet," he ordered, his gaze burning into hers for a second before flicking away.

"Get the hell off me and I may consider it," she muttered, twisting left and right in an effort to dislodge his weight.

"That creature hunts by sound and movement alone. Remain still, and we might escape with our lives."

A soft snarl ran across the wind. She stopped fighting and turned her gaze to the fire escape. A kite-like shape leapt off the second flight of stairs and landed awkwardly near the boxes. It made several odd snuffling noises before turning blind eyes in their direction. Her fingers twitched, pressing the trigger of a weapon she no longer held. The stranger glanced down at her, his odd-colored eyes holding a warning.

It went against her every instinct to remain still, to not fight, and her muscles quivered as she fought the desire to do both. The creature took a lumbering step in their direction. Her breath caught somewhere in her throat and refused to move. At the other end of the alley, the howling wind tugged at the garbage bins. One fell and rattled toward the road, spewing paper and food scraps across the pavement before rolling away. The creature roared, then swung around and ran out of the alley.

The stranger released her and scrambled to his feet. She lurched forward and grabbed his wrist.

"Oh, no you don't. You're not leaving until you tell me what the hell that thing is."

A slight smile creased the corners of his lush mouth. "And what gives you the right to detain me?"

"I'm a cop, mister. You're under arrest."

"For what? Saving your life?" He pried her fingers away from his wrist, his fingers warm and slightly rough against hers. "Sorry, but I have a creature to stop. Arrests will have to wait."

He moved so swiftly that he almost seemed to blur. One blink and he was gone.

The night didn't appear to be getting any saner, she thought sourly. First her partner becomes a vampire, and then she's hunted by a kite-like monster, only to be rescued by a man who could blur his form and move like the wind. What next?

Knowing she probably didn't want an answer to that question, she slowly climbed to her feet. Pain fired up her right leg and her ankle suddenly felt encased in iron. Great, just great. The night from hell and a busted ankle. Maybe the best idea was to just sit here and wait for the cavalry to arrive. The thought made her frown, and she glanced at her wristcom. Four minutes had passed since she'd pressed the emergency beacon, nine since she'd first requested help. Why wasn't anyone here?

She glanced around for her weapon and saw it sitting in a puddle ten feet away. She hobbled to it, doing her best to ignore the protests from her ankle. As she bent down, that weird sliver of heat prickled a warning across her skin.

Jack was behind her.

Slowly, warily, she picked up her weapon and turned around. He stood ten feet away. Blood ran from the wound in his thigh, the flow gleaming darkly against his rain soaked jeans. Fear swept her again. On a night like this she shouldn't be able to even see the blood.

She flicked off the auto safety catch and pointed the gun at him. "I have to take you back. You know I have to."

He smiled. "I'm not going back. I can't. Pull that trigger if you want to."

She didn't pull the trigger. Nor did she lower her weapon. "Why did you really call me here tonight?"

"I've already told you—to ask you to join us."

"And that thing you were with—did it kill the old man?"

He lowered his gaze, but not before she'd seen a brief flash of amusement. A chill ran down her spine. Jack had watched that thing strip the old man of his humanity. Had enjoyed it.

"We all have to feed, Ryan, and society has no use for the dregs." His gaze flashed up again, cold and hungry. If there was any humanity left in her partner, it quickly fled as the vampire rose fully to the surface.

"I'm sorry you won't join us," he continued. "We were a good team."

Were. Not are. She swallowed. It didn't ease the aching dryness in her throat. "Don't move, Jack. This time I'll shoot to kill."

His laugh was a low, almost inhuman, sound. "Perhaps you

want me to wait until the reinforcements arrive."

Sweat trickled down her back, and her palms felt slick against the cool metal of the gun. "That's my plan, yes."

"Ever the optimist." He flashed a familiar smile, all confidence and teeth.

Too much teeth, in fact.

The vampire was getting ready to feed.

"*Don't* make me kill you," she warned softly. Please don't.

The sudden ferocity in his eyes made her take a step back. Even as she did so, he leapt.

Jack had once told her the best way to kill a vampire was to blow its fucking head off.

And that's exactly what she did.

Two

Gabriel Stern leaned a shoulder against the wall and watched dawn color the sky a bright, almost bloody red. The rising sun played across his face and arms, pleasant and warm. But if the gathering clouds were anything to go by, it was going to be a bitch of a day. God, he hated Melbourne in winter.

He crossed his arms, and studied the stark white building across the street. Situated on the western edge of the Central Business District, close to the Law Courts, the building housed both the State Police and the Special Investigations Unit. With the precision of ants, men and woman clad in the stark black of the State Police moved in and out of the building, a tide that was occasionally interspersed by the dark gray favored by the SIU. As yet, there was no sign of the woman whose life he'd saved last night.

"It may be hours before she gets back. You know what the cops are like when one of their own gets shot."

The voice rose like a demon out of the darkness, setting his teeth on edge. Gabriel turned from the window. Though it was still dark in the small office, he could see the old desk, chairs and recording units well enough. Martyn stood in the deeper shadows crowding the far corner, idly sipping a bottle of dark fluid.

Gabriel's stomach rumbled a reminder that he hadn't eaten in over twenty-four hours. He shoved his hands in his pockets and tried to ignore it. "I want the SIU called in on this. Me, specifically."

Martyn's smile was fleeting. "That has been arranged."

A fact Gabriel knew, simply because he'd started the arrangements earlier. Still, there was protocol to follow, if he didn't want too many suspicions raised, and, technically speaking, Martyn was supposedly his one and only link to the Federation, the covert group they both worked for. While Martyn was well aware that Gabriel talked to Stephan, he had no idea just how often. Gabriel intended to keep it that way.

"Good." At least he could get closer to the woman, and maybe he'd find out just how she'd been able to sense the presence of the kite monster last night. From the little information they'd been able to glean about the creature, it was supposed to be invisible to humans—at least until the point of attack. Yet she had sensed it early enough to escape.

"If this interest of yours in the woman develops into an obsession, Stephan's not going to be happy."

He glanced at Martyn sharply. He knew better than Martyn ever would just what Stephan was, and wasn't, going to be happy about. And he knew for a fact Stephan more than agreed with his interest in this woman. So why would Martyn say otherwise?

"Twenty-four people have been killed by the kites. She is the only person to ever escape. We need to know why."

"*We* can sense them. Surely that's all that matters."

"We're an extremely small group, and the kites are growing in number. We can't hope to kill them all, nor can we hope to conceal their existence for much longer."

"Worry about that when the time comes. For the moment, we have more important matters to worry about."

Yeah, like what the hell Sethanon—the man ultimately behind the attacks last night, and someone the Federation had being trying to stop for years—was up to. He glanced back out the window as movement caught his attention. A woman with red-gold hair walked up the steps of the opposite building, her slender figure almost lost in the sea of black clad officers and camera crews that surrounded her.

Sympathy flashed through him. He knew what it was like to kill a partner. He'd done it himself, what seemed a lifetime ago.

Once she'd walked through the main doors, he turned to face Martyn once more. "What intrigues me is the fact she apparently sensed the presence of the kite and her partner, and yet showed no signs of knowing I was there."

"Given you didn't actually talk to her, you can't be certain about that."

No, he couldn't. But instinct suggested that was the case, and he'd long ago learned to trust his instincts. At least when it came to issues like this, anyway.

"When I talked to Stephan earlier—"

"I'm your control," Martyn said, voice sharp. "You're supposed to talk to *me* first."

"I'm reporting to you now."

"In the future, you will report to me, and only me, or disciplinary action will be taken."

He snorted softly. What were they going to do? Pull him off the job? Not likely, if only because it'd take Federation years to get someone else into the position he was now in. And given the number of operatives that had been killed or uncovered of late, maybe the very reason he was still one of the Federation's most effective plants was the very thing Martyn was bitching about— his lack of continuous reports.

Although, truth be told, Stephan himself would have to be classed as *the* most successful. No one, beyond himself and Stephan's wife, knew Stephan's alter ego. Not even Martyn.

"Have you found out any more about Kazdan's disappearance and subsequent reappearance?" Martyn continued.

He shook his head. "Other than the fact he resurfaced about a week ago, no."

"Why was he meeting with her?"

"Trying to recruit her, apparently."

"Do we know why?"

"Not yet."

Martyn grunted. "You'd better get back across the road. I'll contact Stephan and see if we can dig up anything more on Kazdan's recent movements."

To *his* way of thinking, it was more important to find out what was so special about this woman that a man like Kazdan, who was reportedly a general in Sethanon's organization, was forfeited in an effort to try and recruit her. But he said nothing, merely nodded and left Martyn to the shadows.

***

"What do you mean suspended until further notice?" Sam stared at the captain in disbelief.

He sighed wearily and spoke more slowly, as if she were a child with little comprehension, which, after twenty-two hours without sleep, was a little too close to the truth for comfort.

"You shot your partner, Ryan. Blew his brains out. There has to be an investigation, and you're suspended until it's finished."

"Did I mention the fact he'd become a vampire?"

"Several times," the captain replied heavily. "Vampires have rights, same as the next person."

She sighed and rubbed her forehead wearily. Somewhere in the last few hours, her head had begun to ache, and that ache was getting steadily worse. But she knew better than to ask for some pain killers. There was no such thing as rights or fair treatment for a cop suspected of foul deeds. She was lucky they'd fixed her ankle before they'd realized she was the one who'd pulled the trigger on Jack.

"Did I mention he was trying to kill me?"

"Ryan, you blew a hole in his thigh, and then shot his friggin' head off. That's more than self defense, you know."

She shuddered and tried to ignore the bloody images his words bought to mind. He really didn't have to tell her what she'd done. It was a moment she'd relive in her dreams for many years to come.

"The first shot was just a warning, Cap. And I did warn him that the next time I'd shoot to kill, but he didn't seem to believe I would."

"Well, you were partners for five years."

She shook her head, unable to believe what she was hearing. "So, it's perfectly all right for him to try to kill me, but not for me to defend myself?"

"Try to face the fact that we have only your word and a corpse. And while you said you had your wristcom on record, the labs weren't able to pull any images from the unit."

She glanced down at the wristcom. There'd been no indication that control had downloaded information from it, and there should have been. "It was on, Cap. And it was working."

"You may have thought it was working, but the labs say there are neither images nor voice."

So was the unit faulty, or just the linking capacity? "Do they want me to send them the unit? Maybe there's a problem with the satlink?"

He shook his head. "They tested the link. They can read everything A-OK. There's just nothing in the memory about last night."

She took a deep breath and blew it out slowly. "Then just do a DNA scan on his body. It'll back up the fact that he's a vampire."

He hesitated and glanced down at his hands. "We don't have to. His corpse was touched by sunshine when the boys were bagging it. It didn't go up."

How could there be no reaction to daylight? Of all the myths that abounded about vampires, that was the one that had proven to be true. No immunity to daylight. The minute the sun touched them, they burned. "Damn it, I saw his teeth, Cap. He *was* a vampire."

"You might have seen teeth, but the fact is there was no reaction to sunshine."

She stared at him for a moment before asking, "Have you done blood and DNA tests?"

He nodded. "Inconclusive."

"How can a blood or DNA test be inconclusive? Either he was a vampire or he wasn't."

"They're running further tests. Until they come back, you're suspended."

She slumped back in her chair. What the hell was she going to do with herself if she didn't have work to come to every day? "What about the old guy?"

The captain's brown eyes were suddenly calculating. A sliver of unease ran down her spine. Something odd was going down here.

"What old man?" he said eventually.

"Don't tell me you can't find him. I *know* that's impossible."

"There was no other body besides Jack's."

"Surely to God you found blood. There was a ton of it all over the fire escape."

The captain hesitated. His gaze flickered minutely to the security cam in the far corner of the room. She straightened a little. If the captain was suddenly worried about being watched, something odd *was* going down.

"The only blood we found was Jack's."

She stared at him. How could that be possible? The kite-like monster had all but stripped the old man of his flesh. How could all that blood simply disappear?

It couldn't. Not unless someone had cleaned it up. Someone involved in the investigation. Foreboding began to beat in time with the ache in her head.

The captain cleared his throat softly. "We notified Suzy of Jack's death."

She frowned at the sudden change, wondering why he didn't want to talk about that creature.

"She's not happy," he continued softly.

"Well, gee, I wonder why?" She didn't bother trying to hide the sarcasm in her voice. "Might it have something to do with the fact that her husband of three and a half years turns up dead after he'd been missing for weeks?"

"Dead because you shot him."

That wasn't what she'd meant, and the captain knew it. And though guilt rose, she determinedly pushed it away. Guilt wasn't a luxury she could afford right now. Not when she was up to her neck in trouble and sinking fast. "How did she take it?"

"Her reaction was interesting, to say the least."

God, what had Jack's bitch of a wife said about her now? "Interesting how?"

The captain smiled slightly. "She said you and Jack were having an affair. That you'd been casual lovers for some time and that you'd finally given Jack an ultimatum—leave Suzy, or you'd kill him."

She stared in disbelief at the captain. It was evident by the look in his eyes that he didn't really believe it. But others might. She and Jack *had* been close. Hell, most of the people in their squad had presumed they were lovers, a notion that seemed to gain more credibility every time she and Jack denied it. And yet nothing could have been further from the truth. Fact was she rarely saw Jack out of hours.

"You know that's not true, Cap."

"Do you deny having a fight with him the day he disappeared?"

How could she deny it when half the station had probably heard it? "That was over prisoner treatment."

"And degenerated into some serious threats."

She frowned. Even now, she had no idea what that fight had really been about. Jack had been edgy, strung out, all day. But when he'd started beating a suspect more than usual, she'd stepped in—and he'd turned on her as swiftly and as violently as a snake. "I didn't threaten him. You can check the vid tapes, if you like."

"We have, and you're right, the threats didn't happen then. According to Suzy, they happened later, on the way home."

Suzy would say that, because Suzy hated the thought of anyone else being close to Jack. As far as Sam was concerned, it was a hatred that bordered on an obsession. Why, she had no idea.

"Since Suzy wasn't in the car, she can't actually say what Jack and I did and didn't talk about."

"She said Jack told her."

"And I could say Jack told me the sky was green, but would you believe it?"

A smile lifted one corner of his thin lips. "No."

"Then it's her word against mine. You choose who you'd rather believe."

"Unfortunately, it's not for me to choose." Again, his gaze flicked to the camera. "I need your badge, gun and wristcom."

"This is ridiculous," she muttered, leaning forward to unclip her gun from the back of her belt. She thumped it down on the desk with her badge, then undid her wristcom and dropped it beside them. "I should have let him bite me. Then maybe someone would believe me."

The captain made no reply. He slid a piece of paper across the desk. "They want you to undergo psych evaluation. Here are the appointment details. I advise you not to miss it. Your job may depend on it."

"I'm not crazy," she said softly. Beginning to get as mad as hell, maybe, but not crazy.

"It's standard procedure, Ryan."

No, it wasn't, and they both knew it. She leaned forward and picked up the paper. On it was a name, section and time, but beneath it, he'd written a note. *Don't fight this. The suspension order came from the top, and there's nothing either of us can do about it. Use the time to find out what really happened to Jack. Go after those who did this to him.*

She glanced up, and met the captain's gaze. After a moment, she nodded and folded the paper, shoving it inside her jacket. "That appointment is with the SIU. I didn't know they'd taken over psych evaluations."

"Your claim that Jack was a vampire forced us to report it. They're taking over these types of investigations from now on."

"But why is the spook squad doing the psych evaluation as well?"

He shrugged. "Maybe they want to make sure no hidden prejudices are behind this."

"Meaning someone, somewhere, must believe my statement that Jack was a vampire."

"Or maybe they want to ensure you're not seeing bogeys where there are none." He hesitated. "It's not exactly a state secret that vampires are not on your list of favorite people."

No, it wasn't. But that wasn't what this was about. Nor was it the reason Jack now lay on a slab ten floors below them. He was dead simply because he'd tried to kill her.

And as the captain had pointed out, she now had the time to find out why.

But she had an awful feeling the answers to many of the questions surrounding Jack's death would not be found on the streets, but rather here, in the pristine halls of Central Security. An area that was now out of bounds until she was reinstated.

"You'd better go, Ryan. The SIU do not like to be kept

waiting."

She grimaced. "See you around, Cap."

He nodded and began rifling through some papers on his desk. Knowing a dismissal when she saw one, she turned and walked through the door. Surprisingly, security wasn't waiting beyond the door to escort her to her desk and ensure she took nothing more than personal belongings. In the corridor itself, people walked up and down, going about their daily business as if nothing untoward had happened, yet not one of them would meet her eyes. She shook her head, wondering why she was so surprised. She'd shot one of their own, her partner no less. The ultimate no-no in any law enforcement community. The reason behind her action didn't matter to them. She'd crossed a line and would always be judged because of it.

She passed several doors until she came to the office she'd shared with Jack. "Lights," she said, hesitating in the doorway.

A muted glow warmed the room. Jack's desk was as he'd left it. She hadn't touched it simply because she'd always thought he'd be back. She blinked back the sudden sting of tears and glanced across at the clock on her desk. Eight minutes left to find some sort of clue.

She sat down on his chair and rifled through the papers on his desk. Nothing caught her eye. But then, had she really expected a clue to be so easy to find?

"Computer on."

The screen hummed to life. "Voice identification required," stated a soft, sultry voice.

Jack had always preferred his computers to have a feminine touch, where as her preference leaned towards cartoons. Dizzy Izzy, a hot pink fur-ball that had become the newest rage on the cartoon front, was the voice of her com-unit here, while the old Warner Classic, Marvin the Martian, was the current face of her home units.

"Samantha Ryan. Badge number MSF 1079."

"Voice verified. Request?"

"Diary entries for the tenth of May, two-o-four-seven."

"A password is needed before request can be processed."

She frowned. Since when had Jack begun putting security codes on his files? "Suzy."

"Access denied."

Maybe his badge number. "MSF 1045."

"Access denied."

She swore softly. The password could literally be anything. She frowned, trying to think back to that day, trying to remember, something, anything that might provide a clue. "What about . . . vampire?"

"Access denied."

"Afterlife."

"Access denied."

"Fuck," she muttered, and leaned back in the chair. She had to get what she could now, or she'd lose out. Once official word got around about her suspension, she'd be escorted from the premises and not allowed back in.

The computer hummed silently. "Access granted."

She blinked in surprise, then shook her head and smiled ruefully. Trust Jack to use a password like that.

"Transfer all personal files and diaries to outlink 1097. Security access one."

"Transfer proceeding."

What else might she need? She tapped her lip for a moment, staring at the screen. "Are there transcripts of phone calls for May 10th?"

"I have five on record."

"Were those all the calls for that day?" Jack had been something of a whiz at getting around official protocol, especially when it came to calls he didn't want recorded.

"Two were not recorded."

No real surprise there. Jack loved horse racing, and over the years he had lost of fair bit of money to the bookmakers—legal and otherwise. It was a practice that was officially frowned upon, and would have meant instant dismissal if anyone else had found out. "You have the numbers?"

"Yes."

"Send those and the five transcripts to outlink 1097. Security access one."

"Transfer proceeding."

She glanced across at the time. Damn, she was late. "Computer, complete transfer then close."

"Transfer complete. Have a good day." A smiley face appeared on the screen as the computer shut down. Smiling, she opened the drawers and grabbed Jack's spare wristcom. Hers would probably be decommissioned right away, but with Jack's death not yet officially recorded, both his units would still be viable.

She rose and moved across to her desk, quickly gathering the few personal items she cared about—her Marvin the Martian clock, and the big old china mug that Jack had given her their first Christmas as partners—shoving them in a bag as she walked across to the door.

But at the doorway, she hesitated and glanced back. She'd spent a lot of happy times in this office, laughing and caring and fighting. And she had an odd feeling she wouldn't be back to see it again. Tears stung her eyes, and she blinked them away quickly.

"Lights off," she whispered. As the room fell into darkness, she added. "Bye Jack."

Turning away, she headed for the elevators and her appointment with the SIU.

***

Gabriel glanced up as a young doctor entered his office, carrying a bundle of printouts. After pressing a button on the com-screen to black out the screen but not the sound, Gabriel relaxed back in his chair. "Are those the test results for Officer Ryan, Finley?"

The young doctor nodded, and collapsed onto the only chair in the room that was free of books. "Christ, I'm exhausted. Don't know how that woman is surviving, given she's had so little sleep over the last twenty-four hours."

"With Kazdan as a partner, I guess she'd have to be pretty tough." He nodded towards the papers. "What are the results?"

"Well, she's not crazy, but she does hold some deep-seated prejudices against vampires. So deep I doubt even she knows why."

"They're not the results I was talking about."

Finley smiled evenly. "Didn't think you were." He shuffled through the papers and dragged out the middle set of sheets. "These results were interesting, to say the least."

So he was right. There *was* something special about the woman. "Interesting how?"

Finley pushed his thick glasses back up the bridge of his nose. "Well, as you know, when we measure psychic energy, most people come in at one end of the scale or the other, depending on whether they are gifted or not."

"I helped invent those tests, remember?" he said, a slight edge of sarcasm in his voice.

"Ah, yes, so you did." The young doctor cleared his throat. "The thing is no one ever comes in as neutral. It's impossible—

either you have some ability or you don't, simple as that. But this girl has done the impossible."

He frowned. "As you said, that's not possible."

"With all the psychic deadeners we have around the place, there's no way she can be using some form of talent to evade the probes. And yet, she registers neutral."

Finley held out the printouts. Gabriel silently accepted them and quickly leafed through the sheets. As Finley had stated, every test had come out neutral. He stopped at the BP, cardiovascular and EKG charts, and raised an eyebrow in surprise. "Brain activity registers extremely high, considering the readout indicates she'd fallen asleep during some of the tests."

"That in itself would suggest some form of talent at work—if it wasn't for the fact that the psychic deadeners render *any* form of talent useless."

"Unless she has some form of talent that can evade the deadeners."

"Unheard of."

He glanced up from the printouts. "Until now, it was unheard for anyone to come in as neutral."

Finley pursed his lips. "True."

"What do we know of her life before she joined the state police?"

"Basic stuff. She was left in State care at fourteen. Remained there until she was eighteen, and then joined the state police."

"Done a check on her parents?"

"State did, when she joined. They're listed as missing. The case is still open."

He glanced up. "That's not what I asked."

Finley cleared his throat. "No, we haven't done a check on her parents."

"Then do one." He hesitated, and then frowned, rereading the last line of text again. "Body growth immature? What the hell does that mean?"

"Basically, it means that, when it comes to internals, she has the maturity of a fifteen year old."

"Finley, she's twenty nine years old." And, he thought, remembering the firm roundness of her body pressed under his last night, she was certainly built like it.

Finley shrugged. "None of us can explain it—and we ran those tests twice, just in case."

If she had the maturity of a fifteen year old, it suggested

nonhuman background, because most nonhumans had a slower rate of development than humans. Yet Finley's tests had so far picked up nothing other than human in her makeup. "Best guess?"

"That the printouts state the absolute truth."

For a human that was twenty-nine years old? Not likely. "Will you need to run more tests?"

"Definitely. We found some anomalies in her cell sample that need checking out, as well."

He flipped back several pages until he found the blood results. "An unknown chromosome found in cell sample." He glanced at the doctor. "We have any ideas on this one?"

"Not one. As I said, we'd like to run more tests."

He didn't miss the odd edge of excitement in Finley's normally indifferent voice. Obviously, there wasn't much in the way of excitement to be found in the labs of the SIU these days. He smiled slightly, wondering how the young doctor would react if he ever got his hands on a kite. He put the printouts back into order and handed them back. "Where is she now?"

"Room 101."

"Book her for more tests tomorrow. And arrange a pass for her to get back in, as State will have cancelled them all by then."

Finley nodded and headed for the door. Once the doctor had gone, Gabriel pressed the screen again. "You heard?"

Stephan appeared on the screen. His normally strong features were little more than a pale replica, and there were dark shadows beneath his green eyes. Even his normally tanned skin had a translucent quality to it. Fear stirred deep in Gabriel's gut. The one thing the Federation couldn't afford, the one thing *he* didn't want, was for Stephan to get any sicker.

"Yes," Stephan said softly. "Most interesting."

He somehow resisted the urge to question Stephan about the state of his health and tried to concentrate on the matter at hand. But it was difficult, especially when Stephan's visage was that of one close to death. He'd lost one brother recently. He didn't want to lose another, and right now that looked like a distinct possibility. "I wonder if these anomalies are the reason Sethanon tried recruiting her last night."

Stephan shook his head, his expression doubtful. "How would he have known? State insists on medical checks every six months. I checked them out this morning, and they haven't altered until now."

"Which makes me wonder if someone was actually altering

the results before they were placed in the system. Sethanon wouldn't risk the life of an operative like Kazdan unless he knew this woman was a threat in some way."

"That makes no sense. Why would anyone bother altering the results? And why would Sethanon know she was a threat, when, for all intents and purposes, she *is* human?" He hesitated, expression thoughtful. "You know, if we do think along those lines, absurd as they seem, then it *is* always possible that last night was merely some sort of test."

"Which again implies that he knows more about her than what is showing in the medical workups. I think the SIU needs to assign her a guard. Me, specifically."

"People will think it strange that an Assistant Director is assigned guard duty."

He smiled thinly. "They expect strangeness from me."

It was a point Stephan didn't bother refuting. "I'll arrange it."

"Thanks." He hesitated, and then added softly. "When was the last time you ate, brother?"

Stephan sighed and rubbed a hand across his eyes. His fingers were reed thin. He'd lost a lot more weight in the week since they'd last seen each other.

"My stomach rebels every time I try."

"What about liquid?"

"Water I keep down. Anything else—" Stephan shrugged.

He frowned, not liking the sound of it. Stephan had been ill for close to two months now, and he was literally beginning to fade away. And though he'd been under the expert care of the Federation's doctors, they could find no cause. Time, he thought, for a radical change of direction. He had no intention of losing his last remaining brother without a fight.

"I'm going to send a friend of mine to you. I want you to do as he asks, without question."

He groaned softly. "Not that spiritual weirdo you hang out with."

"The very one. I've seen him work miracles, so no arguments." He hesitated, and then added with a grin. "Or I might just call Kathleen in on you."

Kathleen was the matriarch of the Stern clan, a sprite and bossy three-hundred-year-old woman who tended to sweep into your life as carefully as a cyclone. And she was probably the only person his brother was truly frightened of.

Stephan shuddered, a look of mock-horror momentarily lifting the tiredness from his eyes. "God, no."

"Then kindly take note of what Karl says."

"I will, I will." Stephan's smile faded. "And I want you to be careful out on the streets. Attacks have almost doubled in the last week. Sethanon's up to something, and until we know what it is, I've asked that all Federation operations be double-manned."

"Good move."

"That includes you, brother," Stephan added dryly.

'Yeah, right." The day *that* happened would be the day hell froze over. "I'll send Karl over to your place tonight."

Stephan sighed. "Fine. See you tomorrow night."

He nodded and clicked off the link. The computer hummed softly. "You have a call."

"Patch it through, and then get Karl on the line for me." He hesitated slightly before adding. "And run a background check on Samantha Ryan. I want all personal details that can be found." Finley's check on her would run to the academic side of her life rather than the personal. And as one of the SIU's assistant directors, his system had access to a greater range of computers.

The better he knew her, the closer he might get to some answers.

And he had a very bad feeling that he was going to need those answers pretty damn quick.

Three

Sam lay on the sofa, staring up at the ceiling. Night had fallen over two hours ago, encasing the small living room in darkness. And yet, despite her exhaustion, she couldn't sleep. The moment of Jack's death played itself over and over through her mind, a nightmare from which there was no escape. Nor could she escape wondering if there was something, anything, she could have done except pull the trigger.

Yet every time, the answer was the same. Jack would have killed her had she given him the chance. She was certain of that, if nothing else.

But then, she *had* to be certain, otherwise her actions would destroy her. Not so much job wise, but internally. Mentally.

Outside, the rain still pounded, an almost soothing sound when compared to the bass-heavy thumping drifting up from the apartment below. Obviously, Becky and Matt were out again, and their two teenagers were making the most of it. Normally, she didn't mind, but at the moment, the noise grated against her nerves.

She glanced at the clock. Nine-twelve. Sighing, she climbed off the sofa and walked across to the kitchen.

"Coffee, black," she said softly.

The autocook hummed to life, and almost instantly the rich aroma of coffee filled the room. It was an illusion—they'd long ago stopped using real coffee beans, at least in the stuff she could afford, and it almost never tasted as good as it smelled. When the timer chimed softly, she opened the door and grabbed the steaming mug. She then wandered over to her computer desk and sat down. If she couldn't sleep, she might as well put her time to good use and have a look at the transcripts she'd uploaded from Jack's computer.

"Computer on."

As she waited for the screen to blink to life, she stared at the framed drawing sitting next to the computer. It was a sketch she'd done as a child of a woman she could no longer remember. A woman with red hair, blue eyes, and freckles across her nose. Mommy, the childish writing at the bottom proclaimed. Apparently, she'd been clutching the drawing when they'd found her on the steps of the state run children's home. Even now, it was the only true clue to her mother's identity.

"You have mail, Earthling."

She glanced at the screen. Marvin the Martian glared back at her. "Secure files, then open."

The computer hummed for several seconds, and then Marvin was back. "Completed. Files opening."

Split screens appeared. The one on the right listed phone calls, the other diary contents.

"Trace these." She marked the two unrecorded phone calls Jack had made the day he disappeared. The screen went blank, and for several seconds, nothing happened. She swore softly, fervently hoping the department hadn't discovered the illegal lines Jack had set up for her. She needed the unregistered access to their main computers, if only to continue the search for her identity.

Marvin blinked back onto the screen. "Tracing."

She sighed in relief and opened the diary. Jack had made two appointments for the tenth. One was with a Frank Mohern, and the other with a J. C. Dodd. She didn't recognize either name. She touched their names and ordered another trace.

The doorbell buzzed into the silence, making her jump. "Security cam," she murmured, taking a quick sip of coffee to calm the sudden attack of nerves. "Front door view."

Anyone would think she was a rookie on her first day, given the way she was beginning to jump at shadows. And after last night's events, it was natural, wasn't it? God, it wasn't every damn day that her missing partner showed up and tried to kill her. But she certainly wasn't going to talk to the psych guys about it. Knowing them, they'd probably put it down to guilt or something worse.

The com screen flickered, briefly showing the rain swept pavement outside the building before it centered on the man standing at the door. He was big, at least six four, and heavy set. He was also what she'd term *extremely* hirsute—his dark brown hair curled wildly around a beard so thick it hid his features. It was no one she knew, that was for sure.

She leaned forward and pressed the comlink. "Can I help you?"

"I'm looking for Samantha Ryan."

"Why?"

White teeth flashed briefly through the forest of brown hair. "I have a message."

She frowned. Alarms were ringing in the back of her mind,

and she didn't understand why. But it was a warning she'd long ago learned to heed. Flicking the sound off, she leaned back and snagged her bag off the coffee table, then dug around until she found Jack's wristcom. The computer hummed as she attached the two. "Computer, download all files to link 1045." She hesitated, and then added. "Send search results to outlink 1097b."

"Proceeding, Earthling."

Turning the sound up again, she glanced back at the gorilla. "What sort of message?"

"From your partner."

She grimaced and rubbed her eyes. This wasn't trouble, just a nutter. Either that or someone was playing a very cruel hoax. Someone like Suzy, maybe.

The computer hummed its readiness. She detached the wristcom and put it back in her handbag, which she tossed onto the nearby chair, out of the way. "My partner is dead. Leave before I call security."

The white teeth flashed again. "The man you shot was not Jack. Last night was a test, nothing more."

The man was *definitely* a nutter. God, how could Jack not be dead? As the captain had so eloquently put it, she'd shot his friggin' brains out. And Suzy had identified his remains. "You have three seconds before security arrives."

Her finger hovered over the call button, but she didn't press it. Sometimes the words of nutters held a grain of truth, and there was something about this man that almost made her believe him.

Either that or she was suffering from sleep deprivation.

His shrug was almost graceful. "Call them," he said. "But not because of any threat you see in me. Call them because of the others."

Others? What the hell was he? An alarm cut through the silence, strident enough to wake the dead. *Someone had broken into her apartment.* Her heart racing, she reached for her gun, only to remember that they'd confiscated it. And her spare was locked in the safe. She thrust up from the chair and ran like hell across the room.

"Safe open," she hissed.

"Retina identification required."

No time, her mind screamed, even as the bedroom door crashed open. She spun around, catching a brief glimpse of two men wearing black facemasks, before a flash of white arrowed across the shadows. Fear surged, and she threw herself sideways.

Heat sizzled across her hip, and pain flared, short and sharp. She hit the floor with a grunt that turned into a yelp as another flash of light cut through the gloom, slicing through her shirt but missing skin. The wall inches from her shoulder exploded, sending plaster and dust flying.

Lasers. The sonsofbitches had lasers. She pushed to her knees and scrambled behind the sofa. It wouldn't offer much protection against the lasers, only time. Light flared again. A two-inch hole appeared on her right, and the carpet near her feet began to burn.

She had to get out of here before the bastards destroyed the apartment—and her. She shuffled backwards then twisted to look at the door. One of the men was standing there. It left her with only one option—the window.

She lunged to the left and grabbed her boots from the end of the sofa. Then, making sure the sofa still hid her, she half rose and flung the boots towards the kitchen. They clattered against the wall and dropped. Light flared again, spearing one boot as it fell to the floor. The smell of burned leather infused the air. It was a smell that would be joined by burned flesh if she didn't get the hell out of here.

She scrambled upright and dove headfirst for the window. Heat seared the soles of her feet as she flew through the air, but in her desperation to escape, there wasn't even pain, just a great rise of determination. Then the glass was shattering around her, glittering like diamonds even as it cut through her skin, and she was free-falling out into the rain soaked night.

***

The acrid smell of smoke stung the night air. Water sheeted across the pavement, flanked by the silvery-white fire hoses that snaked their way up the stairs and in through the main doors. The flashing red and blue lights of the emergency vehicles gave the small crowd of people huddled at the far end of the street an almost haunted look. Samantha Ryan was not among them.

But Gabriel would have been surprised if she had been. What *did* surprise him was the fact that she was here at all. Not many cops lived inside their patrol zone. Fewer still could afford an apartment in a place like Brighton. The old bayside suburb had once again become the playground for the trendy rich, and apartments like this, so close to the beach, cost more than Samantha Ryan would ever earn.

As Gabriel tried to enter the building, a young man dressed

in the black uniform of the State Police stepped forward. "Sorry sir. No one's allowed inside."

He stopped and impatiently dug his ID badge out of his pocket. "What happened, son?"

The young officer's eyes widened as he took in the badge, and he visibly gulped. He had to be all of seventeen or eighteen years old. Was the state so desperate for officers they were now robbing the cradle?

"Bomb on the second floor, sir."

His gut clenched. Ryan lived on the second floor. Sethanon had obviously made it here before him. He glanced around, but he didn't see any ambulances. That could either be a good or a bad sign. "Anyone hurt?"

The young officer shook his head. "Two apartments were seriously damaged, though."

"Who's in charge upstairs?"

"Captain Marsdan."

Marsdan was the head of Samantha's squad. Why would he be called down instead of the Internal Investigations Unit? Even suspended, she was still a cop whose apartment had just been bombed. That was IIU's territory, not the beat police. Unless, of course, someone high up didn't want them involved.

He nodded his thanks to the young officer and made his way upstairs. Black uniforms were everywhere on the second floor, but again, the average age was little more than twenty. And all of them were still wet behind the ears, if the eagerness in their eyes was anything to go by.

After flashing his badge at the officer manning the door, he stepped into the shattered remains of Ryan's apartment. By the look of it, the front room had taken the brunt of the blast. The wreckage of what once must have been a coffee table and sofa lay partially embedded in the wall to his left. A few twisted metal shelves arched up the wall to his right, framing the hole that now led out into the corridor. The tangled remains of a desk and com-terminal sat in the far corner. What remained of the kitchen wasn't worth salvaging.

But if someone had wanted this place truly destroyed, they hadn't done a very thorough job. The damage was hefty, but the apartment itself was still in reasonable shape, and the furniture was replaceable. So why bother? It was almost looked as if they were trying to cover something up rather than actually destroying anything.

A balding man in his mid-forties stepped forward, suspicion evident in his small brown eyes. "Can I help you?"

Gabriel flashed his badge yet again. The suspicion in the captain's eyes increased.

"Have you located Samantha Ryan yet?" Gabriel asked.

The captain glanced around. Despite his casual stance, the sharp eyes were never still. He had the look of a man desperate to escape. Sethanon had many Government connections—but did they extend as far down as the captain?

"Since when has the SIU gotten involved in such a mundane case as a bombing?"

"Since when have the beat police?" He deliberately put a derogatory edge on the term, wanting to evoke some sort of honest response from the man.

Anger darkened the captain's face. "Since it was one of my damn officers who was hit. Got a problem with that?"

The man's sudden fierceness surprised him. Such loyalty to the ranks was a rarity these days. "Actually, no." He watched a young officer bend to examine a small hole in the floor, then switched his gaze back to the captain and repeated his question. "You found Ryan yet?"

"No. Security reports show she was home, but we've found no evidence of it yet."

If she'd been here, they would have found bits of her by now. "Mind if I look around?"

As an SIU officer, he outranked the captain and had the right to go where he wanted. But he'd discovered very early on politeness cost nothing and gained much.

"I want to know if you find anything."

He nodded. Whether he actually would say something or not was another matter entirely. Stepping past the captain, he moved across to the small hole the young officer had been examining. Squatting, he ran a finger round the edges. The white marker next to it told him forensics had already checked the hole, so he didn't have to worry about fouling evidence. The rim was glass-edge smooth. The hole wasn't a result of the bomb blast, but more likely a laser. He frowned. Lasers were a rarity on the streets. Even the black marketeers had trouble getting hold of them.

The SIU had them. The defense forces had them. So, too, did a few more covert government departments. As far as he knew, Sethanon *didn't* have them.

He rose and moved into the next room. This room, a bedroom, had been shielded from the main blast by the kitchen cooking units. It had more smoke and water damage than anything else. Sodden masses of boxes and clothes laid everywhere. Even the bed was laden down with junk. Samantha Ryan might live in the apartment, but she sure as hell didn't sleep in this room. There wasn't space enough for a gnat to move.

He was about to turn round when the window caught his attention. Why was it broken, when the bomb had destroyed nothing else in this room? Not even the infinitely more fragile light bulb. He weaved his way through the waterlogged boxes. Broken glass had scattered over the layers of junk near the window. If the explosive force of the bomb *had* caused the break, it would have blown out, not in.

He placed his hands on the sill, and, carefully avoiding the sharp shards still embedded in the window frame, leaned out the window. No stairs, and no obvious way of getting to this window from the ground. He glanced up. Another two stories then the roof.

He headed back to the main room. "Captain, have you assigned anyone to the roof yet?"

Marsdan looked up, sudden interest evident in his hawklike features. "No. Why?"

"Might be worth a look. I think someone broke in through the bedroom window before the blast."

Two officers were immediately assigned. He started to follow, but a long slash across the wall under the living room window caught his eye. He walked across to examine it. Another laser wound—and one that looked to have been fired at a moving target.

He rose, and looked out the window. If she'd jumped out this window, then surely she would still have been lying down on the rain washed pavement when the police arrived. No human could survive a fall like that, and she certainly wouldn't have been well enough to get up and run.

Then again, Finley's test results had indicated Samantha Ryan was definitely something more than human.

He watched the rain gust across the pavement below. The fact that the bomb had only destroyed one section of the apartment suggested it was meant to either cover the attack on Ryan, or destroy something specific. Maybe even both. No matter what that something was, no matter if the bomb succeeded in destroying its intended target, she would have had a backup. It would be in this apartment somewhere, and she would be back for it.

All he had to do was sit here and wait.

***

Sam rubbed her arms in the vague hope that the friction might stop her shivering. She was soaked to the skin and so cold she was beginning to lose sensation in her feet, which was probably a good thing, considering the laser burns.

She blew out a breath and leaned out of the shadows again. Across the street, her apartment building had slipped back into dark silence. The flashing blue and red lights had finally left. Also gone were the teenagers masquerading as state police officers, and the solitary gray Ford with its government plates.

She still didn't understand why the SIU had been called down here. Granted, she was under investigation, but the bombing of her apartment was IIU territory, not State and definitely not SIU.

Maybe she *should* have arrested those two prostitutes last night. Maybe then her life would have remained sane.

But it was far too late for regrets. All she could do now was try and figure out what the hell was going on. She studied her apartment building again. All that remained was the solitary blue light hovering near the front steps. It designated a crime scene and warned anyone entering the building not to go near said crime scene. Upstairs, near her apartment, there would be another one, along with a monitor that would activate the moment anyone tried entering her rooms. If the SIU were involved in the investigation, she had no doubt there would be a nonhuman guard somewhere in the vicinity.

Getting around them all would be a problem. She could probably get past the first monitor using the State's override code, but the monitors guarding the immediate crime scene usually had specific codes. The general override code wouldn't work on it. Jack could probably have managed to get past, but she'd never had his aptitude for hot-wiring. But someone else did. Either that or someone from State had given the invaders her security codes. How else could they have gotten past the heat sensors near the windows? It was only thanks to the alarm she'd installed the day after Jack had disappeared that she was alive right now.

A chill ran down her spine, a chill that had nothing to do with the cold and everything to do with fear. The stranger had said Jack was still alive.

Jack had all her old codes.

But if he were alive, why would he want to kill her? And why blow up her apartment afterwards? It didn't make sense. *Nothing* that had happened in the last twenty-four hours made sense.

Including her survival of a two-story swan dive out the window onto the pavement.

She looked up. Hell, she was bruised and sore all over, and her feet burned something fierce from the laser cuts. But she was basically unhurt from the fall, and that was definitely a miracle.

And it would take another damn miracle to get in and out of her apartment without being caught by the State and SIU watchdogs. With her feet burned so badly, she couldn't exactly run.

Sighing again, she wriggled her toes, enjoying the sensation of the not-so-gentle rain washing over them. But sitting in the shadows of the building across from her own, getting wetter and colder by the minute, was achieving nothing.

She had to get into that apartment and retrieve her backup com-unit—if it had survived the blast. It should have, hidden and protected as it was by the mountains of junk in her bedroom.

But Jack knew about her backup system. If her partner was alive, and if he *was* behind the bomb, then that too would be gone. Though she *had* shifted its location since his disappearance, and the new alarm hadn't allowed the invaders time to look around before they'd attacked.

At least she still had the comlink bracelet she'd stolen. And they'd been developed to survive just about anything—even a bomb blast. The files would be safe, as long as Marsdan and his juniors hadn't found her bag—or, at least, bothered to look inside it.

Though just what in hell Marsdan was doing down here with such a gaggle of wet-nosed officers was another point that didn't make any sense. What was wrong with their squad?

She shook her head. She could sit here and mull on questions forever and a day. If she wanted answers, she'd have to move. Grabbing the railing lining the steps for support, she pulled herself upright. Fire leapt up her legs the minute she put any weight on her feet, and for a moment, she thought she was going to puke. Swallowing heavily, she tried to ignore the throbbing rush of pain and hobbled forward as quickly as she could.

Never before had the street seemed so damn wide. After what

seemed an eternity, she reached her building's front steps and grasped the railing as fiercely as a drowning swimmer did a life buoy. Her breathing was little more than hungry pants of air, and her stomach heaved, leaving a bitter taste in the back of her mouth. Maybe her first port of call should have been a hospital. But the staff were required to report laser burns, and she'd have ended up in the hands of the State Police again.

Until she figured out just who was trying to kill her, she intended to trust no one but herself.

The churning in her stomach began to ease. After taking several more deep breaths, she resolutely hobbled up the rest of the front steps. The blue light hovering near the door became agitated, and a stern voice asked for her name and apartment number, adding the warning that she was about to enter a crime area. Like she didn't already know *that*. She flipped open the monitor's control box and punched in the State's override code. The sharp voice stopped, and the globe ceased its whirling. Of course, when the state boys did a link with the unit to check who was coming in and out of the building, they'd know she—or at least, someone with access to the codes—had entered. But hopefully, by then, she'd be long gone.

She edged inside the door, and quickly scanned the lobby. No one around. She limped across to the stairs and looked up. Everest had surely never seemed so high. She grabbed the handrail and began to haul herself up.

By the time she got to the first landing, the pain in her feet was so bad her legs were shaking, and her head spinning. She collapsed in a heap and stared at the rest of the steps in despair. She was never going to make it the rest of the way. Not like this. Sweat dripped down her forehead, stinging her eyes. She wiped it away with the back of her hand, and then groaned as her stomach rolled and rose. On hands and knees, she lurched towards the nearest planter pot. Luckily for the plant, she'd consumed little more than coffee over the last twenty-four hours.

Once she'd finished, she wiped her mouth with the back of her hand, closed her eyes and leaned back against the balustrade. God, she felt awful. And there was still another whole set of stairs to climb.

As she was contemplating how she was going to manage it, the softest of sounds flowed across the silence—a resonance as soothing as the whisper of silk shimmying across a bed.

She opened her eyes and looked up. A man stood at the top

of the stairs, staring down at her. The warm corridor light flared strangely across his back and shoulders, almost giving him the appearance of wings as it cast his features into shadows. A dark angel, she thought, and wondered briefly if death had come to collect her.

Nah. Hell was more likely her last resting place.

He moved, and the angel image fled. What remained was a tall man, with dark brown hair, dressed in a dark gray suit. The color of choice for those in the SIU.

She groaned again. She really wasn't up to another tête-à-tête with the boys from the spook squad—if indeed he was with them.

He walked down the steps, loose limbed yet somehow graceful, then stopped near her feet and knelt down. He reached out but didn't quite touch her right foot. She sucked in a gasp of air anyway. "Don't—"

"I wasn't," he said, voice soft as he glanced up at her.

She knew those eyes. Would have recognized the odd, green-flecked hazel depths anywhere. This was the man who'd rescued her last night.

"What are you doing here?" she muttered, unable to keep the hint of annoyance from her voice. "And how did you find me?"

A dark eyebrow rose. "Haven't you heard? The SIU knows all."

So she'd guessed right—he was with the spook squad. "Let me see some ID."

He reached inside his suit jacket and drew out a small ID card. She studied the photo and eye scan, and then glanced down at his name. Gabriel Stern. Assistant Director, no less.

She handed back the card. "Not a good photo, Mr. Stern."

"They never are. And please, call me Gabriel. I prefer less formality."

She raised an eyebrow. He'd have to be the first SIU officer in history to ever say that—most were sticklers for regulations, and regulations said no first names. She'd never understood why. She doubted if anyone else did, either.

"So why didn't you back up my story about Jack and that creature? You were chasing the thing, for Christ's sake."

His eyes gained an intensity she suddenly found unnerving. Her breath caught in her throat, and for an instant, it felt as if she could simply reach out and touch his thoughts, his soul.

And for some reason, she found that a more terrifying thought than anything else that had happened in the last twenty-four hours.

"I have my reasons," he said after a moment, and looked down to her feet.

She suddenly found herself able to breathe again. Damn, maybe she *did* need more psych tests.

"These are pretty bad burns," he commented into the silence.

The men from the SIU were observant, no doubt about it. "No kidding? And here I was thinking about running a marathon."

He glanced up again. This time the slightest hint of a smile touched his full lips, softening the impact of his eyes. "Maybe tomorrow."

He seemed in no great hurry to move, which was odd. She knew from past experience that SIU breezed in and out of situations before you had time to blink. Him squatting at her feet simply didn't make sense. Unless, of course, he had a motive for doing so.

Her heart began to beat a little faster. Maybe they'd discovered something about Jack's case, something that implicated *her*. But if that was the case, why didn't he simply arrest her?

Swallowing to ease the sudden dryness in her throat, she asked. "What are you doing here?"

He rocked back on his heels slightly. "Direct. I like that."

"I don't care what you like, mister. Just answer the damn question."

If her tone was less than civil, who cared? If he was here on official business, she had the right to know. And if he wasn't, well, what in hell *did* he want?

The slight smile tugged the corners of his lips again. She had an odd impression it was something that didn't happen often. Which would be a pity since even a slight smile transformed his angular features into something worth a second look.

"The SIU have assigned me as a temporary guard. We believe your life might be in danger." He glanced up the stairs, then back at her. "Looks like we were right."

"And just a little late to prevent major damage being done to my apartment."

"We've never claimed to be perfect."

She snorted softly. "Yeah, right. Am I able to get back in?"

He nodded. "I haven't set the monitor yet."

So he *had* been waiting for her. Interesting. "How bad is the damage?"

He shrugged. "Structurally, nothing much."

Which surely meant there was a shit load of damage to everything else. "I want to go have a look."

He didn't argue, simply rose to his feet and held out his hand. She grabbed it gratefully. His fingers were warm against hers, his palm slightly callused. He wasn't just a simple desk jockey then, which again, was odd. There weren't many Assistant Directors who could claim that.

Nor were there many A.D.s who opted for bodyguard duty. Again, she had an odd sensation that someone was setting her up. For what was the question she had better start finding the answer to.

She'd barely stood when the pain hit her, sliding up her legs like a leech, sucking away whatever strength her muscles had left.

"Oh Christ," she muttered, knowing she was falling but unable to do one goddamn thing to prevent it.

He caught her before she hit the ground. "Want me to carry you?" he said, wrapping an arm around her waist to hold her upright.

And place all control in his hands? Not likely. "I can manage," she said tightly. But the longer she stood here, the more the pain swam through her senses and sent them reeling.

Before she blacked out entirely, she had to get the com-unit.

"Only offering."

He shifted his stance slightly, moving around to her left side. She noted a little wryly that he had to bend quite a bit to accommodate her height—or lack there of. The top of her head barely brushed his chin.

She took a deep breath, gathering whatever strands of strength she had left, and hobbled toward the next set of stairs. Though Gabriel was almost carrying her by the time they got to the top, it still felt as if she'd crawled to hell and back.

"Stop," she managed to say through her gasps for breath.

He eased her to the ground. She closed her eyes and leaned back against the wall, trying to drag enough air into her lungs, and trying to ignore the shaking in her limbs. Maybe Jack's motto of doing unto others wasn't such a bad idea. Right now, she'd love to give the bastards who'd shot her some of their own medicine.

"The scabs have broken open," Gabriel said. "You really

should have treatment for these wounds."

She opened her eyes. He was squatting near her feet again, his eyes as remote as his expression. A man well versed in hiding his feelings, she thought suddenly. "I just want to get home."

"What's left of it." He studied her, the green specks in his hazel eyes glittering like jewels in the dusky hall light. After a moment, he asked. "Ready?"

She nodded. He lifted her up again and helped her walk the rest of the way to her apartment. When she got there, she could only stare.

She'd been to more than one bombing, and she knew firsthand the damage they could do. But this time it was different. This time it was her belongings, her privacy, that had been invaded and destroyed.

Pain momentarily forgotten, she pushed away from Gabriel and hobbled into the living room. Everything was either gone or severely damaged. All the books she'd gathered over the years, all the small bits and pieces she'd collected to remember the changes in her life. All gone, or not salvageable.

Clenching her fists, she glanced to where the com-unit had once stood. Even the sketch of her mother had been destroyed. All that was left were small shards of glass that glittered brightly in the soggy remains of the carpet.

"It's going to be a few days before State releases these rooms for cleanup," he said into the silence.

She *knew* how long State would take, for Christ's sake. Unable to decide whether to swear vehemently or simply sit down and howl, she did neither, hobbling into the bedroom instead.

Even this room had not escaped destruction, though here, at least, the cause was more smoke and water. The smell of sodden boxes and wet carpet churned her already agitated stomach. She ran a hand through her sweat-dampened hair, fighting a sudden feeling of despair. God, it would take her days to clean up this mess. And years to replace all that she'd lost. *If* she could replace it. Her gaze touched the stack of boxes that hid her second com-unit. They looked undisturbed, and relief surged through her.

She looked over her shoulder and met Gabriel's gaze. He stood in the doorway, his hands shoved into his pockets, his stance casual yet strangely alert. And the feeling that this man, her supposed protector, was far more than what he seemed hit her like a punch to the gut. He might have saved her life last night, but she knew absolutely nothing about him, let alone if she could trust him. And as she stared at him, she got the distinct impression he was here for reasons other than his official watchdog duty.

"I've arranged accommodation at a small hotel down the road." His voice was soft, almost soothing, as if she were fragile glass about to break.

The only hotel down the road was the Rosewater, which was upmarket and very expensive. Well beyond the usual offerings for someone under protection. "And who's picking up that little tab?"

He raised an eyebrow in surprise. "The SIU, of course."

The SIU obviously had a hell of a budget. "I'll get some things together."

She limped to the wardrobe and opened the door. The clothes inside reeked with smoke, and she screwed up her nose. Still, she could hardly keep wearing the things she had on, and smoke smell or not, these were her only other option. She grabbed a duffle bag from the top of the closet, and shoved in enough clothes to last a week. Surely it wouldn't take any longer to clean up this mess.

But what if it did? What if, by some vicious quirk of fate, they actually charged her with Jack's death? What would she do? God, if the captain didn't believe her, a courtroom filled with strangers certainly wouldn't.

Panic flashed white hot through her body, and for a moment, even the simple act of breathing seemed difficult. She couldn't go to prison. Couldn't be locked up like that. Not again.

She frowned at the thought, wondering where in hell it came from. The only time she'd been in prison was to question suspects. And she *wasn't* going to go to prison now. The truth was out there, and so was the evidence that would prove her innocence. All she had to do was find it—or at least hope they gave her the time to find it.

With the bag almost full, she hobbled across to the stack of boxes that hid her second com-unit. After thrusting the sodden mess to one side, she bent down and disconnected the portable unit from the wall, then put it inside the bag, hiding it underneath her clothes.

When she turned around, Gabriel was at the door, watching her.

"Need a hand?"

Anger surged, but she bit it back, knowing it was futile. He might say he was here to protect her, but the fact was, she was still under suspicion for Jack's murder. There would be other cops out there, cops she couldn't see, also watching her.

She tossed the duffel bag across to him. He caught it deftly, a hint of surprise flaring briefly in his eyes.

"I'm not leaving anything of value here. I know for a fact a cunning enough criminal can get past those scanners." Jack could have, for a start.

And she didn't even want to think about what the hirsute stranger had said. That maybe Jack *was* alive.

Gabriel nodded toward the sea of sodden boxes. "What about these?"

She shrugged. "Just books and junk I've collected over the years and never gotten around to throwing out." She'd have to now, though. The water and smoke damage had seen to that.

"Anything else you want?"

"Handbag, if you can see it."

He turned around, his gaze scanning the front room. She slowly hobbled across, and then stopped beside him. "There," she said, pointing to the leather strap barely visible beneath the half destroyed sofa chair.

He walked across the room. The bag came out in one piece, which hopefully meant everything within it was intact as well. He slung both bags over his left shoulder. "Ready to go?"

She nodded. Weariness rose like a tide, and suddenly it was all she could do to stand there. Pain was beginning to beat through her brain again, and she just wanted to go somewhere, anywhere, to rest.

He walked over and tucked his arm around her waist. It felt good. Safe. Obviously, the last twenty-four hours had affected her brain cells worse than she'd thought, because nowhere was safe right now.

"Let's go," he said, and guided her out of her apartment.

By the time they reached his car, he was almost carrying her. Everything ached so badly, all she wanted to do was just lay down and die.

He opened the door of the standard issue dark gray Ford and eased her inside. She clipped the seat belt into place, and then let her head fall back against the rest. Sweat trickled down the side of her face, but she couldn't drag up enough energy to wipe it away. Closing her eyes, she struggled against the lethargy beginning to take hold, knowing she had to stay awake, stay aware and in control. Trusting no one was a motto she'd lived with half her life—or at least, the half she could remember. Only Jack had broken through the barriers she'd raised—and, living or dead, Jack had now betrayed her.

"You okay?"

His soft question ran through the mist encasing her mind. Energy rose from somewhere, and she opened her eyes. He was in the driver's seat, the car running. She'd heard neither event.

"I'm tired, that's all. Just go."

A slight hint of concern cut through the intensity of his gaze. He nodded, and drove off. As if from a great distance, she watched the streets flit by. Within seconds, it seemed, they'd stopped again.

He opened her door, then bent down and unclipped her seat belt. "I'm calling in a doctor about those wounds on your feet."

She rubbed her head wearily. God, even her fingers hurt. "Just get me upstairs and let me rest. I'll be fine."

"Like hell you will." His mutter ran past her ear as he slipped his arms round her body.

She didn't protest as he lifted her out of the car. Didn't have the energy. She just wanted to rest, to let it all slide away. But not until she was safe. Not until she was alone.

She rested her head against his shoulder as he walked the steps to the hotel lobby. The warmth of his body seeped across her skin, chasing the icy chills from hers. He smelled good, too, his scent a pleasant mix of sage and erotic spices. But a nice smell and a warm, taut body didn't mean he was trustworthy. Gabriel Stern had a mission here with her, and it wasn't the one he had told her about. Until she knew what his motives were, she had to be extremely cautious around the man. No matter how pleasant some sections of her body might find him.

A thin man, his expression slightly alarmed, met them in the lobby and escorted them to the elevator. The doors swished closed, and then they were heading up and up. It finally came to a jolting stop, and she closed her eyes, fighting another bout of nausea. Then she was being lowered, and Gabriel's warmth left her. She forced her eyes open, and looked up.

The edge of concern was stronger in his gaze. "Your two bags are at the end of the bed. I'll be in the next room, making a few calls. Do you need anything?"

"Just rest."

He frowned slightly, then nodded and walked from the room, closing the door behind him. She forced herself upright, reaching for the strap of her handbag and dragging it towards her.

The wristcom was still there. She held it up to the light, looking for any sign of damage. Moisture glistened on the metal surface, but these things had been tested underwater to great depths, so the bit of liquid it endured in her apartment wouldn't have harmed it. There was no other sign of damage, though, which was a relief. If she were alone, she would have started it up, but with Gabriel in the next room, she didn't dare take the chance. If he saw it, he'd take it off her, of that she had no doubt. And probably charge her for theft in the process. The SIU boys were sticklers when it came to the rules.

She put it back, and an odd clinking sound caught her attention. Opening the bag wider, she saw several large shards of china.

She reached in and pulled one out—the handle and a jagged chunk of white china. Pain welled up, pain greater than anything she'd ever felt before. She stared at the broken piece of mug, her gaze suddenly blurred by tears. Everything she'd ever valued was gone. The bomb had destroyed the few precious mementos she'd had of her past, and now it had taken this, the very first Christmas present she ever remembered getting.

She flopped back on the bed and rolled to one side, raising her knees and hugging them close as she finally let go. Tears fell like hot rain down her cheeks to the sheets, slowly spreading out in an ever-widening circle of grief.

Four

A soft knock at the door jerked Gabriel awake. He pushed the hair back out of his eyes, and glanced quickly around. Nothing had changed in the brief time he'd slept. Darkness still held court in the room, but through the windows, the bloody flags of dawn were beginning to stain the horizon. He rose from the sofa and walked over to the door.

"Yes?" he said, one hand on the knob, the other reaching for his weapon.

"It's Karl. Open up."

He would have recognized that gruff voice anywhere, but even so, caution prevailed. He switched on the security camera and looked out. The man standing on the other side of the door could only be described as a square—he was almost as wide as he was tall. Wearing baggy jeans that looked half a century old, a bright yellow Hawaiian shirt, and a red bandanna that barely restrained his wild brown hair, he looked more like an escapee from the circus than one of the country's top herbal healers.

He unlocked the door. "Glad you could make it."

"Didn't know if I would," Karl said. "Stephan has some major problems."

Something clenched in his gut. Stephan wasn't just his brother. He was also the driving force behind the Federation. Destroy him, and you'd come damn close to destroying the Federation. And yet, less than a dozen people knew who Stephan actually was, and only four had constant access to him.

"What sort of problems?" He relocked the door and moved across to the window. The street below was empty of traffic, and no one lurked in the shadows in the park across the road. They were safe from discovery, at least for the moment.

Karl slumped onto the sofa and propped his sandaled feet on the mahogany coffee table. "Won't know for sure until I get the second lot of test results, but it looks like someone's been poisoning him."

Relief eased some of the tension knotting his shoulders. Poisoning was better than some of the scenarios he'd envisioned. "How is the poison being administered?"

"The first tests indicate it's probably through his drinking water."

He frowned and moved across to a chair. "He told me last night that water was the one thing he could keep down."

Karl nodded thoughtfully. "There are about a dozen poisons that are almost untraceable in water, and a few of those effect your system to a point where water is the only thing you can take."

"Is it curable?"

"I think we've caught it before it got critical, so yes."

"Thank the gods," he muttered. He wasn't ready to face Stephan's death. Probably never would be, despite the fact they'd discussed the possibility only a few months ago.

The sound of a soft footstep made him look at the closed bedroom door. Surely she couldn't be awake—not after all she'd been through in the last twenty-four hours. When no other noise followed, he glanced back at Karl.

"How long has the poisoning been happening?"

"At least four months." Karl hesitated, and then lowered his gaze to his steepled fingers. "How many people have constant access to Stephan?"

"Myself, Martyn, Lyssa and Mary." Two of those three he'd trust with his life. And it couldn't be Martyn, simply because he knew poisoning Stephan would not truly kill him. It would only thrust him into life as one of the undead.

"One of those three has to be your culprit," Karl said.

He scrubbed a hand across his jaw. It made no sense. If one of the three had wanted Stephan dead, they could have found far easier ways than this. "When will you get the second lot of test results back?"

"Tomorrow."

"Any chance of tracing the poison back to its source?"

Karl hesitated. "Probably not, but I'll try."

He nodded, then at the sound of another step, glanced across to the bedroom. She was definitely moving around. He rose and walked to the door. Grabbing the handle, he turned it quickly and opened the door—only to hit something solid on the other side.

How much had she heard? He had no desire to explain who Stephan was, and what he meant—to both him and Federation—to someone like her. Someone who, even if unknowingly, might be involved with the enemy.

She rubbed her nose, but her expression was defiant. Which, oddly enough, he liked. "You should be resting. Finley has lots of tests planned for later this morning."

She shrugged, her blue eyes wary. "I heard voices."

"I called a doctor down here to look at your feet." Which, he noticed, she seemed to be standing on just fine. Odd, given that only a few hours ago, they'd been burned so deeply he could literally see bone.

"There's really no need, but thanks, anyway."

He nodded and stepped to one side, waving her past. Tension ran across her shoulders when she spotted Karl, but it just as quickly, fled. He wondered who Karl had briefly reminded her of.

"Karl, Samantha," he said.

She propped herself on the opposite end of the sofa from Karl, reminding Gabriel of a trapped animal. One wrong move and she'd run, of that he had no doubt.

"May I have a look at your feet?" Karl spoke softly, as if he too sensed her desire for flight.

Gabriel caught the wariness in her eyes again. Distrust was part of any good police officer's makeup, but this seemed to run much deeper. So how had she become involved with someone like Kazdan?

She shifted her feet onto the cushions. Karl studied them silently, then reached forward and lightly ran a finger over both wounds. She winced, but otherwise didn't object.

"There's a fair bit of scar tissue, but otherwise, they're fine." Karl raised an eyebrow, his gaze meeting Gabriel's. He shrugged at the unspoken question in Karl's gaze. Four hours ago the wounds had been so bad that she shouldn't have been able to even walk on them—yet walk she had, even though she'd made herself sick doing so. Now they were almost healed. Maybe the answer was tied up in those extra chromosomes Finley had found.

"It'll be a bit tender for a day or so," Karl continued, his gaze moving back to Sam. "But I can give you some oil to help that."

"Thank you," she said softly.

Karl reached into his pocket. She tensed, relaxing only when his fingers came free. Again, Gabriel wondered what had happened to her that distrust ran so deeply.

"Rub a small amount of this oil into your feet morning and night. Should numb the pain and stop the permanent formation of scar tissue."

She took the small bottle with her fingertips, turning it slowly over in her hand as she examined it. Karl rose, and Gabriel walked him to the door.

"I'll talk to you tonight about the other matter."

Karl nodded. "Do that. I have some interesting observations

to share."

He raised his eyebrows, but made no comment and opened the door. "Take care, my friend."

Karl slapped a hand on Gabriel's arm, grinning lightly as he walked past. Moving with a speed and grace that belied his bulk, he quickly disappeared down the hall. After locking the door, Gabriel turned around and found Sam's gaze on him. Uncertainty and suspicion clouded her eyes. She wasn't sure about him, despite the fact he'd undoubtedly saved her from the kite. Was it the natural suspicion of a cop in trouble, or something more?

"I took the liberty of sending your clothes out to be cleaned," he said, walking across to the small autocook. "They're hanging in the closet."

"Thank you." She hesitated. "Tell me, is it usual for SIU to provide such lavish surroundings for those they're trying to protect?"

He smiled. "No. But in your case, I deemed it best."

She raised a pale gold eyebrow. "Why?"

He shrugged. "Because it's the sort of place we don't usually choose. Makes it that much harder for would be killers to find you."

She glanced away, but not before he'd seen the slight sheen of tears in her eyes. Yet, like last night, she'd refused to shed them, refused to give in to the shock and pain of the last twenty-four hours. Why?

"I think I'll go take a shower," she said, and scrambled off the sofa.

He took in her sleek shape as she walked away, finding himself oddly attracted, even though his taste usually ran to women more curvaceous. But maybe a major part of his attraction was not so much the woman, but the mystery she presented. And it was a mystery that ran far deeper than Kazdan's recruitment efforts and his subsequent death.

She was an enigma, but puzzles and problems were his forte. And no matter what it was she was hiding, he *would* uncover it.

As she neared the doorway, he asked, "What do you want for breakfast?"

"Coffee," she said, without turning around. "And toast, or something like that."

She closed the door firmly behind her. A few seconds later came the sound of running water. He selected a breakfast for them both, then made himself a cup of coffee and walked across to the window.

Resting the steaming cup of coffee on the windowsill, he
crossed his arms and leaned a shoulder against the window frame.
Dawn had spread her bloody fingers wide, playing across the
field of clouds. For the moment, at least, the rain had stopped.
He glanced at his watch, then retrieved the vid phone from his
jacket pocket and quickly dialed Stephan's number. The call was
answered on the second ring.

"What's wrong?" Stephan asked, without preamble.

"We safe?" Though this particular number was one only the
two of them knew about, there might have been someone close
by.

Stephan nodded. His face was pale, eyes still ringed by
deepening shadows, and right now, he looked like death itself.
The thought chilled him. He wasn't ready to handle his brother
as one of the undead.

"I'm alone in the study," Stephan said. "Lyssa is upstairs,
asleep."

"I've just talked to Karl. Stop drinking the water. Someone's
poisoning you."

Stephan scrubbed a hand across his jaw. "Impossible. I don't
drink tap water, only bottled, and it's always tested when it
arrives."

"Which means someone is administrating the poison after
it's tested." He watched the implications of this dawn in his
brother's eyes. "Until we know who, I don't want you to drink
anything unless I give it to you."

"That'll raise suspicions."

"Right now, I don't fucking care."

Warmth momentarily chased the weariness from his brother's
gaze. "I'm not going to die on you, little brother, so stop
worrying."

In the park opposite the hotel, something moved. He frowned
and watched the shadows more closely. "Given this attempt is
very close to home, I have every right to worry."

"You'll investigate?"

Who else was there? Most of their immediate family
members were no longer fully functional in the Federation. To
draw them back now would only raise suspicions. "When Karl
gets the full results in." He hesitated, catching another stirring in
the shadows. Someone was definitely down there—but was it
someone intent on harming them, or simply someone taking an
early morning walk? "I have to go. Remember, no water until I
get there."

"Will do."

Stephan's image dissolved. Gabriel pocketed the phone. In that instant, the sun broke through the clouds, and in the shadows of the park, something long and metallic glinted briefly. A gun.

Or worse.

Adrenaline surged like fear through his body, and he flung himself sideways. A second later the window shattered, spraying glass across his back and shoulders. Something thumped behind him, and he twisted around to look. A black ball had lobbed three feet away and was rolling slowly towards him. *A fire grenade.* Knowing he only had a minute at the most before it went off, he lunged forward, wrapped his fingers around the device, and flung it back through the shattered window.

Not a moment to soon.

There was an almost inconspicuous pop, then a blinding flash, and liquid heat was exploding across the air, across his flesh. Ignoring the burning sensation, he crawled towards the bedroom. The door was flung open as he neared. Sam, hair wet and bedraggled, peered out.

"Keep down," he hissed, and noted with relief that she was fully dressed.

She dropped to her knees. Another thump sounded behind them. He grabbed her and rolled them both behind the cover of the bedroom wall.

Heat hissed through the room, curling paint and scorching the fine wool carpet. He kicked the door shut, but he knew it wouldn't offer much in the way of protection. Fire grenades weren't generally designed to ignite into flame, but if the man below kept firing them into the room, the whole place might soon be an inferno.

"Grab your stuff," he said, and released her.

The first thing she grabbed was her com-unit, which definitely meant it was something he should look at, when he had the time. Which sure as hell wasn't now. He stamped out a lick of flames near the door, then rolled onto his knees and crawled to the window.

The shadowy form was still in the park, still watching. They'd have to leave the car. Even though he'd parked it out of sight, there was only one exit from the parking garage, and that was straight onto the street below them. He got his phone out and quickly dialed SIU for assistance.

Two minutes, the impersonal voice on the other end informed him.

Two minutes they didn't have.

Sam crawled towards him, bag slung over her back. "What now?"

In answer, he took his gun from the holster and set it to full laser. He pointed it at the wall and pulled the trigger. Plaster and wood splintered across the room as he blew a hole big enough for the two of them to fit through.

"Now we escape," he said, holstering his weapon.

"I like your methods," she said, a slight smile curving the edges of her generous mouth.

His own smile was grim. He was pretty damn sure the men in charge at SIU *wouldn't*. Property damage was something to be avoided at all costs. It said so in the fine print of every rule book he'd ever read. Of course, he wasn't one for following rule books, which was probably why he was still an assistant director and not something more.

"Keep close," he said, and crawled forward. She tucked herself behind him.

He stopped at the hole and peered through. Though he knew this room should be empty—simply because he'd booked the four rooms on this floor as a security precaution—he still checked. Given the attack, it was highly logical there would be other assailants around. But the room was silent, and he had no sense that anyone was close. He climbed through, stood up and helped Samantha do the same.

The wall that separated them from their own room shook as another incendiary device went off. Beyond that, the strident sound of an alarm. Time to go, before the State and Fire boys arrived.

"We'll take the fire escape and catch a cab back to Central Security."

She raised a pale eyebrow, but didn't argue. Though if the glint in her unusual blue-gray eyes was anything to go by, she'd definitely thought about it. He wrapped a hand around the door knob and slowly opened the door. The corridor beyond was empty, silent.

Smoke was beginning to filter under the door to their room, spreading translucent fingers through the hall. Overhead, the automatic sprinklers chimed softly and dropped from the ceiling, ready for action should the smoke get any thicker. He opened the door wider, and edged out.

"Stairs are four doors down to our right," she said quietly.

He nodded, more than a little surprised that even when half-unconscious, she'd noted the exits. It was the sign of a damn good cop. "Stay behind me."

He kept his back to the wall and moved forward cautiously. The wailing sirens were drawing closer. Surely their assailant would have fled by now. If he lingered too much longer, he'd be an easy target for the State boys. Or the SIU, who should also be close by now.

In the room opposite, a floorboard creaked. He stopped, holding the gun at the ready, staring at the door, straining every sense he had to try and decipher who—or what—approached.

"Gun!" Her warning was little more than a hiss of air, and then her body cannoned into his back, knocking him down and sideways. He twisted, catching her in his arms, breaking her fall with his own body.

A heartbeat later, the section of wall where he'd been standing shattered into a million pieces, showering them with chunks of plaster and wood.

"Two doors back, on the right," she whispered, then rolled behind him.

He turned and fired. The shot burned through the door. A second later there was a heavy thump as something solid hit the floor. "Go," he muttered.

She scrambled to her feet and ran for the stairs. He flicked the gun charge to stun and fired several warning shots, doing little more than singe the paint. Then he pushed up after her.

They made it down the stairs in record time. At the bottom, he stopped and listened for any sort of pursuit. The rapid sound of Sam's breathing was the only sound to be heard over the wailing sirens, but that didn't mean someone wasn't after them.

He cracked open the exit door and peered out. Nothing seemed out of place, and the only sign of movement was the slate gray car cruising to a halt a hundred meters down the road. There would be another around the next corner. It was standard SIU procedure.

He grabbed her hand and led her out. Two men climbed out of the car as they approached it.

"Assistant Director Stern," the first man said, giving them both the once-over. "What's happening?"

"Somebody fire bombed room four-five. Assailant was in the park."

"State is around front, but we'll check. Anything else?"

"Another assailant, possibly two, in the rooms opposite four-five. And check my car. If they knew I was here, they might have tampered with it. I'll have your keys."

The SIU agent handed over the triangular shaped black key-coder. "Yours, sir?"

He tossed the agent his keys, then ushered Sam inside the car. The two SIU officers headed for the fire exit as he climbed into the car.

"Didn't you just break a few major rules?" she said.

He started the engine and glanced at her. The wariness was still very evident in her eyes, but it had been softened slightly by a hint of amusement.

He shrugged. "They've come to expect that of me."

"I noticed they didn't quibble."

Maybe. But that didn't mean the shit wouldn't hit the fan later on. He *had* broken a few major rules, but right now, he didn't care. This case was getting dangerous, and he wasn't about to hang around where it wasn't safe. "At least Finley will be able to get an early start on those extra tests."

"And what about someone starting an investigation as to why I'm being attacked? Not to mention how they found us so quickly at the Rosewater?"

"What do you think I'll be doing while you're having those tests?"

"Good," she muttered, and crossed her arms.

The gentle hum of the engine filled the silence for several seconds. Her gaze was a warmth that he could feel deep inside, but he kept his own gaze on the road. Right now, she was probably trying to figure out whether he could be trusted or not. Which was fair enough, given the situation she found herself in. But if their positions had been reversed, he would have been asking lots and lots of questions, if only because answers didn't come by remaining silent. And sooner or later, if she wanted *real* answers, she would have to not only start asking questions, but place her trust in *someone*. Even if her psych evaluations suggested she not only had a problem with vampires, but trusting people in general.

So why had she trusted Kazdan? If ever there was a man not to trust, it was *that* lying, murdering hound.

"Am I still under investigation for Jack's death?" she asked eventually.

He nodded. "You shot and killed your partner. Did you expect them *not* to investigate?"

"No, but—" she stopped, and sighed. A frustrated sound if he'd ever heard one.

"There's nothing much anyone can do until those test results come back and confirm or deny your story."

"*You* can confirm my damn story."

He ignored the anger in her voice. "Only part of it. Fact is I was long gone by the time you killed your partner."

"You can still confirm the fact that they were trying to kill me."

"But not the fact that Jack was."

She made a sound in the back of her throat that sounded suspiciously like an exasperated growl. He looked at her, but she was now looking out the window and refused to meet his gaze, though the sudden tension in her shoulders made it obvious that she was well aware of his scrutiny.

The rest of the journey passed in silence. He parked in the SIU's underground parking lot and climbed out. She avoided his attempt to guide her across to the elevators, walking by his side but just out of arm's reach. He swiped his pass through the security slot and punched the button for sub-floor twenty-eight. Once they reached the main labs area, he led her to the unoccupied reception area and paged Finley.

"Why all these tests?" She leaned back against the whitewashed walls, and gave him what could only be described as a hostile look.

For all of two seconds, he thought about lying. But if he wanted her to trust him, he had better start giving her some reason to do so. So he shrugged, and said, "Because you did something the other night you should not have been able to do."

She raised an eyebrow. "Something other than having the audacity to save myself when my partner was trying to kill me?"

His smile was grim. "You sensed the kite-monster. You shouldn't have been able to do that."

"Why? You obviously could."

Yeah, but he wasn't about to go into the reasons for that right here. As protected as the SIU was from monitors, there was still the remote possibility that somehow, somewhere, someone was listening.

"The kites are a new find. Few people know of them, fewer still have been able to see them early enough to survive an attack. You did, and we need to know why."

The anger in her blue-gray eyes had died a little, but not the frustration and wariness. "So the psych tests were just a reason to get me down here to do these other tests?"

"Basically, yes."

"At least someone's being honest," she muttered, then gave him a smile that held little real warmth. "Thanks."

He nodded and glanced up as Finley came down the hall.

"You're early," Finley commented, pushing his thick glasses back up his nose.

He wondered why the young doctor just didn't have laser correction or get implants for his eyes. Hell, given Finley's skills in the medical field, he could probably even do the procedure himself.

"How small do they make microchips these days?"

Finley's expression was one of surprise. So was Sam's.

"The *largest* they make them is pinhead size. Those ones are rather outdated, of course."

"Can they be inserted into a human body? Used to track movements?"

Finley glanced at Sam. "Yeah. Want me to look for one?"

He nodded. They'd been found too quickly at the Rosewater. They hadn't been followed there from Sam's apartment, nor had he told anyone that they were going to be there. Only Karl had known, and even he didn't know who Sam was.

Which left them with Sam herself.

"Let you know what I find." Finley stated, and waved her ahead of him.

He nodded and turned, heading for his office. He had to call Karl, and then he had plans to make. There was a traitor in the Federation's midst, a traitor intent on taking the life of *his* brother. It wasn't going to happen. Not if he could do anything to stop it.

He had no idea who was behind this particular attempt, but he *would* find the culprit.

And then he'd kill him.

Five

Sam leaned back in the well-padded armchair and watched Finley walk out the door. In some ways, the doctor reminded her of a dragonfly—he was always darting about from one machine to another, as if he couldn't remain still for more than a few minutes. And he was about as skinny as one of those insects, too.

She glanced at the monitor on the far wall. It was nearly nine. Four hours she'd been here, being poked and prodded and shoved inside huge, impersonal machines. And she'd really had just about enough. None of this would find any answers. Not the answers *she* wanted found, anyway.

Her gaze dropped to the ID tag sitting on the nearby table. She frowned, reached forward and picked it up. Finley had given it to her earlier, warning that she'd need it if she wanted to go to the restroom. She'd thought he'd been joking, until she'd actually tried to go. Anyone would think the toilet seats were damn gold.

She turned the card over and caught sight of some writing in the left corner. Security clearance level three. Her heart began to beat a little faster. It was probably the minimum clearance you needed to move around the SIU halls, but upstairs, in the areas governed by State, level three would get her into the morgue.

Dare she?

Her gaze went to the door through which Finley had disappeared, and she smiled grimly. How could she not? She needed answers, and this tag would at least help her get some.

She clipped it on, rose and walked across to the door. Finley glanced up from the com-screen as she entered the outer room and gave her a distracted smile. Her own smile was easy. Jack had once told she could act right up there with the best of them. She hoped like hell he was right.

"Restroom again," she said. They'd been feeding her enough fluid over the past few hours that she knew he'd accept the explanation.

He nodded and returned his attention to the monitor. She moved into the hall and stopped. It was still deserted, and the silence was almost intense. Finley had told her that only a skeletal staff worked here during the day. The SIU, with its task of investigating all matters relating to the paranormal, tended to have its normal working day during the night, which meant there would be few people around to question or stop her. All she had to do was hope no one in the know was watching the monitors.

She turned left and headed up the corridor. The elevators came quickly into view, the doors opening as she neared. She stepped inside and swiped her card, as she'd seen Gabriel do earlier. Then she pressed the button for sub level three. For a moment, there was no reaction, and her breath caught. What if she'd been wrong about the pass? God, the last thing she wanted was more damn trouble landing on her shoulders.

Which undoubtedly was what she'd get by doing what she was doing. But, damn it, trouble brought about by searching for answers was worth it. It was the doing nothing that was driving her crazy.

The doors decided to shut, and the elevator moved up. She sighed in relief and watched the numbers zip by. At upper-fourteen, the elevator stopped and the doors opened. She peered out. The corridor was silent and quite dark. Obviously, no one had reported in to work up here yet, which had to be good news for her. Unless, of course, security noticed her presence and decided to do something about it.

She studied the ceiling, looking for monitors. One . . . two near the elevator, and at least one halfway down the hall. But if she kept to the walls, out of the light sensor range, maybe she'd escape notice long enough to get to the morgue and take a look at Jack's corpse. *If* they hadn't processed him—though it would have to be something of a record if they had. Technology might have made everyone's job simpler, but things still seemed to take the same amount of time, if not longer.

She walked along the corridor, keeping as close to the thick shadows crowding the wall as possible. Above her, the security cam's hummed as they tracked her movement, but no lights came on, and more importantly, no alarm had sounded. She found the entrance to the morgue, and swiped her card. The door clicked open. In the morgue's outer rooms, bright light flared, making her eyes water.

Cursing softly, she quickly stepped inside and shut the door. "Light's dim," she hissed. Instantly, the glare became a muted glow. She glanced around. Though she'd only come down here when absolutely necessary, that was still often enough to know the general layout of the place. Mark Righter, the medical examiner, had a desk in the far corner. More than likely he'd be handling Jack's examination himself.

She rifled through the papers and files sitting on his desk, but Jack's file wasn't among them. Surely they couldn't have finished the autopsy already? Frowning, she swung around and headed for the morgue. She didn't have time to do a proper search for the file. Finley would soon notice she was missing. Before the alarm was raised, she had to get in, and have a look at Jack. She had a feeling Assistant Director Gabriel Stern would be canny enough to guess exactly where she'd gone.

The sickly strong scent of antiseptic punched her senses the moment she entered the room. Behind it, elusive and yet just as powerful, was the smell of death. She shuddered and quietly closed the door. The morgue was long and silent. Shadows crowded the far corners, despite the dim glow of the lights. Her gaze went to the where the dead lay waiting, and after a moment's hesitation, she walked across the room. The freezer units were categorized alphabetically. Jack's was about halfway along the wall. She grabbed the handle, and then she stopped and took several deep breaths to calm her suddenly churning stomach.

She could do this. Had to do this, if she wanted to start finding answers.

Gripping the handle tightly, she pulled the drawer open. Jack's body, cold and white, slid out to greet her. Her gaze went to what was left of his head, and her stomach rolled in revulsion. She let go of the drawer and backed away, desperately trying to control the urge to be sick. It wasn't as if she'd never seen a dead body before, for Christ's sake.

But this *was* the first time she'd seen anyone she'd cared about down here.

And absolutely the very first time that person was down here because *she'd* shot them.

For a reason, she reminded herself severely. She'd had no other choice, of that she was certain, even if she was certain of nothing else. And if she wanted to know why Jack had forced that choice, then she had better control her damn stomach and get back to examining the body.

Before AD Stern and his cronies came in here and dragged her away.

Taking another deep breath, she walked up to the drawer. And saw that death had frozen a look of disbelief on what remained of Jack's face.

Oh God . . . no.

She staggered away and threw up in the nearest trash can.

"You okay?" The question rose out of the semidarkness, the voice familiar and filled with concern.

She groaned. Just what she needed. Gabriel finding her before she'd had a chance to overcome her nerves and look at Jack.

"I'm fine," she muttered, digging into her pocket to grab a handkerchief and wipe her mouth.

"There's a water fountain in the outer office. Would you like a drink?"

That had her looking up. He'd leave the room, leave her with the body? That went against every rule in the book, but then, Gabriel Stern didn't seem to care much about the rules. Not when ignoring them suited him better. "Yes. Thank you."

He nodded and turned around. She watched him walk back through the door, and then she pushed away from the desk and walked back over to Jack.

Trying to ignore the look on his face, trying to ignore her rebellious stomach, she studied the rest of his body. Jack naked was nothing new to her. Men and woman shared the same change rooms up in State, and once she'd recovered from the initial shock, even embarrassment, she'd become as indifferent as everyone else to it all.

Yet she could never remember Jack being *this* white. He'd always prided himself on his tan—he'd never cared about how out of fashion it was deemed these days. Surely death hadn't stolen *all* his color.

Gabriel came back through the door and crossed over to her. He handed her a cup and studied the naked form in front of them.

"What are you looking for?" he asked.

"I don't know." Sipping the water, she let her gaze slide down Jack's body. His left hand rested on the flat of his stomach. His wedding ring was missing, which in itself was not unusual, given the morgue staff would have secured any possessions before they placed him in the drawer. What *was* unusual was the fact that his finger showed no telltale mark of him ever having worn a ring.

Her gaze moved down, and she frowned. Where the hell was the knife scar? He'd received the wound in their first year as partners and had worn it as a badge of valor ever since, refusing to have skin grafts. It made no sense for it to be gone now.

But before she could open her mouth to mention it, the lights in the outer office went off. And they wouldn't have done that unless someone had ordered it. Why would someone from State, or even the SIU, have done such a thing when it was obvious someone was in the morgue?

Gabriel touched her arm in warning and pointed to the examination tables on the far side of the room. She nodded, slid Jack's drawer back home, and followed him across. The morgue lights went out as she hunkered down beside Gabriel. Someone moved in the outer office, sliding drawers open and closed. Searching for what?

Minutes dragged by. She shifted, wondering why Gabriel didn't do something. Whoever was in that office had to be up to no good if they'd turned the lights off, so why not call in the police? Hell, they were squatting in a building filled with them.

She shifted her weight again, and then stopped as the morgue door eased open. Heat prickled across her skin, and once again her senses seemed to explode outwards. The two men entering the room where vampires . . . and yet not.

The sensation slithered away. She shuddered, not understanding what was happening, not even understanding the information the weird attack had given her.

Gabriel's hand touched her knee. Warmth and strength seemed to flow from it, fighting the chill suddenly encasing her body. She glanced up and saw the concern in his eyes. Fear suddenly slammed into her heart. She could see his eyes, see *him*, as clearly as if it were light, not pitch black. *What the hell is happening to me?* She had a sudden feeling that Finley's tests, and Gabriel himself, might be able to provide an answer, but now was not the time to ask.

Biting her lip, she turned her gaze back to the two men entering the room. Dressed in black, they almost merged into the darkness. One of them carried something over his right shoulder—a sack of some kind. Both of them stopped just inside the doorway, their gazes scanning the darkened room. If they were vampires, how could they not see her and Gabriel? Or hear the beats of their hearts? How could these men not know they were here?

Because they obviously didn't. They moved as one, walking silently across the room to Jack's drawer. For some reason, she wasn't entirely surprised. The weirdness had started with Jack. Somehow, he was the key to it all.

Gabriel squeezed her knee lightly and motioned to the left, holding up three fingers. She nodded. Placing her cup on the floor, she silently counted to three, rose and scooted around the edge of the room, coming in on the two men from the left.

They were so intent on trying to bag Jack's body that neither man became aware of their approach until it was far too late.

"Police," she said softly, grabbing the arm of one of the strangers and twisting it back behind his back. "Don't move."

He was obviously hard of hearing, because he not only moved, but came out swinging. She ducked under his blow, and then hit him. Not exactly ethical, but hey, he was possibly a vampire, and she was already suspended.

He went down like a sack of potatoes. She frowned and glanced at her clenched fist. She hadn't hit him *that* hard. She looked across to Gabriel. He had the second intruder by the neck and was holding him slightly above the ground.

It took a lot of strength to do something like that, more strength than most humans normally had. But then, Gabriel Stern worked for the SIU. They weren't big on employing normal type humans.

"Remind me never to tackle you when you're angry," he said, his expression grim. But as he met her gaze, a slight hint of amusement touched his eyes.

This, coming from a man who appeared intent on choking his suspect to death. "Ah . . . hadn't you better loosen your grip at little? Don't want to kill him before he can answer a question or two."

He glanced at the felon for a moment and shook him a little. The man made an odd sort of gagging sound. Gabriel smiled grimly. "He can breathe," he said. "He's just a little blue around the edges. Nothing to worry about with his type."

"What on do you mean by his type? Are they vampires?"

"No. Thralls."

He dug his cell phone out of his pocket and made a call for backup. Given no chance to ask what a thrall was, she glanced down at the man near her feet and toed him lightly. Still out cold. She obviously packed quite a punch. He hadn't even twitched.

"I guess I've landed myself in a shit load more trouble," she said, once Gabriel had hung up.

He met her gaze, his eyes intense, thoughtful. Once again she was left with the distinct impression that Assistant Director Stern was a man with his own agenda.

"Maybe," he said after a moment. His gaze went back to the felon. Not releasing his grip in any way, he asked. "You going to talk?"

The man gurgled.

"I'll take that as a yes." He let the felon's toes touch the floor. "I'm about to release my grip a little. Twitch, and you're dead, understand?"

Jack had nothing on Gabriel Stern when in came to menace, that was for sure. Though he'd kept his tone light, the threat hung like a noose in the air. She had no doubt that he meant it. Obviously, neither did the felon.

"Who sent you?"

The felon took several deep breaths, and then croaked, "Sethanon."

The name meant nothing to her, but it was one Gabriel obviously recognized. His expression was grim as he asked, "Why?"

'To collect Kazdan's body."

Gabriel glanced at her for a moment. He didn't look entirely surprised by this news, and she wondered why.

"Why do you want Jack's body?" she asked, keeping her voice soft. The man was in a bad enough state as it was. If they threatened him too much more he might just faint.

"I don't know."

Gabriel tightened his grip again. The felon flapped his arms in agitation, a frantic look of fear twisting his face. "I'm telling you, I don't know. I'm just a runner. I do what I'm told. They don't tell me nothin'."

"Really?" Gabriel's tone implied disbelief, even though the fear in the felon's eyes suggested he *was* telling the truth. "Where were you supposed to take the body?"

"To a warehouse in Carlton."

"Address?"

"Five ten Rathdown Street."

Footsteps sounded in the outer room, and the lights once again came on. Help had arrived. She half expected him to release his grip on the felon, but again, he went against the norm, tightening it instead.

"Time?" he continued flatly.

The morgue door opened, and five gray-suited men filed in, weapons at the ready. On seeing them, they holstered their guns and approached.

The felon gagged a little, struggling to breathe. "Ten . . . ten thirty."

"Thank you." Releasing his grip, Gabriel pushed him into the arms of the nearest gray suit. "Detain these two for further questioning."

Two other gray-suits approached the unconscious man at her feet and unceremoniously dragged him away. Obviously, the SIU didn't give a hoot about prisoner rights. Jack would have been right at home with these boys.

Her gaze darted back to his body, and she bit her lip. This wasn't Jack. She was sure of that much. A damn good imitation maybe, but still not the real thing. Which begged the questions, where was the real Jack, and why in hell did he need a clone?

Gabriel walked around the drawer and touched her arm, his fingers like fire, sending heat past the thickness of her sweater, down onto her chilled skin.

"Langston, I want you and Renolds to stay here and guard this body until I arrange for its transfer down to the SIU vaults. No one is to touch it, not even State."

She glanced at him in surprise. His expression was grim. "Come on," he said, and tightened his grip on her arm, hauling her from the room.

"You came here to check whether this was really Jack, didn't you?" he said, once they were clear of the room.

She nodded. There was no point in denying the obvious.

"And?"

"And it's not."

When the elevator opened, he swiped his card and punched the button for sublevel fourteen. "What makes you so certain?"

"His lack of tan, a missing scar." She hesitated. "The fact that he has no mark or indentation on his finger from his wedding ring."

Indeed, that was the most telling. Jack's love for Suzy was almost as obsessive as Suzy's was for him. In the three years since his marriage, she'd never seen him take the ring off. Even if he'd lost it during the ten days he'd gone missing, there would have been a fading band of white on his finger.

She blinked suddenly. *Suzy.* Why had she implied that jealousy was the reason behind her shooting Jack? Suzy of all people would have been aware of the truth. She knew how little they saw of each other after-hours, if only because Jack had spent all his spare time with *her.*

Unless, of course, she was involved in Jack's schemes, whatever those schemes might be. Maybe the first person she should talk to when she got out of here was Suzy Kazdan.

The doors slid open, revealing the SIU foyer. Finley was

waiting at reception for them.

"Next time she wants to go to the restroom, have someone escort her." Though Gabriel's voice was even, a hint of censure ran through it.

Finley flinched. "I've posted security at the lab doors."

Gabriel nodded. She met his gaze and saw the anger burning bright in the intense depths of his eyes. He might not have said anything about her running off, but he would eventually. She smiled grimly. If he'd read her file, and he probably had, he'd know following orders had never been a strong suit of hers, even though she had the rep for being a by-the-book cop. Given the slightest chance, she'd be out of here.

"I have a ten thirty meeting I have to get to." Though he was talking to Finley, his gaze was still on her.

She shifted uncomfortably and glanced at the clock. He was really going to have to fly if he was going to get to Carlton on time. Though the suburb was only a few minutes from the CBD, the traffic in the city at this hour was hell.

"Watch her until I get back."

Finley nodded. Gabriel turned and walked away. As much as she wanted to go with him, she knew it was pointless to ask. He wanted her here, in Finley's hands, to find out why she could see the kite monsters when no one else could. And what Assistant Director Gabriel Stern wanted, he apparently got.

A situation that was about to end, she thought grimly.

Finley cleared his throat, and then he nervously motioned her up the hall, towards the labs. She knew she could get past Finley. Once the doctor got his nose into his computers, his attention would wander. Security was another problem altogether.

Not to mention the fact that she had to get out before Gabriel got back. The man seemed to know the workings of her mind altogether *too* well. With him around, there would be no escape.

She had, at best, a couple of hours. And once she was free, Suzy Kazdan was the first port of call. And that lying bitch would tell her exactly what was going on.

Or there'd be hell to pay.

Six

Gabriel glanced at his watch as he ran across Rathdown Street. Ten twenty. He was cutting it close. Whoever was waiting for the two men would probably be there by now.

But there had been nowhere else to shift shape except the park. Any closer and he could have run the risk of being sensed by those waiting inside the warehouse. He bent his arm back and forth, trying to ease the slight ache. It had been a long time since he'd flown so hard, so fast. He was out of shape—something Stephan had warned might happen.

Still, given his work, and SIU's policy of not flaunting your abilities in public, he'd had little chance of late to get in some flight time. And by the look of things, it was a situation not likely to change in any great hurry.

He dodged a car trying to do an illegal right-hand turn, and headed toward the warehouse. In reality, it was an old red brick factory that somewhere along the line had been converted into apartments. Now though, it was abandoned and waiting for a new owner to refurbish it. Given the scarcity of housing this close to the city, it was surprising that hadn't happened already.

The light breeze whistled through the smashed windows on the upper floors and rattled the loose roofing atop the front veranda. It was a forlorn sound that jarred uneasily against the noise and rush of the morning traffic.

He took the front steps two at a time and stopped when he reached a wrought iron gate. Beyond it, there was a long tunnel that opened out into an expanse of sunshine and grass. From where he stood, the courtyard seemed—and felt—empty. He twisted the handle and pushed the gate open. Then he studied the red brick walls on either side of the tunnel, making sure there were no alcoves or doors. There weren't, so he moved down cautiously.

No one waited in the courtyard. The sun shone on the pond that dominated the center, making the water sparkle like diamonds. In the surrounding patch of lawn, weeds had overtaken the grass. Surprisingly, there was very little litter, just the occasional glitter of glass shards.

He lifted his gaze, studying what remained of the windows that looked out onto the courtyard. The place looked, and felt, uninhabited. But if he went out into that sunshine, he'd be a sitting duck for anyone who might be hiding within the buildings. And unless he did, he'd never know if there was anyone up there to worry about.

He swept his gaze across the silent apartments, and then sprinted across to the nearest set of stairs. Silence greeted him. If anyone *was* here, they obviously didn't care about, or hadn't yet noticed, his presence.

He searched the entire first floor and found nothing but debris and dust. Stopping near the stairs, he stared down at the pond and wondered if he'd been taken for a ride. It wouldn't be the first time a suspect had lied so convincingly he'd believed him. And it *was* ten forty-five. Whoever the two men had intended to meet should have been here by now.

Unless, of course, they were stuck in traffic.

He pushed away from the railing. There were only a half dozen apartments on the second floor, so he might as well take a look. He headed up the stairs to the next floor. In the third apartment, he found a body.

After checking the remainder of the apartment to ensure no one else was around, he squatted beside the remains and felt for a pulse. Nothing. Not that he'd expected one. The smell of death, of ripe and rotting flesh, was beginning to permeate the still apartment air.

He rolled the corpse over. It was male, probably in his mid-fifties, and his bloated face was somewhat familiar, though where he'd seen him he couldn't remember offhand. Frowning slightly, he patted down the man's body. No identification card, no wallet, nothing that might even hint at who he was. So why had this body been dumped here? It wasn't exactly the best of hiding spaces, especially when the gates were unlocked and these apartments were so accessible. Maybe—

His thoughts came to an abrupt halt as the stale air found life. He dropped and swung around. Two men approached, one carrying a large club that already arced towards his head. He raised his arm and blocked the blow, but the force of the impact sent a shudder through the rest of his body. Ignoring the resulting pain, he surged upwards and struck out with a clenched fist. The blow smashed into the stranger's face, and bone and cartilage gave way. No vampire then, he thought, as the man staggered back, blood pouring from his shattered nose. A vampire would have been fast enough to avoid such damage.

The second man moved in, fists swinging. Gabriel ducked

several blows, and then he threw one of his own. The man went down like a ton of bricks. He frowned. He was fast, and he definitely had more speed and strength than mere humans, but this was almost too easy . . .

The stale air stirred again, warning him of another approach. He spun, catching a brief glimpse of two men before something smashed into his head and the lights went out.

***

Sam sat on the toilet seat and stared up at the ceiling. Time was growing short, and her hopes of escape even shorter. Finley was watching her closer than a shark did a potential meal, and he had two gorillas as assistants. Hell, they'd even come into the restroom with her, just to check that there were no vents or other likely escape routes present. They were back outside now, but if she sat here much longer, they'd been back in, wondering what was going on.

She bit her lip, her gaze sweeping the entire roof for what seemed like the hundredth time. Lots of ceiling tiles, and not one vent. Who could believe that? Christ, people were always escaping via the air ducts in movies. Just this once, couldn't fact have followed the lead of fiction?

Sighing, she rose and turned around. But just as she was about to push the button, she noticed one of the ceiling tiles above her head, near the wall, had a broken edge. They were fibro—or whatever fire retardant material it was they were using these days—not proper tiles. And beyond the broken edge, metal gleamed.

Her heart began to race. She didn't know much about buildings, and she'd never even thought about the fact that the building probably had a suspended ceiling to allow for all the cabling and ducts. But if the electrician and air-con guys could move around in the void between the suspended ceiling and the actual one, she certainly could.

First though, she had to try to get up there. She flipped down the toilet seat cover, climbed from there onto the paper dispenser. Then, with one hand pressed against the wall for support and hoping like hell the dispenser would hold her weight long enough, she rose onto her tiptoes and tried to flip the tile back. But she was several inches too short.

She swore softly. After taking a deep breath to calm the anxiety clutching her stomach, she eased off a shoe and tried to move the tile that way. Her second attempt was successful, and the tile plopped to one side. The void beyond was dark, but it certainly looked like there was at least crawling space.

If she could get up there.

If she could get over her fear of enclosed spaces.

If she could achieve both of those things, all she'd have to worry about was not putting a foot—or more—through a tile and letting everyone know what she was up to.

Piece of cake, she thought wryly.

Taking another deep breath, she carefully hooked her leg over the stall wall and clambered up. Luckily, whoever had designed this building had installed strong partitions rather than the usual paper-thin ones. Maybe the designer figured a building housing the SIU and State Police needed decent toilet walls, just in case officers needed to throw a suspect or two around. Which wasn't the joke it appeared to be, because she'd certainly seen Jack do it.

Once her butt was securely parked, she eased along the top of the stall until she neared the wall. Then carefully, slowly, she rose and looked through the hole.

Darkness and dust. God, just the thought of clambering up into it had sweat breaking out across her brow. She had no idea where this fear of small, dark spaces had come from. The State psych guys reckoned it was probably the result of a childhood trauma, but since she could remember zero about her childhood, that wasn't much help.

And standing here thinking about it wasn't doing the fear any good, either. She needed to escape, and this was her only method. End of story, no other choice.

She gripped the steel bracing on either side of the tile and tested it for strength. It didn't bend, but then, if it supported the guys who maintained the ducting and cabling, it was more than strong enough to support her. And this testing was merely another way of avoiding the inevitable.

She took another deep breath and pulled herself up into the darkness. Almost immediately, sweat broke out across her brow, and her stomach began to twist. She licked her lips, but otherwise ignored the fear as she waited for her eyes to adjust to the darkness. Thankfully, it didn't take long.

The void was a mess of ducts, cabling, wires, and all sorts of building rubbish. She studied the crisscrossed lines of metal supports, trying to compare them with what she knew of the building's layout. The concrete mass that was the core area wasn't that far away, since this building, like many of its era, tended to have all facilities crowded around the main core. Which meant the elevators were in the center, with the stairs and restrooms on either side of the shafts. But making her way toward the elevators wasn't a good option, as that was probably the first place they'd look once they realized she was missing again. Which left the stairs. But how did she get there? Especially when most of the offices on this floor were locked down tighter than Fort Knox. She doubted the security pass she'd been given would give her access into any of them. And given that the security measures here in the SIU section of the building were far tighter than those in the State Police section, the key coder she had hidden in her boot would probably raise alarms rather than open doors.

Her gaze settled on a mass of pipes not that far away. Surely that was the men's restroom. And, like the ladies, it was close to the stair area. If there was no one in there, it might be her best bet.

She blew out a breath, drew her legs fully into the void and shifted the tile back into its position. With her one spot of light gone, the darkness seemed to close in, pressing down on her with the consistency of glue and making it hard to breathe.

She swiped at a trickle of sweat running down her face, her hand trembling. It was ridiculous, this fear. There was nothing in the darkness that could harm her—nothing but fear itself. And if she didn't move, and move *now*, she'd blow her chance to escape. Finley's goons would surely be wondering what the hell was taking her so long.

Besides, the enigma that was Assistant Director Stern would surely be on his way back from that meeting soon. And he'd have no doubt as to what she was doing in the restroom—he seemed to know the workings of her mind entirely *too* well.

With that thought to stir her on, she shifted onto her hands and knees and began to shuffle forward, trying to make as little noise as possible. It felt like she was moving with the speed of a gnat.

Sweat dribbled down her face and leapt off the end of her nose, the small droplets splattering against the grime covered metal. Every motion stirred dust, until the air was filled with a thick, choking cloud that was almost impossible to breathe. Or maybe it was simply the fear sitting like a lump in her throat that was making it hard to breathe.

She licked her lips, and concentrated on the pipes, trying to think of reaching them and nothing else. Not the weight of the darkness. Not the choking dust. Not the looming, threatening walls of the core.

When she finally neared the pipes, relief surged, and the need to get out of this darkness was so fierce it was all she could do not to rip off the nearest tile and plunge down into the restroom. Which would be absolutely stupid when she had no idea how safe it was down there. She carefully eased up the nearest tile and looked down. She was above the washbasin area. There didn't appear to be anyone in the men's, but just to be sure, she eased the tile up a little more, and listened carefully. No sound. Good.

She took the tile off completely, then stuck her legs out the hole and dropped down. With her feet safely on the floor, the trembling began. She bent over and took several deep breaths. Lord, her heart was beating so damn fast anyone would think she'd just run a marathon. But at least it was over—or the worst part was, anyway. Compared to climbing through the void, getting out of the building itself would surely be a cinch.

She splashed her face with cold water, shook the dust and cobwebs free from her hair and walked across to the door. The corridor beyond was small and turned left about six paces away. Given the core layout was the same as State's section, the corridor would pass the stairs before going on to the foyer section and elevators.

The elevators dinged as she stepped out of the restroom. She froze, listening, but luckily, no one came her way. But it was warning enough that if she didn't get out of here quickly, someone would spot her. Luck had never been a long time friend, and right now, it felt like she was pushing her limits. She walked on until the stair door came into view, and she swiped the ID card through the slot. The door beeped, and then opened. The stairs were as silent and as empty as the corridor. She let the door close quietly, and then she began her run up the stairs to freedom.

***

Gabriel woke in the arms of a dead man. Not the walking dead, but the *dead* dead. The pungent aroma of decay told him it was the corpse he'd discovered in the apartment before someone had tried caving in his skull.

He shifted slightly, trying to ease the persistent ache in his ribs. But the minute he moved, every other ache began screaming for attention. Mostly, though, it was his head that hurt. And the insistent, steady thump of music some fool insisted on playing so loudly wasn't helping any. He stopped the thought and frowned. *Music?* There'd been no music anywhere near the abandoned building. He'd been moved, obviously.

He opened his eyes and saw only darkness. He reached out and felt the confines of his prison. His fingers brushed across warmed metal. He had maybe a foot of breathing room above his head and about the same on his left side. The dead man and a tool box of some kind shared most of the room on the right-hand side. The space near his feet was so tight he couldn't straighten his legs to relieve the cramp beginning to settle in across his thighs.

He was, he realized suddenly, in the trunk of a car, and heading God knew where. One thing was certain—he'd be as dead as the man beside him if the car reached its destination with him still locked inside. He'd seen four men, but there might have been more. Either way, it wasn't good fighting odds.

Shifting around a little, he felt for the trunk's catch. The throaty roar of the engine—what he could hear of it over the music—told him the car was one of the older models that still ran on gas rather than hydrogen or electricity. With any luck, the owners wouldn't have bothered updating to the newer thumbprint coded locks.

Luck was with him. The trunk had a key lock on the inside, which in itself suggested the owner was a vampire and also explained why absolutely no light was getting into the trunk. Obviously, it had been fitted out for emergency escapes from sunlight.

He reached down to his boot, but the sudden movement had red fingers of fire lancing through his brain. He cursed silently and waited for his vision to clear. Obviously the fools had done some serious damage when they'd tried to cave in his head. There was blood on his face—he could feel it crusting, tightening his skin. The right side of his head felt heavy, as if the hair there was weighted down. More blood, probably. Stephan was going to give him hell—especially given his warning that all missions were to be double manned.

He carefully drew the knife from his boot, flicked it open and inserted it into the lock. Several twists, and there was a soft click. It was all too easy, really. But then, if he'd been a vampire, he would have made sure any lock imprisoning *him* was damn easy to open in the event of a lost key or sign of trouble.

He inched the trunk open. Bitumen met his gaze. The speed

at which it zipped past told him they had to be doing at least a hundred, which meant they were beyond the city limits and out on some freeway.

He opened the trunk a little more. Sunlight danced though the leaves of the gums arching over the road. The rich hint of humus, of moisture and damp earth, told him they were up in the hills somewhere, while the tree ferns huddled beneath the gums suggested it was more the Dandenong's than Macedon.

Why head up this way with the stranger's body? There were certainly better places to dispose of a corpse than the picturesque but heavily populated Dandenong ranges, and ... His thoughts came to a sudden halt as the car went into a slide. Tires squealed, and the smell of burning rubber briefly overrode the smell of death. The force of the stop smashed him into the side of the car, and for a moment, everything went red. The trunk tore from his grasp, swinging open, then crashed down again, barely missing his fingers as the car came to a shuddering stop.

He groaned and tried to roll over onto his back. Couldn't. The stranger's body had been forced hard up against his own. He elbowed some room, and then rolled over. Taking several deep breaths to calm the churning in his gut, he tried to concentrate on what was happening beyond the confines of his dark prison.

Footsteps. And voices talking softly. Savagely. Then the trunk swung open, and light poured in. He blinked, throwing up a hand to shade his eyes against the sudden glare of sunlight. But the shape silhouetted by the sunshine was one he knew well.

"Glad to see you're alive and well," Karl said, and held out a hand to help him up.

He accepted it gratefully. Right now, it felt as if he'd become a punching bag for some fool wearing boots. He climbed out, but it was only with Karl's help that he made it over to the side of the road.

"How many fingers am I holding up?" Karl asked, as he squatted down in front of him.

"Three," he guessed, looking down the road towards the car rather than at Karl. Four men were lying face down in the dirt, guarded by Karl's oldest son, Harvey. He returned his gaze to his friend. "I don't mean to sound ungrateful, but why the hell are you here?"

There was tension around Karl's eyes, despite his smile. "The bond of the twin, my friend."

He groaned softly. As if his brother didn't have enough to

worry about. Then he realized exactly what Karl had said and glanced up in surprise. "He told you."

Karl nodded and handed him a cell phone. "Call him."

He did. Stephan answered almost immediately. "Are you okay?"

He scrubbed a hand across the raw edge of his face. Fresh blood mingled with old, and his hand came away smeared red. "Better than I look."

"You going to make it tonight?" Concern mingled with relief through Stephan's soft voice.

"Yes." He might feel half-dead, but come hell or high water, he'd drag himself to that meeting. He still had a poisoner to net and a brother to save.

"Good. You have a problem, though."

Only one? That would be something of a miracle. "What?"

"Ryan's skipped."

He swore softly, though in truth, he wasn't really surprised. The need to break loose, to find answers herself, had been very evident in her eyes earlier. He just hadn't thought she'd succeed in getting past SIU's security so easily.

"I'll find her. See you tonight."

He hung up and handed the phone back to Karl. "You took a risk, bringing Harvey in on this."

Karl shrugged. "I was with Stephan when he sensed you were in trouble. With the poisoner obviously being someone close to home, he didn't want to trust your safety to just anyone. So I came."

He rubbed his ribs. Christ, it hurt to breathe. "And Harvey?"

Karl handed him two tablets. "Painkillers." Once Gabriel had swallowed them, Karl added, "Harv was in town signing up for extra university courses, and I was supposed to pick him up and bring him home once I'd finished with Stephan. He's been itching to get into some action for a while now, and this was safer than some of our operations."

True. Lord only knew how many had gone sour recently—which again, pointed to someone close to home. But which of the three?

"You going to take those four back to Federation headquarters?" He indicated the prone forms on the road.

"Yeah, but not before I look after these wounds of yours."

Karl began swabbing the blood away from Gabriel's face. He grimaced and pushed his friend's hand away. "I'm fine.

Really."

"Yeah, right," Karl said, voice dry. "Doesn't mean a thing that you look like a pin cushion that's born the brunt of too many pins."

"You're exaggerating again, my friend. No one could look *that* bad." Even though he certainly felt *that* bad.

Karl smile. "Maybe I should get a mirror. Or maybe I should just leave you alone and let Stephan take care of you tonight."

He raised an eyebrow. "That a threat?" If it was, it was a damn good one, because if he looked as bad as Karl was suggesting, Stephan would ban him from field operations. He'd threatened it more than once already, particularly after Mathew, their youngest sibling, had been killed a year ago.

Karl's smile widened. "Could be. Your choice."

He quit fighting the inevitable and bore the rest of Karl's ministrations in silence. And at least the salve Karl applied liberally over his face and ribs eased the pain somewhat.

"I want you to have a quick look at the body in the trunk," he said, once Karl had finished. "His face seems familiar."

Karl nodded and wrapped a hand around Gabriel's arm, helping him up. The pain killers had kicked in, and the aches were little more than a distant promise of pain yet to come. But given the strength of that muted ache, he'd be lucky if he could move tomorrow. The bastards really had stuck the boots in once they'd knocked him out.

"You're lucky shapechangers have strong bones," Karl said, expression grim. "Any other man would be in the hospital right now."

"Forgive me if I don't feel particularly lucky," he muttered, and rolled the corpse over. "You recognize him?"

Karl frowned slightly. "Hard to say for certain, with the face so bloated, but it looks a lot like Dan Wetherton."

The Minister for Social Services. No wonder the face had seemed so familiar. He'd been in the news a lot lately, raising hell about the amount of money the Government had allocated to Science and Technology in the latest budget offering.

"Looks like someone wanted him out of the way."

"But this man's been dead for two or three days. Wetherton was on the news last night."

He frowned at the corpse. He didn't doubt that Karl had the right man, but if Wetherton was on the news, who was this? Another clone? The second in as many days? That was more than just a coincidence.

Something big was obviously going down.

He studied the body a moment longer, and then asked, "Wetherton's in town tomorrow, isn't he?"

Karl nodded. "Premier's meeting."

"Take this one back and run genetic tests. I'll see if I can arrange for a cell sample to be snatched from Wetherton."

Karl raised an eyebrow. "No one's ever been able to clone a human to the point where mannerisms and behavior are an exact match. They might be genetically identical but there are *always* differences."

He smiled grimly. "But if someone has succeeded, we need to find out who and why. Especially if those people are connected to Sethanon."

"True." Karl hesitated, and then added. "I'd like to get hold of a cell sample from Sam Ryan, too."

No one would be getting anything from her if he couldn't damn well find her again. "Why?"

"Haven't you noticed her eyes?"

He frowned. "They're blue." And quite pretty, even when they were glaring at him.

"Bright blue, ringed by a fine band of shifting, smoky gray." Karl hesitated, his expression curious.

"So?"

"So, eyes that color were one of the few tangible signs of a Shadow Walker."

He snorted softly. "Shadow Walkers never existed. It was simply another name humans gave to vampires."

"Oh, they existed all right. But their numbers were few, and they were thought to have been killed in the Race Wars."

"Which was fifty years ago." The Race Wars had pitted humans against many nonhuman races. It was a war that cost billions of lives, and yet, in the end, provided no clear winner. Humans still ran most Governments, but nonhumans had at least won recognition—the right to vote, to take a hand in the decision making process. Most were happy with that. Some, like Sethanon, were not.

"Sam's twenty nine. She can't have Walker blood in her."

"Why not? Her parents would certainly be close to the right age to have at least some Walker blood in them."

"There's no record of her parents. She was abandoned as a teenager."

"Everyone has parents, my friend. There'll be a record somewhere."

You'd think so, but apparently no one in State, and no one in the kids' home she'd spent her teenage years in had ever been able to find it. Which, in itself, posed several interesting possibilities—but her being the offspring of Walkers certainly wasn't one of the ones he'd come up with. "Birth records don't state race, and Walkers were never one of the declared races, even after the wars."

"No, but they existed, even if in extremely small numbers. Eyes like that aren't a freak of nature; they're the one tangible sign of the Walker race."

"Why are you so revved up over the possibility that Sam might have Walker blood?" Especially when they were nothing special? While they supposedly possessed the ability to wrap the merest wisp of shadow around their bodies and disappear to the human eye, it had to be nothing more than a vampire trick. Though Walkers *could* apparently move around in daylight, where vamps couldn't, which would have made them better spies. He'd heard that the government *had* used them extensively during the Race Wars, but he'd found no evidence of their existence, let alone use, in all the searches he'd done over the years. Which is why he, like many others, believed the Shadow Walker legend was mired in the reality of vampires.

"Walkers were more than just shadow dwellers, my friend," Karl said, an undercurrent of excitement edging his normally serene tones. "Much more."

He raised an eyebrow. "Finley has been running genetic tests on her, and while he has found some anomalies, I very much doubt Walkers are on his lists of possibilities."

Karl frowned. "Doing those sorts of tests at the SIU labs could be dangerous. Computers are not safe conveyances of information. How often have you told me that?"

"Quite a lot. But given the amount of genetic tests we regularly do, I doubt whether these are going to raise any immediate interest."

"Unless, of course, someone out there doesn't want the test results to be known."

He ran a hand through his matted hair. He didn't have the time to be standing here arguing about the existence of mythical creatures when there was so much he had to do before the meeting with his brother tonight. And on top of all that, he now had to find Sam. Yet something held him to the spot. Maybe it was the conviction in Karl's voice. Maybe it was the knowledge his friend's hunches was very rarely wrong.

"Why would anyone else be interested in the tests?"

"Why would anyone try to kill her?" Karl countered. "Someone must know, or suspect, that she is more than what she seems. If that's the case, they may well be watching what is happening at the SIU."

"What if I send you a copy of all of Finley's tests so far? Then you can check them out for yourself." And give them a secure back up.

Karl nodded. "And once you finish your meeting tonight, drop by. I have some books you might need to read if she *is* a Walker."

Something to look forward to, for sure. "I might have to drag her along with me."

"Even better. I can run a few tests of my own."

"If you can convince her to oblige. She's getting a little sick of being a guinea pig."

Karl smiled thinly. "I think you'll find that young woman has a desire to know the truth."

When it came to her partner and what had happened to him, maybe. But when it came to herself, definitely not. She hadn't even asked why they were doing all these extra tests. Hadn't even shown the slightest bit of curiosity. It was almost as if she didn't care.

He straightened and returned his gaze to the kidnappers. "Will you need help with those four?"

"Harv and I can manage." He hesitated, and again Gabriel noted the tension around his friend's eyes. But before he could ask about it, Karl added, "You'd better get back before someone starts missing you."

He nodded. "You going back to Stephan after this?"

"No. It would raise suspicions in the wrong quarters." Karl pulled a small bottle of pale green liquid from his pocket. "Give him this when you see him tonight, and make sure he gets some water. I won't have a chance to get there until tomorrow."

He held up the bottle. The green liquid was thick and shiny. "What is it?"

"A medicine designed to flush the toxins from his system. If we've pinpointed the right poison, it should work pretty fast."

"How's he doing? Health wise, I mean."

"He's weak, but he'll survive."

Relief surged through him, relaxing muscles he hadn't even realized were tense. "I'll see you later tonight, then."

Karl nodded and moved back toward the prisoners. Gabriel glanced at the license plate number of the car he'd been locked in, taking note of it for later investigation. He then called to his other shape and leapt skyward on brown-gold wings.

* * *

Sam climbed out of the taxi and slammed the door shut. As the vehicle zoomed away in search of another fare, she stepped onto the pavement and stared at the house across the road.

Even on a relatively bright day like today, the squat, almost ugly, red brick dwelling sat in shadow. Surrounded by tall gum trees, it hunched in the middle of the block like some forgotten troll. For some reason, Jack had loved it. Think of the possibilities, he'd said. All that land to expand on, all that room to move in.

Three and a half years later, the place was as still as ugly as the day he'd bought it. Uglier, as it had also begun to fall into disrepair. And the land he kept raving about was a mass of weeds and rotting leaves.

The houses on either side had well manicured lawns, perfectly trimmed garden beds and spotlessly clean driveways. But then, in an upper middle-class suburb like Mulgrave, you expected nothing less. Jack had to be driving them insane.

Smiling slightly, she crossed the road. The minute she stepped into the shadows of the house, it was as if she'd stepped into another world. The everyday whine of cars, of people talking and dogs barking, faded away, leaving only an uneasy sort of hush. She glanced up, studying the branches far above. Odd that there were no birds in any of the trees. Even though it was winter, there should have been sparrows and starlings, at the very least.

She walked up the steps and knocked on the front door. Then she stepped back, waiting for an answer. After a minute or two of silence, she knocked again. She'd checked earlier to see if Suzy had gone back to work. She hadn't, and she wasn't expected to be back for at least another week.

Still no answer. Frowning, she turned and headed for the backyard. All the windows along the side of the house had their curtains drawn, so she couldn't sneak a peak inside. The overgrown look had gone into overdrive around the back. Weeds climbed the fences and dominated the garden beds. She shook her head. It was hard to believe Jack had let it get to this state. At work, he was practically a freak when it came to tidiness.

She knocked on the back door. Again, no answer. Of course, there was always the possibility Suzy had gone shopping or was visiting friends, but instinct told her that wasn't the case. There was an edge of awareness in the stillness that suggested someone was home.

She bent down and slid the wire-thin key-coder out of its specially designed sheath inside her boot. Though they were officially frowned upon, a good half of the State's enforcers used them. This particular one Jack had given her a few weeks before he'd disappeared, claiming it would open any lock currently in use. At the time, neither of them had thought she'd be using it to break into *his* house.

The coder beeped softly. She slid it back home in her boot, and then cautiously opened the door. The kitchen lay in darkness, and the air that rushed out to greet her was stale, as if the house had been locked up for several weeks.

She edged into the kitchen and looked around. Dishes lay in an untidy pile in the sink. Judging by the thick layer of scum on the surface of the water, they'd been there for some time. A half-filled coffee cup sat abandoned on the table, and one chair lay flat on its back, as if someone had gotten up in a hurry.

She moved into the next room. There were no other signs of a hasty abandonment, but it was obvious no one had been in the living room for some time. She walked across to the coffee table and picked up a newspaper. Dust stirred, tickling her throat. Coughing slightly, she studied the date on the paper. May sixteenth. Five days after Jack had disappeared.

If appearances were anything to go by, Suzy hadn't been in the house since then. Yet that simply didn't make sense. Surely she must have been here when Jack—or his clone—was shot. How else would headquarters have gotten hold of her so quickly?

Dropping the paper back to the coffee table, she turned and headed for the study. Dust lay thick on the furniture in this room, too. Two monitors sat abandoned on an otherwise bare desk. Several photos lined the walls—all of them of Suzy. Sam sat at the desk and opened the top drawer. Empty. So were the next two.

Frowning, she stared at the monitor for a moment, wondering what to do next. Anything useful had obviously been cleaned out of the study, so there was a good chance every other room had been cleaned out, too. But the only other room that might hold something was the main bedroom. Even the tiniest scrap of paper might provide a clue, and while Jack was generally a neat freak, Suzy wasn't.

She checked the remainder of the house as she made her way up the hall to the main bedroom. The place was empty, despite her feeling to the contrary. Relaxing a little, she allowed herself to remember the pride in Jack's voice when he'd first guided her through his ugly duckling house. Remembered his wonder at all the space when all she'd seen was wasted space. Lord, they were so completely different. Maybe that was why they'd been such good partners. And good friends, at least during working hours.

So why had he tried to kill her?

Tears stung her eyes, and she blinked them back. Damn it all, the man she'd shot *wasn't* Jack. It was a clone who didn't deserve her guilt or her tears.

Maybe Jack himself didn't even deserve them.

The bedroom was a mess. Blankets were strewn onto the floor, and clothes lay everywhere, the ironed mingling with the dirty in drifting piles. But the dust that lay thick on the furniture through the rest of the house was absent here. A coffee cup sat on the dressing table, its contents half-consumed and just beginning to congeal. Someone had been in here recently, and if the clothes were any indication, had packed in a hurry.

She stepped across several clothing mounds and made her way into the master bathroom. No trace of Suzy's makeup—a telling sign, if ever there was one. From what Jack had said, she had a veritable mountain of the stuff she used night and day. It had obviously gone with Suzy—wherever that might be.

She turned and crossed to the bedside table, opening the top drawer. Undergarments greeted her—Jack's, by the look of it. She poked through the drawer, just to ensure there was nothing else, and a slight edge of white caught her eye. She pulled it out. It was an empty envelope, addressed to Jack. She flipped it over. The sender was an R. C. Clarke—the same man who rented the rooms above the Chinese restaurant where this mess had all begun. No wonder the name had sounded familiar. Jack must have mentioned it at one time. Clarke was obviously someone she'd better start investigating.

But why had Jack kept an empty envelope? That he had suggested it had some value, which made no sense, given everything else of value had disappeared. Unless it was something he'd forgotten.

Frown deepening, she folded the envelope, and slipped it into her pocket. Then she grabbed the drawer and pulled it out, tipping the undergarments onto the floor as she flipped it over. Nothing taped on the bottom. She studied the base for a moment, and then noticed a slight scrape along one side, and a broken edge in one corner.

She tapped the bottom and heard the slight echo, as if the drawer were hollow. And the actual depth of the drawer certainly didn't match the depth of the sides. Maybe a false bottom? She stuck her little finger into the hole and gently tugged. The top layer came away, revealing a two inch hiding hole. Several digital disks gleamed softly in the half-light. She shoved them into her pocket with the envelope.

Out in the hall, a floorboard creaked—a sound so soft that if it wasn't for the strange hush over the house she might not have heard it. Even then, she might have passed it off as nothing more than the normal creaking of an old house, but there was a sudden prickle of heat across her skin, and the wash of awareness through her mind.

A vampire and a shapeshifter had entered the house.

She reached back for her gun, and then realized she no longer had it. Her gaze went to the bed. Jack had often said a gun was the natural extension of his arm. Even in the bedroom, he would have had one within reach.

She knelt down and felt underneath. Her fingers slid across the metal slats, then touched something slick and cold. Smiling grimly, she peeled the weapon away from its hiding spot.

Only it wasn't just any old gun—it was the latest in laser development, a Y-shaped weapon that molded itself to your palm and could blow a hole the size of a football field in the side of a building.

She frowned as she peeled the tape off the weapon. Where had Jack found the money to buy something like this? You certainly couldn't get these legally, and they were worth a damn fortune on the streets.

As she checked to see if the weapon was loaded, another floorboard creaked. Mouth suddenly dry, she grasped the weapon and walked carefully to the door. The silence was so deep she could hear breathing—not hers, someone else's.

They were close. Maybe even right outside the bedroom door.

She set the gun to immobilize, and then clicked the safety off. The sound, though whisper soft, seemed to ricochet through the hush. In the hall, someone chuckled softly.

A chill ran down her spine. No one in their right mind would laugh like that. Not unless they were very, very sure of the outcome. With the gun clinging to her palm like a limpet, the barrel barely visible between her clenched fingers, she took a deep breath and stepped from the bedroom.

Seven

Gabriel strode down the pristine halls of SIU, trying to ignore the surprised looks that came his way. He felt like shit, and as Karl had already pointed out, he looked like it, too. But hell, did everyone have to look so damn amused once their initial shock had worn off?

His office door slid open long before he neared it, revealing Finley, who had several reams of paper clutched close to his chest.

"They told me you wanted to see me, sir."

He smiled grimly. What he'd actually said was that he'd like to wring the doctor's scrawny little neck for letting Ryan escape. And he had promptly been reminded that the woman was his responsibility, not Finley's. A truth he couldn't argue without explaining why he hadn't been here to mind her.

"I told you to watch her, Finley."

The young doctor pushed his glasses up his nose and stepped back, allowing Gabriel room to pass.

"I assigned two guards. I just didn't expect her to escape through the false ceiling."

No one did, least of all him. But he was beginning to think they should expect the unexpected when dealing with Samantha Ryan. He crossed to the small wash area and flicked on the tap. "How many tests did you manage to run?"

"Several." Finley peeled the printouts away from his chest and shuffled through the top layer. "We haven't yet been able to pin down that extra chromosome. Tests so far indicate it's something we haven't come across before."

He studied his reflection for a moment. Dried blood had matted his hair into a free-for-all of weird shapes, and a deep cut near his right cheek was beginning to swell his eye shut. Stephan was going to be really pleased to see the state he was in, especially after his request that Gabriel take a partner with him on missions.

He ducked his head under the cold water, rinsing the blood away, then grabbed a towel and returned his attention to Finley. "I thought we'd just finished cataloging all known species, human or not."

"That's the thing—known species. You can be pretty sure there's a heck of a lot of species out there that we haven't seen, let alone cataloged."

The kites were one of them, that was for sure. And they were one secret the Federation wouldn't be able to keep much longer. With the recent rise in kite attacks, the SIU would soon have to be notified and brought in.

"Are you trying to tell me Ryan's not human?" Given what *he'd* seen of her so far unnoted skills, he suspected this was a very real possibility.

Finley shook his head. "I'm just making a point. If there are nonhuman species out there we haven't yet seen, why shouldn't it be the same with humans? Especially in this day and age, when gene manipulation and cloning is a government funded research program?"

Even so, it was odd to find a human chromosome they couldn't categorize. Unless, of course, they were looking for something only partially human and long thought dead. "Finley, do you believe Shadow Walkers ever existed?"

The young doctor pushed back his glasses and pursed his lips. "To be honest," he said eventually, "no. My father once told me he worked with a man who could hide in shadows, but I always presumed he meant a vampire."

Finley's father had worked for the military. Covert operations, if he recalled correctly. "Did he ever mention Shadow Walkers?"

"No." Finley hesitated, his expression curious. "Why the sudden interest in a myth?"

"No reason." Maybe Karl was barking up the wrong tree, for once. "What about the microchip?"

Finley dug into the reams of paper and pulled out a small, flat container. "Found it under the armpit. Been there for some time, I'd say."

He walked to Finley and took the container, holding it up to the light. The microchip looked to be little more than a speck of dust. "What can you tell about it?"

"Well, it's one of the military's, though they stopped using this type some twenty years ago."

Sam would barely have been nine. Why would they insert something like this in the side of a child? "What did they use them for?"

"Tracking, usually. Every soldier has one, even today."

"Were Ryan's parents in the military?"

Finley shrugged. "We haven't been any more successful in finding information on her parents than State was."

Maybe his own search had been more successful. Once Finley

left, he'd check. "If this device is still active, is there anyway for us to track the signal back?"

"We can try."

The look on the young doctor's face told him results were doubtful. "What about someone continuing to track us through it?"

"As long as you leave it in that container, you're safe."

Good. Because he fully intended handing it over to the Federation's experts to see what *they* could make of it. "Mind if I keep this awhile?"

The young doctor shook his head. "We got all the information we can off it."

"I'll need a copy of the test results sent to my com-unit, too."

"Already done, sir. We'll update as we go."

At least Finley was efficient, even if he wasn't so observant at times. "Thanks."

The doctor nodded and quickly exited. Gabriel studied the chip a moment longer, then shoved it in his pocket and walked across to his desk. "Computer on."

The com-unit hummed softly. "Background check on Samantha Ryan complete. Results inadequate."

He frowned. How could search results be inadequate? "Explain."

"No record of Samantha Ryan until the year two-o-three-two, when she was placed into state care by person or persons unknown. No record of parents, though a certificate of birth was filed in two-o-eighteen. No country of origin recorded on certificate. No doctor's signature."

"That can't happen." That it *had* spoke of government forces being involved somewhere along the line. Either that or someone had purposefully erased nearly all record of her past, which again could only have been managed by someone in power.

He leaned back in his chair and stared at the screen thoughtfully. "Have you tried military records for the time frames mentioned?"

"Military records for that period are not available for general searches."

Sometimes these computers were as dense as any human. "Do a priority one search through all available government records, military or otherwise." He hesitated, tapping the desk lightly. It wasn't likely he'd get back to this office any time soon.

He had too much to do. "Send search results, a copy of Ryan's current file and any updates to outlink 5019. Security access one."

"Transfer proceeding. Search proceeding. Director Hanrahan wishes to speak with you."

He scrubbed a hand across his eyes. The day was definitely getting worse. "Put him through."

The director's familiar features came on-line. "I want an update on the Ryan case."

He watched the Director's heavy jowls flap like sheets in the wind and barely controlled a smile. With all the weight Hanrahan had lost lately, he looked more like a basset hound than ever. "Investigations are still proceeding, sir."

The director's heavy-lidded gaze flicked to the right of the screen—a warning there was someone in the office with him. Who?

"Why haven't the investigations been wrapped up? Ryan admitted shooting her partner. It's a matter of record that she made several threats towards him. What's the problem?"

He frowned. That's the first *he'd* heard of any threats. "Ryan claims her partner was a vampire, and that she killed him in self-defense."

"Poppycock. The woman knows the trouble she's in and is just spinning you a line. State is getting restless over this. They want a result, and so do I."

There was an edge to the director's voice that didn't make sense. Almost an urgency. Something was obviously wrong. For a second, he considered storming Hanrahan's stronghold. But the Director's eyes, green slits barely visible beneath the heavily curtained lids, seemed to warn against it.

"When I find out what's going on, you'll be the first to know, sir." Which was the truth, in more ways than one, he thought grimly.

"Not good enough, Stern. You have until tomorrow to wind up your investigations and hand the woman back for prosecution."

Prosecution. He snorted softly. So Sam's fate had already been decided—she was being shafted big time. The question he had to answer now was why. And there was precious little time to do it in. "You'll have my final report tomorrow afternoon."

Hanrahan nodded. "See that I do."

The screen went blank. He swore softly and leaned back in his chair. Someone wanted Sam out of the way, someone powerful enough to put pressure on Hanrahan to wind up an investigation.

He had to find Sam, and fast. Not that he had any intention of handing her over to anyone—at least until he'd sorted out the puzzle she presented. But where would she have gone? Where would he have gone, in the same situation?

Jack had been her partner for five years. Given their work, the stress and long hours it often entailed, as well as the fact they were rumored to have been lovers, she had to have known him better than anyone. Except maybe, his wife.

Which is exactly where *he* would have started. He swung back round. "Computer, do we have an address for Jack Kazdan?"

"Subject currently has two addresses listed—nineteen Lincoln Street Mulgrave, and apartment eight-eleven, fifteen Russel Street Melbourne."

He raised his eyebrows. *That* end of Russel Street was right near Federation Square and considered prime real estate. Kazdan, like Sam and her Brighton apartment, should never have been able to afford to rent a *bathroom* in that area, let alone own an apartment.

Maybe the two of them had something other than sex happening. "Which address is listed as his permanent address?"

"Mulgrave."

Great. It might be only a ten-minute flight in normal conditions, but the wind was picking up. He rolled his shoulders slightly. The muscles protested faintly. If he flew any more today, there'd be hell to pay tomorrow. But flying was quicker than driving, and he had a suspicion he'd better get to Mulgrave promptly or risk losing Ryan for good.

He stood and headed for the roof.

***

The hall was empty. Sam bit her lip and pressed back against the wall. Slowly, carefully, she edged along to the next doorway. After silently counting to three, she quickly stepped inside, her gaze sweeping the semidarkness. Nothing.

Tension slithered through her limbs. They were here, somewhere. She could feel them—a whisper of heated evil that burned across her skin. She moved on to the next room, but it, too, was empty. She flexed her fingers and tried to relax a little. The last thing she needed right now was to blow someone else's head off.

Another board creaked, this time in the kitchen. It didn't make any sense. She'd checked the house and had found no one, though she *had* stupidly left the back door open. But the vampire, at least, shouldn't have come in from outside. They *couldn't* move round in daylight—it was the one myth that was true.

Yet Jack's body, or at least, his clone's, hadn't burned when touched by sunlight. And no matter what the captain said, he *was* a vampire.

She stared at the kitchen door for a moment longer, then took a deep breath and kicked it open. Two people sat the table, drinking coffee, totally unconcerned by her sudden appearance. One was a man she didn't recognize—he was the vampire she'd sensed. The shifter she'd sensed was Suzy. Sam frowned. Why had she never noticed this before? Or had she been too busy hating to observe the almost translucent quality of Suzy's skin— the sure sign of a shifter?

"Well, well, if it isn't the little cop killer," Suzy said, her tone dry, but her eyes stormy with hatred.

The tension in her limbs increased, though not because of Suzy's words. The vampire's expression was one of amusement. Either he hadn't yet seen the weapon in her hand, or he simply didn't care because he knew she'd never have time to use it.

Heat washed over her skin, whispering secrets to her mind. A second vampire was behind her.

She spun, pressing her finger against the trigger even as she did. The weapon bucked as it fired, throwing her back against the wall. A blue bolt of light hit the second vampire square in the chest. He made no sound, just fell down in a heap, gasping for air and clutching at his chest.

Behind her, a chair lightly scraped across the tiles. She swung back round and fired a second shot. The blue bolt hit the first vampire in the side of the head. He went down fast, hitting the ground with bone jarring force. She swung around, centering the weapon on Suzy.

"Unless you want to end up lying next to your coffee-swilling friend, get up and drag this thing into the kitchen for me." She lightly toed the vampire at her feet and then stepped back.

Suzy rose, hate warring with fear in her eyes. Moving with a model's grace, she walked across and grabbed the second vampire by the arms. With some effort, she dragged him to the table, and dropped him next to the first vampire.

Sam stepped back into the room and kicked the door shut, ensuring no on else could sneak up on her. "Now sit back down."

Suzy did. "How dare you come into my house and assault my friends like this."

She snorted softly. "Say that with a little more venom and I might just believe these two are actually your friends."

"What are you here for, Samantha? Come to finish the job you started with Jack?"

"The man I shot wasn't Jack, and we both know it."

Amusement flickered through the hate. So she'd guessed right. Suzy *did* know about the clone.

"And that's your defense? It wasn't Jack but a *clone?*" Suzy gave a mocking, hard-edged laugh. "They're really going to believe that."

"They will when I produce the real thing. Where is he?"

"Like I'd really tell you if I knew."

She knew, all right. The cynical half-smile touching her artificially full lips said as much. "Then tell me why you came back here today?"

"I live here, remember?"

Not recently, she hadn't. Maybe she'd come here to collect something Jack had forgotten—like a certain set of digital disks. She frowned. If Jack was a vampire, it made sense he'd keep Suzy near to do his daytime work. What didn't make sense was the fact he'd sent two guards, both of them vampires.

Apparently, they *could* move around in sunlight. But how? Her gaze flicked down to the two men. There was enough light coming in through the kitchen window and back door to cause them discomfort, yet their skin remained a pasty white, untouched by the slightest hint of burn.

It also appeared *shiny.* As if someone had taken a roll of cellophane wrap and stretched it tightly across their faces.

Had someone figured out a way to enable vampires to move around in the sunlight? Foreboding began to beat through her. If that were true, it could be a very, very *bad* thing.

"Don't move, Suz. Or I *will* shoot, love of Jack's life or not."

Suzy gave her a mutinous look and crossed her arms. A sign of rebellion and compliance in one action, she thought grimly. She knelt next to the men, and lightly touched the first vampire's face. He glared at her, brown eyes promising death—or worse—when he could move. Not that she was planning to hang around until then. His cheek felt as shiny as it looked and sort of wet.

She looked at the vampire she'd shot in the head. What looked like skin had peeled away from the wound near his temple. She grasped it, and lightly pulled. With a weird sucking sound, a three inch sliver came away.

Though it felt like real skin, the odd shininess suggested it was some sort of plastic-like substance. She shoved it into her pocket. Maybe Gabriel would know what to make of it—once he'd finished throwing the book at her for escaping his noose yet again. She rose and returned her gaze to Suzy.

"Time to cut to the chase. I know, and you know, that Jack's alive. I want you to arrange a meet. Midnight tomorrow at the Dragon and George." Hopefully, that'd give Gabriel enough time to calm down, and her enough time to convince him this was a good move.

"He won't come."

"Oh, I think he will. Especially if you tell him I have the disks."

Suzy's gaze narrowed. There was nothing pretty about her face now. In fact, she looked like the harridan Sam had always thought her to be. "That's theft, officer. Those disks belong to me."

Suzy didn't ask which disks, she noted. "So report me."

Suzy didn't respond to that, and Sam half-smiled as she added, "Just give the message to Jack."

"Why, so you can kill him all over again?"

"If it's another clone rather than the real Jack, most certainly. And if it's not the real Jack, the disks are history."

"He'll kill you, you know."

The venom in Suzy's rich voice sent a shiver down her spine. "If he tries, I'll shoot his brains out. Again."

One of the vampires on the floor moved. Though it wasn't much more than a fingertip, it was warning enough that the immobilizing effects of the laser were starting to wear off. She backed to the door. There was no way in hell she wanted to be around when those two got mobile. She might still have the laser, but they were both pretty pissed off, and she'd lost the element of surprise. Plus, there was Suzy. Three against one weren't good odds, whether or not she was armed.

"It was such a pleasure to see you again, Suz."

Suzy didn't reply, merely glared. Grinning slightly, Sam backed out the door. And realized about a heartbeat too late that someone was standing behind her.

***

Her reactions, Gabriel thought, were almost too fast to be human. Though he hadn't spoken, much less made a sound, she seemed to sense his presence behind her. She leapt away with almost vampiric speed and spun, her left hand raising so fast it seemed to blur.

It was then he saw the deadly Holcroft laser clenched between her fingers.

"Whoa. I'm on your side, remember?" He raised his hands and watched her blue eyes. With most people, the pupil dilated a little before the trigger was pulled—not much of a warning, but generally, it was the difference between life and death. Of course, as he was beginning to discover, she wasn't most people.

Luckily, it was recognition, not the need to kill, that sparked in the depths of her eyes. She lowered the laser, but didn't entirely relax. Neither did he.

"How did you find me so quickly?" Despite her question, she didn't really seem all that surprised to see him there.

He shrugged. "It wasn't all that hard to guess where you might go." He hesitated, hearing movement inside the house. Footsteps, receding slightly. "Suzy's obviously home."

She grimaced. "Yeah. And she's not alone. Can we get out of here?"

"Why? What have you done now?" From inside the house came an odd sound—like someone was scuffling around on the floor. He glanced down at the weapon in her hand. Obviously, she'd used it to immobilize one of Suzy's companions.

"They attacked me. I defended myself." She hesitated, her bright gaze searching his face, lingering a little on the side that held the bruises. "You can't go in there."

"Why not?" Given he was supposed to be in charge of the investigation against her, he was duty bound to go inside. Of course, he and duty weren't often the companions they were supposed to be—not that *she* knew that.

She hesitated. Deciding, he guessed, whether or not he could be trusted. Something he had a feeling wouldn't happen fully unless he reciprocated. And *that* wasn't going to happen any time soon. Hell, the only people he completely trusted were his twin and his immediate family.

"I've asked Suzy to arrange a meeting with Jack. If either of them suspects your mob is involved, they won't come."

By "your mob" she obviously meant SIU rather than the Federation, as very few people knew of his involvement with the Federation. But such a meeting could prove very interesting indeed. At the very least, it might just prove how much Kazdan, and ultimately Sethanon, knew about the Federation's infiltration of the SIU.

"Kazdan's smart enough to realize the SIU would have to be involved. He'd be more suspicious if I *wasn't* there."

She tilted her head slightly, her expression a mix of curiosity and dislike. "You don't like him."

And that was obviously a mark in her bad books, despite the fact that Jack had tried to kill her. "No. I don't," he said, a little sharper than intended.

She raised a pale eyebrow. He rubbed a hand across his rough jaw, wondering where the sudden rush of anger had come from. "Look, I've got a cab waiting out front." He'd arranged for one to be here, so she wouldn't question how he'd arrived. "I think we need to go somewhere and talk."

She nodded. "Preferably somewhere with food. I'm starved."

If she thought it strange he was using a cab rather than an official car, she certainly didn't mention it. "Fine. But first, tell me who's in there with Suzy."

Her hesitation was brief, but nevertheless there. He couldn't say he entirely blamed her. So far, he'd given her no real reason to trust him.

"Two vampires. Guards, I presume."

And somehow, she'd bested not one, but two of them. Something no *human* should have been capable of—even when armed with a Holcroft laser. The human eye and brain just weren't designed to assimilate the speed with which a vampire could move. That was why most humans thought vampires could disappear into shadows. Fact was, they couldn't and didn't. Humans just couldn't see their movements.

Usually, the only vampires killed by humans were the newly turned, the careless, or those so fed up with eternal afterlife they virtually committed suicide. From what he'd seen of Kazdan, the two guards he'd sent with his wife would be the best. Yet Sam had beaten them.

Maybe Karl was right after all.

"Why did you leave them alive?"

Her eyes widened and color leeched from her face, only to be quickly replaced by a flush that spoke of anger. Her fingers clenched and unclenched around the laser. He watched her warily. Her psych profile suggested her hatred against vampires ran so deep that her response when confronted by one would be to shoot first and ask questions later.

She might have shot, but she didn't *kill*. A huge difference.

"I wanted to give Jack some reason to trust me."

"If it wasn't for Jack, would you have killed them?"

She glared at him. "What do you think?"

He thought not. Somehow, the profile and the computers had gotten it wrong. She might hate them, but she wouldn't kill them, not unless forced to. As she had been forced to kill Kazdan's clone.

"I think it's time we get something to eat." He stepped back and motioned her to go first.

After a moment, she did. The bright yellow cab waited out front, stopped right behind an old caddy with darkly tinted windows. A vamp wagon, if he ever saw one. He frowned slightly, studying the car as he opened the cab door for her. When he'd walked past it earlier, he could have sworn he'd felt heat coming from the engine. But that didn't make sense—not if the two men inside were vampires.

"Did the vamps arrive in that car?"

She glanced at him over the roof of the cab, and then glanced at the car. "I don't know. It wasn't here when I arrived, though."

Odd. But as they were probably being watched by those still inside the house, he resisted the impulse to inspect the car. Instead, he climbed in the cab and fed the computer the address of a restaurant in the Southgate entertainment complex. It was owned by a good friend, and he knew it would be safe to talk there.

The seat belt sign flashed. He buckled up, and then glanced across at Sam. Her color was still high, and she refused to acknowledge his stare. At least she no longer held the laser. Maybe she'd put it away to avoid the temptation to shoot him. Where had she gotten the weapon in the first place? At Kazdan's? And if so, how did *that* fiend get hold of it? Through Sethanon, or through his sources on the street? Either was a pretty frightening thought.

The cab sped away, electric motor humming through the silence growing between them. He returned his gaze to the road and watched the traffic roll by. It took just over half an hour to get to Melbourne. The cab rolled to a stop near Princess Bridge. He swiped his credit card through the debit slot, then climbed out and walked around the cab.

She stood on the pavement, arms crossed, eyeing the mid-afternoon crowds somewhat pensively. "When you suggested we talk, I thought you meant to go somewhere quiet."

"What can be quieter than standing alone in a crowd of

strangers?" He led the way to the steps leading down to the promenade. Han's restaurant sat in the shadows of the bridge, overlooking the Yarra River.

She flashed him a surprised look, a smile almost touching her lush lips. "Is that a quote from Kuchoner?"

He nodded. "A great poet and something of a favorite of mine." He noted the surprise that flitted across her face and smiled grimly. "What, I'm with the SIU, so I'm not allowed any interests outside the paranormal?"

"Well, that's the rumor, and from what I've seen, the truth."

"Then you haven't seen enough."

"Obviously."

He opened the restaurant door and ushered her through. Inside, it was dark, the only light coming from the rainbow sparkle that played like stars across the ceiling. But in an hour or so, when the restaurant officially opened for evening trade, candlelight would join the stars and help provide the intimate, magical atmosphere that made Han's so popular.

"Gabriel, my friend." A big man loomed out of the darkness, arms opened wide. "It is so good to see you."

He allowed himself to be engulfed, and he briefly returned Han's embrace. "And you, old friend."

Han stepped away, wide grin barely visible beneath his bushy, handlebar moustache. "And who is this pretty little lady?"

"Samantha Ryan," she said, and held out a hand.

"So formal," Han mocked, and caught her fingers, holding them still as he bent down to kiss them.

Gabriel could almost feel the heat of her blush. She cleared her throat and snatched her hand back as soon as Han released it.

Han raised an eyebrow, amusement evident in his brown eyes. "What can I do for you both?"

"We need a meal and somewhere to talk."

Han nodded. "The dragon room is safe. I shall cook you something and bring it in."

Safe meant he had both psychic and electronic dampeners in place, preventing anyone from using either means to listen in. "Thanks, Han."

The big man nodded and walked back into the darkness. Gabriel guided her through the tables to the small room at the back. He pressed the button to one side of the door, switching on the special effects inside the room, then opened the door and ushered her through.

Her gasp was almost inaudible. He glanced at her, half-smiling as he closed the door. "Amazing, isn't it?"

She nodded, her gaze on the myriad of tiny dragons that danced and played across the roof. "They look so real."

"They're the latest in holographic technologies. Han is something of a pioneer in the field." He walked across to a center table.

She followed him. "So what's he doing running a restaurant?"

He lit a candle and motioned for her to sit. She took the chair directly opposite his. He hoped it wasn't a sign of things to come. "He still dabbles in the field, as you can see." And running a restaurant was far safer than active service in the Federation, which was where Han had honed his holographic skills.

She leaned back and asked, "What do you want to talk about?"

He smiled at her directness. "Honesty."

Her blue eyes glittered like ice encrusted sapphires in the candlelight. There was anger there, as well as suspicion. Yet he had a sense that she was also controlling herself very tightly, and he wondered why. "I've been nothing but honest with you."

"Have you? Then tell me why you went back to your apartment to retrieve the com-unit you've been hiding in your bag. Tell me what you found at Kazdan's, besides that laser, that makes you so certain he'll come to this meeting tomorrow. And tell me why someone is setting you up for a murder rap."

"What?"

Despite the edge in her voice, she didn't seem all that surprised. "I have orders to wrap up my investigation, and hand you over for prosecution, by tomorrow afternoon," he informed her. "That order came from the top."

"The bastards." She rubbed a hand over her eyes, and then looked up again. "What do you intend to do?"

"That very much depends on you."

"And just what is it you want me to do, Assistant Director Stern?"

The sarcasm in her voice suggested that someone, at some time, had tried using their authority to get her into bed. The sudden coldness in her eyes suggested the outcome had not been favorable—for either party.

He held her gaze. "I want you to help me with a problem. In return, I'll help you find what's behind Kazdan's attempt on your life."

"What about your orders to hand me over?"

He shrugged. "I was never much one for following orders."

Her gaze returned to the dragons for a moment. He sat back in the chair and waited.

"You want me to trust you," she said softly. "And yet you're not willing to trust me."

He raised an eyebrow as her gaze returned to his. There was something in those bright depths that seemed to run straight through him, diving deep into his soul. It was partly a recognition of fate—a sense that this woman, for good or for bad, would play an important part in his future. But it was also something else, something he couldn't even begin to name. Yet it was *that* something that made him trust her, even when common sense, and everything he knew about her, suggested extreme wariness. Which was why what he was about to say what might well end up being a bargain with the devil herself.

"What makes you say that?"

"The tests. We both know they're not just psych and psychic evaluations. You've run the whole gamut, right down to biological. Why?"

"I told you—we want to know why you were able to see the kites."

"But it's more than that now."

He nodded. "When Finley ran the original tests, we found a few interesting anomalies. For a start, you registered neutral in the psychic tests, and that can only mean you have a talent strong enough to avoid detection, yet still be able to work in the presence of the psychic deadeners."

She raised her eyebrow, but offered no comment, simply tapped a finger lightly against the tabletop as she waited for him to go on.

"Finley also discovered an unknown chromosome in your cell sample. As yet we haven't been able to track it down." He didn't mention her developmental immaturity. It would be something she'd surely be aware of.

She frowned. "How can I have an unknown chromosome running around my body?"

"We don't know. That's why we're running extra tests."

She fell silent for a long minute, and then lowered her gaze to the table. "What's the favor you want of me?"

He hesitated as the door opened. Han came into the room, carrying a tray full of bread, meats and rice. "Best I could do in a hurry," he said, putting the tray on the table.

"Thanks, Han."

The big man nodded. "I shall keep a watch out for you."

"Thanks." He waited until Han had left, then reached out and grabbed a thick slab of bread. "A friend of mine is being poisoned." That the friend was also his twin was a fact she didn't need to know. "Through the water. Only a very few people, myself included, have access to him."

She helped herself to a plate of the thick sliced lamb and aromatic rice. "If it's being administered through the water, it could be anyone."

He shook his head. "He doesn't drink tap water, and the bottled water is fully tested before he goes near it."

"Your friend must be very important for such measures to be taken."

"He is." He was the only brother he had left.

She frowned, tilting her head slightly to one side, her expression thoughtful. "How can I help, then?"

"I think I'm too close. I've known these people all my life. I don't know if I can be clinical enough to choose the killer amongst them."

"And you want me to be your fresh set of eyes?"

He nodded. "You're a police officer, as well as an outsider. You might see what I don't."

"That's a hell of a gamble on my integrity. How do you know I won't pick someone randomly and be done with it?"

Good question. And the truth was, there was no good answer to it. Nothing except instinct and something deep inside that said he *had* to trust her. "How do you know I won't shoot Kazdan on sight and save the State the costs of a trial?"

She blinked in surprise. "Jack's done nothing illegal."

Yeah, right. Maybe she didn't consider trying to kill her illegal, but he sure as hell did. And that was only the tip of it. "Kazdan's a commander in an underground organization run by a man known only as Sethanon."

She paled a little. "What sort of organization?"

"An organization that believes humans have no right to be running the world when they are not the superior race."

"Jack said a war was about to begin," She hesitated, licking her lips slightly. "A war in which man will play no part, and yet ultimately be the loser."

If Sethanon won, that would certainly be the truth. "When

did Kazdan say this?"

"The night he . . . his clone tried to kill me."

So they *were* gearing up for war. Maybe the kites were nothing more than a warning shot. "So he *did* try to recruit you that night."

She shrugged. "I'm not so sure. It seemed more of a test of some kind. I just didn't get the feeling he seriously tried to enlist me."

He reached for a plate, and heaped on some meat. Maybe it *was* a test—to see if the clone could pass the muster of someone who knew the original intimately. But if that were the case, why not just test the clone with Suzy? Maybe it was something to do with Sam's extra chromosome and the psychic abilities they'd yet to pin down.

That in itself suggested Kazdan knew more about Sam than maybe she did herself.

"If Jack was right about the war, then who is the other side?" She hesitated, her gaze thoughtful as she stared at him. "It's you. You're with them, aren't you?"

He nodded. He hadn't wanted to go this deep, but now that she'd made the connection, it couldn't be avoided. He just had to hope his instincts about her were right.

"I'm with an organization known as the Federation. It's a conglomerate of races that oppose Sethanon's ideologies."

She abandoned what remained of her meal and leaned back in the chair. "I've been with State for over ten years, and I've never heard of either Sethanon or the Federation. Why?"

"The Federation originally formed after the Race Wars. It was basically meant to be a union for 'other' races, to ensure we got fair treatment in the wash up after the war."

"Then why haven't I heard of it?

"Because there is no real need for us to be active these days. By and large, other races have a fair deal. We have no wish to rock the boat."

"But this Sethanon does?"

"Definitely. He surfaced about sixteen years ago. Since then, he's tried several strikes against us. Nothing major, just tests of strength, I think. Our biggest problem is that we know as little about him today as we did back then."

Her gaze had narrowed. "You keep saying we. I take it then, that you're not human."

He grimaced. He definitely hadn't meant her to pick up this

much. "No. I'm a shapechanger."

One pale eyebrow rose. "You look human."

He snorted, irritated by her response. He'd expected more from her, for some reason, though he shouldn't have. The psych tests showed her prejudices clear enough. "I am."

"That's not what I meant—"

"I *know* what you meant." Why did humans continue to seek differences when, basically, they'd all come from the same stock?

"No, you don't. You think I'm being biased when I'm not."

"Then what *did* you mean?"

"Shapechangers' generally have a spark of wildness in their eyes that suggest their dual nature. Same as the constant shifting from one human form to another gives shapeshifters a translucent quality to their skin." She regarded him steadily for a moment, and then shook her head. "Don't judge me until you know me, Gabriel."

It was interesting she'd noted the differences between shifters and changers. Most of the population wasn't even aware that they were two distinct groups. It would be intriguing to see what she made of the meeting tonight.

"I apologize."

She nodded. "These friends of yours—they're a part of this Federation, too?"

"Yes."

"Then they're nonhuman species, as well?"

"Some of them, yes." He wondered if this one fact would alter the way she dealt with them.

She glanced at the dragons for a minute, then nodded and returned her gaze to his. "If I agree to this, what happens to Jack?"

So they were back to Kazdan. The bastard certainly didn't deserve the regard with which she seemed to hold him. Even after the attempt on her life, she still cared what happened to him.

"What happens tomorrow night depends very much on what he does. At the very least, though, he should be charged with the attempt on your life."

"But you don't intend to arrest him tomorrow night."

"No." But only because he wanted him tracked. If Sethanon planned a war, it was high time they found out more about him and his organization. Kazdan's reappearance made him the ideal starting place. "Why are you so certain he'll turn up tomorrow?"

She grimaced, and then reached back into her pocket.

"Because I have these."

He accepted the three silver disks and the envelope. "Know what's on them?" he asked, holding the envelope up to the ceiling. It wasn't as empty as it looked.

"No. But the disks were hidden in the false bottom of a drawer. Suzy came back specifically to get them."

"Have you tried reading them?" He frowned, and tilted the envelope to one side. What looked like a strip of plastic was embedded along one edge.

She shook her head. "Haven't exactly had the chance. And my com-unit is back at the SIU with my stuff."

"Han's probably got one we can use. Wait here." He rose and went in search of Han. The big man was in the kitchen, and he directed him to the portable unit in his office. Sam's frown deepened as he handed her the unit.

"There's not enough light in this room to run this unit."

There was a touch of reluctance in her voice, and he had to wonder if it was simply a matter of knowing what was on the disks and not wanting him to see it, or whether she didn't want to pry into Kazdan's affairs any more than necessary. But that didn't make any sense, not if she wanted answers.

Maybe she wasn't after answers. Maybe she just wanted her partner back.

He glanced at the ceiling. "Hologram off. Lights on."

A bell chimed softly in the distance. The dragons fled, and bright light filled the room. "Problem solved," he said.

Her eyes narrowed at his unspoken challenge, and she took the disks back. He picked up the envelope and carefully tore off an edge, revealing the tip of thin plastic he'd noticed earlier. He clutched it between two fingers and lightly tugged. After a slight resistance, it came free, and he held it up to the light. It held a series of images, though they were far too small to pick out any detail. Han probably had a scanner they could use, but Gabriel didn't want to involve his friend any more than he already had. Han might support the Federation, but he was no longer an active member. They could wait till he got home—or to Karl's.

He put the strip back in the envelope and placed it inside his jacket. Sam was frowning at the com-unit.

"What's wrong?"

"The unit won't read the disks."

He pushed the edge of the unit around until he could see the screen. Disk error, it stated. "You put them in the right way?"

Her look was pure irritation. "Nah, I put them in upside down for the hell of it."

"Then maybe they've been coded."

"Why would Jack bother coding data disks?"

He shrugged and leaned back. "Maybe for the same reason he hid them."

She shook her head. "It doesn't make any sense. Jack's a computer whiz. If he wanted to hide something, he could do it far easier than messing around with these things." She nudged a disk with her fingertip. "For a start, they're too easily damaged."

Maybe the information was too explosive to be held on any com-unit. No computer was safe—not from the government, not from any number of hackers. If Jack were a hacker himself, he'd be well aware of that fact.

"The SIU system might be able to decode them." And it had the added advantage of having trackers installed, so if someone *did* get interested, they'd get some warning. Not that that had stopped information leaks in the past, but right now, they had little other choice. "We should also go take a closer look at Jack's clone."

She nodded. "And talk to the two men who were trying to nab him."

"That too." Though he personally didn't hold much hope of getting any information out of them. As thralls—humans who were shackled to the life of their vampire masters, but not actually vampires themselves—they would die before they betrayed their masters. They had no other choice.

"When do I get to meet your friends?"

He raised an eyebrow. "Does that mean we have an agreement?"

Her hesitation was briefer this time. "Yes." She held out her hand.

Her fingers were long and slender and seemed to get lost within his. "Then you meet my friends tonight."

"And afterwards, you'll help me find out what Jack's up to?"

"And stop him."

Her gaze dropped to the table. "And stop him," she agreed softly.

Why was she so loyal to the bastard? And why did she cling to the notion that talking to Kazdan would solve anything? There was only one person in the world that Kazdan looked out for—

himself. If she held any notion that the two of them were really friends, she was deluding herself.

"Let's go," he said, rising.

She nodded, gathering the disks and shoving them back in her pocket. He followed her out the door, wondering what she'd do when the time came to kill Kazdan.

Eight

The feeling hit the minute Sam left the elevator and walked into the lobby. A wash of heat, followed by the certainty that there was a shifter nearby, which was a given, considering these were the halls of the SIU. Except for one thing. This shifter *felt* bad. Like Suzy had felt bad. Like the thing that had attacked her on the rooftop had felt bad. She stopped and stared down the hallway to her right. It was in the labs.

"You okay?"

Gabriel's soft question made her jump. She stared up at him for a moment, then swallowed and nodded. "This is going to sound odd, but there's a shifter down in the labs."

"Could be anyone. There are over twenty shifters currently working for the SIU, you know." Even so, he stared down the hall, hazel eyes filled with concern.

"I know, but this feels . . . wrong." So wrong it was beginning to leave a very bad taste in the back of her mouth.

His frown deepened. "Let's go take a look."

She nodded. The sensation grew stronger as they approached the labs, until it felt like her whole skin was itching. The door swished open as they approached. There was no one inside.

"Odd," he murmured, moving across to the com-unit. He ran a finger along one edge of the screen, and then held it up to her. "Blood."

She hoped it wasn't Finley's. Hoped it didn't mean he was dead. As much as she loathed the tests, Finley himself had been okay. She reached back for the laser and saw Gabriel had already drawn his gun.

"The shifter is in the next room," she said quietly.

He nodded and walked to the next door. She followed, keeping to the opposite side of him.

There wasn't a sound to be heard. Even the hum of the test units seemed silenced. Soft light washed through the room, giving the walls a waxy appearance. She glanced up at him. He motioned to the left, and then held up three fingers. She nodded and began to silently count. At three, she moved in, laser raised.

Two people looked up from the com-screen. One was Finley, the other a woman with bright blue hair and a body any wrestler would be proud of.

Finley raised an eyebrow in surprise. "You have a problem,

Assistant Director?"

"I think we might," Gabriel's voice was cold, his weapon centered on the young doctor. "Don't move."

Heat washed a warning across her skin. This was the shifter, not the real Finley. The woman moved. Almost as if it were in slow motion, she saw the gun in the woman's hand, saw her finger curl round the trigger. Sam raised the laser and dove to her right, firing as she fell. The blue bolt missed by a hairsbreadth, zinging past the woman's ear and exploding into the cabinets behind her. Almost simultaneously, she heard Gabriel's gun bark, a sound that was echoed by the shifter's weapon. A bullet hit the floor near her toes, tearing away a huge chunk of carpet and concrete.

She scrambled to her feet and saw the shifter lunge at her. She dodged and fired the laser. Again she missed, the blue bolt bouncing off the wall near his head and sizzling back along the desk. Then he was on her, his weight hitting with the force of a tree. She struck the floor with a grunt, the air forced from her lungs as she took the brunt of his weight. Then his hands were grabbing her, trying to pin her arms. She swore, avoiding his hands even as she punched him with her free hand. Though her blows landed with enough force to jar her arm, he didn't react, simply shifted his weight so that suddenly it was hard to breathe. She bucked, trying to move him, but he was as unmovable as a brick wall. Her lungs began to burn with the need to breathe. He caught the hand that held the weapon, his grip bruising her flesh as he forced her arm back over her head. Cursing him softly, and wasting precious air in the process, she drove her free hand between them and grabbed his testicles, squeezing hard. He yelped in surprise, simultaneously jerking back and releasing her arm. She bucked him off, and then fired the laser at this face, freezing his body and his expression of pain.

She scrambled to her feet. Gabriel swung round, weapon raised. The blue-haired woman lay at his feet, pinned by the foot he ground into her throat. Yet another sign how little the SIU cared about prisoner rights.

He seemed to relax slightly as their gazes met. "You okay?"

She nodded, then bent and lightly touched the shifter's neck. He had a pulse, which was good. Despite the fact that she'd had the gun on stun, firing at such close range could often prove deadly. Or so she'd read. She walked over to Gabriel.

"You know either of these two?" he asked. The woman

shifted her arm slightly. Gabriel pressed a little harder on her throat, and all movement stopped.

She stared at their blue-haired prisoner. The woman had a hole blown clear through her thigh, and blood poured down the side of her face from another wound near the hairline. Yet, despite this, it was anger and hate, not pain, that filled her dark eyes as she glared at up them.

"No," she replied. "You?"

"This one," he said, pushing his heel deeper into the woman's throat. "Goes by the name Ruby Lee. Works part time down at *The Body Beautiful Gym*, and the rest of the time as a high class thief."

Ruby Lee obviously wasn't human. Otherwise she'd be suffering a crushed larynx right about now. "What the hell is a thief doing sneaking into the SIU?"

"Good question." He motioned to the machines lining one wall. "Why don't you go see if the real Finley is alive so we can find out."

She nodded and walked across to the machines. The young doctor was in the third unit. Squeezing in beside him, she lightly touched his neck. His pulse was steady and strong, but he had a decent sized egg on his skull. He'd probably have a hell of a headache for several days to come.

"Hey Finley, you okay?" She pinched his cheek, trying to get some sort of response. A soft groan was her only reply. She climbed out the machine and walked back to Gabriel. Three men and a woman, all clad in SIU gray, had joined him.

"Finley's alive, but he's out of it for the moment."

He nodded and glanced at the woman in gray. "Take these two to security, Briggs, and get the medics in here for Finley. And watch the woman carefully—she's something of an escape artist."

Briggs nodded and motioned to one of the men to help her with the woman. The other moved across to the shifter.

She watched them leave, and then looked at Gabriel. "I was under the impression shifters could take only one alternate human form, with the second identity being ordained when they were young. So how come this shifter was able to walk right in and take Finley's form?"

"Because there's a strain of shifter that can take alternate forms at will."

She raised an eyebrow. "That's something of a well kept

secret, isn't it?"

He shrugged and crossed to the com-screen. "Why prejudice humans against shifters any more than necessary, especially when multi-shifters are rare?"

"Sounds more like a case of keeping the human race ignorant."

"Ignorance is bliss, isn't it?" His attention was on the screen, his reply almost absent.

"Not from what I've seen." She leaned forward, her face close to his. As she stared at the screen, her nostrils filled with his warm, spicy aroma. "That's gibberish."

"Indeed." He glanced up as two medics entered. "Finley's in unit three."

She waited until the two medics, carrying Finley on a stretcher, had left. "Have you tried retrieving anything?"

"Computer, update on test results for Samantha Ryan."

"Voice identification required."

"Stern, Assistant Director. Badge number 5019."

"Voice verified. Request processing."

The com-unit hummed softly. "Results for test subject Samantha Ryan unavailable."

"Why?"

The com-unit hummed for several more seconds. "Results for test subject Samantha Ryan unavailable."

"Sounds like it's been looped."

He nodded. His gaze, when it met hers, was grim. "Someone doesn't want us nosing around your genetic history."

"Put like that, I'm not sure if I do, either." She glanced back at the screen. "How could they simply walk in here and do that? I thought the SIU had a top security system."

"We have retina and voice ID, but sometimes that doesn't mean much."

Not when shifters could take alternate forms at will. But even without that ability, no system was truly safe. Jack could have gotten in here. *Had* gotten in here, if the drunken boast she'd overhead one night was true. "But why would they bother stopping anyone getting access to my files? I'm not so special."

"Aren't you?" He leaned back in the chair, and studied her for a moment. "You sensed the kites. You sensed the fact that Jack's clone was a vampire. And despite the psychic deadeners we have in place, you knew the shifter was in here."

The intensity of his gaze cut right through her, stirring

something deep in her soul. Suddenly uneasy, she cleared her throat and looked back at the screen. "I was tested for psychic ability when I entered the academy. I came up with a big fat zero."

"Most talents come on with full maturity."

She shot him a quick look. His gaze was calculating, thoughtful. *He knows.* That's what the second set of biological tests had been about. They'd obviously discovered what she'd known since she was fifteen. That she'd never fully mature as a woman. Never have children of her own. Not unless she had a complete uterus and ovary transplant. And even then, the children would never *really* be hers.

"You obviously know that can't be the case here. I'm twenty-nine. A little past puberty, I think."

He shrugged. "Shapechangers tend to mature a lot later than humans. My two sisters were well into their thirties before they actually started menstruating."

That was really a little more info than she needed about his sisters. "But I'm human, not a shapechanger."

"But maybe that unknown chromosome we found has delayed your development in much the same manner."

She shook her head. "They ran all manner of tests on me when I was fifteen. They all came up with the same answer. This was it, this was all I was going to get."

He raised an eyebrow. "You resent it, don't you?"

She snorted softly. Of course she resented it. Having a family of her own had been the one dream she could remember clearly through the fog that was her childhood. "You don't know how lucky you are, having sisters and a family. I have nothing. Not even memories."

He leaned forward, covering her hand with his. His touch was warm, comforting, and yet at the same time, electric. As if they were two opposing currents that had briefly merged and become one stronger identity. Her gaze jerked to his. If he felt the elemental surge of energy between them, there was no sign of it in his eyes. Only compassion.

And in many ways, that was the more frightening response. This man seemed to understand her entirely *too* well.

"Maybe the answers we seek lie in the past you can't remember."

She frowned. "What do you mean?"

He squeezed her hand briefly, and then leaned back in the

chair, his expression thoughtful. "Finley found a microchip in your side. Military in design, and probably inserted when you were about nine."

She touched her side. He'd told her he was merely taking a skin sample for further tests. Odd she hadn't picked up the doc's lie. She'd always been able to pick up Jack's slightest variation of the truth.

"Why would someone want to put a microchip in me, especially at that age?"

"I don't know. All we know is that it was used to track your movements."

"That makes no sense." A cold sensation ran over her. It wasn't caused so much by the fact that someone had wanted to trace her movements twenty four hours a day, but that Jack might have been involved. He had always known where to find her. But if she believed he was involved, she'd also have to believe their friendship was nothing more than a lie, a setup from the beginning. She couldn't, *wouldn't,* believe it.

Jack was her friend. Just about her only friend.

"Can you remember anything about your childhood? Your parents?"

She shook her head. "The only thing I had was a hand drawn picture of my mum, but the bomb destroyed it. The doctor's at the home said I must have undergone some severe trauma to forget my past so completely."

"And you've never bothered trying to rediscover that past?"

"Of course I have. That's why Jack set me up an unregistered link into State—" She broke off as he smiled grimly.

"So that's why you went back to retrieve your com-unit. You sent yourself some of Jack's files."

He didn't miss much. "Yes." There wasn't much point in denying it now. "But I haven't had the chance to look at them yet."

"Then we'll make time later tonight." He glanced at his watch, and then pushed upright. "We're late for our dinner date with my friends."

"What about my bag? And what about Jack's clone?"

"We'll collect your bag on the way out. As for the clone, he'll still be here tomorrow. This is more important."

More important to him, maybe. "And the disks?"

He glanced at the com-unit. "I don't think we should risk it. Someone's obviously got a line in here, someone who doesn't want us to discover any more about you."

Someone with enough clout to get two saboteurs into the heart of the SIU. But no matter where they went, they would still face that problem. She'd witnessed Jack hacking into enough systems to place tracers to know how easy it was. "If someone's trying to stop us, they'll be watching the lines into your place and mine."

"Maybe."

A sudden hint of amusement played round his full lips. She frowned at him. "What's so funny?"

"Maybe Jack will help us."

"Yeah right. Hand over the disks so he can translate them for us." She snorted. "That's really going to happen."

"That's not what I meant." He hesitated, considering her for a moment.

Something in his eyes made her remember that this was a man with an agenda of his own. Made her remember her vow not to trust anyone. He might have saved her life, but that didn't mean she should completely trust him.

"I mean," he said. "We should visit Kazdan's apartment and try using his computers to read the disks."

She stared at him, wondering what in hell he was talking about now. "I went to Jack's place. I told you, it was stripped."

His expression wasn't altogether friendly. "I said apartment, not house. Surely you remember his apartment? You must have visited it at least once or twice."

His tone insinuated they'd been doing more than simply visiting. She clenched her fingers, but she somehow resisted the urge to hit him. This wasn't the first time she'd heard these accusations, so she should be used to them by now. But for some reason, the fact that it was Gabriel voicing what was generally assumed as fact hurt her more than it ever should have.

"Jack and I never visited that apartment. I never even knew it existed." It was on the tip of her tongue to refute his insinuation, but she held back. No one else had ever believed her, so why should he?

"Really?" His raised eyebrow hinted at disbelief. "You were partners for five years, and you never knew he had an apartment near Federation Square?"

"I was his partner, not his keeper." She frowned. "How in hell could Jack afford an apartment in a precinct like that?"

"Same way you can afford to own an apartment near the

beach in Brighton."

The blood drained from her face, only to be replaced by a rush of heated anger. He didn't trust her. Not entirely, at least. Despite his earlier words, he still suspected she was involved in something with Jack.

"I inherited that apartment when I turned twenty-one. I have no idea who my benefactor was, and the attorney wouldn't reveal his identity." An edge of anger crept into her voice, despite her efforts to remain calm. "The only previous owner I could find said he sold it to the Panjet Corporation. They've refused to answer any of my queries over the years." She hesitated and clenched her fists. "You can accuse me of Jack's murder, you can accuse me of being his lover, but don't you *ever* accuse me of being crooked."

"And yet that's how it looks." His voice still held an edge, his eyes still intense. Yet something in his manner suggested he believed her. "And it is something they will bring up in court, if this ever gets that far."

"Let them. I have nothing to hide."

"Maybe. Maybe not." He held out a hand. "Shall we go?"

It was on the tip of her tongue to tell him to go to hell, but she had a feeling she needed his help far more than he needed hers. Someone out there was setting her up for a fall, and like it or not, he was the only thing that currently stood between her and a prison cell.

Nodding briefly, she ignored his outstretched hand and brushed past him, walking to the door. One thing was certain— Jack had better provide some answers tomorrow night, or she might just be tempted to shoot him again.

***

Sam climbed from the car, shouldering her bag as she stared up at the three-story building in surprise. With its soaring white pillars and vast expanse of windows, the house looked as if it belonged in America's Deep South, not sitting here among the gums in the genteel suburb of Toorak. Although it *was* part of what was commonly called Millionaires Row. And the other houses on this block were even more extravagant in design than this.

She glanced at Gabriel as he moved around the car. "You didn't tell me your friend was wealthy."

He shrugged. "It isn't important."

When someone was trying to poison him, it was. Wealth

was often a motivating factor. "You've seen his will? Investigated his beneficiaries?"

His smile was somewhat grim. "There are two. His wife, Lyssa, and me." He motioned her up the stairs. "And if it *is* Lyssa, wealth won't be a motive. This house is hers—it's been in her family for several generations."

She raised an eyebrow. He was an heir? Why? "That's some friendship you have there, Assistant Director."

His gaze met hers. "Yes, it is. And I have no intention of losing it."

He pressed a button near the door. A bell chimed softly in the distance, then the security screen came to life.

"Gabriel." The woman was young and blonde and had a voice that could only be describe as sultry. "You're late."

"Sorry, Lys. Trouble at work."

"I see you've bought some of it along with you." The blonde sighed dramatically. "Come on in."

The door clicked open. She glanced up at Gabriel as he ushered her inside. "Your friend's wife an actress, by chance?"

A smile touched his lips. "Anyone would think so."

"How did she know I was one of your assignments?"

"One cop shooting another is big news these days. Your face has been plastered all over the media, I'm afraid."

So much for the right to an unprejudiced trial. She took off her coat and handed it to him so he could place it in the cloak closet, but she kept a grip on her bag. The hallway in which they stood was all white marble and gold fittings. And it was all real, all worth a king's fortune. His friends were obviously more than just plain old wealthy.

"This way." He caught her elbow, his touch light but warm as he led her down the hall. Their footsteps echoed through the silence, and the air was chill, almost stale. Maybe this part of the house wasn't used much.

It wasn't until he opened a set of French doors and ushered her into a smaller hallway that any real warmth came into the house. In this section, the walls were a mellow sandstone color and the doorways a rich turquoise. The floor was wood—real wood, not that plastic stuff they'd used in her apartment—but covered by a runner that was red, gold and turquoise diamonds. Even the air smelled different—warm and rich, with the scent of sandalwood combined with a faint hint of lime.

"I like your friend's taste in colors."

He nodded. "We spent a lot of our youth over in Santa Fe."

She raised an eyebrow. "Then why the southern influence in the front half of the house?"

"Because that's the way it's always been, and Lys doesn't want to go against tradition. It's only used for functions."

He ushered her through another doorway. Heat prickled a familiar warning across her skin and she stopped. He glanced down at her, one eyebrow raised in query.

"Your friends include a vampire and a shifter?"

He nodded. "There's also a shapechanger and a human."

There was? Then why couldn't she sense them? Why was this talent of hers, if indeed it was an emerging talent, picking up some nonhumans, and not others?

A man appeared in the doorway, his smile of greeting dying a little when his gaze met hers. "Samantha Ryan," he said. "What a surprise."

"I'm sure it is," she said dryly. Obviously Gabriel hadn't warned his friend that she was coming.

The two men briefly embraced. He was about Gabriel's height, maybe a little taller. His eyes were a vivid green, and his hair was black, but, like Gabriel's, it had a tendency to flop untidily across his eyes. Maybe they went to same barber. Even their build was similar, though the loose hang of the stranger's clothes suggested he'd recently lost a lot of weight.

"Karl sends his regards," Gabriel said softly. He took two small plastic bottles from his pocket and handed them to his friend. One looked like water, the other a pale green fluid. She guessed it was medicine of some kind.

The bottles disappeared into the other man's jacket pocket. Gabriel turned towards her. "Sam, this is my friend, Stephan."

She shook his offered hand. Despite the almost skeletal appearance of his fingers, his grip was firm. "Sorry to land on you like this. Gabriel should have warned you I was coming."

Stephan's expression was wry, as if the unexpected was an every day event when it came to Gabriel. "Yes, he should have. But you're welcome all the same. Come in, and meet the rest of the family."

He ushered her inside. Three people turned to look at her. "This is my wife, Lyssa" Stephan said. "Then we have Mary, and Martyn's over there near the fire."

She nodded politely at the three of them. Close up, Lyssa looked even younger than she had on the com-screen, and she had the figure to match her face and voice—except for a slightly rounded stomach. Pregnant, she thought, and wondered how different birth was for shifters.

Martyn was thin and pallid and looked like the typical vampire. Only he wasn't the bloodsucker she sensed. That was Mary—an older woman, probably in her mid-fifties, with steel gray hair, a face that looked well lived in, and kind blue eyes.

"Dinner's ready," Stephan continued. "So let's head into the dining room."

Gabriel placed a hand on her back, his fingers seeming to burn deep into her spine as he guided her into the next room. As he pulled her out a chair for her, she murmured her thanks, and was glad he decided to sit beside her. There was a sense of anger in the air that she didn't like. Oddly enough, the main source was the two women.

Mary sat opposite her, Lyssa to her left—an arrangement that left her with an uneasy feeling of being penned. Something about the two of them felt *wrong*. Though she couldn't explain it, the sensation gnawed at her, churning her stomach.

Martyn sat next to Mary, his gray eyes unfriendly as he studied her. Gabriel had obviously misjudged his friends. They were never going to loosen up in the presence of a stranger. Not enough, anyway, for her to be able to glean any real insights about them. Of the four of them, the only one not showing any sort of animosity towards her was Stephan.

"You should have told us you were bringing a celebrity, Gabriel. I would've dug out my autograph book."

Though Lyssa's tone was even, there was something in her manner that was far from friendly. It was almost as if she knew Sam and hated her.

"I didn't bring her here to be cross-examined," he said, annoyance in his soft tones. "No office talk, remember?"

"Oh, come on, don't be such a pooper." Lyssa's sultry tones were lightly teasing, but her blue eyes were sharp, almost icy. "You surely can't expect to bring along such a controversial guest without us asking a question or two."

His gaze met hers, and in the hazel depths she saw concern. But she wasn't entirely sure that the concern was for her. Maybe he thought she'd shoot the lot of them if they said too much. She smiled grimly and nodded at his unspoken query. Questions couldn't hurt, and they might just give her an insight or two into the people at this table. Although it was already obvious that the only one he was *really* close to was Stephan.

"Go for it, folks," she murmured.

Mary shook out her napkin, and then asked, "Did you really shoot your partner?"

The older woman's voice was steeped in concern, and little lines of tension ran around her blue eyes. If she didn't know better, she would have thought Jack's fate was somehow important to Mary. But if that were the case and Mary had been involved with Jack somehow, surely Jack would have mentioned it sometime during the last five years. Then again, he'd certainly never mentioned the apartment. Maybe she hadn't known Jack as well as she'd thought.

"I didn't shoot Jack. I shot his clone."

Mary snorted. "And State's buying that defense?"

"Apparently not, considering I'm still suspended."

Stephan gave Mary a look that quickly silenced any other questions she might have had, and then he leaned forward, interest bright in his green eyes. "Why was the clone attacking you?"

"I don't know." She glanced up as an autocook unfolded from the ceiling, and a large silver tray began to descend. "But the clone was a vampire, and it had every intention of killing me."

"A vampire?" Stephan glanced at Gabriel. "When did Kazdan become a vampire?"

She raised an eyebrow in surprise. "You know Jack?"

"Know of him." He regarded her steadily for a minute, his green eyes intense. "Was Kazdan a vampire before he disappeared?"

"No." There was something in Stephan's manner that reminded her of Gabriel. Maybe it was the way he leaned back in his chair, casual yet on guard.

"Interesting." He glanced at Gabriel again. "That means Kazdan was cloned after he turned."

"It would appear so," Gabriel said quietly.

"That's not possible." Martyn's voice was scratchy, almost harsh on the ears. "To produce a clone the same age as Kazdan in two and a half weeks, they would have had to use a tremendous amount of accelerant. So much so, the clone would soon have aged past Kazdan, and be of no use."

"Hang on." She frowned at Martyn. "Why does the clone have to have been produced after Jack was turned? Couldn't it have been turned, same as Jack?"

"In theory, yes. In practice?" Martyn hesitated, shrugging a thin shoulder. "There have been government trials, all unsuccessful. No one can figure out why."

Why in hell would the government be spending money trying to turn clones into vampires? Then again, why in hell was the government trying to produce the perfect clone at all? Wasn't it enough that they were able to make all the spare parts humanity could ever need?

"Anyone would think you men actually believe her clone story." Mary shook her head. "A clone has the same genetic makeup as the original but that's it. No one's ever found a way to imitate the workings of a human's mind." Mary hesitated, staring at her for a moment. Anger radiated from the woman, a wave so heated it was almost visible. "If she thought it was Jack she shot, then it was. A clone would not have had the same behavior patterns. She would have seen a difference."

For some reason, her shooting Jack mattered to Mary. And if Jack was connected to this Sethanon, as Gabriel suggested, then maybe he'd better start investigating Mary. "There was no obvious difference, believe me."

The silver tray settled on the table. The rich aromas of fresh breads, spicy curries and fresh vegetables filled the room, and while she would normally have dug in, right now, her stomach turned. She really didn't feel like eating. The feeling of wrongness was growing, gnawing at her like a dog with a bone. She just wished she could figure out what, exactly, was wrong.

Lyssa and Mary reached for plates. Martyn produced a small flask from inside his jacket pocket, and then poured a viscous, dark looking liquid into a wineglass. Blood, she thought, a chill running down her spine. If he was also a vampire, why hadn't she sensed it? And why had Gabriel said two of his friends were a shapechanger and a human, when what she was sensing suggested one shapeshifter, and possibly two vamps? She couldn't even begin to guess what Stephan was, but if he was part of this Federation of Gabriel's, it was possible he was also nonhuman. So who was the human? Her gaze swept the lot of them. She had no idea, and yet she doubted Gabriel was lying.

Her gaze came back to Mary, and her confusion deepened. Instinct still insisted that this woman was a vampire, but the fact that she had a plate loaded with food, and was in the process of devouring it, meant she couldn't be. Vampires couldn't eat food— or at least, couldn't keep it down. Another myth that had proven to be true.

What the hell was going on with her? Why was she sensing things that were obviously wrong?

"Curry?" Gabriel asked.

His sudden question made her jump. He frowned, but otherwise made no comment.

"No thanks," she said. "I think I'll stick to vegetables." The way her stomach was churning, she didn't dare try anything spicy.

He nodded, and handed across the platter of vegetables instead. She spooned a small selection onto her plate and put the platter back onto the tray.

"How long have you known Jack?" Stephan asked, breaking the brief silence.

She glanced at him. There was nothing in his tone but polite interest, but something in the intensity of his gaze suggested he was judging her. Because she'd come here with Gabriel? Because she'd obviously gained his trust enough to meet his friends? Obviously, Stephan had no idea just how little Gabriel really trusted her.

"We became partners just over five years ago."

"And you knew him well?"

"Yes." Or she thought she had. But the dawning of every day seemed to bring out more and more she hadn't known.

Mary snorted softly. "We all heard the news reports. They were lovers, for Christ's sake. Of course she knew him well."

Lyssa shifted on her chair and angrily speared a piece of meat off her plate. The sudden viciousness behind the movement left Sam with no doubt that Lyssa was not the gentle soul she looked.

She switched her gaze to Stephan. For some reason, she sensed it was important that this man, if no one else, believed her. "We were friends—good friends. Nothing more, nothing less."

He nodded, green gaze flickering briefly to Gabriel.

Lyssa jumped into the brief silence. "And were you also such good friends with his wife?"

Her smile was grim. "She was a bitch." And would probably get on extremely well with Lyssa.

The young blonde pursed her lips, eyes glittering with an odd mixture of jealously and hate. And the way she held her mouth stirred a memory. They'd met before, though where she had no idea

"Jealousy speaks," Martyn murmured.

She abandoned the pretense of eating and pushed her plate away. Mary, she noticed, was the only one who was really making any attempt to eat, shoveling in the food almost desperately.

"My partner's clone was trying to kill me. I shot him. End of story." At least for now. She hesitated, sweeping her gaze across the four of them. "Why don't we talk instead about this Sethanon Jack is supposedly involved with?"

Mary almost choked on her food. Martyn slapped her several times on the back, and then glanced at Stephan. As did Lyssa. It was almost as if they were looking for direction.

Which would make Stephan the leader of this little group. Maybe even of the Federation itself.

"What do you know of Sethanon?" he asked quietly.

"Only what Gabriel has told me." She looked at the man in question. His hazel eyes gave little away, as usual. "Which was nothing much, believe me."

Mary stood up quickly, her chair scraping across the wooden floor. "I think I've got something stuck in my throat. Please excuse me."

Lyssa rose. "You okay? Let me help."

Mary waved the offer away. "I'll be fine. I won't be a moment."

Sam watched her walk out the door, and the sense of wrongness jumped about ten degrees. She shifted, trying to deny the urge to get up and run from this house. She was a police officer, for Christ's sake. She'd been in a hell of a lot tougher situations than this.

So why did she feel that if they didn't all move soon, they'd die, right where they sat? It didn't make any sense. The house was well protected—the security cams and sensors near the front gate and front door were top of the range. No one would get near the house without Stephan being warned.

But what if the threat was from inside? What if the poisoner was about to take one step up the killing ladder? Her gaze went to the doorway. Maybe she should follow Mary and see just how bad the food lodging in her throat was.

"I need to go to the restroom." She gathered her bag off the back of her chair and stood.

Gabriel regarded her for a moment. Though there was no emotion in either his face or his eyes, she nevertheless sensed his concern. Or was it mistrust?

"Turn left out the door. Guest bathroom is the third on the right."

She nodded her thanks and walked out. The hall beyond the two rooms was quiet. She turned left and headed for the bathroom. Once she found the correct door, she opened it and peered inside. No one was there. Frowning, she turned and listened, trying to get some feel for where Mary might have gone.

She could hear the men talking—not so much their words, but the gentle rhythm of their voices. Water cascaded to her left, a soft sound that failed to soothe. Above her head, a board creaked. Was someone walking up there, or was it just the inherent noise of an old house? She didn't know, but the feeling of wrongness seemed to be coming from that direction.

She continued on down the hall until she found the stairs. Placing her foot on the bottom step, she paused and looked up. Nothing but shadows waited above—yet the sense of dread was getting fiercer. Something was very wrong, and she couldn't shake the feeling that if she didn't hurry, they would all die. Was there really danger upstairs, or was this weird certainty of death a sign that the stress of the last few days had finally pushed her over the edge? Probably the latter, she thought grimly.

Still, it couldn't hurt to keep investigating. She kept close to the wall as she climbed, her gaze scanning the darkness, watching for any sign of movement.

Nothing.

She reached the landing and stopped. The floor was in darkness, except for a thin strand of light coming from a room midway down the hall. She licked dry lips and headed in that direction.

Once near the door, she stopped and reached back for the laser. Maybe it was an overreaction, but she still felt safer with the weight of the weapon in her hand. She reached out with her free hand and slowly pushed the door open.

The room held a large autocook and little else. Heat itched across her skin, a warning that someone, or something, was near. The sensation of danger grew, pricking across her skin like stinging bites, though she could see nothing that presented an obvious threat.

She edged into the room. The com-unit attached to the autocook hummed softly, and cool air washed across her fevered skin. The room was fairly big, and shadows lurked in the far corners.

Gun raised, she eased past the autocook. Mary wasn't hiding in the far corners. Nothing was, beyond two small desks and another com-unit—this one attached to security screens. Obviously, this room also doubled as a security center.

She clicked the safety on and clipped the weapon back onto her belt. There was nothing here that could possibly be a threat to anyone's safety. Maybe she was misinterpreting the weird sensations flowing over her. She turned, and out the corner of her eye, she caught a flash of light. Frowning, she bent and looked under the desk. Green numbers glowed back at her. A timer, counting down.

Fear leapt into her throat, and squeezed tight. She edged closer and got down on her hands and knees. On the back wall, held off the floor by tape and almost totally hidden by the position of the desk, sat two small, dust covered plastic cylinders. White wires joined them, and these were connected to a small plastic timer.

Her heart seemed to shudder to a stop. She'd seen something like this once before. They were touch sensitive and almost impossible to defuse once they'd been set. The one time she'd seen someone try, it had blown half a city block apart. Someone wanted to make *very* sure of their deaths.

Air stirred, brushing past her face. She glanced up. The door was swinging shut.

"No!"

She leapt up and ran for the door, but it closed too quickly. She grabbed the handle, twisting it. Locked. "Mary! Open up."

There was no answer. Nor did the door open. She pounded the panel in frustration, but her fist sank deep. It wasn't wood, but an imitation used to sound proof rooms. She felt the wall—it too was spongy. Great. Just great. Stepping back, she unclipped the laser and fired it at the lock. Nothing happened.

Which meant the room was shielded. The laser wouldn't work within the room's confines.

She swung around and stared past the autocook to the desk. The bomb had obviously been hidden there a while, which in turn suggested that Stephan didn't have regular sweeps for this sort of thing. But why would he when he had all the other security measures in place? And even if they did do sweeps, most didn't detect this sort of bomb—it had no metal parts. As far as she knew, they were still working on a detector to cater for this type.

Had Mary placed it here? If so, why set it off now? What

had happened in the last hour that had made her flip the switch?

Not that the answers to those questions mattered now. She had to find a way to warn Gabriel and get everyone out of here. With the room shielded against lasers and the door locked, her only real option was to try her com-unit. Maybe she could find his cell phone number and call him. If that failed, she could call State and alert them.

She dug the com-unit out of her bag and sat down, positioning the unit on the floor so she could keep on eye on the timer. A small light on top of the com-unit flashed—a warning that the solar batteries were low. Hoping like hell the power would last, she opened up the unit. Marvin glared at her.

"Satlink unavailable, Earthling."

She glanced at the lightly glowing numbers. Five minutes and twenty four seconds to live. She swallowed heavily. She'd have to use a land link and hope like hell the lines weren't clogged.

She dove across to the com-unit attached to the autocook and disconnected the land line. Then she grabbed her com-unit and quickly connected it, waiting impatiently for Marvin to react.

"Landline available."

"Find the cell phone number of Gabriel Stern, Assistant director SIU."

Marvin crossed his arms and tapped his foot. She glanced across to the timer. Four minutes fifty-three seconds.

"No number available."

She swore. "What about his home number?" Maybe he diverted his private calls to his cell phone.

Marvin stopped tapping again. "No number available."

Her gaze went to the timer again. Four minutes twenty-two seconds. Sweat began to bead her forehead. "Damn it, try calling the SIU switchboard."

It seemed to take forever to get a response. In reality, it was precisely eighteen seconds.

"Special Investigations. How may I help you?"

The softly feminine voice was deceptive, as was the image of the dark-skinned beauty on the screen. The SIU, like most major Government departments, had gone completely computerized some ten years ago. "I need to get a code four-one message to Assistant Director Gabriel Stern." She only hoped the SIU system would recognize the State's *officer in danger* call sign.

"Assistant Director Stern is not currently in his office."

Sweat trickled down her nose. She swiped at it with her sleeve and glared impatiently at the woman on the screen. "I know. I repeat, this is a code four-one message. Put me through to his cell phone."

The computerized image was silent for a moment. "Unable to process request without Assistant Director Stern's consent."

"Well, for heavens sake, contact him."

She glanced at the lightly glowing numbers. Three minutes, forty-five seconds. She sat back on her heels and closed her eyes. There was nothing else she could do now but wait.

And pray.

Nine

When Sam left the room, Gabriel leaned back and waited for the questions to start. While he hadn't really expected Mary or Martyn to relax in her presence, he certainly hadn't expected the current depth of their hostility, especially from Mary.

No one involved in any sort of law enforcement liked cop killers, but there were mitigating circumstances here, and Mary's attitude made no sense. Not unless she was somehow involved with Kazdan.

Martyn leaned forward, gray eyes intense. "What the hell happened to your face?"

He raised an eyebrow. It wasn't the question he'd expected from Martyn. "I was following a lead and got ambushed by four men."

"How unlike you." Martyn's dry tone was edged with a note of amusement. "Your attention diverted by your little cop killer?"

"Clone killer," he retorted. "Kazdan himself is very much alive. We have a meet tomorrow night."

"Is that wise?" Stephan rested bony arms against the table, his expression one of concern. "Kazdan's already tried to kill Ryan twice. This may be just another set up."

"Maybe. But we have something he wants." He met his brother's eyes and saw the warning there. *Don't say too much.* "It's also gives us an ideal opportunity to tail him."

Martyn snorted. "If he's a vampire, he'll sense anyone that gets too close."

"It's still worth a chance." Besides, Kazdan wouldn't sense a shapechanger flying high. Nor would he expect it, unless forewarned.

"You realize, of course, that this whole thing with Ryan might be a setup." Martyn leaned back in the chair. "She might be nothing more than a plant, a mean's for Kazdan, and therefore Sethanon, to learn more about the Federation."

"She might." But he personally didn't believe it. He'd seen the need to know, the need to understand what had happened to Kazdan, in her eyes. That couldn't be faked, no matter how good an actress she might be.

"But you believe in her?" Stephan asked softly.

He looked at his brother. "I've bet all our lives on it."

"Why, I do believe you like the girl." Lyssa's voice was gently mocking.

He barely glanced at her. "That has nothing to do with my reasons for trusting her."

"Right. Just remember that she shot her last lover. Don't get too close." Her soft voice held a cynical edge.

"I have no intention of doing so." His cell phone vibrated against his side. He pushed his chair back and rose. "Sorry, I have a call."

Mary walked through the door as he neared, face pale, as if she'd been sick. He waited for her to pass, and then stepped into the semidarkness of the next room. He flipped open the phone. SIU's digital secretary smiled at him. "Yes, Christine?"

"I have a code four-one call from a Samantha Ryan on line. Do you wish to accept it?"

Code four-one. State speak for officer in trouble. His heartbeat accelerated. "Yes."

Sam's image came onto the small screen. "You have to get . . . friends . . . of here . . ."

Her image was fading in and out, and her voice was going with it. "Sam, repeat message." Why the hell was she calling him? And why was the transmission fading in and out?

She licked her lips. Even on such a small screen, he could see the fear on her face.

"Bomb . . . house. Upstairs . . . . Cook . . ."

Her image faded as the connection cut out. He swore and spun around, racing back to the dining room. "Stephan, get everyone out of this house. Now," he added, as his brother opened his mouth to ask why. "We haven't got much time."

Stephan nodded and rose. Gabriel ran for the stairs. 'Cook' had surely meant autocook. Though why the hell would she go in there? He took the stairs two at a time and headed down the upstairs hall. The room holding the autocook was locked. He quickly punched in the code, and the door clicked open.

She all but fell into his arms. "We have less than two minutes to get out of here."

His gaze swept the room behind her. "That should be more than enough time to diffuse a bomb."

"Not this fucker." She grabbed his arm and pulled him away from the door. "Its touch sensitive. We have to get out of here."

He couldn't ignore the plea in her eyes or the urgency in her voice. And she'd been with State long enough to have seen a bomb or two. He had no choice but to trust her judgement. Grabbing her hand, he ran for the front door.

As they exited the house, he saw Stephan and the others ahead of them, running for the front gate.

"Come *on!*" She tugged him forward, desperation evident in every movement.

They were halfway to the gate when thunder rumbled ominously, a low sound that rapidly gained momentum. Then there was a flash and heat, terrible heat, as the world around them went momentarily red. The ground rose in a wave of grass and dirt, surging past their feet, chased by a wind that was fast and furious. He dove towards Sam, pushing her to the ground, covering her body with his.

The actual sound of the explosion hit last and was accompanied by the debris and dust, jettisoned through the air by the blast's force. Bricks and glass and deathly sharp bits of wood became missiles that rained around them. He cocooned her against him, her body shuddering against his and her heart racing as fiercely as his own. Yet, she didn't make a sound, keeping the fear he could almost taste tightly leashed. Several large chunks of inner wall speared the ground, one so close to their heads it plunged several strands of Sam's red-gold hair deep into the earth. Another shaved his calf muscle, drawing blood as it smacked into the earth near his feet.

Then silence fell. For a long moment, he didn't move, wanting to be certain it was over, that it was safe. Then he rolled to one side and stared. Devastation lay behind them.

A crater lay where the mansion had once stood. Whoever had set the bomb had sure as hell wanted to be certain there was nothing left, not even bits for the bomb squad to find.

"Someone really hates your friend, don't they?" she said quietly.

He glanced at her. Her cheek was grazed, a wound that contrasted starkly against her pale features. He reached out, gently brushing some dirt away from the weeping sore. She flinched away from his touch, so he let his hand drop and glanced back to the ruins. "How did you find the bomb?"

"I was following Mary. I thought she went into the autocook room, but when I went in, it was empty." She shrugged lightly. "Someone locked me in."

Mary was the only one to leave the room, the only one who had an opportunity to set a bomb and lock the door. But why would she do such a thing? And why come back into the dining room once she'd set it? That amounted to suicide and simply didn't make sense.

"How well do you know Mary?" she asked.

He shrugged. "We all grew up together."

"But she's a lot older than the rest of you."

He nodded. "By about fourteen years. She was more a baby sitter than a friend, at first."

"How long has she been a vampire?"

He glanced at her sharply. "She's not. She's human. Martyn's the only vampire in the group."

She frowned, her blue eyes uncertain. "When I first walked into that room, I sensed a shapeshifter and a vampire. I thought Martyn looked like a bloodsucker, but it was Mary I sensed."

Was the answer that simple? Was it Mary, one of the two people he would have sworn it couldn't be? He closed his eyes for a moment, listening to the approaching footsteps, knowing four people walked towards them but hearing the steps of only two. Vampires carried themselves lightly. Martyn and Mary weren't making any sound.

And yet, as youngsters, they'd often teased Mary that her footsteps were heavy enough to register on the Richter scale. The change must have been recent—surely either he or Stephan would have noticed it otherwise. So who had she shared blood with? Who had performed the ceremony and supervised her first steps into the world of the night? If it had been a vampire aligned with the Federation, they would have heard about it.

And why would she want to kill Stephan? Had that been the price of becoming immortal?

It didn't make sense. But none of this was making sense—not the attempt on Stephan's life, nor the attempts on Sam's life.

He stared at the smoking ruins for several seconds, and then ran a hand through his hair, prying free several twigs. "Stephan is the shifter you sensed."

Confusion flitted across her face. "I thought he was the human."

He frowned. "What?"

"Lyssa's the shifter I sensed, not Stephan."

His frown deepened, even as a feeling of dread began to build in his gut. "Lyssa's a changer. Her other form is a cat."

"Then why—"She hesitated. "I'm getting the same sort of feeling from her that I got from that shifter who took Finley's form in the lab."

No, he thought. *No!* "You're wrong."

"Maybe." She shrugged and shifted her gaze away from his. "After all, this talent, or whatever it is, is fairly new. Maybe I'm just reading it wrong."

But she'd been right about the kites, about Kazdan's clone, and the shifter in the lab. Odds were she was right about this, too. He closed his eyes again. Lyssa *wasn't* Lyssa—what other explanation could there be for Sam sensing a wrongness about her? God, this could shatter his brother's spirit. Completely. "You sure?"

She nodded. "As sure as I was about the others." She hesitated again, concern flaring deeper in her eyes. "Why, is something wrong?"

Everything, he thought bleakly, then shook his head. "No, nothing." Nothing beyond the fact that the woman his brother loved, the woman who was now carrying his brother's child, was *not* the woman he'd married.

Somehow, he had to separate them, had to find out what had happened to the real Lyssa. There was always the chance, however slight, that she might still be alive.

"You two okay?"

Like a soothing breeze in the heat of the night, Stephan's voice rose out of the darkness. Gabriel glanced up. His brother had stopped a pace away and was wraithlike in the darkness.

"Someone wants to make very sure you die, Stephan." He let his gaze rest on Lyssa for a moment. She'd stopped just behind his brother, face pale and eyes haunted. Either she was a very good actress, or she hadn't known about the bomb.

Maybe both.

"Why would someone do this?" Lyssa whispered, the shake in her voice matching the shock in her eyes.

"That's what we've got to find out." He returned his gaze to the house. With so little left to burn, the flames were beginning to die down. "I think it might be wise for you to go on a business trip."

"Might be." Stephan's voice was dry. "At least we won't have to worry about packing."

Despite his brief attempt at humor, relief and anger mingled freely in the vivid green depths of his brother's eyes. "Alone, I mean."

Stephan's gaze narrowed, but after a moment, he nodded.

"What about Lyssa and Mary?"

"I'll arrange a twenty-four hour guard." Martyn said, and then he hesitated and shrugged. "Accommodation might be a problem. If this is Sethanon's doing, he might know all our safe houses."

Mary was standing just behind Martin, staring at the crater, a glazed look of horror on her face. Maybe she hadn't known the power of the bomb.

Damn it, it made *no* sense that she would even set it. If she was behind the poisoning, why make such a public attempt of murder when the poisoning appeared to be working?

"Take Mary and set her up in apartment three seventeen." Stephan's voice was even, despite the anger in his eyes. "We only acquired it three days ago, so it should be safe. Lyssa can stay with relatives."

He meant *their* relatives, not *her* relatives. And she would be safe in the Stern compound. Question was, were *they* safe from her? How safe was it even showing her the location? But he couldn't dispute Stephan's decision, not without telling him why. And there was no point in doing that until he knew for sure that Sam was right. He'd just have to call his old man and have him keep an eye on Lyssa.

In the distance, sirens howled, drawing closer. People in dressing gowns hovered near the front gates or peered out windows from surrounding houses. Stephan glanced over his shoulder, studying them. "State's on the way. We tell them nothing."

"They'll want to know how we escaped," Sam's soft voice soft held a hint of annoyance.

"We know nothing, and we tell them nothing. This is our business, not State's." Stephan glanced at Gabriel. "Not even SIU."

Sam looked ready to argue. He brushed his hand against hers and shook his head when she looked at him. Her gaze was mutinous, but after a moment, she nodded. He pulled the cell phone from his pocket, and handed it to Stephan. "Let me handle State. Why don't you ring the old man and make arrangements for Lyssa to go home?"

Stephan nodded and moved away a few steps, drawing Lyssa with him. Gabriel watched him for a minute longer, and then rose stiffly to his feet. Three black squad cars swept up the driveway, headlights spearing the darkness, targeting them in brightness.

"Now the fun begins," Sam murmured.

He glanced at her. Her face was still pale, and her eyes were ringed by shadows of gray. She looked exhausted, beaten. Yet her gaze held an edge of steel that told him she would battle on until she got the answers she needed. Kazdan certainly didn't deserve the loyalty she gave him.

He held out a hand to help her up, and after a moment, she accepted it. Her fingers were like ice against his own. He shrugged out of his dinner jacket and placed it around her shoulders.

"Thanks."

He nodded. "Let's go face your fellow officers."

She drew the coat tight across her chest, a gesture that was defensive more than an attempt to keep out the chill wind. "Only if we must."

He could understand her reluctance—especially with the spectre of Jack's death still hanging over her head. But regardless of what happened, regardless of whether he eventually cleared her of blame, the fact was, she'd shot the man she thought was her partner. And they would always judge her by that one action. She could either live with it or quit.

He hoped it was the former. A recent survey by State showed that many disgraced officers spiralled down a self-destructive path. Sam, like those others, appeared to have nothing but her job in her life. He'd hate to see her step onto that same path.

"We must," he replied softly.

She took a deep breath and blew it out slowly. Then she nodded and walked forward, her body a slender shadow against the brightness of the lights.

Martyn cleared his throat. Gabriel looked back at him.

"Don't trust her," Martin warned softly. "Just . . . watch it. She's been Kazdan's partner for five years. She might be a whole lot more."

This coming from someone who'd long been infatuated with the woman who may have just tried to blow them all to bits. He studied Mary for a moment, and then nodded. Because in truth, he *was* worried about the depth of Sam's determination to find out what her partner was up to. She might not love Kazdan, and she might well have shot him to save herself, but she certainly still cared about him. Who knew what would happen if Kazdan ever tried to subvert those feelings?

"Just get Mary to that safe house and keep a watch on her.

Then you'd better send out a warning to our other operatives."

Martin nodded. "I'll be in contact once we've settled."

He nodded, and then he turned and followed Sam to the squad cars.

***

Sam leaned a shoulder against the roughened trunk of an old silky oak and watched Gabriel walk towards her. He'd spent the last hour or so speaking to various levels of officialdom, and for the most part, had managed to keep her out of it. Which she sure as hell didn't mind. The lieutenant who'd briefly interviewed her had made his opinion of her quite clear. She'd shot her partner. She deserved to be lying in bits, not sitting in a squad car sipping lukewarm coffee. Not long after *that* pleasant experience, she'd abandoned the car, and her coffee, and retreated to the shelter of the silky oak. At least trees didn't judge.

"You okay?" He stopped, and held out a steaming mug of coffee.

She accepted it gratefully. "Once I warm up a little, I will be." She wrapped her fingers round the plastic mug and studied the black-clad figures swarming the crater. "They going to let us go anytime soon?"

"We can go when we please. I'm just waiting for SIU to deliver another car. Not much left of the old one, I'm afraid."

She nodded. She'd noted one of the doors wrapped around the trunk of a Sugargum earlier. Who knew where the rest of the vehicle was. "What's the plan when we get the car?"

His hazel eyes were suddenly enigmatic. "We visit Jack's apartment."

She frowned. "Is that wise? He might be home. And if he isn't, he sure as hell will have the place alarmed."

"He's a vampire. He won't be home at this hour of the night. Alarms I can get around."

Maybe normal alarms he could. But he didn't know Jack, didn't know how devious he could be. "That end of the Central Business District tends to be high security. We may not even get in."

His sudden smile held a cynical edge. "I'm SIU. I can get in anywhere." His gaze ran past her. "Car's here."

She glanced over her shoulder. Two gray Fords were pulling to a halt near the black squad cars. "I really don't think raiding Jack's is a good idea."

"Is that a professional or personal opinion?"

Annoyance ran through her. He obviously still believed she was somehow linked to Jack. That her actions, her reluctance, were an attempt to protect him. Maybe she'd have to shoot Jack again just to get Gabriel to believe anything else.

The thought shook her. Jack was her *friend*. She refused to believe anything else, even if the mounting evidence was to the contrary. At the very least, he deserved the chance to explain his motives—to explain why his clone had tried to kill her. Gabriel was here only because he wanted to find out more about her ability to sense the kites. To do that, he had to keep her out of prison. Friendship certainly didn't enter into the equation.

"Let's get out of here," was all she said, as she pushed past him and headed for the car.

Two gray clad SIU officers greeted them with polite nods. One handed over a key coder. That was it. No questions about what had happened to the previous car, and no forms to fill in. Jack was right. SIU was a law unto themselves, and, through Gabriel, it was a world she was getting sucked into deeply. And something told her only death would now free her from its grip.

She climbed into the car and crossed her arms, trying to ignore a sense of trepidation. In one respect, Gabriel was right. They had to find out what was on those disks, and Jack's computer might be the only one capable of reading them. But Jack would know by now that she'd taken them. He wouldn't take a chance on her not knowing about the apartment. He'd anticipate it and be ready.

Gabriel started the car and drove away smoothly, heading for the city. She watched the bright lights draw closer, and with every mile that passed, the sense of danger grew.

They arrived too soon for her liking. She climbed out of the car and looked up. The building was little more than a wall of black glass that acted like a mirror, reflecting the myriad of lights from Federation Square. Black marble steps led up to the foyer doors, which were also black glass with gold fittings. The whole place reeked of money. How could Jack afford to own an apartment here? He earned the same salary she did, and she wouldn't be able rent a bathroom in a place like this. Besides, he'd been having trouble keeping up with the payments on his Mulgrave home. If he owned this, why would he even bother?

Gabriel headed up the steps, and she reluctantly followed. A doorman, dressed in gray and gold, nodded politely and keyed open the huge glass doors.

She shook her head. How could anyone at State have missed this? If SIU had known about the apartment, surely State must have known—and that, in itself, suggested the apartment was legit. Anything shady would have brought down an investigation quicker than Jack could fart.

Their footsteps echoed sharply in the cavernous foyer. The huge reception desk was actually manned, rather than having the usual hands-on computer help. The tall blonde woman smiled as they approached, and her smile didn't falter when Gabriel flashed his badge.

"Could you tell me if the occupant of apartment eight-eleven is currently in?"

The woman looked at her monitors. "No, he's not."

"Good. We need you to open it up for us."

"I can't do that, sir."

"Yes, you can. I have a warrant."

He pulled out his cell phone and pressed a few buttons. The woman studied the screen for a few minutes, and then nodded. "I can use the cleaning code to give you access, but the time will still be limited to half an hour. I'm afraid there's nothing I can do about that—I haven't got the clearance to change the programming."

"Half an hour will do."

The woman pressed a white button near the monitor. "I've called the elevator. It will take you straight to the eighth floor. Mr. Kazdan's apartment is on the right."

"Thank you for your assistance."

The woman nodded. "I will, of course, have to call Mr. Kazdan and inform him of your warrant and search."

"And you will, of course, inform us when Kazdan enters the building."

The blonde nodded a second time. Sam walked over to the elevators. Once the doors slid open, she stepped inside. Gabriel followed.

"I thought you didn't want Jack to know we're here," she said, as the elevator began to rise.

He shrugged. "All we need is enough time to see what's on those disks. I doubt whether Kazdan will actually turn up."

"Don't underestimate him," she said softly. "He has a mind as fast as his temper. He'll be ready for a move such as this."

His eyes were a subtle green under the elevator's soft light. Green and cold, she thought.

"I don't underestimate anyone," he said.

Including her, obviously. While his distrust rankled, she understood it. Hell, even she wasn't certain where her loyalties should lie.

The elevator came to a smooth halt on the eighth floor. He looked out and then motioned her forward. The door to Jack's apartment slid open as they neared. She hesitated in the doorway, her stomach churning as she stared down at the line where the carpet's plush gray carpet met the rich burgundy carpet of Jack's apartment. If she stepped past that line, what she discovered might forever alter her relationship with the one person she'd allowed closer than arm's length.

"You intend to stand there forever?" While Gabriel's voice had no inflection, his eyes held a hardness that suggested he understood her sudden reluctance to enter.

"We only have half an hour," he continued.

He touched a hand to her back, but didn't push. She licked her lips and stepped inside. The room was sparsely furnished. A large leather sofa faced the ceiling high wall of glass running the length of the apartment. An entertainment center covered the wall to her left, and a black glass dining table sat in the middle of the room. The apartment had no kitchen or autocook. Maybe it was fully serviced—not that a vampire had any need for it. Two doors led off the main room, and both were closed.

She shoved her hands into her pockets and walked across to the window. The faint strains of a jazz band drifted up from Federation Square. The whole place was ablaze with light and sound and people enjoying life. It was a feeling so different from the one she was getting from this apartment that it might as well have been another world

She rubbed her arms and turned around. "The com-unit must be in one of the other rooms."

He nodded and waved a hand toward the only two interior doors in the apartment "Care to pick one?"

Both looked identical, but the carpet leading up to the one on the left had definitely seen more traffic. "Left door."

She followed him across the room. The door slid open silently, revealing another large expanse of carpet, and a big round bed draped in red silk. She walked over and lightly touched the sheets. Real silk, not fake. While it went with the feel of the apartment, it didn't go with what she knew of Jack. So who was the genuine article? The man who owned this apartment, with its bed big enough to hold a party in and the million-dollar view, or the rough, friendly man who'd been her partner these past five years?

"Right door first time," Gabriel murmured, as he walked across to the com-unit. "You sure you've never been here before?"

His hazel eyes were cold, and cynical. He still wasn't entirely convinced that she and Jack were only friends. On some level, he still thought they were involved—not as lovers, perhaps, but as conspirators. It was a belief she could at least live with since time and evidence would prove her innocence.

She hoped.

She ignored his question, dug into her bag and got out the disks. "Let's hope the computer's not security coded."

He accepted the disks as he sat down on the chair. The com-screen came to life, revealing a dusky skinned, large busted woman with the most amazing green eyes. Sam smiled. At least she was clothed. Most of the digital personalities she'd seen Jack use were of the wild and free variety.

"How may I help you?" a husky voice asked.

"Translate data disks."

"Translation proceeding."

She raised an eyebrow. No security code, not even voice-key security. Why? Was Jack so confident no one knew about this apartment that he just hadn't bothered?

"Translation finished. Do you wish to view results?"

He glanced at her. "Wouldn't have a spare disk in your bag, would you?"

She hesitated, and then dug the wristcom out of her bag. "I have this. Almost as good."

"I'm surprised State didn't request this back when they suspended you."

"They did. This is Jack's."

He gave her a half smile as he attached the wristcom to the com-unit. "Obviously, they weren't watching you closely enough. You should never have been able to get something like this out of the building when suspended."

She shrugged. "But I didn't leave right away. I went down for psych evaluations."

"Same thing. If you ask me, someone in State was giving you time."

She remembered feeling surprised when she'd walked out of the Cap's office to find no escort. Had the Captain given her the only help he could, time alone to sort through Jack's desk and maybe find some clue? If he had, it would suggest he knew more than he was saying. She frowned. She really had to find some way to catch him alone.

"Computer, display results, then download all three translations to wristcom . . ." Gabriel hesitated, glancing at her.

"1045," she supplied.

"1045," he repeated.

"Proceeding. Disk one currently on screen."

She placed a hand on the back of the chair, and leaned over Gabriel's shoulder. Disk one was little more than a series of names, with monetary amounts next to them.

"There are a few government officials on this list." She reached past him and placed a finger on the screen. "Isn't Dan Wetherton the Minister for Social Services?"

He nodded. "He may also be very dead."

"When did that happen? I didn't hear anything on the news about it—not that I've had much chance to listen to updates recently."

Amusement flitted briefly through his eyes. "That's because, officially, the minister is alive and very well."

She took a moment to absorb this. "Another clone."

"Another clone," he agreed. His breath brushed warmth across her face. "It's interesting to note that Wetherton's donation is a lot larger than some of the others."

"Paying for life? Or maybe a form of afterlife?"

"Maybe." He paged down, stopping when he came to more well-known names. "Rob Garbott, the State Minister for Police and Emergencies. And David Flint, our newly elected Prime Minister."

She frowned. "Isn't Flint against cloning?"

He nodded. "Look, though. No donation amount. His name is highlighted instead."

"And Garbott's been ticked. Wonder what that means?"

"Maybe you could ask your partner when you see him tomorrow night." Though the comment was made in the blandest of voices, she had a feeling he was being sarcastic.

"Maybe I will." She leaned forward again. "General Lee Hagan. He's also highlighted."

"Hagan's a very influential figure in the army. He's also a key figure in the military's investigations into cloning and gene manipulation."

She began to get a very bad feeling about this list. "You don't suppose they're being set up for some type of hit?"

"It's possible. Maybe if they can't subvert them willingly, they just intend to kill them and replace them." His gaze met hers, his expression grim. "If that's the case, this is Sethanon's doing, not Kazdan's."

She had to agree. Jack was never one to sit around and plan, especially to this degree. He was more your react now and think later type of guy. "If they intend replacing these men with clones, it would have to mean they've found a way to imitate the original's behavior patterns."

"And Wetherton might just be their first success story." His expression was bleak when he glanced at her. "Let's see what's on the other disks. Computer, display data from disk two."

"Displaying," intoned the sultry voice.

Another list came onto the screen. "More names and donations," she muttered. "Surely they can't all be paying money to be cloned."

"They're not." Gabriel pointed to the right of the screen. "Wetherton had the number P1-c after his name. These are P4-v."

"C for clone, v for vampire?"

"It may be as simple as that."

"Why would anyone pay money to become a vampire?"

"Why not? Man spends billions of dollars every year trying to cheat death—something a vampire has already achieved. Given the choice, what would you choose?"

"Better death than life as a bloodsucker."

"Not all vampires are evil. Not all vampires take sustenance from humans to survive."

The edge in his voice suggested this was more than just an opinion. "And you? Given the choice, what would you do?"

He shrugged. "That would depend very much on what, or even who, I had to live for."

She frowned. "So if you loved someone enough, you'd take the change? Isn't that a little sick?"

"As I said, depends on your reasoning."

"You've done it, haven't you?" she said, unable to stop the hint of revulsion creeping into her voice. "You've performed the ceremony that will enable you to make the change when you die."

His eyes showed a faint hint of surprise. "I haven't, but a

close friend has. Not for love, but for reasons I can well understand."

"Stephan. You're talking about Stephan." Why she was so certain, she couldn't say. But in the two days she'd known Gabriel, she'd seen him interact with many people, both work colleagues and friends. With Stephan, there had something more than friendship. With him, there was a bond that went much, much deeper.

"I can see why you're a good cop." A brief smile tugged the corners of his lips. "And yes, it was Stephan I was talking about."

"What about Lyssa?"

A veil came down over his eyes. For some reason, Lyssa was not someone he wanted to talk about right now.

"Her, too," he said, looking back to the screen. "Computer, display translation disk three."

"Displayed."

The third disk was not a list of names and donations. It was a series of pictures, and the subject was Lyssa.

"Looks like someone's setting her up for a hit," she said. "They've obviously been following her around."

"Maybe."

There was an edge to his voice that suggested anger, though it hadn't yet reached his eyes. "What I want to know is how deeply Kazdan's involved in all this."

From the sound of it, he was talking about something other than a hit. She'd even go as far as to guess that he was talking about an event that had already happened. But that made no sense. Lyssa had been just fine this evening—unless he thought the bomb had been primarily aimed at her. Though why go to all the trouble of photographing her movements if you were simply going to blow the shit out of her?

"I don't understand—"

He touched a finger to her lips, halting her question. "Listen," he said softly.

For a moment, she could hear nothing beyond the sound of their breathing. Could feel nothing but the warmth of his finger against her lips. Then, slowly, she became aware of a faint hissing sound. It sounded for all the world like a snake had moved into one corner of the room.

Only no snake could get into a building like this.

And no snake she knew of smelled like overripe gym shoes.

"Fuck—gas."

She glanced at him sharply. "What?"

"That noise—it's some kind of gas being pumped into the room." He grabbed the wristcom and disks, and then scrambled to his feet. "Let's get out of here."

She didn't argue. Gas leaking into a room was never good. Gas leaking at a time when they'd be using the com-unit and normally not notice could only be a trap. The bedroom door slid open. Vapor hissed into the main room, thicker and more noxious than in the bedroom. She held her breath and ran for the front door, only to see it slide shut. The locks clicked firmly into place, a sound that ricocheted across the hissing, as sharp as death.

Trapping them like rats in a stinking prison.

Ten

"It hasn't been half an hour yet, has it?" Sam pulled uselessly at the handle, and then got out the key-coder Jack had given her.

"No."

The key-coder flashed red. It couldn't break the lock. She slapped the door in frustration and turned, watching a puff of pale yellow vapor creep fog-like across the carpet. "I think we'd better contact reception and see if she can open the door again. And fast."

He already had his cell phone out. "No answer," he said after a moment. "Any idea what's behind door two?"

The vapor began to catch at her throat. Fighting the desire to cough, she tried to breathe as shallowly as possible. "Bathroom, maybe?"

"Maybe. Come on." He touched her arm, guiding her across the room.

The vapor was thicker near the doorway. It tore at her throat and seeped down to her lungs, burning like fire. Dizziness swept through her, and for an instant, everything blurred. Only Gabriel's light touch kept her upright, kept her moving.

The second door swept open. He pushed her through, and then slapped a hand against the control on the wall. The door shut, momentarily locking the vapor out. She took several deep breaths, then bent over and coughed long and hard.

"You okay?"

His hand touched her back, its warmth contrasting starkly with the ice creeping over her skin. She nodded and straightened. His eyes were red-rimmed and watering, and his face was the color of milk.

She looked around, noting the shower and wash basin. "It is a bathroom."

"And service room, by the look of it." He handed her the disks and wristcom, then stepped past her and pressed a button on the wall. The response was the soft hum of machinery. "Service lift. And this . . ." He tapped a circular panel on the wall. A small door gently rocked. ". . . would be the laundry chute."

She wiped the tears away from her eyes. Vapor was beginning to seep under the door, curling like yellow strands of rope round her feet. "Neither of which will help us get out of here."

A bell chimed softly. He pressed another button and a door slid open, revealing a three-foot square elevator. He glanced at her.

She swallowed heavily. He surely couldn't mean for them to climb in there. It looked too small for one, let alone two. A shudder ran through her. Too small and far too enclosed. "The two of us won't fit in there."

"No, but one of us has to stay behind to close the door and send it down anyway. Get in."

She didn't move. Couldn't move. "What about you?"

"I'll use the laundry chute. Come on, the vapor's getting thicker."

The yellow strings were beginning to wind their way up her legs. Legs she couldn't force to move. "That chute looks all of a foot in diameter. You're, what, six two, six three?"

"I'm a shapechanger, remember? A hawk will fit down the chute easily enough. Get in the lift."

She licked her lips, and then edged forward. The closer she got, the smaller the space looked.

"Isn't there another way to get out of this place?" she asked, balking at the last moment. She knew the question was inane, that she was only delaying the inevitable. But once she climbed into that lift, and the door closed, there would be only darkness and fear.

"You know there's not." He hesitated, coughing. "Get in. I'll meet you down at the bottom."

She wet her lips again, and then slowly climbed in. The metal seemed to weigh down on her, as heavy as the gathering darkness and colder than her skin.

"You will be there to let me out of this thing when it stops, won't you?"

He nodded. "Don't worry. These things almost never fail."

The way her luck had been running lately, almost was *not* the best of odds. Still, she had no more choice this time than she had the last time she'd faced her fears and the darkness. He shut the door, and the darkness grew tighter. The lift hummed, and then it dropped. She squeezed her eyes shut and hoped like hell she didn't have to spend more than a few minutes inside this metal coffin.

***

Unable to spread his wings or do anything to even guide his descent, Gabriel plunged down the dark tube and prayed there was something soft near the bottom. At the rate he was descending, a broken neck was a very real possibility.

Light speared through the darkness. A circle washed by red

became visible, and past it, layers of mauve and blue material. He plunged beak first into the middle of the material, then flipped onto his back, wings flying outwards from his body and loose feathers pluming skywards.

For several heartbeats, he simply lay there, staring up at the red-washed ceiling, too stunned to do anything. Gradually, he became aware of the musty, almost sickly scent of humanity rising from the material beneath him, and he realized the red light washing through the darkness came from the exit sign to the left of the clothes hamper.

Then he remembered Sam. He had to get her out of that elevator, in case the vapor found its way down the shaft.

After changing to human shape, he climbed off the mound of damp and dirty laundry. As he moved, a spasm locked the muscles in his back. Pain ripped through his body, and for a minute, he couldn't even breathe. He clenched his teeth and hoped he hadn't done anything serious. Hoped it was just a momentary problem. The pain began to ebb, and he took several deep breaths. The spasm in his back eased, and it became little more than a muted ache that radiated down his left leg. He ignored it as best he could and limped forward quickly.

The door led out into a long, dark hallway. Light, little more than a splash of yellow, beckoned down at the far end. He limped on. Voices edged across the silence. One he didn't know. The other's was Kazdan. He limped closer to the door and stopped, listening.

"The boss isn't going to like this."

The speaker's voice held a hint of Irish-brogue. If he was an operative of Sethanon, he wasn't one the Federation knew about. None of those were of Irish descent.

"Let me worry about that." Kazdan's voice held a hint of impatience. "How long will it take for the apartment to clear?"

"Another five minutes."

"Good."

Footsteps broke the silence, a tattooed beat of violence. He edged forward and peered through the small gap between the door and the jamb.

A long metal table dominated the view. On it, a wiry black man sat, flipping a dagger from end to end, catching it neatly between thumb and middle finger. *Eddie Wyatt.* He smiled grimly. He'd had a run-in with Eddie some years ago, when the vamp had gone on a killing spree. He'd gotten off on a technicality and had promptly sought revenge against his accuser—Gabriel. He watched the thug's hand as he deftly caught the dagger. Five years, and only the thumb and one finger had grown back.

Still, he was lucky it was only his hand that had been chopped. It should have been his friggin' head. But SIU had been feeling generous that day. Because Eddie had no previous history of violence, they'd let him escape with only a minor penalty. In doing so, they'd created a headache for themselves. Eddie Wyatt was the chief suspect in the recent bombings of several SIU buildings. But up until now, informed opinion said he'd fled the country.

A second man stood further down the table, barely within his restricted line of sight. Taller, but with the same wiry build as Eddie, this man had blond hair and a somewhat scraggly ginger beard. No vampire, then, as vampires tended not to be able to grow beards. But no human, either, if the almost feral gleam in the man's green eyes was anything to go by.

Kazdan was nowhere in sight, but his heavy steps were audible. Three men, at least two of them vampires. Not good odds for an attack when he wasn't one hundred percent fit.

He shifted slightly, trying to ease the ache in his left leg. Kazdan's pacing stopped. Gabriel froze, wondering if the vampire had caught the sound of a pumping heart. If he was close to the door, it was a real possibility, even though Kazdan was very young in vampire terms and still had to be learning how to handle his newfound senses.

"We don't dare wait any longer. That bitch at reception is bound to wake up soon and raise the alarm. We have to get the disks and Ryan out of here."

Eddie slipped off the table, the movement almost languid. "The boss wanted her left alone." He flipped the dagger one final time and shoved it into a sheath attached to his right wrist. "He ain't going to like this."

Gabriel raised his eyebrows in surprise. Sethanon wanted Sam left alone? What exactly did that mean? That she was somehow involved with Sethanon?

"You're working for me now. You do as I say."

Kazdan's voice was sharp with menace. He wondered what Sam would think if she could hear him now. And why did Kazdan want her when his orders were obviously to the contrary?

"What about Stern?"

"Take him straight to the car. He and his brother were slated for termination at the end of this month, anyway."

Brother. Only three people beyond their immediate family

knew Stephan and he were brothers. Mary, Karl, and Lyssa—the original Lyssa, that was. Whether the shifter taking her place knew depended on just how long she'd been by his brother's side. But if Kazdan knew, then it had to mean that one of those three was involved with him.

And if both he and Stephan were slated for termination at the end of the month, did that mean that Mary had orchestrated tonight's bombing attempt alone? But why?

He listened to the receding sound of their footsteps, but he didn't move until silence had returned. He pushed open the door and limped in. The kitchen was long and full of gleaming metal benches and appliances. It was also empty, for which he was grateful. He walked through a doorway to his left and down another corridor. The service lift door came into view. The doors hadn't even fully opened before Sam scrambled out. She fell into his arms, her whole body shaking, alternatively coughing and sucking in huge gulps of air.

Even though she still wore his jacket, her skin felt like ice. This wasn't an effect of the fog; this was fear. He wrapped his arms tightly around her and held her close. After several minutes, the trembling in her limbs began to ease, but her heart still raced.

"Why didn't you tell me you were claustrophobic?" he asked softly.

She took a shuddering breath. "What good would it have done? You know there was no other way out."

If he'd known she was so terrified of small, dark places, he might have tried to find another way. "How long have you had this fear?"

"For as long as I can remember."

"Have you talked to the psyche guys about it?"

"Yeah. They put it down to a childhood trauma." She shrugged, feigning a casualness that was almost instantly belied by the tremor that ran through her slender form.

"You okay now?" He hoped so, because Kazdan had probably entered the apartment, and it wouldn't take him long to discover his trap had failed.

She sniffed, and then nodded. The top of her head brushed across his chin, and silky strands of red gold tickled his nose. He smoothed her hair down, feeling the dampness near the crown and sides.

"Then we'd better get moving," he said, though if Kazdan had not been a threat, he could easily have stayed here, simply holding her. It felt good. *She* felt good.

She pulled away slightly. "There's a problem?"

His gaze focused on her lips, watching them move as she spoke. "Kazdan."

She tensed. "Jack's here?"

"Yes," he said, a little more sharply than he'd intended. "He wants the disks."

And you. He frowned suddenly. The tone Kazdan had used when speaking about her was not the tone of a friend. Enemy, yes, friend, definitely not. So why was he so keen to get her back?

She met his gaze. The ring of shadows around the blue of her eyes was more pronounced than it had been a few hours ago. "Why can't we just confront him now?"

"Because he has company. I can't fight three nonhumans alone." Though with her help, he certainly had a better chance. She'd apparently gotten the better of the two vamps at Kazdan's house, and she still had the laser. But there was a niggling concern in the back of his mind about her relationship with Kazdan. A niggling that said don't trust her when it comes to him. "We're better off getting those disks out of here."

She nodded. "We still have the meet tomorrow night anyway."

He let her go and stepped back. "I doubt that Kazdan will show up."

She shrugged and turned away. "We'll see, won't we?"

He led the way forward. When they reached the foyer, he crossed to the reception desk. Both the doorman and the receptionist lay unconscious on the floor behind the desk. He felt their necks, relieved to discover both had steady pulses. Given Kazdan's reputation, that was something of a miracle—though perhaps it was simply a matter of not wanting to shit in his own backyard.

"They okay?" she asked, though her gaze was on the elevators rather than the victims.

"Yeah." He rose, and got out his cell phone. "Why don't you head outside? I'll call in the troops." Kazdan and his cronies would be long gone by the time the SIU got here, but the apartment itself might yield something useful.

He made the call, and then followed her out the door. But halfway down the steps, he stopped. One of the men with Kazdan was a bomber. The car sat right in front of the building, State plates conspicuous. And Kazdan had ordered his men to take him down to the car. He'd said Gabriel had been slated for termination anyway. At the time, he'd thought they'd meant Kazdan's car, but it could easily have been his own.

"Sam, wait."

She turned, one eyebrow raised in query. He got his car key-coder out and pressed a button. The car purred to life.

"You don't think they'd go to that extreme, do you?" Though her voice held a hint of doubt, she stepped back to the partial cover of the foyer entrance.

He smiled grimly. He'd underestimated Kazdan once already tonight. He wasn't about to make a second mistake. He pressed another button and ran a fingernail across the screen. The onboard computer responded, and the car edged forward, wheels turning away from the curb.

Then it exploded.

Deadly metal missiles were flung in all directions. He dropped and saw Sam do the same. Heat and flames hissed through the night air, scorching several Elms that lined the curb. The glass door behind them shattered, showering them with glass.

He scrambled to his feet, shook free the glass, and then grabbed Sam, helping her rise. The blast would draw Kazdan and his cronies down to the ground. They had to get out of here—fast.

"There's a taxi stand just around the corner," he said.

She nodded. Her expression was remote as her gaze went back to the car. Only her clenched fists gave any sign of emotion. He touched her arm, trying to get her to move, and she looked up. There was something almost chilling in her gaze. Something decidedly *unhuman*. Then she blinked, and the moment was gone.

"We have to go. Now," he said.

She nodded again and followed him down the steps.

***

"He tried to kill me." Again, Sam added silently, and shook her head in disbelief.

In the passing gleam of headlights, Gabriel's eyes seemed fired with gold. "Maybe. Maybe not."

She frowned. "What do you mean?"

"I mean he keeps missing. It could be intentional."

"That car bomb definitely would have killed us." But why would he have set it in the first place? If he'd been so certain they'd escape, why wouldn't he have rigged the service elevator? It was the only other way out of the apartment.

He shifted. The plastic covering the cab's back seat squeaked in time with his movements. "Think about it. You escaped the kite, something no human has ever been able to do. Two men break into your apartment and bomb it after you escape. They trace us to the hotel and let themselves be seen before they firebomb us."

"That still doesn't explain the car bomb." Even as she said it, she had an uneasy feeling he was right.

"It does if the bomb was meant to take out only me."

That made a little more sense. If the gas in Jack's apartment had been meant to knock them out, not kill, it would be easy enough to take Gabriel down to the car and blow him up. It still didn't explain why they'd bother, though.

A trickle of moisture ran down the side of her face. She wiped it away and glanced down at the smear on her palm. Blood. She had cuts all over the place from the glass that had flown everywhere. So did Gabriel. It was just as well the cab had plastic covers in place.

She looked out the side window. They were traveling over the Bolte Bridge, and the lights of the Western suburbs stretched out below them, firefly bright in the darkness. Thousands upon thousands of lights. Millions of people, living side by side uneventfully. Why couldn't fate have given her one of them as a friend? Why did it have to choose a nutter?

She crossed her arms and tried to ward off a chill. Maybe fate had nothing to do with Jack becoming her partner and friend. Maybe it had all been planned from the very beginning.

"Why would he do something like that? Threaten me, but not kill me, I mean."

"You claim to know him so well. You tell me."

She frowned. She'd seen Jack push suspects until they were so afraid they'd do just about anything he wanted. Hell, that's why they'd argued the day he'd disappeared. Was that what he was doing here? Pushing her? For what reason? What did he want that he couldn't just ask for?

"I don't know." It was an answer to both his question and her own.

He shifted again. There was something oddly angry in the movement. "Answers are going to be damned hard to come by if you keep refusing to face the questions."

She glanced at him. His hazel eyes were as emotionless as his face. Yet, she could feel his anger, almost as if it were a blanket about to smother her. Gabriel Stern was pushing her as much as Jack, and his reasons were just as unclear.

She studied the river of lights again. "Where are we going?"

"Karl's."

The weird looking hippie he'd introduced her to earlier. "Why?"

"He might be able to enlarge the filmstrip I found in the envelope.

"And?" she asked, sensing there was more.

"It's a safe place to rest for the night."

Yeah, right. Any of the dozen hotels they'd passed along the way would have been just as safe. He was going to Karl's for a specific reason.

They cruised onto the Tullamarine Freeway and headed out past the airport. The taxi didn't stop until they'd reached the expensive farmland region beyond the satellite city of Sunbury.

She climbed out and looked at the sky. Away from the aureole glow of the city lights, the stars shone bright and crisp. She turned until she found the Southern Cross, and then smiled. When she was very young, someone had told her the cross was a symbol of her freedom, something that could never be taken away. But like everything else in her past, the memory of who had told her that was gone. Only the cross remained, a symbol that was oddly comforting, even now.

The taxi reversed back down the dirt driveway. Gabriel walked over to where she stood.

"Your friend must have a bit of money to own farmland this close to Melbourne," she said.

The house itself didn't scream money, as Stephan's had. Granted, it was large, but the worn bricks and ramshackle appearance gave it an air that was more homely than expensive. What made it expensive was the location—smack in the middle of a top farming region.

"He's one of this country's top herbalists and grows all his own materials." He pressed a hand to her back, his fingers warm against her spine as he guided her forward.

The door opened as they approached, though no one appeared to have actually opened it. She raised an eyebrow and glanced at him. He smiled and pointed to the small camera perched in the entrance's corner.

"Security-com," he said. "I've spent a bit of time here."

More than a bit of time, if security gave him no-questions access at this time of night. He ushered her into a large living room warmed by one of the biggest log fires she'd ever seen. It was fake—had to be. The only trees that could be cut down nowadays were plantation stock, and it was considered something close to criminal to use such wood for fires. Besides, from this angle she could see one of the jets near the end of the log. Still, it created an illusion that was both inviting and comforting, and the warmth of the gas heating filled the room without being uncomfortable.

Karl came through a doorway at the far end of the room, tea-towel in one hand and a dripping bowl in the other. "Have a seat while I finish these. Won't be long."

Her interest was piqued by the long rows of books on the shelves behind the two sofas, and she walked over to take a look. She collected paperbacks, and that in itself was expensive enough. Karl's books were hardcovers and literally worth a King's ransom. Subject matters ranged from herbs to genetics and painting to history. Anything and everything. Fiction books were relegated to bottom rows, and judging from the amount of dust gathering, hadn't been touched for a while.

Karl came back into the room. "Drink?"

She moved around one of the sofas, and sat down. "I'd love a scotch and soda." She had a feeling she was going to need something strong—had a feeling she wasn't going to like the information Gabriel had come here to get.

Karl nodded. His wild brown hair, unfettered by a bandana, swayed in all directions. "Gabriel?"

"Just a beer will be fine. Where's the family?"

"Visiting Jan's folks. Her old man's not well."

She frowned and watched Karl pull a beer out of the bar's fridge. That last statement was a lie. It was obvious in the way his gaze had dropped, in the tension that had briefly curled his fingers. But if he and Gabriel were such good friends, why would he lie over an inane matter like that? Was it because of her presence? Or something else?

"So, tell me, what's wrong," Karl continued softly.

Gabriel looked at her. His eyes were still shuttered. This time the anger she sensed in him was not aimed at her. "Someone blew up Stephan's house."

Karl was still for the briefest of moments. That alone gave away his shock. Like Gabriel, his face was impassive. "Anyone hurt?"

"Fortunately, no."

"Lucky." Karl handed them both a drink and sat on the chair between the two sofas. "What did State have to say?"

Gabriel's brief smile was grim. "That we were lucky."

"Anyone with you, besides Stephan?"

It was a question that seemed to be loaded. Something was going on, something she didn't understand, but Karl obviously did.

Gabriel hesitated. Anger and disbelief warred briefly in his eyes. "Martyn, Mary and Lyssa."

"Ah."

Again, a simple statement that contained a lot of meaning. She crossed her legs in irritation. Damn it, she was getting more than a little tired of people keeping her in the dark. She gulped some of the scotch. The liquid burned down her throat and began to warm the cold pit in her stomach.

"How are those feet of yours?"

She met Karl's eyes. Something more than polite interest lurked in the brown depths. He was suspicious, but not exactly of her. *That* made about as much sense as Jack pulling his punches. She swallowed another mouthful of scotch, and then said, "Fine, thanks." Her gaze went to Gabriel's. "Now that we have the niceties over with, why don't you tell me why we're really here?"

He regarded her steadily. "I told you in the cab." As if to emphasize his point, he dug the envelope out of his pocket and placed it on the coffee table.

"You evaded the subject in the cab," she corrected. "I want the truth this time."

Karl snorted softly. "Told you."

She glanced at him. He raised his glass in a salute, a grin splitting his thin lips. "Don't take none of his crap, lass. He's a man used to playing his cards close to his chest. You have to push to learn."

"Believe me, she pushes," Gabriel muttered, then leaned forward, his hazel eyes suddenly intense. "Okay then, I brought you here because Karl wants to run a couple of extra tests."

She groaned. "What sort of tests?"

As she spoke, a soft ringing started. Gabriel rose, digging the cell phone out of his pocket as he walked into the other room.

The tension level leapt about ten degrees. Why, she had no idea. She took another gulp of scotch, but it did little to ease the sudden, uneasy churning in her stomach.

"News!" Gabriel called from the other room.

Karl pressed a button on the arm of his chair, and a panel slid aside on the wall opposite the sofas. A vid-screen came to life.

" . . . current reports suggested the toll could be as high as one hundred. While the State offices held only a skeletal crew, the SIU was fully manned."

The camera zoomed in on the devastation behind the female reporter. It looked like some voracious giant had come along and taken a huge bite out of one side of the building. Flames gleamed in the darkness, their golden light highlighting the paper and other bits of rubbish that still drifted like snow to the ground. The rest of the building, while still whole, looked like it had been shaken by a severe quake. Windows were shattered, lights were out, and fires burned.

She covered her mouth, trying to deny the horror. She'd been listed for night shift this week—another team would have taken her and Jack's place. She wondered if the captain was alive. Wondered if those who had taken her place had been killed.

Gabriel came back in. His face was white, and his eyes were bleak. "I have to go."

"Hanrahan?" Though Karl's voice held no emotion, she could see the sympathy and concern in his brown eyes.

He nodded. "He was apparently in the building at the time of explosion."

"Keys," Karl said, and threw them across. "And remember, they'll have the blocks up. You won't get near the place unless you're in human form."

Gabriel nodded. She scrambled to her feet, and his gaze swung to her, hot with a pain she couldn't understand. "You stay here."

"I'm coming with you."

"No." His voice cracked, as if he were barely controlling his pain. "It's too dangerous for you there."

Karl stood. "If he was dead, you would know."

"That's just it. I don't—either way."

He walked out the door. A few seconds later, an engine fired to life, and then a car sped away. She glanced across to Karl. "What was that all about?"

Karl considered her for a moment, and then sighed. "Hanrahan's not only Gabriel's boss. He's his brother. His twin brother."

Eleven

Sam blinked. Not even the most irrational of minds would think that the two men came from the same family tree, let alone be brothers. "They can't be."

Karl's smile was grim. "Hanrahan's a shapeshifter. His true form is similar."

"So why isn't he a shapechanger like Gabriel? How can twins have two totally different talents?"

"Both talents are strong in their family." He shrugged. "Twins aren't always identical, so why would their talents always be identical?"

"Makes sense, I suppose." She swallowed the last of her drink and held out the glass. "I don't suppose I could have another."

"I think we both need one." Karl accepted her glass and moved back to the bar.

She sat back down and watched the vid-screen. There were still lots of people pouring out of the partially destroyed building, and there were plenty more milling around a safe distance away. That was surely a good sign, especially since the State police offices only had a skeletal staff on at night. But she guessed it depended on just how much damage was done to the underground floors.

"It's sometimes better not to watch."

Karl held out her glass. She blinked away a tear and accepted it with a nod of thanks. "I need to know—"

She stopped. He was right. She didn't need to see this. There was nothing she could do to change what had happened. Nothing she could do if someone had died in her place. Nothing she could do to ease the sense of guilt that would probably haunt the rest of her nights.

"Turn it off." She took a large swallow of scotch. At the rate she was consuming the alcohol, she'd end up drunk in no time. And maybe that would be a blessing.

The panel eased shut over the images, and Karl sat back down. "Want to talk about the tests and why I want to run them?"

"Let me guess. I can see the kites, and you want to know why." Her voice had a sarcastic edge. She glanced at the liquid, then shrugged and took another drink. What the hell. Maybe if she offended him enough, he'd throw her out of the house, and that too, might be a blessing. Alone, she just might be able to start finding some answers instead of stumbling into blocks all the time.

Karl considered her for a moment, his brown eyes curious and friendly. "Actually, no. I'm more interested in the fact that you may have Shadow Walker blood in you."

She blinked. She'd wanted honesty, and Karl was certainly giving it. "Shadow Walker? What the hell is that?"

"A race that died out some fifty years ago."

"If it died out, how can I have it?"

"Maybe someone kept it alive."

Maybe it was the alcohol, but his answers weren't exactly making sense. "What do you mean?"

"I'm not really sure myself."

He wasn't trying to avoid an answer—he simply didn't know. Both his body language and her own innate ability to sense a lie told her as much. And yet that same innate ability was telling her something was very wrong. She shifted and tried a different tack. "So what is a Shadow Walker?"

"It's a very rare race that is said to be vaguely related to the vampires, without possessing their need for blood to survive."

She hastily swallowed more scotch, and then asked, "Why are they called Shadow Walkers?"

"Because, like vampires, they could disappear into shadows."

Which was definitely something she could *not* do. "Why the hell do you think I might have Shadow Walker blood in me?"

"Because of your eyes."

She raised her brows. "My eyes waver between blue and gray. Nothing special in that."

"Walkers supposedly had eyes the same as yours."

She snorted. "So does half the population of Melbourne. Blue eyes are very fashionable at the moment."

"Maybe." He shrugged. "Are you prepared to take the tests?"

"Why the hell not." It couldn't hurt, and maybe one of these damn tests might eventually give her some clues to her past.

"Good. We'll start them in the morning."

"Why not now?" Morning was only a few hours away.

He smiled. It made his almost fierce features look gentle, fatherly. Yet there was a haunted light in his kind brown eyes. "Because, my dear, you look dead on your feet, and you're bleeding onto my sofa. You need a shower, some patching up and sleep. In that order."

She glanced down. Blood was oozing from the graze on her arm, dripping steadily onto the sofa. She shifted her arm, letting it drip onto her clothes. "Sorry."

He shrugged. "Come on, let's get you sorted out."

She watched him rise and move into the next room. The sense of wrongness was growing, and though she didn't understand why, it was something she couldn't ignore. Biting her lip, she grabbed the disks and the wristcom from her bag, then rose and walked around to the bookcase. Kneeling, she carefully slipped them behind the dust-laden fiction books on the bottom shelf. Maybe it was a silly precaution. Maybe she was just being paranoid, but she felt safer with both items hidden. With a final look to ensure she'd left no telltale smudge near the books, she turned and followed Karl into the next room.

***

Gabriel pushed his way through the large crowd of people, and ducked under the yellow police tapes. Before he'd taken two steps, a young police officer caught his arm and hauled him around.

"I'm sorry sir, but no one's allowed any closer."

He bit down on his impatience and flashed his badge. "Any word on causalities yet?"

"Not that I've heard. But they've set up a temporary headquarters over near those vans." The young officer pointed towards several white vans parked half a block down from the smoking building.

"Thanks," he said, and strode past the emergency vehicles and the fire-hose armed men and women who poured water onto the flames. The night was warm, as if the explosion had blasted the chill from the air, and a trickle of sweat ran down his cheek. The red and blue emergency lights cut through the white of the spotlights, washing color across the white-clad backs of men and women who were still helping survivors from the damaged building. Thankfully, there seemed to be plenty of them. But an eerie silence still hung over the entire area, as if everyone working here feared a raised voice would bring on yet another disaster. His gaze traveled the long line of ambulances.

Stephan had sensed it when he'd been kidnapped, had known enough to send Karl to the rescue. Surely if Stephan were dead, he would feel the sudden emptiness, the loss, deep inside. It shouldn't matter what form that death had found him in—be it as his identical brother, as the green-eyed, black-haired leader of the Federation, or the hound-dog figure that was Hanrahan. Surely he should *know*.

Mike Reynolds, Hanrahan's secretary, glanced up as he approached.

"Any news on Hanrahan yet?" He stopped and studied the screen in front of Reynolds. It was a list of missing persons. Hanrahan and Finley were both on the list.

Reynolds shook his head. "Hanrahan apparently got a warning and called an emergency evac about three minutes before the bomb exploded. He ordered all his personal staff out, but he refused to leave himself until he was sure the building was clear."

How very much like Stephan. He scrubbed a hand across his eyes. "What about Finley?"

"We know most of the lab staff got out, but their exit points are around the other side of the building. I'm still waiting for a report on them."

"Much known about the bomb itself?"

Reynolds laughed sourly. "Yeah, it went off."

But the building still stood. Surely that was a good sign that injuries would be far lower than the men behind this bombing had intended. Damn it, why did he feel nothing but a peculiar emptiness when it came to Stephan? Did that mean his life was over, and afterlife had begun? He shoved his hands into his pockets. "Any idea where the bomb was placed?"

"It was a car bomb. A couple of state boys noted the driver acting suspiciously. When they tried to question him, the guy simply took off. He drove his vehicle through the security gates, into the parking garage and right into a side wall."

Which would explain why one side of the building seemed to have taken the brunt of the damage. "How badly damaged were the SIU floors?"

"The parking garage and the first three SIU levels mirror what's happened above ground, but the rest seem in reasonable shape."

Stephan's office was on the third of the underground levels. He scrubbed a hand through his hair. "Is the building structurally sound?"

"First reports say yes, because the bomb hit the middle of the wall, rather than the core or one of the main outside supports. They're still in there checking, though."

He nodded. "Have they set up a morgue?" Not that he actually wanted to visit such a place—but with the emptiness that resided inside him, he might just have to.

Reynolds shook his head. "They're ferrying the dead to hospitals. Michael is checking for identities as they're being loaded into ambulances, though." He hesitated and handed Gabriel a sheet of paper. "These are the confirmed deaths."

He scanned the list of names. There weren't many, thank God, maybe twelve in all. Hanrahan wasn't among them. "No unidentified?"

"A couple, both woman." Reynolds grimaced. "We're lucky we got that warning. It saved a lot of lives."

He just had to hope it had saved the one life that mattered to *him*. "Any idea who the warning came from yet?"

Reynolds shook his head. "It went directly to Hanrahan's office, apparently. It would have been recorded, but as yet, we can't access the network."

If Sethanon was behind this bombing, why had there been a warning? There hadn't been one in any of the other SIU bombings. To give one now didn't make any sense.

A phone rang, and Reynolds answered it. After a few minutes of arguing with whoever was on the other end, Reynolds hung up and looked at Gabriel.

"They've just helped a heap of people from the Lang's Lane exits. The fool in charge won't send me the list of names until he clears it with his boss. Don't suppose you want to head over and check it out for me?"

It was a better option that waiting here for some sign of his brother. "I'll give you a call back with the names."

He made his way out of the van. The night air, despite its residue of heat, seemed crisper, cleaner. Or maybe it just seemed that way because Hanrahan wasn't yet on the confirmed dead list. There was hope yet.

He walked around to Lang's Lane. Thirty or more people huddled near the end of the lane, watched by two officers in black. He frowned, wondering why they weren't being taken straight to an ambulance. A good third of them were bleeding or looked dazed, and one of the men was supported by a woman half his size. All were wearing the SIU gray, though none were faces he recognized.

He approached the most senior looking of the two State officers and flashed his badge. "What's the problem, Officer? Why aren't these people being taken to medical help?"

"There's been a report of a gas-leak up near Spencer. They're shifting the medical teams to a new position. We've been told to wait, as this position is fairly secure."

"There's no medical unit that can come down to help these people?"

The officer shook his head. "They've called for more medical staff—I know they're sending teams over from St. Vincent's and the Freemason's. Even the Mercy is sending help. Until they get here, and until they tell us the leak is clear, we have to stay put."

"Over on King Street we have a doctor checking the identities of the wounded and dead as they're being loaded into the ambulances. Call your people and tell them you're moving there." He hesitated, and then added, "Some of these people need help urgently."

The officer looked set to argue, but he glanced at the people behind them and nodded. Gabriel moved across to the second officer. "These were the only people to come out of this exit?"

The towheaded officer nodded. "These are the last, we think, but until they give us an all-clear from the gas leak, we can't go back in to check."

He nodded. If there was a gas leak, then they had to stop it quickly, especially with the small fires still burning inside the building. "Do you have the names and badge numbers of these evacuees? I need to send a copy to our people."

The young officer hesitated. "We've been told all requests for information have to go through headquarters, but I guess these *are* your people . . ." He glanced furtively at his partner, and then quickly showed Gabriel the list.

He scanned it through to Reynolds, and then smiled his thanks at the young officer as his partner approached.

"They've given us the okay to move them. We could do with your help, sir, if you aren't too busy. As you said, a couple of them are in pretty bad shape."

He nodded. "I'll take the man being supported by the woman. You two help the others."

The woman glanced up as he approached. Her face was a mess, the entire left side raw and bleeding, her eye was shut and swollen, and her lips were split and puffy. Her body didn't look much better. Her gray suit was torn and stained black by dirt and dried blood. Even the arm that supported her companion was bloody and bruised. But for all that, there was a look of intense elation in her gray eyes. Staring death in the eye and escaping had that sort of affect on you.

"Agents Layton and Byrne, from the Director's office," she said, mellow voice cracked and edged with pain.

His heart rate leapt. "See any sign of Hanrahan?" he asked, trying to remain calm as he slipped a shoulder under Byrne's, taking his weight off Layton's injured arm.

Layton shook her head. "But Byrne here was with him, last I saw him. Maybe he can tell you what happened once he's lucid."

It was the closest he'd come to finding his brother, and hope soared. The two officers began moving the others off. "You okay to walk, Layton?"

Her sudden grin was cheerful. "I just escaped a bombing attempt basically unharmed. Believe me, I think I could fly right now."

Byrne groaned softly as Layton moved away. Gabriel shifted his grip, and then glanced down.

And found himself staring into his own hazel eyes.

"Don't react," Stephan whispered urgently. "I'll explain when we're alone."

Don't react? When he'd been half convinced he'd find his twin under concrete? The sheer stupidity of the request made him shake his head. For an instant he wasn't sure whether to hug Stephan fiercely or throttle him. In the end, he did neither. Stephan knew how he felt. He could see the relief and love reflected in his twin's eyes.

"You'd better explain," he muttered. He shifted his hold again, and followed the two officers.

"And so had you, brother. So had you."

Stephan's voice faded. Gabriel wondered what he'd meant. His twin's eyes were closed, his breathing shallow. Sweat beaded his forehead and ran down the side of his face, scouring clean channels across his blood-smeared chin. Fighting not the pain of his injuries, Gabriel knew, but rather for the strength to maintain Byrne's image.

But why Byrne's? Why not Hanrahan's, an image his body was used to?

Frowning, he dug out his cell phone and quickly dialed. "Michaels, I'm bringing across some wounded. With the gas leak being investigated, you're the closest medical help I can think of."

Michaels almost looked relieved. "I'd rather treat the living than check the dead, I can tell you. I'll be waiting."

"We're on our way." He shoved the cell phone into his pocket and hurried on.

"As I've said before, I'm not going to die on you," Stephan said quietly. "Stop worrying."

"Like you wouldn't, if the situation was reversed?" He kept his voice low, his gaze sweeping the people in front of them.

Stephan's smile was a mere ghost, something Gabriel felt deep in his heart rather than actually saw. "I'm the oldest. It's my job to worry."

He snorted softly. "Yeah, right."

It took what seemed like hours to reach Michaels. Gabriel curbed his impatience, watching Michaels tend to the two more seriously injured women before waving him over to look at Stephan.

"What's the verdict?" he said, once Michaels had given his brother the once over and bandaged him up.

"Like the rest of them, he's lucky. His right arm's broken, his legs are severely bruised and his ankle's either badly sprained or broken—can't tell without x-rays. There's nothing wrong with him that a few days in the hospital won't fix, though."

"No hospital," Stephan muttered, eyes still closed.

Probably hiding the fact they were hazel rather than Byrne's natural blue. No matter what Michaels said, the stress of the injuries had to be bad if it was preventing Stephan from doing a full shapeshift. And if he couldn't fully shift, he had no option but to avoid the hospital and the ever-prying doctors.

Michaels frowned. "Sorry, Byrne, you've got no choice. That ankle needs looking at."

"No hospitals," Stephan repeated. "Stern, make sure they don't take me there."

"The man has a morbid fear of hospitals," Gabriel explained apologetically. "It's all in his file." It wasn't, but who was going to check? The whole com system was down right now . . . he stopped the thought cold. They wouldn't attempt to bomb a whole building just to prevent him from getting Sam's tests results . . . would they?

Maybe, just maybe.

He scrubbed a hand across his jaw. The day was getting worse, not better.

"If you don't get that ankle fixed he may never walk properly again," Michaels continued.

"Only if it *is* broken." Besides, Stephan was a shapeshifter. His body retained the memory of itself, and it could heal any number of broken bones, no matter how shattered, a whole lot faster than any doctor possibly could. "I have a friend, a physician. Retired, but still willing to keep his hand in. I'll take him there."

Michaels glanced over his shoulder as a string of ambulances came around the corner. "I guess we have no choice. He's obviously lucid, so we can't take him anywhere against his will. He's all yours."

"I'll go get my car. Take care of him until I get back."

Michaels nodded. Gabriel squeezed his brother's shoulder, then rose to fetch Karl's car.

***

Gabriel booked a hotel room in the middle of Saint Kilda, a trendy district that held a dark heart of criminal activity. The manager asked no questions, and he turned a blind eye to Stephan's condition—the main reason he'd chosen to come here.

Given the dilapidated state of the place, he had no doubt that if someone came looking for them, it would take only a buck or two for the manager to spill his guts. But it didn't matter, because they wouldn't be here all that long. Just a day or so, until his brother regained his strength.

He lowered Stephan to the bed, then locked the door and crossed to the window. The hotel fronted the esplanade, and their room looked out over the bay. It also had a damn good view of the hotel's front entrance. He checked the street, drew the blinds closed and dragged a chair up close to the bed.

"We safe?" Stephan asked, without opening his eyes.

"Safe as we can be."

Stephan sighed, a soft sound full of relief. His body began to shimmer, to blur, and for an instant resembled play dough being molded by invisible hands.

Then the shimmer died away, and his own image faced him. "You don't know how good that feels."

"I can imagine," he said wryly. "Now tell me why all that was necessary."

Stephan shrugged. "For awhile I've felt that the usefulness of Hanrahan's image was coming to an end. Too many people were beginning to suspect he was my alter identity. Especially since both Hanrahan and I appeared to be suffering the same mysterious ailment."

Gabriel propped his feet on the end of the bed, and leaned back in the chair. "Who, precisely?" Certainly he'd never heard any whispers about it.

"Lys knew, naturally enough. But I think both Mary and Martyn suspected, and I'm sure Byrne knew something was wrong—even if he didn't know what."

"Is that why you've taken his image?"

Stephan nodded. "I needed a new identity, and he fit the criteria. No immediate family, few friends. A loner who loved his work."

"Did you kill him?"

Stephan's smile held a hard edge. "I'd planned to, but my offices were right under where the bomber hit, and we were both caught in the rubble—him more than me. I doubt there'll be much of him left to find—but I left some of Hanrahan's personal effects, just to be sure."

Gabriel nodded. If there was enough left to perform DNA tests, there might be problems—though it was nothing they hadn't handled before. When the real Hanrahan had died in a boating accident, Federation had altered the tests long before the coroner saw them.

"Tell me about the warning you got."

Stephan rubbed his eyes. "Line trace said the caller was female, probably in her mid-thirties. She was calling from a phone booth in the Dandenongs."

Odd. The four men who'd beaten him up had been hightailing it up there before Karl stopped them. Did that mean Sethanon had a hideout up there? "What did she say, exactly?"

"That the SIU building was about to be bombed. I had five minutes to live."

Reynolds said the bomb had gone off three minutes after Hanrahan received the call—obviously, the State boys questioning the driver of the bomb car had disrupted his plans. Then he frowned. "*You* had five minutes to live? Isn't that a little strange? Why not say you had five minutes to evacuate the building?"

"I have no idea, and at the time, I was too busy trying to trace the call and check authenticity to worry about it."

"Did she say anything else?"

"She told me the make and number of the car. I looked out the window, saw the car, and ordered the evac."

"Were you the reason the State boys investigated the car?"

"No. That was sheer chance. I had some of our own people headed up there, but they arrived far too late to prevent this tragedy."

No one could blame the State boys for simply doing their job, though. It was just an unfortunate sequence of events. "I don't suppose you recognized the voice?"

Stephan shook his head. "Voice scanning was in progress, but the system just didn't have long enough before it all went to hell."

Had the call come from the woman supposedly impersonating Lyssa? Or perhaps even Mary, using some form of voice modulator? Though why would either of them warn Stephan if they were involved with Sethanon or Kazdan? It didn't make any sense. But nothing about this situation made any sense.

And with the computer network down, and who knew what information destroyed, any chance of a crosscheck of the woman's voice against Lyssa's or Mary's was gone. His only option now was checking whether either woman had left their safe houses near the time of the warning. "Any idea who might be behind the bombing?"

"It's probably Sethanon."

He frowned. If Sethanon could get a shapeshifter into the labs to lock away Sam's files, he could easily have arranged to have a car drive into the side of the building and explode. What didn't make sense was the why. In the past, he'd tended to be a little more subtle. "I think he's smart enough to realize bombing the SIU will only make it stronger—past efforts to destroy us have certainly proven that."

"What are you saying? That it could be any one of the hundreds of people who have a gripe against the SIU? None of them have gone *this* far for revenge before."

"No. Personally, I think it's Kazdan."

Stephan opened an eye and regarded him steadily. "Why?"

He told Stephan of the conversation he'd overheard between Kazdan and the blond shapechanger. "I think Kazdan's getting tired of the middle management yoke. I think he wants more. I think he's intending to use Sam to get it. And Eddie Wyatt is working for him, not Sethanon."

"The SIU bomb certainly had Eddie's style. And if Kazdan intends using Sam in his overthrow plot, it suggests he knows more about these abilities she seems to have."

He nodded. "It also suggests Sethanon knows. He arranged for Kazdan to be her partner, after all. Maybe he wanted to keep an eye on her."

"That would suggest she's somehow linked to Sethanon."

It seemed that way, but gut instinct said she wasn't involved with him. Not yet, anyway. "Sethanon wanted her watched but otherwise left alone. I think we need to find out why."

"Where is she now?"

"With Karl."

Stephan frowned. "He seemed a little tense last time we met. Has he got family problems or something?"

He frowned, remembering the tension around Karl's eyes. "Not that I know of."

"Odd." Stephan's gaze drifted shut again. "He kept glancing at his watch and checking to see if his cell phone was on. When I asked what the matter was, he said his wife had gone to visit relatives in New South Wales and was due to call at six. He said he had to catch the call or she'd kill him."

New South Wales. Not to Jan's parents, who lived on a farm half an hour's drive away from Karl's.

Gabriel closed his eyes for a moment and took a deep breath. "Did you tell Karl that Hanrahan was your alter identity?"

"There was no need to tell him."

And yet Karl had known. He could only have found out from one of three people—three people he shouldn't even know. Gabriel pulled out his cell phone and quickly dialed Karl's number. The phone rang several times. Either no one was home or no one was in the position to answer it. He swore and shoved the phone back into his pocket.

"What's wrong?"

He stared at his brother bleakly. "I think I've just handed Sam over to the enemy."

Twelve

Sam stirred, vaguely aware of movement. Rough vibrations ran through the metal floor beneath her, bruising her back and rattling her teeth. Darkness encased her. She couldn't see.

Old fears rose, threatening to overwhelm her. She swallowed and forced them back. Now was not the time to panic. Not until she knew what was going on, anyway. It was obvious she was no longer in bed at Karl's place. Not unless it had suddenly converted to a car.

Two men were speaking close by. One voice seemed familiar, though she couldn't exactly place where she'd heard it before. Beyond that, music, though it was barely audible above the throaty roar of the engine. She frowned. It sounded like *Ennui's* latest hit, *Silence*. Jack's favorite tune.

Her heart began to beat a little faster. Maybe she'd done the right thing in following her instincts, and hiding the disks at Karl's.

She shifted slightly. Almost instantly, an ache sprang up her arms and settled into her shoulder blades. She tried to rub the sore spot, only to realize her hands were tied behind her back. The ropes were tight, chafing at her wrists. She shifted her feet. Also tied. Something rubbed across her face, making her nose itch—a cloth of some sort. She took a deep breath, and then blew it out. The black cloth puffed away from her face, momentarily giving her vision. She was in a van of some sort. Out the back window she glimpsed golden pines, and then the cloth settled back into place.

The vibrations through the floor stopped. Doors slammed shut, and then the door near her feet opened. Hands grabbed her roughly. Her immediate instinct was to fight, but until she knew exactly what was going on, it made more sense to play possum. She went limp, feigning unconsciousness.

Hands slipped under her shoulders, and suddenly she was free from the metal flooring. Gravel crunched and more doors opened.

"Any problems?"

Jack's voice, coming from a doorway to her left. So, she'd been right. He wasn't dead, and he *was* mixed up in whatever was going on. For a moment, it felt as if someone had knifed her heart.

"No trouble whatsoever." The slight hint of Irish brogue in the speaker's tone was definitely familiar. She'd heard it before—on the phone, asking to speak to Jack.

"Take her down to the holding cells. We'll let her sleep it off for a few hours."

The man near her head grunted, and the two men moved off again. They carried her down a flight a stairs, and into a room that smelled musty and old. But it was occupied. She could hear soft conversation to her right—female voices.

Another door creaked open, and she was thrown none too gently onto a mattress. The cloth over her head was pulled away, taking with it more than a few strands of hair. She bit back her yelp of pain and kept her eyes closed. The two men moved away, and the door slammed shut.

She waited several minutes before opening her eyes. Her prison was a red brick room, maybe ten feet long by six feet wide. The door was metal, with a small barred opening in its middle. She looked behind her. There was another window on the back wall, probably a couple of feet in diameter. Big enough to crawl through, if it wasn't for the thick metal crossbars.

Sunlight streamed in, warming the chill from the air. She'd obviously been out some time, because the sun seemed to be riding high in the sky. She swung her feet off the bed and stood. The red walls swam momentarily, and a bitter taste rose to the back of her throat. She swallowed and tried to ignore the churning in her stomach. Whatever drug they'd used to knock her out, it obviously didn't agree with her system.

The rope around her ankles was thick and tight. If it weren't for her boots, it would probably be cutting off her circulation. She blinked. *Her boots?* She was dressed—still wearing the same clothes that she'd worn last night. Had they re-dressed her, or had she never undressed? All she could remember was getting to the bedroom after Karl had bandaged her wounds. She had a vague memory of the softness of the mattress, but she couldn't remember stripping or climbing into bed.

Had Karl drugged her drink? Had Jack been at the house all the time, simply waiting for Karl to do his dirty work? If that were true, then maybe the SIU bombing had saved Gabriel from being captured—or even killed. Or maybe he was the reason it had been bombed—to get him away from Karl. And her.

She shuffled to the window. There wasn't much to see outside, just several feet of concrete and another wall, this one bluestone. A breeze whispered in, carrying with it the stench of rotting rubbish. Maybe her cell was near a dump of some kind.

She shuffled back to the door and peeked out. The main room was full of shadows. The two women were still talking in one of the cells to her right. To her left, a set of stairs curved around a wall and disappeared. No one stood watch.

She looked at the door lock. Key coded. The decoder was still in her boot—she could feel the end of it digging into her ankle beneath the ropes. If she could somehow get it, she might be able to get out of the cell. Then all she had to do was find out what Jack was up to.

She shuffled back to the bed and sat down. Twisting her legs up beside her, she leaned sideways, and reached with her fingertips for her boots. Her shoulders cracked, and pain slithered down her spine. She bit her lip and reached a little more, trying to get closer. No matter what she did, she couldn't touch more than a fingertip to the top of her boot. There wasn't a hope in hell of pulling anything out.

She cursed and slammed her feet back to the concrete. Then she stared at her boots for a moment. Why didn't she just take them off?

If there was enough leeway in the rope to do a shuffle walk, surely there was enough leeway to kick off a boot. Raising her legs off the floor, she forced her left leg a little in front of the right. The rope rolled off the top of her boot and bit into her leg, sawing at her flesh. She ignored it, and tried to catch her left heel with her other boot. After a few minutes, she managed to hook the heel and force the boot off her foot, though the effort left her whole body trembling.

She dropped her legs back to the floor, took a deep breath, and blew it back out, lifting the sweaty strands of hair off her forehead. Then she took a look at the damage. The rope had dug deep into her leg, and red trails of blood were beginning to wind their way through the flower patterns in her socks. And rope burns *hurt*. It felt as if someone was holding a flame to her ankles, burning her flesh. But she had no time to sit and feel sorry for herself. First, she wanted to find out who else Jack was keeping locked up, and then she had to get the hell out of here.

She rose and shuffled over to her boot. The rope around her ankles was looser, though not enough to actually get it off. She crouched down, and felt around the inside edges of her boot until she found the decoder. She carefully pulled it out and shuffled back to the door.

The key-coder beeped after several seconds, and the door clicked open. She peered out. No one lurked in the shadows. She pushed the door open with her shoulder, and then she headed toward the cells at the far end of the room.

The talking stopped as she neared. She hesitated, listening. Inside the end cell, someone breathed heavily, short sharp gasps that spoke of fear.

"Hello?" she whispered. "Detective Samantha Ryan, State Police." She was suspended, but that wasn't a point these women needed to know right now.

A white face appeared at the barred window to her right. "You're here to rescue us?"

She snorted. Some rescue. She was tied up tighter than a turkey on Christmas day. "Not exactly. Step back, ma'am."

She turned around and placed the decoder on the lock. The door clicked in response. She pushed the door open and shuffled in. The two women inside looked at her for a moment, and then they shared a glance. It wasn't hard to see the disappointment in their eyes. Neither were tied, which wasn't a good sign. At the very least, it meant Jack was very, very sure of his security.

"Officer, you seem to be in worse trouble than we are," the woman with the white face said.

"For the moment, I'd have to agree." She held out her tied hands. "I don't suppose one of you ladies could get these ropes off?"

The older of the two stepped forward. She had long brown hair swept into a ponytail and held by a red and purple scarf. Her loose fitting pants were also purple, while her jumper was vibrant white. Karl's wife. She had to be, because there was no other explanation for his betrayal of Gabriel. Even in the brief time she'd seen them together, it was obvious they shared a deep friendship. At least now she understood the anguish she'd seen in Karl's eyes. To save his wife, he had to kill a friendship he held dear.

The other woman in the cell was someone she knew. "Lyssa," she said, surprised. "How the hell did you get here? I thought Stephan was sending you to stay with his old man?"

Surprise flitted through Lyssa's blue eyes, followed quickly by pain. She took a deep breath, and then released it in a sigh that was somehow mournful. "I have not seen Stephan for at least six months. Nor have I met you, officer."

"But . . . I saw you, yesterday." She hesitated. Gabriel had said some shifters were multi-shifters. The Lyssa she'd seen with Stephan was definitely a shifter. She was getting no such reading from this woman, though that didn't mean she wasn't a shifter. This talent of hers seemed to be very selective about who it did, and didn't, pick up.

"That wasn't me, officer."

"Obviously not, if you're here."

The ropes finally came off. She rubbed her wrists, then shook her legs to get the circulation going properly again. Big mistake. The rope burns began to ache with renewed vigor.

"Those wounds need tending," Karl's wife commented. "They'll get infected, otherwise."

Right now, infection was the least of her worries. "Has Jack been down here? Said anything to you two?"

Both women shook their heads. "We're fed through the slot in the door three times a day," Lyssa said. "They escort us to the showers once a day, and they bring in a box load of books and magazines every week. But it is always the same two men, and neither will answer any of our questions."

So Jack had no obvious intention of harming them. He just wanted them out of the way. She glanced at Karl's wife—Jan, if she remembered correctly. "How long have you been here?"

"Just a day."

Snatching her had to have been a last minute plan—maybe a result of Sam unexpectedly finding the disks. And if Jack knew Gabriel was close to Karl, it would be an easy enough guess that, sooner or later, he would take her there.

She looked at Lyssa. "They haven't said anything to you, in the six months you've been here?"

"No," Lyssa hesitated, her hand drifting down to her stomach. It was only then that Sam noticed the telltale rounding. "I fear my child will be born with Stephan never knowing."

She obviously didn't know about the shapeshifter taking her place. Nor was it the time to really tell her. "Believe me, I fully intend to get us all out of this before that ever happens."

But first, she had to find out what Jack was up to. She bent down and picked up the ropes. "I'm going to have to lock you back in for now. Jack obviously has no intention of harming either of you, and until I know what he's up to, and where exactly we are, I don't want to do anything that may jeopardize that situation."

The two women nodded. She spun and walked out of their cell, carefully locking the door again. Then she made her way back to her own cell. Retrieving her boot, she slipped it back on then shoved the decoder back. The ropes she flung under the bed, just in case she needed them later. Then she sat on the bed and waited.

The sun was well on the way to setting by the time the two men came back. They glanced at her hands and feet, then at each other, surprise evident in their expressions. One stepped back and pulled out a gun, motioning her to follow the other man.

She climbed off the bed and followed the taller of the two men. He led her up the stairs, then down a long corridor remarkable only for its antiseptic whiteness. A door swooshed open at the far end, revealing yet another corridor. Their footsteps echoed hollowly, as if it were metal flooring hung in space rather than anchored to the ground. Another door opened and they finally entered a room.

It was sparsely furnished—containing only a white desk and two cheap-looking chairs. Her escorts stopped and motioned her to sit. She chose the chair in the farthest corner and watched the first man walk round the desk to the com-screen.

"She's here."

"Send her in. I want you and Roston to remain outside."

Roston. The man with the Irish brogue—the man who'd called Jack several times in the week before he disappeared. He had blond hair, a scraggly ginger beard, and green eyes that were feral and full of anger. A shapechanger, she thought, and one not in full control of his other nature.

The door behind the desk slid open. Beyond it, she saw warm amber walls and a tapestry depicting two knights at battle, one dark, one light. Oddly fitting, given the situation. Jack had often considered himself something of a dark knight. But was she the light? Or something else entirely?

Roston motioned her into the room. She rose and entered. Jack stood at the far end of the room, hands behind his back, staring at another picture rather than facing her. The door slid shut, and the lock clicked home, trapping her in the room with a probable madman. She looked quickly around. No windows through which to escape, and very little in the way of loose furnishings to grab as a weapon—which certainly was deliberate.

Jack finally turned around to face her. He looked no different from the last time she'd seen him. No different from the clone she'd shot. Only his gaze gave the game away. It held a coldness that went beyond anything she'd ever seen before.

He was a vampire with an agenda all his own. Not her partner. Not her friend.

"How nice of you to join me," he said.

Her smile was thin. "Why? Were you falling apart?"

"Still seeking sanctuary in humor when faced with tough situations, I see." He motioned her to a chair that was firmly bolted to the floor. "Please, sit down."

"Thanks, but I prefer to stand." At least she could run if he tried to jump her for a little sunset refreshment. "Why aren't you in the land of nod, like all good little vampires should be at this hour?"

He smiled. There was nothing nice about that smile. "Sunshine may be dangerous to a vampire's health, but that doesn't mean we can't move around during the daylight hours." He quirked an eyebrow at her. "Have you learned nothing in the years we've been together?"

She crossed her arms and leaned against the door. "I've learned that friends can't be trusted."

"Ah." He gave a small smile, swiveled his chair around and sat down. "Come and sit. I promise not to jump you."

She remained exactly where she was. A small vein near his temple pulsed slightly in response.

"If I wanted to harm you, I could have well and truly done it before now."

"But you didn't want me harmed. You wanted me scared." As Gabriel had suggested. Her gaze roamed the features that were so familiar, and yet somehow so foreign. "Why, Jack?"

Surprise flared in his eyes and just as quickly died. He leaned back in his chair. "You never were a fool."

Yes, she was. She'd called this man her friend. Had trusted him beyond common sense. "Just answer the question."

He shrugged. "You have talents. Granted, they're just developing and not yet understood, but they are talents that will be quite formidable, nonetheless."

Talents suggested more than one, and as far as she knew, she only had the one. How would some weird ability to sense things like the kites help him in whatever mad scheme he had going on here?

"That makes about as much sense as you becoming a vampire," she retorted. "Speak English, Jack. Or has turning robbed you of that ability?"

The vein ticked a little harder. Maybe it wasn't such a good idea to make him angry, but in the past, an angry Jack had always been a verbal one. He'd give away more than he intended if she got to him.

All she had to do then was survive it.

The chair thumped forward again. "I plan a take over. This war is not happening soon enough for my liking. You, dear friend, will assist me in achieving my goal."

She raised her eyebrows. "Is this war you're talking about the one in which the human race will be the loser?"

"Yes."

"Well, in case its escaped your notice, I'm human. Guess which side of the line I tend to fall on?"

His smile was smug, like that of a rat that'd just eaten the cat. "You're anything but human, my dear Samantha."

She stared at him, uncertain whether she should believe him or not. Jack could lie with the best of them, but usually, she could tell when he was. He wasn't lying now. She clenched her fists. Damn it, she *was* human, despite what that unknown chromosome Finley had found might reveal. She was human. Nothing more, nothing less.

"What is the one thing you have wanted?" he continued softly. "The one thing you have searched for all these years?"

He knew the answer to those questions. He'd helped her search the records often enough. But was he also the reason she'd found nothing?

His smile grew, as did the coldness in his eyes. He leaned forward and slid a sheet of paper across the table towards her. "Part one of the answers. The first link in the trail to who you really are. Please, feel free to look. It's only a taste of what I know."

She stared at that sheet of paper, her throat dry. It was tempting, so very tempting. The desire to know who she really was, to know who her parents, who her grandparents, were—to find whatever kin might still be out there—was something she'd lived and breathed since she'd been a teenager and awakened from a nightmare and found herself abandoned in the shelter. If the information was all that he promised, she'd want more, there was no doubt about it. She didn't know if she was strong enough to resist the lure once she'd taken a bite.

Better by far to refuse straight out.

She met Jack's gaze. "Since I seem to be your guest, it's impossible for me to discover whether the information on that sheet is the truth or lies."

"The sheet tells no lies."

"But you do, Jack."

His mouth narrowed to a slash of anger. "I've told you no lies today."

She considered him for a moment. So far, he'd done nothing to hurt her. If he hoped to enlist her in his mad schemes, he might just hold off using force for a while. Maybe she should push his generosity and see just how far he was willing to go.

"All right then. Who attacked me in my apartment, and why bomb it afterwards?"

His eyes were green slits that conveyed both malevolence and amusement. A chilling combination.

"My men attacked you. We bombed it to destroy your computer and the files you downloaded." He hesitated then shrugged. "I forgot about the second damn com-unit."

"So that's why we were attacked at the hotel?"

He nodded. "I was hoping you'd panic and leave it behind. I should have known better."

"What is in those files that you don't want me to see?"

He smiled coldly. "That's something you'll never know, since I now have your bag and the com-unit."

But she still had his wristcom and the backup files. Or did she? Had they found them at Karl's? She forced a sweet smile. "But you don't have your disks, do you?"

The vein tripped into triple time. "A point I was going to raise. Where are they, Samantha?"

He hadn't found them, then. Good. "Where do you think?"

He cursed. "I thought you'd have more sense than to give them to the spook."

"He was trying to help me, you know."

Jack laughed harshly. "Stern is no more trying to help you than I am. He wants you for his own ends, and you're a fool if you believe otherwise."

Maybe. But right now, she knew which of the two men she trusted more. "What about the kite, then?"

He smiled. "Reflex test. No human can outrun those things, yet you did."

"Maybe I'm just very fast when I'm scared."

He raised an eyebrow and said nothing. She shifted, suddenly uncomfortable under his knowing gaze. She didn't *want* to be anything else . . . didn't want to be related to the very things she'd loathed for as long as she could remember.

"How do you know about me, about my past?"

"Sethanon told me."

Sethanon. The great evil. The great unknown. "And why the hell would he know or even care about me?"

"Because he fears what you might become."

She snorted. "Yeah, right. A would be dictator with hordes of dark monsters at his command fears one lone cop who's a few cogs short in the memory department. Nice try, Jack."

His cold smile widened. "I was appointed your watchdog five years ago by Sethanon. Before me, there was Rachel, your blonde neighbor for several years. Before that, I believe there was a boy named Raul. Brown hair, buck teeth. You went through training together."

She stared at him. She'd never told him any of that. Had she lived in a fish bowl all her life, unaware, yet never alone? It was a frightening thought. She swallowed heavily.

"Then who's trying to set me up for your murder? And why the clone?"

"Sethanon, again. It would seem some of your searches were getting a little too close to the truth for his liking. He wants you off the force and away from their computers. Having you 'kill' me was a method of ensuring that."

All that would ensure was that she'd end up in prison. Though she guessed that *would* keep her well away from the State's computer system. "Why try and take the clone back then? It was your men in the morgue, wasn't it?"

"Yes. Reliable help is not readily available these days, I'm afraid." He gave her a thin smile. "The clone was pumped with accelerant. Even on death, the accelerant keeps working. In a day or so it would have been very obvious it was not me."

"And what about the other clones?"

He raised his eyebrows. "What other clones?"

"Wetherton, for a start."

"And why would you think Wetherton is a clone?"

"Hard to think otherwise once I'd stumbled across his dead body." The fact that it had been Gabriel who'd discovered Wetherton's body was something Jack didn't need to know.

He smiled his cold smile. "Which would explain why orders to get rid of Wetherton have come down from the top. I'm afraid he's about to have a horrible car accident. There won't be enough DNA left to make a check."

"Why make someone like Wetherton a clone, anyway? He was on his way down the ranks, not up."

"Because he's still a government minister, and there are certain things only a government minister has access to."

"Like what?"

He raised an eyebrow. "So full of questions today, aren't you?"

And while he was answering them, she was going to keep on asking. "So where does Suzy fit into all this?"

His gaze narrowed. "She's my wife."

And will do as I say, go where I go, she thought sourly. For the first time, she began to feel a little sorry for Suzy. The woman was a bitch, but not even the biggest bitch deserved a bastard like Jack for a husband.

So why had it taken *her* five years to see Jack for what he really was?

Maybe she'd always known. Maybe she just wasn't willing to admit it. Wasn't willing to lose a friendship she'd valued above everything else.

She shifted her weight from one foot to the other. "Why is this Sethanon so interested in stopping my quest to find out who I am? And if he fears me so much, why not just kill me?"

Jack smiled. "Maybe those are questions you should ask him."

She raised an eyebrow. "You don't know, do you?"

He crossed his arms on the table and leaned forward. "You will help me, you know, and I don't care if it's willingly or unwillingly."

She let her gaze drop to the paper in front of him, considering it for a minute. "Was I ever anything more than a job to you? Did you ever even consider me a friend?"

He returned her gaze and smiled. For just a moment, there was something more than a chill in his eyes. But that brief moment of sadness was gone almost as quickly as it had appeared. "You stand before me unchained and free of drugs. I'm giving you the choice to join me willingly. Friendship, Samantha, nothing else."

She looked at her toes and blinked back the sudden sting of tears. He was rotten to the core, but he was still her friend. Her only friend. Damn, she hated life sometimes.

"I can't make the decision right now, Jack. I need time to

think." Time to plot an escape. She hesitated, looking at the paper again. How could she leave this room without knowing what was on it?

She couldn't. With a sigh of defeat, she walked over and picked it up. Jack laughed softly; a sound full of victory. At that moment, she didn't care.

The paper was a birth certificate. Her birth certificate, but not the one she'd seen—not the one State held. This one had four names in her father's side, and four in her mother's.

She frowned up at Jack. "This makes no sense. How can I have four of each parent?"

His expression was filled with gloating. "The answers, dear friend, will come when I have your answer. A simple yes or no is all I need."

"I need time to think," she repeated. She carefully folded the certificate and shoved it inside her pocket. Amusement flared in his eyes. He thought he had her. Thought he could reel her in as simply as that, which proved he didn't know her as well as he thought he did.

"You have until tomorrow morning to make your decision. After that, I'm afraid I'll have to try other methods."

She had no desire to find out what those other methods were. She knew Jack too well. They wouldn't be pleasant. The door behind her swished open.

"Take her back to the cells," Jack said quietly. "Make sure she is fed tonight, and bring her back in the morning."

Two men entered. She ignored them, her gaze still on Jack.

"Tomorrow we shall find out just how well developed your abilities are," he said. "And I'd rather have you as a willing accomplice, Sam."

She smiled, even though it felt as if something was breaking inside. She had no intention of being here tomorrow, and by escaping, she'd kill the one true friendship she'd had. A friendship that was nothing more than a lie.

"See you tomorrow morning, Jack." Hopefully with a gun in her hand and the SIU at her back.

Thirteen

Gabriel stormed into Karl's home. Though Karl hadn't answered the phone, he was home, sitting on the sofa in the dark. He raised his hands, as if in surrender.

"I had no choice," he said, voice soft and cracked with pain. Gabriel saw the tears in his eyes. It was that, more than anything else, that stopped his anger.

"They have Jan," Karl continued.

He sighed and ran a hand through his hair. Then he slumped onto the sofa beside his friend. "Fucking hell. Why didn't you tell me?"

Karl grimaced. "They were monitoring all my lines. They shot Jason's dog and threatened to do the same to Jason if I tried to warn you in any way."

Jason was Karl's youngest—barely ten. The loss of his pet would certainly shatter the poor kid. "Then why not use a public phone? Or go to one of the neighbors?"

"They said they were going to call at six, and every half ten minutes after that. They said if I didn't answer, they'd kill her."

He shook his head. After all Karl had seen with the Federation, he should have known better than to trust the word of a man like Kazdan. "Have they called?"

"Yes."

"And?"

Karl closed his eyes. "They were supposed to call back an hour ago with the details of her release."

"I'm sorry I dragged you into this, my friend."

Karl shrugged. "I knew the risks when I joined the Federation. Jan and I discussed it. I just didn't think they'd go for my family rather than me."

"Sethanon probably wouldn't." To date, Sethanon had confined his attentions to only active operatives of the SIU and the Federation. "This is Kazdan's doing."

"And Kazdan's worse?"

"Much worse." Sethanon seemed to have limits, lines he wouldn't cross. Kazdan appeared willing to go to any length to get what he wanted. And right now, that was Sam. "Are the kids really with Jan's folks?"

Karl nodded. "School holidays, remember? They go up there for the week Jan can't get off. I've sent Harvey up there to guard them."

However much Karl felt Harv was ready to join Federation, Gabriel doubted that Karl's eldest had the training or the skill to deal with the likes of Kazdan's men.

Karl's brown eyes were full of torment as he continued, "They won't release her, will they?"

"I doubt it. Jan's proven valuable. He might find other uses for you."

"Bastard," Karl muttered, then took a deep breath. "I thought something like this might happen. That's why I bugged his car."

He stared at his friend for a long moment. "You bugged his car?"

"And the cretin with the gun. I used the new plastic type—detectors can't pick them up."

"Then why are you just sitting here?"

"Because I knew you'd realize something was wrong. I knew you'd come here first."

He grimaced. "I should have picked it up far earlier than I did." Karl's tension should have been warning enough. He'd just been too preoccupied with his own problems to be concerned. He sighed heavily, and rose. "Let's hope the cretin and the car go to wherever they're holding Jan."

Karl clasped his fingers together, cracking them loudly. "And if Jan's not there, it will be my great pleasure to thump the information out of the fellow."

"To think you were a pacifist a mere ten years ago."

"Reality has hit me since then." Karl walked to the bar and pulled a small tracer unit from behind a whiskey bottle. "Used the long-range type. We should be able to pick up a signal from the city."

"Then let's go find some heads to smack."

***

The evening meal came and went. Sam sat on the bunk and watched the shadows creep further and further into the cell. Outside, a storm was brewing. She could smell the hint of rain in the air, could see the occasional flash of light weave its way across the darkening sky. Electricity seemed to buzz through the air, a sense of power that tingled across her skin. She breathed deep. Energy flowed through every pore, every muscle, filling her with that power. It was almost as if she were one with the night—one with the storm.

The shadows flowed into the darkness of true night. She

rose. The only light she could see in the room beyond was the one coming from the cell that held the two women.

Why were there no guards? It was unlike Jack to be so careless. She glanced at the ceiling, and saw what she'd failed to see earlier. Small monitors that were hidden within the lights themselves.

Jack knew she could get out. Knew she'd talked to the two women earlier. So why hadn't he taken the decoder? Maybe he wanted her to escape. Maybe he'd given her the time and the chance as another test.

Frowning, she stared at the dark light bulb. Why was she seeing the monitor now and not before? Was it somehow linked to the sensation of power that ran through the storm-held night, the power that burned across her skin? Or was it something more, something to do with the extra abilities Jack seemed so certain she had? Was that the real reason he'd given her until morning? Not to let her think, but to see if she could escape and how far she could get?

Even if this *were* nothing more than a test, she had no choice but to run with it. She had to get the two women out of here. Then she needed to find out just what Jack was really up to.

She slipped the decoder from her boot and pressed it against the lock. The click of it opening seemed as loud as the thunder rumbling overhead. She frowned and slowly opened the door. A slight whine sounded as the monitor tracked across the cell and focused on her.

She swallowed to ease the sudden dryness in her throat. She shouldn't be able to hear something like that. The energy of the storm was somehow heightening her senses. The night was as clear as day, and sound had become something she could almost touch.

Was this one of the abilities Jack had mentioned? Or was the fear laying like a stone in the pit of her stomach lending wings to her imagination?

The light from the cell at the far end of the long room beckoned like a beacon, but if Jack was watching, that was the one place she couldn't go. First, she'd have to take out the monitors, and whoever was watching them.

She turned left and headed for the stairs. The monitor buzzed into the silence, following her movements. She ran up the winding, open staircase and tested the handle on the door at the top. Unlocked. She grimaced. It was a test for sure. Jack wouldn't allow his men to be so careless.

If he wanted her to go this way, it was the one way she couldn't go. Surely there was another way out. She turned and leaned against the banister, studying the room below. Her gaze stopped when she came to a vent close to the floor halfway between her cell and the cell of the two women. From where she stood, there didn't appear to be any screws holding it in place. It was simply sitting there.

It was almost too good to be true. Maybe even a trap. And yet, the vent hadn't been disturbed any time recently. The rust and the dirt that caked the cover would have revealed any sort of recent movement.

Jack knew of her fear of tight spaces. It was the last place he'd expect her to try.

The monitor would have to go. Otherwise, they'd see what she was up to and be down here before she could escape. She pulled off her boot and took careful aim. Luck was with her. The bulb shattered, and the soft whine of the monitor faded. Would the watching guards come down to investigate? Or would they give her time so they could see where she went?

She retrieved her boot and moved back to the door. The two corridors beyond were dark. Monitors buzzed to her left and her right. She stepped out, and then hesitated—more for the watchers than anything else.

After a moment, she headed left. When she was directly under the monitor, she stopped. Gripping the end of her boot tightly, she swung it hard at the light bulb. Glass shattered, spraying across her face and hair. She jerked her head away, closed her eyes, and then shook her head. Glass fell to the floor, as soft as rain. When she opened her eyes again, the monitor lay at an odd angle, one wire torn away from the base.

She repeated the process with the monitor down the other hall, and then she went back to the cellar. With any luck, Jack would think she was destroying the monitors as she went, and he'd hold off any attempt to stop her until it was too late.

She crossed to the vent and squatted down. Air stirred, heavy with the scent of the oncoming storm. She forced her fingers through the wire grate covering the vent and tugged hard. Dirt and rust sprinkled across her fingers. She tugged again and felt the grate give slightly. After several more attempts, it came free. She lay on her stomach and peered inside. The walls were damn thick, if this vent was anything to go by. It was more a small tunnel than an actual vent, and it was at least three feet long. It was also large enough for her to squeeze through, and it led directly outside, not to some sort of duct, as she'd presumed. At the other end, there was a small square of concrete and the bottom of a bluestone wall. Neither gave any indication of what else she might find. She'd have to risk squeezing through.

She pushed forward. The walls closed in instantly, pressing against her shoulders and tearing at her shirt. She shuddered, trying to ignore the image of being trapped like a rat in hole, as she wriggled and forced her body through the vent until she reached the end's opening. She shoved the wire covering off, dragging it back into the hole with her before peering out

Trash bins lined the wall, overflowing with paper and food wrappers. To her right were half a dozen large buildings, some with lights glowing brightly, some dark, and further down the slope were several cars. She knew how to hot-wire a car. Jack had taught her.

To her left was a high wire fence. It was electrified. She could hear the high pitched whine running through the wire, could feel the dance of power—a sensation that was similar yet somehow different from the touch of the storm.

She pushed the rest of the way out and climbed to her feet. Beyond the whine of the fence, beyond the thunder of the approaching storm, someone breathed. A guard was close by. His cologne stung the air, a sharp mix of spices that tickled her nose.

After taking a deep, calming breath, she stepped around the corner. The man was alert, his gun raising so fast it was little more than a blur. But with the night seeming to feed her energy, she was much faster. She clenched her fist and smashed him in the mouth before he could fire the weapon. Like the man in the morgue, he went down like a ton of bricks. She caught him, grunting under the sudden strain of his weight, and slowly lowered him to the ground. She'd hit people before, had hit Jack more than once, and often in anger. Never had she gotten a reaction like this. So what had changed? Had *she* changed in some way, or was it something to do with the weird sense of power running through the night?

She grabbed the man's gun—a laser, just like the one she'd found under Jack's bed. If she could turn off the power running through the fence, the laser would slice through the wire as easily as a fish through water. The slope beyond was tree lined and rocky, but a pregnant woman desperate to see her husband again would have no trouble climbing it.

She stepped over the guard's body and walked to the next corner. No guard, but a monitor on the far corner. If she shut it down, Jack would know where she was. She didn't want that just yet.

She moved back to the vent side of the building. Where was the main power source? Did it come in off the State's resources, or was there a generator of some kind here? Her gaze came to rest on a small structure on the far side of the encampment, close to the parking lot. Generator, she thought, and housed in that building. Why she was so certain, she wasn't sure. Nor did she have the time to worry about it.

After squeezing back through the vent, she walked down to the cell that held the two women. Both glanced up expectantly when she opened the door.

"We heard the noise and hoped you would come," Lyssa said softly, rising from her bed.

"You're going to have to climb through a rather small vent." She glanced at Lyssa's stomach. "Though if you're a shapechanger, it might be easier to simply shift shape."

Lyssa rubbed a hand across her stomach. "I can't. No changer can, when they're pregnant. It's too dangerous for the developing child."

She raised her eyebrows, but didn't argue. "It's going to be tight."

"I would crawl across glass on my hands and knees, if that's what it took to get out of here."

Which was basically what she had to do. "Then follow me." She led them back to the vent. "Jan, you first."

The older woman got down on her stomach and slithered into the tunnel. It was a tight squeeze, and it was only after several minutes of indelicate pushing that Jan made it through to the other side.

"Okay," Jan whispered, and moved back from the vent.

Sam glanced at Lyssa. "Ready?"

Lyssa nodded and began to push herself through the small gap. Although she was much smaller boned than Jan, she was six months pregnant, and her stomach scraped firmly against the rough bluestone walls. She gasped several times, and slight smears of blood touched the blue-gray stones. But she didn't stop. Once her belly was free at the other end, the rest of her slid through easily.

Sam squeezed through after them, and as she climbed to her feet, she listened to the night. Nothing stirred. The strengthening wind bought with it no sound of movement. Safe for a few minutes longer. She led the two women around the corner and checked the pulse of the man she'd belted. Alive, but still out cold.

"You know how to handle one of these?" she asked, handing the laser to Lyssa.

Lyssa nodded, flicking the safety off and sighting the fence. Sam touched her hand, halting further movement.

"The fence is electrified. You shoot now, and they'll know."

"Then what do we do?"

Lyssa's blue eyes studied her for a moment, trusting and yet shrewd. Something in her gaze reminded Sam of Stephan. Even Gabriel. A determination to do what had to be done, perhaps.

"You do nothing but wait here. I'll turn off the power."

"And if we're discovered?" Jan asked, a hint of fear in her voice.

"You shoot. Don't hesitate."

Lyssa nodded. "How will we know when the power's off?"

Her smile was grim. "I intend to make a lot of noise once it is." Hopefully that would draw Jack's attention away from this area. "Once you hear it, you run, and you don't look back."

Again Lyssa nodded. Pain haunted her blue eyes.

"You okay?" she added.

Lyssa hesitated. "I scraped my belly pretty badly getting out." She shifted her hand, revealing a large, bloody tear on the front of her shirt.

"But the baby's okay?"

Lyssa smiled. "Oh yes. The child is an ox. It's just his mother who's the weakling."

"Will you make it up the hill?"

"I made it out of the vent, didn't I?"

That she did. Sam squeezed her shoulder gently. "Just be careful. Once you're clear of this area, contact Gabriel, not Stephan."

Alarm flitted through Lyssa's pale features. "Why?"

She hesitated. She had no right to tell Lyssa about the bomb or the shapeshifter—such information was better coming from someone close. "There have been several attempts on your husband's life. Gabriel has him hidden, and only he knows how to contact him."

The tension in Lyssa's body eased a little. "I know they'd planned for such an event. I'll contact Gabriel first."

"What about my husband?" Jan asked softly. "He should know I'm free, before he's forced to do something by that . . . that monster."

Karl had already been forced down that path. "Wait and see what Gabriel says."

Jan nodded. Sam rose and nudged the unconscious felon with her foot. "If he moves, if he even blinks, shoot him. Don't hesitate."

Tension leapt into the silence, sizzling through the night, but it was coming mainly from Jan rather than Lyssa. The younger woman might look frail, but Sam had a suspicion she was far more dangerous than she looked.

"Good luck, ladies. Hopefully, I'll see you both a bit later."

"May fortune smile kindly on your ventures tonight," Lyssa said softly.

She smiled. The God of good fortune had looked the other way her entire life, so why should that change now? She stepped past them both and moved back to the corner. At the far end she stopped, studying the six buildings critically.

The minute she stepped out into the open, the monitors would have her. And if she didn't do it soon, Jack would send people to look for her.

The fastest route was a direct route. By the time Jack realized she wasn't actually going for a car, she'd hopefully have figured out some way to get rid of the generator. After taking a deep breath to calm the nerves fluttering in her stomach, she ran out of the shadows and into the open. The monitor failed to respond for a second, and then she heard the hum as it clicked into action and began tracking her movements. With a bit of luck, Jack would think she'd come from the main doorway.

She raced across to the nearest building and stopped in the shadows. Her heart raced as fast as a steam train, and her breaths were little more than short gasps—from fear, more than exertion. In the distance, thunder rumbled. Behind that came the pounding of distant rain. Closer, the soft crunch of gravel as someone walked towards her. To her left, on the far side of the nearest building, the soft exhale of air, and a bittersweet smell began to taint the storm-held freshness. Someone was smoking rat-weed, the newest sensation on the drug scene. He was the one to go for—the drug, for all its much vaunted heightening of senses, often had the opposite effect.

The footsteps drew closer. Time to go. Keeping to the shadows as much as possible, she ran across to the next building. With her back pressed hard against the wall, she waited. A man appeared, and then stopped. He studied the shadows where she'd stood only moments before, then raised a hand to his ear.

"She's not here."

So they definitely were tracking her. The man turned, staring straight at her. She froze, barely daring to breathe.

"I'm telling you, she's not here," he repeated.

How could he not see her, when she could see him as plain as day? What game was Jack playing now?

"I don't care what the monitor said, she's gone. Check the other screens."

He moved on. The sound of his steps faded into the distance, yet she couldn't move. What the hell was going on? Foreboding beat a quick tattoo through her heart. Taking another deep breath, she moved on. The smoker was around the far corner.

"Hey, you," she whispered.

He spun, weapon raised. Faster than the first, but still not fast enough. She knocked him out, eased him to the ground, and grabbed his weapon. Another laser. Jack kept his men well armed, if nothing else. She wondered where he'd gotten the money.

She moved on. There was a monitor on the corner of the next building. She raised the laser and shot it. Sparks flew across the darkness, firefly bright. She sighted at the monitor farther along and took that out, too. Then she turned and ran back the way she'd come. Keeping to the side of the buildings and to the shadows, staying out of the range of monitors, she headed for the hut that held the generator.

Shouts rang through the silence, but they were coming from the area where she'd shot out the two monitors. A man appeared from the building to her left. She raised the laser and fired several shots. He went down with a gurgling sound that shuddered through her mind. She'd hit his larynx, probably made him mute. Still a hell of a lot better than death, she thought, shoving the horror of it from her mind. The door to the generator room was locked. Taking aim, she switched the laser to full and shot the lock to smithereens. The door slammed back with the force of the blast.

Inside it was dark and unguarded. Two large generators sat

on the concrete floor, and a small control board was to one side of them. There were far too many buttons on the board. She had no idea which was the right one to turn off the electricity to the fence, and it could take forever to find out. With no time for finesse, she put the laser on full and shot the hell out of the board. Metal and plastic flew, then white light exploded, punching her backwards and snatching the breath from her lungs as she was flung back against the wall. She hit the floor with a grunt. For several seconds, she struggled against the blackness threatening to snatch her mind into unconsciousness. Smoke hissed through the gloom, and red fingers of flame licked the remains of the board. Coughing slightly, she studied the generators. Sparks flew into the darkness, diamond bright against the fire. Electricity tingled across her skin, wild and somehow free. From the storm, not the generators, which were still working. She took aim again and shot them both. Then she ran like hell for the door.

She barely made it.

A gigantic rush of heated air picked her up and threw her sideways. She hit the ground hard, tasting dirt as she slid along it. Heat licked across her back, burning deep. Realizing her shirt was on fire, she rolled, dousing it. Another explosion shuddered through the air. She cowered against the ground, throwing her arms over her head, trying to protect it as deadly spears of wood and metal arrowed through the air. Flames leapt upwards, a gigantic ball that lit the night sky.

If Jan and Lyssa didn't see or hear that, something was definitely wrong with them. Jack wouldn't miss it, that was for certain.

Ignoring the pain of the burns on her back, she scrambled to her feet and ran for the parking lot. She didn't get ten feet before Jack's voice rose from the darkness like a demon from the grave.

"No further, Sam. You've done enough damage for one night."

Jack appeared out of the darkness to her right, holding a laser as powerful as her own. Jack, the vampire, faster than she'd ever be. She swore. The two women needed time to get up that hill and get away. Somehow, she had to provide it.

She fired haphazardly in his direction, and then dove sideways. Blue-red light burned across the ground inches from her feet. She scrambled to her feet and kept on running.

"I don't want to hurt you, Sam."

No. Just use her. Willingly or not. Heat sizzled across the

night air. She leapt for the corner of the nearby building. Sparks flew, gold and white fireflies that danced across her face as the laser blasted a hole inches above her head.

Malevolence stung the night, and evil, then the sound of running steps. Her so-called friend, approaching fast. Shuddering, she scrambled back up and ran on.

"Stop. This is my last warning."

She ignored it, ignored the sense of danger throbbing through her veins. Ignored the spectre of death hovering in the storm held skies. There was a car only a few feet away. Ten seconds was all she needed to get in, hot wire the com-unit and get the car going. Ten seconds. Surely that wasn't asking much.

She didn't make it. Heat blasted into her back, throwing her to the concrete. Her head smashed against the pavement and stars danced before her eyes. She bit back a cry of pain, fighting to stand, fighting to run. To no avail. Her back was locked in fire, and her body refused to obey her wishes.

The last thing she heard before the darkness closed in was Jack's gentle sigh.

Fourteen

Gabriel walked to the edge of the roadside. Nestled in the valley below them was what looked to be a small military encampment. There were seven long red brick or bluestone buildings in all, surrounded by a high wire fence. He had no doubt the fence would be electrified. The men who'd taken Sam were somewhere below them. Whether she was still there was another matter entirely.

He glanced around as Karl joined him at the edge. Hands shoved deep in the pockets of his jacket, Karl studied the camp for several minutes then met Gabriel's gaze. "What do you think?"

"I think it's far too quiet." There were very few lights, except for the couple on the building at the far edge of the camp. There was no movement, no guards that he could see. Everything suggested it was a trap, with a capital T.

"If they'd found the bugs, surely they would have destroyed them."

"Maybe." Maybe not. They were dealing with a warped mind. Kazdan could do anything. "I might take a flight down and see what I—"

The rest of his words were cut off as an explosion ripped across the night. Flames leapt high, burning into the sky as metal and wood flew like sparklers through the camp.

He dropped to the ground, followed almost instantly by Karl. The lights in the far buildings went out, and several shouts could be heard above the noise of the explosion.

"Someone's hit the generator," Karl commented.

He nodded. Maybe someone who wanted the fence taken out. Otherwise, why bother?

Laser fire lit up the night, brighter than the fire. "Someone's heading north, if those shots are anything to go by."

"And someone else is heading up this hill," Karl said. "Listen."

For a moment, he heard nothing, and then came a soft heel scuff, and the sharp clatter of rock tumbling down the slope. He tapped Karl on the shoulder, and then pointed to the right. Karl nodded, and rose to his feet, moving away as silently as a shadow.

Gabriel shifted shape. The wind tucked under his wings, thrusting him up past the tree line. Whoever was climbing the hill wasn't very fit. He could hear their panting as clearly as he could smell the acid tang of the fire.

He swept down the slope, wings brushing the highest tips of the gum trees. Rodents scattered, their high pitched squeals of terror music to his hawk hearing. He ignored them, gliding on. Shadows ran through the trees just ahead—female, rather than male. Their shapes alone told him neither was Sam. Yet both were shapes he knew. He dove through the trees, changing as he neared the ground.

"Lyssa," he called softly.

She turned with a cry of relief, all but falling into his arms. "Oh thank God, Gabriel. I thought I'd never see you again."

He frowned. The woman in his arms was trembling with fear, and the front of her shirt was covered in blood—blood that he could smell more than see. She was also more drawn, and a hell of a lot skinnier, than the Lyssa he'd seen only yesterday.

The second woman stopped and turned around. It was Jan, as he'd half expected. "You okay?" he asked, over Lyssa's head.

Jan nodded but wrapped her arms around her body, as if in an effort to stop her sudden shivering. The bushes to his left rustled. He tensed and then relaxed as Karl stepped through. Jan ran to him. Karl hugged her so tightly Gabriel thought he'd squeeze the life out of her.

He stepped away from Lyssa, holding her at arm's length, his gaze searching her pale face. "Tell me what happened."

"A police officer freed us. She told us to run up this hill."

Relief coursed through him. Sam, surely. "She's still down there?"

Lyssa's blue eyes regard him curiously. "You know her?"

"We're working together." As Lyssa would have known, had she actually been the shifter who'd spent the last few months at his brother's side. He glanced at Karl. "We have to get them out of here." Before Kazdan came looking for them—before Sam got caught again.

He touched Lyssa's arm and helped her up the slope. Karl all but carried his wife. Maybe the sudden relief of seeing him had sapped all her strength. But it seemed to take forever to reach the top. He bit back his impatience, his need to go find Sam, and helped Lyssa over to the car. Family came first, and Lyssa, the real Lyssa, was family.

When she was safely settled in the back seat, he closed the door and leaned on the top of the car, watching Karl help his wife into the front.

Karl met his gaze once she was in. "Thank you," was all he said.

They'd been friends for a long time, and Gabriel knew that the simple thank you encompassed a whole lot more—like, thank you for letting me help, thank you for trusting me again. He nodded. He'd confided in Karl on all but his brother's secrets for nigh on ten years, and his brother had trusted Karl with the one secret that mattered. Now that Karl had proven to be vulnerable to attack, they'd have to arrange for the information about Stephan to be wiped from his mind. But that didn't mean he was no longer worthy of trust or friendship. And had the situation been reversed, had it been him in Karl's position, he would have done exactly the same thing. Most men would have. And most men would *not* have taken the risk of bugging his threateners. That more than anything told him where Karl's allegiances truly lay.

"I want you to get the rest of your family and get the hell out of Victoria. Go to New South Wales or Queensland or wherever for a while. Tell no one—not your company, not Jan's folks, not your folks." He hesitated, then got out his cell phone, handing it across. "I'll call you when it's safe to return."

Karl took the phone and nodded. "What about your lady friend?"

"I'm going down to get her."

"Not Sam—I mean the woman in the car."

"Lyssa?" He'd never told Karl about Lyssa. She was part of Stephan's life, a secret his brother wished kept for safety's sake. Only Mary and Martyn had known. And one of them had betrayed her to Kazdan. "Take her with you. For now, that's best."

He bent and lightly tapped the window. Lyssa wound it down and studied him expectantly. "You're not taking me to Stephan, are you?"

He shook his head. "Not yet. Not till it's safe. Stephan will kill me if I lose you now."

"Is he all right?"

"He's fine. Don't believe the news reports, no matter what they say. I'll let him contact you as soon as I can." He shifted slightly to let Karl climb into the car. "You're safe with Karl and his family. I'll see you in a couple of days."

She nodded solemnly. He glanced back to Karl. "Be careful."

"I'm not going to lose anyone else to that creep," Karl muttered. "And you're the one who should be careful. He seems to know an awful lot about your family and your friends."

He nodded. As they drove away, he shapechanged, winging his way down the mountain after them to ensure they got away safely. Then he wheeled around and headed back to the camp. Kazdan was on the move.

He saw two men carry Sam to a large white van and put her inside. Kazdan climbed in after her, and the van moved off. Several other cars were lined up in the parking lot. Men scurried ant-like from the buildings to the vehicles, carrying all manner of equipment. No one made any attempt to fight the fire.

Fire trucks were approaching fast, but he doubted if they'd be in time to stop the clean out. And while he'd love to know just what Kazdan was up to down there, Sam had to be his first priority, because she seemed to be Kazdan's first priority. With a flick of his wings, he headed east, after the first van.

They drove for about an hour. The wind grew stronger, buffeting his wings and carrying with it the salty tang of the sea. He studied the horizon. Beyond the dusting of house lights, beyond the trees that danced and swayed to the music of the breeze, he could see the ocean—a blanket of foam washed blue-black. They were nearing Western Port Bay.

Kazdan turned before he got to the beach road, heading inland for several miles, finally slowing as he approached an isolated farmhouse.

Gabriel drifted closer. A familiar tingle ran through his limbs, a warning that he was approaching a changer shield. Why would they have something like that way out here? It was the sort of device used to protect military installations, not isolated farmhouses. He flicked his wings, soaring left, wondering just how large the shield was. A blue-white light speared out of the darkness below him. Before he could turn away, before he could react in any way, it hit, flaring bright against his chest.

He couldn't move. Couldn't fly.

All he could do was watch the fast approach of the ground as he plummeted towards it.

***

Pain washed through every muscle, every cell. Sam's whole body ached. It felt as if it were being stretched, being invaded somehow. Sam groaned, and even that hurt. Her throat felt like sandpaper and was as dry as a desert. Her tongue seemed swollen and rasped harshly against the roof of her mouth.

Boot heels echoed softly against metal, coming towards her. She tried to open her eyes, but they felt so heavy they might have been weighted down by concrete. It took several attempts before she managed to open them, and even then, her vision was reduced to mere slits.

The harsh light made her blink back tears.

"I did ask if you'd do this the easy way," Jack said, somewhere to her left. "It would have been so much better."

The warmth had gone from his tone, leaving only harshness. Or maybe it had always been like that, and she'd never noticed it before now.

"What have you done?" Her question came out a cracked whisper. She tried to swallow, but she couldn't. Maybe he'd sucked all the moisture away, as easily as he sucked the life from others.

"Nothing much, yet. There are plenty of tests left to try."

He sounded almost jovial. The footsteps came closer, and then she could see him. His smile, like the light in his eyes, was one of a conqueror about to demolish his foe. Had she been able to draw enough moisture together, she would have spat at him.

"This isn't exactly a good way to get me to help you," she said. "I think it's achieving the opposite."

His smile was serene. "By the time I'm finished with you, my friend, you'll be begging me to let you help."

He certainly didn't know her very well if he thought she would ever beg. Still, the viciousness behind his words shook her. This man, this demon, called himself her friend, yet he was more than willing to tear her apart. "Why are you doing this?"

"Because I prefer to be a leader rather than a follower. Because I'm sick of pussyfooting around." He motioned to someone beyond her line of sight. "Now, lie back and enjoy the ride."

Like hell she would. She lashed out, trying to catch him unawares. Metal bit into her wrist, cold and hard, stopping her arm from rising any more than an inch or so. Similar metal clamps bit into her ankles and neck.

Jack laughed. "I'm not foolish enough to let you loose a second time. You'll stay here until I've finished."

"Damn you for this, Jack." Damn him for destroying a friendship she'd held dear. Even if it was a friendship based on a lie, *she'd* believed in it.

His laugh was edged with sadness. "I was damned a long time ago, Sam. Now I must live with it the best I can."

Heat began to creep through her fingers and toes, a tingling warmth that made her skin itch, made her heart leap uncomfortably in her chest. Then pain hit, sucking at her strength, leeching away her consciousness. Soon there was nothing but a well of darkness, and she fell into it screaming.

***

He was in a boat that rocked gently back and forth, a soothing sensation that failed to ease the alarms ringing in his mind, forcing him towards consciousness. The breeze pulled at his hair cooled the warm moisture trickling down his face and back. Somewhere above him, leaves sighed, and branches groaned under the increasing strength of the wind.

He became aware of something hard biting deep into his stomach. To his left, wood splintered, a sound not unlike the cracking of a tree branch.

Confused, wondering where the hell he was, Gabriel opened his eyes. The ground was a good twenty feet away, rising and dipping in sickening motion.

He closed his eyes, and then opened them again. No difference. He looked to his left and saw the long arm of a tree reaching towards him—and realized he was wrapped around it, arms and legs dangling on either side. That's what was biting into his gut—the shattered ends of an offshoot branch.

He twisted slightly and looked up. Smashed branches gave evidence of his descent, but the tree had undoubtedly saved his life. With the speed he'd been going, if he'd hit the ground, he surely would have died.

Somewhere off to his right, brush rustled. He stilled, listening. Something beeped, and then a voice rose from the silence like a ghost from the mist.

"I told you, I haven't spotted a goddamn thing. You sure he came down this way?"

The silence seemed to stretch, jarring against his nerves. Then the searcher spoke again, closer this time. "Okay, Okay, I'll do another sweep."

A man stepped into the clearing below him. Short brown hair, balding on top, and a hawklike nose. Danny Fowler, Gabriel thought, gun for hire. He'd disappeared from the circuit five or six months ago, and like everyone else, he'd presumed Danny's violent past had finally caught up with him. If he was now working for Kazdan, then something big was going down. Fowler was a loner from way back.

He watched Fowler walk across the clearing and disappear

into the thick shrub. After several seconds of silence, he grabbed the tree branch, flipping his legs over. Wood caught at his stomach, tearing deep gashes. More pain flared across his shoulders as his arms took the brunt of his weight. The tree branched dipped slightly, and the crack of wood splintering echoed across the silence, as sharp as a gunshot. Cursing softly, he dropped to the ground, landing catlike, his fingertips digging into the dirt to steady himself. Hot lances of fire shot up the backs of his legs, and moisture began to run down his spine. He ignored both, listening. Shrubs moved to his left. He ducked behind the trunk of the gum that had saved his life.

Fowler reentered the clearing, his gun—a standard laser rifle—raised, and his beady eyes narrowed as he sighted. He studied the clearing for several seconds, then relaxed and glanced up at the tree. Even from where Gabriel crouched, it was easy to see the understanding dawn in Fowler's eyes. He had to act now, while he still had the advantage of surprise.

He launched himself at Fowler. The short man aimed and fired. The shot hissed though the air, burned past Gabriel's ear, and hit the tree trunk. He didn't have time for a second shot, because Gabriel was on him, tackling him to the ground and forcing the weapon out of his grip. Fowler cursed and punched, his blows landing thick and fast. Pain rolled through Gabriel, but he ignored it, ignored the blows raining on his body, and, with as much force as he could muster, chopped his hand down on Fowler's windpipe. Fowler was dead before he even knew it.

Gabriel blew out a breath, climbed off Fowler's body and patted him down. There was a knife strapped to his left wrist, and a small two-way in his right jacket pocket. He took the knife, squashed the two-way under his heel and stripped off Fowler's jacket. Then he tore off the bloody remnants of his own shirt, and dragged the body into the bushes.

Using what was left of his shirt, he wiped the blood off his stomach and back. The wounds on his stomach were a good quarter of an inch deep each, and oozing steadily. He could also feel warm stickiness across his back and down the side of his face. Trophies from his descent through the tree, no doubt. There wasn't anything he could do about the bleeding right now, other than hope there were no feline shapechangers in the immediate area—they'd smell his scent a mile off. He tossed the bloodied shirt on top of Fowler's body and covered both with leaf litter.

After pulling on Fowler's jacket and zipping it up, he grabbed the rifle and checked the laser's charge. Nearly full. Good. He turned and made his way to the bushes where Fowler had first appeared. A faint path wound its way through the trees, heading down the hillside.

He followed it carefully, listening intently to the sigh of the wind, alert for any hint of pursuit or discovery. He was halfway down the hillside when several buildings became visible through the trees below. Squatting, he studied them. It looked like an everyday farm, only this farm, unlike most others, had a helicopter pad, complete with a silver bird. It also had a sentry guarding the entrance to its driveway. The slight shimmer in the air near the guard's box suggested the gates themselves were an energy field.

As he watched, a car pulled up to the guard's box. The car's windows were tinted so dark it was impossible to see the driver. Meaning the passenger was possibly a vampire. The sentry walked across, talking to the driver for several minutes. Then he stepped back, and the shimmer of energy died.

The car drove on and came to a stop near the front porch. A woman climbed out, then hesitated, her gaze searching the hillside. Mary, Gabriel thought, surprised. Mary, who was supposed to be a vampire and yet was standing there in the full sunshine. She turned, studying the trees in which he hid. Perhaps she'd sensed his presence. She'd always been intuitive that way.

After several seconds, she headed for the front door and disappeared inside.

He continued down the hill. As he neared the fence, energy zipped across his skin, as sharp as a knife. He picked up a rock near his feet and gently tossed it forward. One foot away from the fence line, there was a sharp whine, then a flash of white light, and the rock shattered. The remaining dust drifted to the ground. He picked up another rock, this time aiming far higher. The result was the same.

So, they didn't only have the front gate guarded by an energy field. The generators had to be either in the sheds or underground, because they weren't anywhere else that he could see. Given that the sky was also shielded, the front gate was obviously the only way in and out, at least until the generators were knocked off-line.

Which meant he'd have to take out the guard. Keeping low, he raced along the fence line until he was level with the sentry box. Then, getting down on one knee, he sighted the laser on the tree just behind the box and fired. There was a sharp crack, then the branch he'd aimed for fell almost gracefully to the ground. The guard scrambled out, weapon raised.

Gabriel sighted again and fired. The guard dropped and didn't move. He waited several seconds, not sure whether there was a second guard inside. When no one appeared, he made his way down to the road.

The guard was dead. With a hole the size of a fist shot through his gut, it came as no surprise. Knowing the guard would have done the same to him given half a chance, he stepped over the guard's body, feeling no remorse, and entered the sentry box.

A half-eaten sandwich and a tattered Playboy magazine rested on the shelf near a small com-screen. He moved over to the unit and watched the images flickering on the screen. Mary came into view, walking swiftly along a corridor that curved to the left, gradually taking her out of the camera's sight. The image flickered and changed, this time revealing a room filled with coffin shaped boxes. After several seconds it changed again, sweeping across the front of the farmyard.

No one was about—at least, no one he could see. He had no doubt there *would* be guards. It was just a matter of where. All he had to do was get into the house. He pressed a button on the com-unit. Nothing happened. The energy field remained in place.

"Computer, disengage gate."

The computer hummed softly, and then a metallic voice said. "Please confirm identity."

He swore softly, then spun and walked out to the fallen sentry. Ignoring the stench of burned flesh, Gabriel rolled him over and patted him down. In the shirt pocket he found what he was looking for—a security tag.

He dragged the body to the back of the sentry box, then went inside and swiped the card. The computer hummed.

"Gate disengaging. Twenty seconds before field is reengaged."

He pocketed the security card, and headed through the gate. The farmhouse was as quiet as it had looked on the screen, and the closer he got to the old building, the more obvious it became that the farmhouse hadn't been used in some time. The place smelled of neglect, dust and mildew. So why had Mary gone in there? And where had Kazdan gone? And the trucks?

He ducked past a window and walked quietly along the front porch, stopping near the door. Through the wire mesh he could see half a room. Faded daisy wallpaper hung in tattered strips from the walls, swaying gently in the breeze. Dust gathered in the corner, along with an old mouse trap, the cheese long gone.

Yet, the room wasn't as empty as it looked. Someone breathed softly, a whisper sound barely distinguishable from the sigh of the wind. Like him, they were standing close to the door, close to the wall.

He waited, not moving. After several long minutes, the watcher muttered. Then soft steps crossed the wooden floors, and a chair squeaked. Stepping back, Gabriel raised the laser, sighting along the wall until he reached the approximate position of the squeaking chair. Then he fired. The acid smell of smoke and burnt wood stung the air. After a moment, the smell of burnt flesh began to taint the air.

He kicked the door open and rolled through, gun at the ready. No angry shots greeted his arrival. The guard lay slumped over a com-unit, half his chest burned away.

Gabriel did a quick check of the rest of the room, noting only one other exit. He rose and walked across to the com-unit. This one had print identification. Old fashioned, but still reasonably effective in an outpost like this. He grabbed the dead man's hand and pressed it against the screen. The door to his left clicked open, revealing the corridor he'd seen Mary disappear down.

He approached it warily. The corridor was long and white, and it wound down several levels before flattening out. He stepped forward and peered over the handrail. No one below, either. Still, it was better to be safe than sorry. He kept his back to the wall as he moved down.

The corridor did a sharp right at the bottom of the ramp. Halfway down were two doors, both closed. He eyed them, unable to ignore the uneasiness beginning to weight his gut. Something just didn't feel right. It wasn't like Kazdan to be so haphazard with his security.

He checked the laser's charge—half full. Probably not enough to handle the trouble he sensed waiting ahead. Keeping the weapon at the ready, he moved forward. The sensor above the door to his right blinked to green as he neared, and a heartbeat later, the door silently opened. He stopped, body tense, ready to retreat or attack. The only sound he heard was the soft hum of the air-con. He dug the security card from his pocket, and tossed it into the room. There was a quick whine, like that of a motor gearing to life, then a white flash. The card flamed briefly as the laser burned it, the ashes falling softly to the floor. Obviously, there were movement-sensing laser rifles inside, which meant that while it was definitely a room he should investigate, it was a no-go for now.

The other door was locked. He edged past it and continued on. The corridor curved to the left, and another door came into view. The sensor above the door flicked to green as he approached, and the door opened, revealing several long rows of coffins.

The uneasy sense that something was wrong was growing. It had been far too easy to get this far. Kazdan was up to something—or was he giving the man too much credit? Surely if Kazdan was aware of his presence, he would have stopped him before now. Still, despite the sense that he was walking into trouble, he really only had two choices—and retreat had never been an option he'd favored.

After taking a deep breath, he dove through the doorway, coming to his feet behind the first row of coffins, laser-rifle primed and ready to fire. No white flash greeted his appearance. Inching upwards, he swept the laser's sight across the room. No one. Frowning, he relaxed a little and glanced at the nearest coffin. Metal, not wood. Odd, because metal was usually only used to contain the newly turned. After checking the room a second time, and noting the exit across the far side of the room, he slowly opened the coffin.

The woman inside was little more than a teenager, with long blonde hair, rich brown skin, and a build that could only be described as voluptuous. Why would Kazdan be recruiting people like this? Sure, the girl was pretty, but the softness in her face suggested she'd led a sheltered, easy life. How would someone like this help him start—or maintain—a war? Wouldn't it make more sense to recruit people he could use as bullet fodder? Even then, as one of the newly turned, his creations would be next to useless for several months. Their thoughts would be consumed by the desire to feed, even as they tried to understand the onslaught of new abilities, new sensations that were often a fast track to madness for the freshly turned vampire.

He lifted the woman's hand, and felt her wrist for a pulse. After a several minutes, he found it. A single beat, unsteady, weak, but nevertheless there. The girl was still turning. It would be another day or so before the unsteady beat settled into its regular pattern of one beat every three minutes, and only then would she wake. Was this girl one of the names on the list? What price had she paid to join the ranks of the undead? And why?

He turned and looked at the other coffins. If he'd had the time, he would check them all, but he didn't have time. Kazdan was gathering an army, and it didn't really matter if that army was filled with women as soft as the blonde. What mattered was how many more he'd created.

And if Sethanon was as all-powerful as they'd presumed, why would he let a lieutenant build an army like this right under his nose?

He frowned and closed the coffin lid. The SIU would have to be called in to decontaminate the place. But first, he had to find Sam. And Kazdan. He hefted the rifle to a more comfortable position then walked across to the next door. Again the sensor opened it as he approached.

The room beyond was silent, but he had a bad feeling someone was in there, waiting. He dove through and rolled upright, rifle at the ready. And found himself staring into the barrel of a laser cannon.

"Don't move, Gabriel dear, or I'll blow your beautiful eyes through the back of your fucking head."

Fifteen

Voices broke through the darkness, voices Sam knew, voices she was beginning to fear—for with them came the onslaught of more tests, more pain. Better by far to remain in the secure safety of dark unconsciousness. Yet something within her struggled through the layers of pain, struggled to hear and understand. Gradually, the words became clearer.

"You keep on with these tests, and you'll kill her." The speaker was a woman. The sultry tones were familiar, even if the worry that edged her words wasn't.

"She is more than any of us had guessed. More than even Sethanon guessed. She is our key."

Jack's voice, cold and hard.

"And she will be no damn good to us dead!" Anger filled the woman's voice. Visions of Stephan's wife, Lyssa, swam through Sam's mind. But if this woman was Lyssa, how did she know Jack? And why was she here—wherever here was—defending her? "Look at her, Jack—she's barely alive. Look at the heart monitor."

She could almost feel Jack's scowl. "I only have two or three tests to go."

"Two or three tests we don't need. Unless, of course, it is your intention to kill her."

"Why the sudden concern?" Jack's voice held a mocking note. "I thought you couldn't wait to get her out of my life?"

Sam frowned. Why would Lyssa want her out of Jack's life? This was making no sense—her thoughts stopped. There were two women called Lyssa. The one she'd met at Stephan's place, and the one she'd rescued from Jack's cell. This was the first Lyssa, the fake, Sam was sure of it.

So why was the fake defending her? Especially given the hostility the woman had thrown her way at Stephan's?

"That's before I saw her in action myself. I owe her my life, Jack. If she hadn't found that bomb Mary set, I'd be paste right now."

Jack snorted. "Have you seen the stupid bitch?"

"No. Stern advised Stephan to separate us, and he tried to send me to some military compound."

"Then maybe he suspected you."

"Suspected his best friend's wife? Not likely."

"Stern's no fool. You must have said or done something to raise his suspicions."

"And maybe it was your precious little partner that made him suspicious. If she could sense the presence of the kites, sense the clone was a vampire, why couldn't she sense I'm not who I'm supposed to be?"

"None of the tests I've performed show any true strength in that field."

They hadn't? Then what the hell was he looking for? What had he found, if not her growing ability to sense some human races?

"And yet she knew Mary was up to no good, something I wasn't aware of even though I'd practically lived with the ungrateful witch for the last six months."

That sounded like Suzy. Even the haughty iciness in her tone was all Suzy. Were she and the fake Lyssa both in the room?

"You never were the most observant person in the world, my love."

My love? There was only one person he called that—Suzy. Then memory hit. Suzy was a shifter, and since she was currently alternating between her own voice and Lyssa's, she was obviously capable of multiple images. Obviously, she was the woman who'd been impersonating Lyssa.

Yet, it was odd that Jack would allow his wife to live with, and undoubtedly make love to, another man. He wasn't the type to share.

"I was observant enough to see Karl leave the mansion. It got you Sam's com-unit."

"But not observant enough to realize Martyn was watching you. It's thanks to Mary you didn't get caught. Half our current problems would be over if you'd simply poisoned Stephan when you were supposed to."

"It's not my fault it wasn't working fast enough."

"I told you to increase the dosage."

"And I told you it was too damn dangerous." She paused, and Sam could well imagine her tossing her long hair haughtily. "He's dead now, so it doesn't matter."

Stephan was dead? When did that happen? She remembered the anguish in Gabriel's eyes when he'd learned that Hanrahan might have been caught in the SIU bombing. How would he cope losing his brother and his friend? Not well, she suspected.

"No thanks to you," Jack all but snarled.

"Damn it, look at the monitors—she's weakening. If you want her help to overthrow Sethanon, you're going to have to stop these tests right now."

Jack cursed softly. "You're right. I need to find Mary, anyway. She's supposed to be here with the final times for the PM's schedule. The boss will be peeved if I don't confirm in the next hour or two."

The edge in his voice suggested Sethanon was someone you didn't want angry at you. So why was Jack attempting a take over? Surely that would piss off Sethanon a hell of a lot more than being late with a schedule.

"So the hit's still going ahead?"

"What Sethanon wishes, Sethanon gets. At least until I'm completely ready to take over."

Suzy sniffed. "The longer you wait, the more chance there is of discovery, especially with Stern nosing about."

"Some things can't be rushed, my love. Why don't you find me someone to eat, while I go make some phone calls?"

"And her? You can't leave her here."

"I'll get Roston to take her to a cell. Let her sleep it off for a while."

Their voices faded, leaving her spinning in the wash of darkness and pain. Her whole body tingled, as if every nerve ending, every cell, had been forced to life, waking and stretching to discover new boundaries. The beat of her heart was an unsteady drum that pounded in her chest, echoing past her ears, and vibrating the cold metal table beneath her. But it was a rhythm that was weakening.

Time was something she lost all sense of. It might have been hours, or it might have only been minutes, before she became aware that she was no longer alone in the room. Became aware that another heart beat in unsteady time with her own.

"Samantha."

The voice was soft and deep and pulled at the darkness of her past. She had a sudden image of a boy, green eyed with red-gold hair. Saw him laughing as he shouted for her to catch him if she could.

But this was no boy. This was a man.

"Samantha, you must listen to me."

She frowned. The man's voice sounded vaguely familiar. She had another vision, this time of the hirsute stranger who'd come buzzing at her door just before the first bombing. But why would he be here? Or was her mind merely playing games to pass the time?

"No games, Samantha. Listen to me."

He was reading her thoughts, and so had the red-haired boy of her childhood. She'd felt no fear back then, nor did she fear him now.

"You cannot die, Samantha. It would kill us both."

Better death than swimming in this sea of pain. And how would her death kill that shaggy stranger? Or the red-haired boy?

"Samantha! Listen to me. Grasp my hand."

A hand touched hers. Warmth radiated across her fingers, through her skin. But she could barely even breathe. Her lungs were burning, her mind spinning. The simple act of clasping a hand seemed the equivalent of climbing Everest right now.

"Fight, Samantha. You've done it your entire life. Don't give up now."

Who was giving up? Wasn't she just facing fact? Still, determination rose from God knew where at his comment. She concentrated, focusing her thoughts, her strength, on her hand. Through the haze of white-hot pain, she moved her fingers and clasped them within the stranger's warm grip.

"We are part of the whole, Samantha. Two halves, each the same but very different. I cannot be if you are not."

The stranger's words made no sense. It didn't matter. The warmth of his grip flooded her system, washing away all the pain. It soothed the throbbing ache tearing her cells apart and eased the unsteady pounding of her heart. Soon there was nothing in the darkness but the need to sleep, the need to recoup her strength and just rest.

The warmth of the stranger's touch disappeared. "No," she mentally whispered.

His smile was a sun, rising brightly in the darkness. "I am never far away, Samantha." A hand caressed her forehead—it was the touch of a loved one, not a lover. "Roston will be here in a moment to take you to a cell. Rest for an hour, and then wake. Get Stern and get out of here."

Gabriel was here? And how could they escape a cell without a key-coder? Jack had taken hers when he'd stripped off her shoes to place the sensors.

"Here." The stranger slid something metallic gently through her sweaty hair. "Use this pin. It's old fashioned, but it's still effective enough, at least on the locks round this place. Stern will know how to use it, if you don't."

He said Stern like it was a curse. As if this hirsute man and Gabriel were old foes.

Again she felt his smile. "That we are. And I would leave him to rot in hell except for the fact you would come back to rescue him."

She probably would. If only so he could back her story and clear the ridiculous murder charge hanging over her head.

"One other thing, Samantha."

What?

"Kill Kazdan if you get the chance. He deserves nothing more than death for doing this to you." The binding around her limbs and neck loosened. "Keep well, little one."

"Bye," she whispered. Suddenly, she had a vision of the red-haired boy, tears streaming down his face and desperately fighting the grip of the two doctors holding him down, screaming good-bye as they dragged her away.

***

"Ease the laser to the floor, Gabriel, then kick it across to me."

He had no choice but to obey. The cannons were renowned for their hair triggers. He'd be dead before he twitched. Slowly, carefully, he lowered the rifle to the floor. At least he still had the knife. If he got Mary talking and kept her talking, she might just relax enough for him to use it.

"Imagine meeting you here."

Her smile was almost weary. "Move across to the chair. Twitch the wrong way, and I will shoot."

He did as she asked. He rested his arms on the table's surface and silently studied her. She seemed to have aged almost overnight. Her full features looked haggard, her skin pallid and somewhat shiny. Even her blue eyes, usually so warm and full of life, looked haunted.

"Why," he asked softly.

She grimaced and sat down on a packing crate, the laser gripped steadily and still aimed between his eyes. "Why become a vampire, or why betray the cause?"

"Both."

Her face became bitter. "Look at me, Gabriel. I'm old. You and Stephan remain eternally young while I just fade away."

"Shifters and changers have longer life spans than humans. We do age, Mary. Just at a slower rate." All of which she knew and obviously didn't like.

"Yeah, but once I'd held such dreams . . ."

For an instant he saw the glimmer of tears in her eyes and realized, with a sense of shock, those dreams had involved either Stephan or himself. Or even both.

"We never knew," he said softly. And even in her most insane moments, she surely couldn't have thought that both of them would ever love her.

Her soft snort was caustic. "No. You never did. I was the trusted nanny, the trusted friend. Never in line to be the trusted lover."

What could he say? She spoke a truth he could not deny. She was a friend they'd shared their life with, but never their hearts.

"Your silence says it all." Her tone was bitter, eyes hard.

He shrugged. "I'm sorry."

"Yeah, right." She shifted the cannon slightly. The laser hummed briefly to life then faded again as the pressure on the trigger eased. "The worst of it was watching Stephan fall for Lyssa, knowing all the while that my chances with you were also slipping away. Then, finally, you met her."

Her? Her who? "There's no woman in my life."

"So I can just jump right in and fill the void of loneliness, huh?" She laughed bitterly. "I saw you with her. You don't fool me."

The only woman she'd seen him with was Sam. Why in hell would Mary presume them to be lovers? Unless she was so consumed by jealousy that any female in his life—colleague or friend—would fuel her insane anger. Maybe that was the reason behind her attempt to kill them all at the mansion.

"So when did you decide to betray all that we believe in?"

She shrugged. "Three years ago."

Which would have been about six months after Stephan had married Lyssa. And about the time Mary had gone on an extended cruise—a ruse, obviously, as it was undoubtedly the time she'd been turned. "Why join Sethanon?"

"I didn't join Sethanon. I joined Kazdan. I realized that if love was out, I wanted power. Kazdan offered it to me."

She was a fool if she believed Kazdan would share a piece of the humanity pie. "You were one of our inner circle, Mary. One of the two we trusted."

"And yet, how much did I ever really know? You and Stephan play your cards very close to your chests. I was your runner, not your lieutenant." She paused, anger touching her expression. "You never even told me that Stephan was Hanrahan. Odd, considering how much you supposedly trusted me."

Yet, knowing them as she did, she should surely realize that that was the exact type of information they would keep close. "So who did tell you?"

She grimaced. "Who do you think?"

"Kazdan." And if Kazdan knew, did Sethanon? Or was that the sort of information a man intent on claiming a throne might keep to himself? He had to hope so, because otherwise, the Stephan who ran Federation was going to have to go the way of Hanrahan. "Not even Martyn knew about Hanrahan, Mary. You're not alone there."

"Martyn didn't grow up with you. I did. You never fully trusted me. You never told me all I needed to know. That hurts, Gabriel."

She knew enough to get Lyssa kidnapped and to train the replacement so impeccably that no one had picked it up until Sam came along. No wonder so many of their missions had gone sour—Mary, who'd been in on most planning sessions, had obviously passed the information on to Kazdan, who'd promptly arranged a neat little ambush.

"Is that why you decided to blow us all up at the mansion?"

She grimaced. "You made me angry, defending that woman, touching her and looking at her all the time. Someone like her had no right to what you refused me."

And that made about as much sense as nearly everything else she'd said so far. "So you decided to set off the bomb that had been placed there to take out Stephan later in the month." It was a guess, but it was a pretty safe one, since Kazdan had said both he and Stephan were due for termination. It would have been very easy for Mary to time the explosion with his and Stephan's biweekly meetings.

She nodded. "As I said, I was angry."

What she was was insane. "How did you ever hope to live through the force of that blast?"

"No one told me it was that big."

He shook his head, unable to believe she could be so stupid after all she'd seen in her time with the Federation. "So, Kazdan offered you eternal afterlife and great wealth, and you jumped at the opportunity."

"Look at me, Gabriel. I didn't want to be some old hag you

looked after out of pity. I didn't want to die living in some poorly heated nursing home, surrounded by dozens of old geezers who can't even hold their own water."

Neither did he, but he doubted he'd ever abandon all he believed in just to gain life everlasting. Besides, in the end, even vampires died, many by their own hand. Few were able to face the weight of the years, the weight of watching life come and go while they remained eternal. Sooner or later even they had to face the choices they'd made in their long life.

And if the haunted, almost hunted, light in Mary's eyes was anything to go by, she was only now realizing that herself.

"We paid you well. And we would have looked after you."

Her smile held a hint of sadness. "I know you would have. But that's not what I wanted."

What she wanted she could never have had. Not from Stephan, and not from himself. "And has Kazdan kept his end of the deal?"

The sadness increased. "Oh yes. Afterlife is more than I ever imagined."

By the mocking note in her voice, he guessed her discoveries had been more bad than good. So many people discovered too late that vampirism was more than just eternal life and fast reflexes. It was never walking in the sun without head to toe total protection, never tasting the tang of wine, or enjoying the richness of food for no more than the few minutes it took for it all to come back up. It was watching those you love die of old age and ending up eternally alone. At least Stephan had gone into the ritual with his eyes wide open.

He studied her for a minute longer, seeing the tiredness, the edge of fear, behind her haunted blue gaze. Then he leaned back in the chair and carefully shifted his hands off the desk.

"What now?" he asked softly.

"Now, I'd better get you to Kazdan."

He painstakingly eased the cuff of the jacket over the knife sheath. The laser shifted, and he stopped, waiting until Mary appeared to relax again.

"You don't have to give me to Kazdan. You can just turn around, walk away, and let me take care of him for you."

"Then I'd be left with the problem of making a comfortable living. I've thrown my lot in with Kazdan. Now I must live with it."

The cuff came free of the sheath. He pulled the knife out

with his fingertips. "Stephan and I would look after you."

She laughed, a short, angry sound. "Do I look like a fool? After all I've done, do you really think I'd believe Stephan would let me live?"

He shrugged and gripped the knife, getting ready to throw it. He'd only have one chance. He'd better be accurate the first time.

"I'm sorry, Mary," he repeated, voice soft. Sorry he couldn't love her. Sorry he had to kill her.

He studied her for a moment, fixing her image in his mind, seeing beyond the layers of anger and warped jealousy to the gentle soul that must still be somewhere within her. She'd cared for him and Stephan as youngsters, guided them as wild teenagers. He'd never thought he'd be repaying all those years with death.

She nudged the laser toward the door. "Rise carefully and go through there."

Good-bye, my friend, he thought, then rose and threw the knife in one smooth movement. He didn't wait to see the result, but launched himself straight at her.

She was fast—but not as fast as he. The blade punched through her wrist rather than her heart, but the shock of the blow made her drop the laser. He hit her a heartbeat later, knocking her sideways, away from the weapon. He threw out an arm as he rolled to his feet, snagging the laser and firing quickly.

There was no sound, just a bright flash of white. Mary's brains, and the wall immediately behind her, became nothing more than black dust.

He turned and walked to the door, refusing to look back. He didn't want his last image, his last memory, of her to be that of a headless corpse.

The corridor beyond was quiet. Darkness shadowed the corridor to his left. He headed right, figuring that whatever Kazdan intended with Sam, he wouldn't be doing it in the dark. Or at least, he hoped he wasn't. He'd barely walked ten feet when the man in question suddenly appeared.

"Laser down, Stern."

He was tempted, very tempted, to simply blow the bastard's brains out. Even though Kazdan had his gun aimed and ready, it would be a close race. But with Sam still hostage, he simply couldn't take the risk. For the second time that day, he eased a laser to the floor.

"Suzy," Kazdan murmured, his gaze never wavering.

Kazdan's slender, dark-haired wife appeared around the corner. She carefully picked up the cannon.

"I'd love to kill you right here and now," Kazdan said conversationally. "But unfortunately, you have something I want."

Gabriel hadn't a clue what that could be, but he wasn't about to argue about anything that saved his life. "Then maybe we could make a trade."

Kazdan smiled, revealing bloodied canines. Gabriel hoped the neck he'd been feeding on wasn't Sam's.

"She's mine, Stern. Always was."

Maybe. And maybe Kazdan was misjudging the depth of Sam's strength, the depth of her will and honesty. She couldn't join with Kazdan—not willingly. If there was one thing he'd learned over the last few days, it was that evil simply wasn't a part of her makeup.

"If you believe that, then you are a fool."

Kazdan's eyes narrowed. He'd guessed right. Sam wasn't a willing partner in anything.

"Where are the disks, Stern?"

He raised his eyebrows. Sam had obviously hidden them. He wondered when she'd found the time. "Somewhere safe."

Kazdan's growl was a soft sound of anger and frustration. "I can shoot you right here and now."

"Then you'll never get the disks, will you?" He studied Kazdan steadily, wondering just how important those disks were to his schemes. "I want to see Sam. I want to know she's okay before I tell you one damn thing."

Kazdan considered him for a long moment, and then glanced at his watch. "Can't hurt, I suppose. Suzy, check him."

He watched the woman approach, debating whether he should grab her and use her as a hostage. But he wasn't entirely sure Kazdan wouldn't just shoot them both and be done with it. Suzy patted him down briskly and efficiently, but she made no attempt to undo the knife sheath. It was empty and useless, anyway.

"Clean," she said, stepping back.

Kazdan nodded. "Keep moving, Stern. And remember, one wrong move and I will kill you. I'm not that desperate for the disks."

He smiled grimly. The mere fact he was still alive proved how desperate Kazdan was to get those disks back. Hands raised, he continued down the corridor, taking note of the twists and turns as he was herded down several sets of ramps. They approached a series of holding cells, and a sentry opened a door as they neared. He was relieved to see Sam asleep on the bunk inside.

"You have until dusk, and I want those damn disks."

The door slammed shut, and the lock rasped home. He listened to the sound of their footsteps fading into the distance, and then he knelt beside the bunk. There were bruises on Sam's face, on her arms and shadowing her neck, contrasting starkly against her half unbuttoned white shirt. They were not the sort of bruises that came from a beating—these seemed to come from an internal source rather than an external.

He'd seen photos of men and women with similar bruising. Ten years ago, in a vague attempt to understand the mechanics behind shapeshifting and shapechanging, the government had run a series of cell investigations, using well-paid volunteers. Though the machines were specifically designed for the task, the tests themselves were too invasive. Ninety-eight percent of the volunteers died after several hours, their hearts simply exploding under the pressure. To this day, no one really understood why. Similar tests had been performed on humans beforehand, with no such causalities, and certainly none of the bruising evident on Sam.

And if Kazdan knew the truth about Sam's past, knew what she was and what she was capable of, why would the bastard risk her life and put her through these tests? What did he hope to achieve?

He gently touched her swollen cheek. She stirred, murmuring something he couldn't catch.

"Sam," he said, carefully brushing the sweaty strands of red-gold hair away from her eyes. Though she obviously needed the sleep, they had to figure a way out of here before Kazdan came back.

Her eyes opened, but her gaze was unblinking, that of a sleeper still caught in a dream. The shadowed ring around her iris was stronger than ever before, the gray almost consuming the blue. "Ten minutes," she mumbled, reaching out and touching his hand, her fingers as cold as his were warm.

He glanced at his watch. If she wanted ten minutes, then she would have ten minutes. Entwining his fingers with hers, he sat on the floor beside the bunk, leaning his head back against the wall as he waited for her to wake.

***

Gabriel's warm hand gripped hers, callused and strong, and somehow very comforting. Rather like the man himself, Sam thought. On the few occasions Jack had touched her, his grip had been cool and clammy. She'd always hated it and had tried to avoid it.

Pity she'd never taken it as an insight to Jack's true personality. She opened her eyes. Gabriel watched her, his gaze intense and concerned.

"You okay?" His voice was soft, yet she sensed the anger in it. Not at her, but perhaps at what had been done to her. Which was odd really, when they were neither partners nor friends.

"Yes." She felt like shit, but there was little to be gained by stating the obvious. Besides, she was alive, and that was more than she'd thought possible an hour ago. "How did you get here?"

"Karl bugged the men who took Jan. We arrived at the first camp in time to see you loaded into a truck. I followed you here."

And had obviously gotten caught. She wondered what had stopped Jack from killing him outright. "Did you see Jan and Lyssa?"

"Karl has them. I'll contact him when all this is over."

"Good." At least something had worked out the way it was supposed to. She studied their entwined fingers. She made no attempt to remove her hand, nor did he. For that, she was glad. There was something very comforting about his touch. "I'm sorry about your brother. I'm sorry about Stephan."

His hazel gaze was suddenly warm and sent a shiver skating across her skin. "Stephan's fine."

He didn't seem too worried—or upset—about his brother death, which was extremely odd. "Jack said Stephan was dead."

"Because both he and Mary know Hanrahan was Stephan's other identity."

"But Hanrahan was killed."

"Sort of."

How could someone be "sort of" killed? She rubbed a hand across her eyes, wondering if her inability to understand had something to do with the ache still in her head. "Did you know Jack's wife is the one impersonating Lyssa? She's obviously a multi-shifter."

"That surprises me. I didn't think Kazdan was one to share."

"I don't think he is. I think he was ordered to."

"No wonder he wants to take the throne and kill Sethanon."

"He's not the only one Jack plans to kill."

He frowned at her. "What do you mean?"

"Mary was coming here—"

"Mary's dead," he interrupted, voice sharp.

Her gaze flicked across his face, and she sensed the pain under the calm exterior. "You killed her."

"She gave me no choice."

Had she given him another option, would he have taken it? She suspected not—not when Mary had almost killed his brother. "When did you shoot her?"

The edge in her voice obviously caught his intension, because his gaze intensified. "Maybe fifteen, twenty minutes ago. Why?"

"Because she was apparently confirming details of the PM's itinerary. Sethanon's planning a hit sometime today."

"A hit or a replacement?"

She shrugged. Either was possible, given what they'd seen on Jack's disks, though she couldn't see what simply assassinating him would achieve. Better to replace him and have background control.

He climbed to his feet and offered her his other hand. "Can you move?"

There was only one way to find out. She placed her free hand in his and climbed slowly to her feet. The small room spun several times, and for an instant, it felt as if her stomach were crawling up her throat. She swallowed heavily and asked, "Do you know the PM's schedule?"

He shook his head. "But my brother will. SIU works with the Fed and State boys when it comes to official government visits. Are you going to fall if I let you go?"

She shook her head. He released her hands, but he watched her warily for a minute or two before he moved across to the door and tested the handle "Locked tight."

She pulled the pin the hirsute stranger had given her out of her hair, but its shape caught her by surprise. It was an abstract man and woman, standing back to back, one dark, one light. The image was similar in theme to the tapestry in Jack's office, but this particular image was one she'd seen before. She just couldn't quite place where.

"Here, try to open it with this."

He accepted the pin, a sudden, rueful smile catching the corners of his lips. "This will test my skills."

According to her hirsute friend, it wouldn't. She wondered who the man was and how he knew so much—about her, about

Gabriel, and about what was going on. Was he one of Jack's men? Or perhaps one of Sethanon's?

But why would Sethanon—or even one of his or Jack's men—want to help her?

Gabriel squatted in front of the door, his gaze intent as he shoved the pin into the lock and began to carefully turn it. After a few minutes, there was a faint click.

They were free of the cell. Now all they had to do was get out of this complex.

Sixteen

"When I was led down here," he said softly, as he rose, "there was a guard stationed to the left of the door. I couldn't see anyone else, but that doesn't mean there won't be."

Sam nodded. "You take out the first guard, I'll look for others." She could do that, even if she felt like shit. He didn't ask if she was capable, which was refreshing. She'd only have to break a nail with Jack and you would have thought she was dying. Obviously fake concern, she now realized.

He grasped the handle, held up three fingers and counted them down. Then he thrust the door back hard. There was a grunt and the sound of something hitting the floor. Gabriel followed through fast. She ducked to the right. A guard stood at the far end of the room, rifle rising as he turned to face them.

"Gabriel, shooter at ten-o-clock!" she warned, dropping to the ground.

He tore the gun from the grip of the unconscious guard near his feet and fired. The second guard went down with a muffled cry.

She hobbled over to the second guard's prone form and scooped up his rifle. With her back against the wall, she studied the corridor beyond, listening and watching for any sort of alarm. Gabriel patted down the two men.

"Found a set of keys," he said softly, stopping on the opposite side of the doorway. "Might be of use."

"Could be the keys to his house or even his mailbox, for all we know." She kept her voice as low as his. "Chances are they won't be car keys."

"Luck's got to fall with us sometime."

Luck was something she'd learned never to rely on. "Do we go for a phone or a car?"

"I can't risk phoning Stephan from here. Too dangerous for him and for us."

"Car, then. Know where we can find one?"

He hesitated, face suddenly grim. "Yes. And I know where we can get the keys." He held up three fingers again.

She watched his countdown. At three she moved out, keeping low as she swung left. No one in sight.

"This way." He motioned to the corridor leading off to the right.

She followed him, almost running to keep up with his long strides. By the time they reached the top of the looping corridor, sweat was trickling down her back, her muscles ached and she felt lightheaded. When he stopped to investigate another door, she leaned against the wall and desperately tried to catch her breath. Jack's tests had sapped all her strength. She felt as unsteady as an umbrella in a windstorm.

"You okay?"

Her gaze rose at his concerned question. Worry was very evident in his hazel eyes, which was natural, since he was using her as much as Jack. He was just being nicer about it. She nodded Weak or not, she had to go on. Had to stop Jack.

"You look sort of gray," he said

"So would you if you'd had a near death experience." The concern in his gaze got stronger, and she forced a smile. "Go. I don't think we have that much time to play with."

He nodded and moved through the door. She covered his back, scanning the room, weapon at the ready as she watched for any sign of movement. But there was no life here, only the dead—either in coffins or as a headless corpse sprawled on the floor. *Mary.* That's where he intended to get the keys. She touched his arm. He glanced down at her, eyes bleak. He hadn't wanted to see her like this, she realized.

"I'll do it."

He hesitated. "I'll watch the exits."

She walked over to Mary's body. The one good thing about laser weapons was the cleanness of the death—there was no blood, and in this case, no head. Her stomach turned at the thought, and she kept her eyes averted from the blackened neck stump as she rifled through the dead woman's clothes. She found a set of keys in her right jacket pocket, and a disk in her left.

If Mary was supposed to be confirming the PM's route, then maybe this was it. Maybe luck *was* with them, for a change.

She rose, and they moved cautiously into the next corridor. Five minutes later, they were outside. It was almost too easy.

"Chopper's gone," he noted, pointing to the empty helicopter pad. "Kazdan's obviously taken off already, though I'd like to know how, given it's daylight, and he wasn't wearing a full protection suit."

"They've developed some sort of second skin that protects them from the UV rays. The vamps in Jack's house were wearing it. I snagged a piece." Though God only knew what condition it'd be in after being in her pocket all this time. She unlocked the car door, then tossed the keys across to Gabriel and climbed in the passenger side.

"That's obviously how Mary moved about in daylight." He glanced at her. "It's not a good development."

"Exactly what I thought." She placed the disk into the onboard computer. The screen hummed to life, revealing an itinerary. She quickly scanned through it.

Gabriel headed for the gate. The slight shimmer that indicated an energy field disappeared as they neared. Obviously it had been designed to keep people out, not in.

"The PM's got three appointments left," she stated. "He's having lunch with the Premier at a restaurant called Henry's, and then he's off to open the new shuttle port. Lastly, the state opera, tonight."

"It'll be the shuttle port," he said, grim certainty in his voice. "There's been a lot of opposition to it, and there'll be plenty of reporters present. Sethanon likes an audience."

She glanced at the clock. "Then we have three hours and twenty minutes to arrange some extra security and get there."

"Call this number—" He hesitated as she grabbed the onboard phone, and then gave her the number.

After several rings, there was a cautious, somewhat croaky, "Hello?" The screen remained static—whoever it was, they weren't chancing the vid-screen.

"Stephan, Gabriel."

The screen came to life, and a second Gabriel stared back at her. Only the way he held himself also reminded her of the Stephan she'd met at the mansion.

"Hi Ryan. Nice to see you back in safe hands."

His voice was different than Gabriel's—deeper and filled with command—but there was something in his tone that suggested familiarity. Yet, she'd certainly never met this man before. Or had she? Given the fact that the Stephan who ran the Federation was a shapeshifter, was it possible that he was one of those rare multi-shifters? Was Gabriel's twin not only Hanrahan, but Stephan as well? It would certainly explain how Hanrahan could be dead but Stephan was alive.

"Nice to be back in safe hands," she said, somehow resisting the impulse to add that she was, as yet, unsure just how much safer she was in Gabriel's hands.

His gaze went to Gabriel. "What's up?"

Gabriel didn't take his eyes off the road, which was just as well, given the speed they were traveling. "We think Sethanon's planning to switch the PM sometime during the shuttle port opening. Kazdan's the executioner."

Stephan ran a hand over his shadowed jaw. "Security's tight. SIU, State and the Feds are all involved."

"Kazdan has a full run down of the security plans. Mary handed them to him."

Stephan's eyes hardened. "She's dead, I gather?"

"Yes."

"Good."

In that instant, Sam saw another difference between the two men. Saw why Stephan, not Gabriel, was the leader. There was no remorse, no regret, in Stephan.

"You heading there now?" he asked.

"Yes, but its going to take us a couple of hours. We're over near Western Port. How much pull has Byrne got?"

Byrne was on the Director's staff, if Sam remembered rightly. But if Stephan was Hanrahan, why not just use his alter-ego again?

"Enough. I'll start phoning around. Call when you get to the port."

The vid-screen went static. She glanced across to Gabriel. "Why not use Hanrahan?"

"Hanrahan's dead."

"He's obviously not, because he was just on the phone."

He gave her a sharp glance. "What gives you that idea?"

"Karl told me Hanrahan was your brother. The Stephan we just talked to obviously is, but his mannerisms, and the fact that he knew me, suggest he's also the dark haired, green eyed Stephan we met last night. Given that Stephan is a shifter, it isn't hard to put two and two together."

Amusement briefly touched his lips. "We're going to have watch what we say around you. You're far too quick."

She wasn't that quick. It had taken her five years to discover her partner was a lying bastard. "So why you can't use Hanrahan?"

"Too many people were starting to suspect Hanrahan. It's better he dies."

"So Stephan *is* a multi shifter?"

Gabriel just shook his head. "See if the disk has a security map of the shuttle port."

In other words, she thought, don't ask any more questions.

She brought up the menu and studied it. After a few minutes, she found a floor plan of the shuttle port. "If they're going to make a switch, they'll have to distract security long enough to do so."

He nodded. "And it won't happen where there are lots of people."

"That cuts out the hanger. The official ribbon cutting's in there."

"It'll probably happen either just before or just after. Have they got entry or exit routes marked?"

She pressed the screen several times. "Yep. He does a walk through the terminal, inspects the Control Center, opens the port, and then shuffles off in his car."

"What's the position of Control Center?"

"Towers at the end of the terminal. Reached by express lift or stairs."

"Ten to one that's where the switch will happen."

She frowned. "They'll have to be quick."

"True. But the lift will only hold ten or so people, and there's nowhere to run once you stop it. Perfect situation."

"Jack still has his mad bomber friend."

"Who will no doubt cause a spectacular disturbance, drawing away the press and most of the security."

"Won't Stephan warn the SIU and the Fed's about the threat? Wouldn't that be enough to stop the visit?"

"They'll up security, but I doubt they'll stop the opening. The PM's waged a major battle against the greens to get these shuttle ports running, and I doubt an unconfirmed threat would be enough to stop him from opening them."

"But the threat is more than unconfirmed. Jack's definitely going to the airport to kill the PM. I heard him say so."

He glanced at her. "I'm afraid the word of a cop under investigation for shooting her partner is not going to be taken seriously—especially when she states that same partner is one of the men behind the threat."

Good point. "So it comes down to us stopping him," she said grimly. "How fast does this baby go?"

"Why don't we find out?" he said, and pressed the accelerator to the floor.

***

Gabriel glanced up as a shadow fell over the security-com he was studying. Without even looking he had a fair idea who the shadow belonged to.

"Byrne," he said, annoyed, but not entirely surprised to see his brother standing in the middle of the Shuttle Port's' main security center. "What the hell are you doing here?"

Stephan, in his Byrne persona, leaned wearily against the center's outer wall. "Kazdan owes us. I've come to claim the debt."

A debt *he* could have easily claimed for them both. Given the energy it took to maintain a new image, his brother was a fool to risk coming here when he was still injured. But there was no point in saying anything, because there was no swaying Stephan once his mind was made up. "You stay here. You don't go out there." He pointed to the main terminal below them.

Stephan's smile was one of agreement. "Where's Ryan?"

He split the screen, tuning in to Sam's wristcom. The stairs in which she stood were brightly lit and empty. "In the Control Center stairwell. I'm about to head for the elevator mechanic's room."

"She's alone?" Stephan frowned. "A bit risky, isn't it?

He shook his head. "Kazdan will expect a guard in the stairs, but he'll run if he hears any more than that. He certainly won't expect to see Sam there. Might give her—and us—a slight advantage."

"Let's hope you're right. I'll take over here." Stephan hesitated, his frown deepening as he jabbed a finger at the slender figure in the center of the screen. "What the hell is Lyssa doing here?"

Gabriel glanced at the screen. It was undoubtedly Lyssa's form, but this woman's walk was different—less graceful, more energetic. And given the real Lyssa was safely tucked away, this was obviously the replacement. But if she was a multi-shifter, why would she wear this form here? Surely she'd have to be aware that the SIU and the Fed's would be here? He paused. Maybe that was the entire idea. Kazdan would have found out by now that his prisoners had escaped. Maybe they were planning to frame the *real* Lyssa for the attempt on the PM's life. The video evidence would be undeniable, especially since few authorities knew about multi-shifters.

He gripped his brother's shoulder. "That's not Lyssa."

Stephan glanced at him sharply. "Why would you say that?"

"Because the real Lyssa is safe with Karl. That's the imitation you've been living with for the past six months."

Though his face went pale, anger burned deep in his brother's eyes. "You knew, and you didn't tell me?"

"I wasn't sure until a few hours ago." He pulled out his gun and checked the clip one final time. "I'll explain later. Right now, I have to go catch our traitor."

"When all this is over, we talk."

When all this was over, he was taking a holiday. He tapped the wristcom one of the State boys had given him, unlocking the audio pin and placing it behind his ear. "Keep an eye on her. I'll be in touch."

The Lyssa imitation had taken a corridor that led to two places—the workers lounge and the refuelling depot. With the careful placement of one or two bombs, the depot would provide one hell of a light and sound show, which was why Stephan had arranged for extra security there.

After exiting the security center, Gabriel ran down the corridor, made a sharp right and continued on. The workers lounge came into sight, but there was no one in the immediate area. He slowed and pressed the wristcom. "See her?" he asked softly.

"Just gone into the ladies room."

He studied the door to his left. Would a terrorist stop for a quick bathroom break? "Check the plans. Is there a large vent of some kind connected to the bathroom?"

"Hang on."

He crept forward while he waited. Once he neared the door, he pressed his back against the wall and pressed his fingers against the door, slowly opening it. He heard soft cursing and then the harsh rasp of metal against tile. She was up to something in there, for sure.

"One vent," Stephan said, "It connects to vents that lead to depots one and two."

Both of which were well covered. Even if she succeeded getting into the depots without being caught, she wouldn't get much further. There had to be something else, something they were missing. "Where else does the vent go?"

"Heads back past the kitchens and up to the main air conditioning unit."

"No other vent openings beside the kitchen?"

"Nope."

Then what the hell was she up to? A soft, metallic thumping indicated she was climbing into the vent. "Keep an eye on the vents at the depot. Inform security I'm heading down to the kitchen."

He eased the door closed and ran for the stairs. State police swung towards him, guns raised, as he entered the lower level. They didn't shoot though, which meant Stephan had been in contact with them. He dug out his ID, flashing it as he ran past.

The kitchen was dark and still. The exit lights gleamed brightly, lending a ruddy glow to the darkness. He quietly closed the swinging double doors and waited for his eyes to adjust.

"Vent's near the crockery shelves," Stephan said.

Gabriel clicked the audio off, letting his brother see and hear but not speak. He had no idea how acute the imitation Lyssa's hearing was, but given she was a shifter, he wasn't about to take a risk. The vent was still in place. He squatted behind a bench that offered him cover while still allowing him to see most of the kitchen.

After several minutes, metal scraped, and the grate covering the vent clattered to the floor. He drew his gun. With a soft grunt, Lyssa appeared, slithering from the vent to the floor like a small sack of potatoes. She climbed to her feet near the far end of his bench and headed toward the stoves. Once there, she began to turn on the jets. A soft hissing filled the air.

Gas, he thought. They were going to blow the kitchen, not the more obvious fuel depot. He rose and held his gun at the ready.

"Not another step, Lyssa."

She jumped and swung around. The red light reflecting from the overhead emergency beacon made her pale features seem harsh. "Gabriel. What are you doing here?"

"I might ask you the same question." She had something in her right hand, and though he couldn't make out what it was, it appeared the wrong shape to be a gun. "Drop whatever you're holding," he ordered.

A smile touched her lips. "I don't think so."

He clicked the safety off. "I mean it, Lyssa. Drop it."

"Ah, but if I do, we're both dead," she said, her amusement more evident this time. "It's a grenade, and the pin is out. It'll cause enough damage by itself, but in a kitchen flooded with gas—" She shrugged.

The kitchen would go up like a rocket, and Kazdan would have his diversion. He motioned toward the stove. "Turn the jets off and step away."

"As I said, I don't think so." She ducked, moving away with a speed that surprised him. White light flared, followed by the

flash of a laser. While he had no idea where the weapon had
come from, he was mighty glad it was a laser—it was the one
weapon that wasn't likely to ignite the gas. The bright light
whizzed past his head and bit into the wall behind him, showering
him with concrete dust. She'd missed by several feet—maybe
she couldn't see too well in the dark.

She scrambled around several benches. He waited, his laser
aimed toward the main doors. Except for the vent and the
emergency exit to his right, it was the only way out. When she
reached the bench closest to the door, she stood and fired several
shots, then raced for the exit.

She never had a hope. He fired. The laser's blue-white light
cut silently across the darkness, and arrowed into her back. She
gasped, her arms flung wide, but her hand was still clutched
around the grenade as she was thrown to the tiles. He pressed the
audio button as he ran towards her. "Get the medics down here."

"Show me her face," Stephan said tightly.

Obviously, he feared it was Lyssa who lay dying, but Gabriel
felt no rancor at his brother's disbelief. If the situation had been
reversed, he'd be asking the same thing.

She was gasping for breath, still struggling to move. He
removed the laser and the grenade from her slack grip, noting
that the pin on the grenade hadn't been pulled. He put them on
the bench, well out of her reach, and squatted beside her.

"Don't move," he said gently. "The medics are on their way."

She gaze swung towards him. Her features were in the midst
of change, Lyssa's features fading into that of the dark haired
women he'd met only a few hours before. Kazdan's wife, as Sam
had said.

"Tell him I'm sorry," she gasped. "I didn't want him to die . . .
He was good . . . to me . . ."

Surprise rippled through him. He had no doubt that she meant
Stephan, and he wondered if Kazdan knew his wife had fallen in
love with the man she was supposed to kill. "So it was you who
sent the warning to the SIU?"

She licked her lips. "I didn't want to be responsible for all
those deaths, no matter what *he* said."

"You'd better leave the bitch," Stephan stated into his ear,
his voice deadpan and tightly controlled, "and head over to the
Control Center. Ryan hit the alarm button about a minute ago. I
sent two State boys over, but we've since lost contact with them
all."

Gabriel swore and headed for the exit.

***

Sam shifted her weight from one leg to the other, trying to ease the ache in her feet. She needed something, anything, to happen; otherwise she was in serious danger of falling asleep. She glanced at her watch. Three-o-five. The PM was obviously running behind schedule. Why couldn't a politician actually do something right and keep on schedule just this once?

She stifled a yawn and checked the forty-four for the umpteenth time. It wasn't a weapon she'd normally use. She didn't like the feel of it, nor did she like the kickback. Still, beggars couldn't be choosers. Security operation or not, no one was standing ready with an arsenal of weapons. They'd taken what had been available, and Gabriel had taken the only laser weapon.

She put the magnum back in its holster and wondered what he was up to. He was supposed to contact her when he'd reached the elevator mechanic's room. So far, her wristcom had been worryingly silent. Maybe there were problems, though she'd heard no noise, no sound of gunfire.

Shifting her weight to her other leg again, she wondered how Jack planned to get into the port. Security was locked down tight. No one was getting in or out without the proper ID. Still, if the Wetherton clone was on Jack's side, maybe getting ID wasn't a problem. Ministers could get such things, even a minister on the way out.

Sound whispered across the silence. She cocked her head, listening intently. After a few moments, she heard it again—the creak of a metal step. Someone was walking up the stairs

The lights went out. She squatted and pressed back into the corner. Another faint creak whispered through the darkness. Carefully, she drew her gun, clicked off the safety, and held it in a two handed grip, aiming for the top step.

Down below, someone breathed. She could hear the whisper of his breath, sighing in and out of his lungs. Could almost hear the beating of his heart, a steady vibration far slower than her own.

When had her senses become so acute?

The landing immediately below creaked. She tensed and waited. So, too, did the man below her. His breathing was a short, sharp sound that spoke of fear. After a minute, he continued towards her. She tensed, her finger tightening fractionally on the trigger.

A head appeared—brown hair, brown skin. No one she knew. Metal glinted in his left hand.

"Police," she said "Drop your weapon and put your hands up,"

He jumped. Then, almost as if in slow motion, she saw his fingers tighten around his gun, saw the brief flash of white sear the darkness, and the ripple through the air as the bullet came at her. She rolled to one side, and then half rose and fired. The retort shuddered through her arms, the sound of the shot a cannon that rebounded through the silence.

The impact threw him back down the stairs. She rose, walked over to the railing, and carefully peered over. The stranger lay on the landing below and he wasn't moving.

But someone else was.

Feet pounded up the steps—four men, at least. She scooted up to the next landing and pressed the alarm on her wristcom. One or two men she could cope with. Four was asking for trouble.

She waited in the shadows. The men stopped on the landing below, one of them cursing softly. Tension leapt into the air, so thick she could almost taste it.

They edged forward. She caught a glimpse of blond hair as the stranger tried to figure out where she was. She informed him by firing a warning shot that skimmed his head. He jerked back, but others appeared over the railing, returning fire. They missed her position by several feet. Maybe they couldn't see her too well in the shadows. She silently ran up to the next landing.

Where the hell was her backup?

With all the security running around this place, she'd have thought there'd be someone close enough to help her out. Maybe she should just hightail it up to the control center. The State boys were up there. At least the odds would be more even, though in reality, the gunshots should have had them out and investigating by now.

She listened to the four men below. They were creeping up the stairs again, heading for the next landing. The Control Center was only another two flights up. Damn it, why hadn't anyone come out to investigate the gunshots? Surely they couldn't have missed the retort of the magnum? But she had no idea just how noisy a control center was. Maybe it was impossible to hear a gun as loud as the forty-four.

The door above her opened as she reached the next landing.

Light flung itself down the stairwell, making her blink. A lanky fellow in the State's black uniform entered the stairwell.

"About time," she muttered. Then the sudden silence hit her as odd. As did the officer's amused expression.

Too late, she saw the gun in his hand, heard the muffled retort as he fired. She dove sideways, but not fast enough. The bullet tore through her shoulder, throwing her back hard against the wall. Pain ran like fire through her body, sucking the strength from her legs. As she slid down the wall, she stared at the lanky stranger walking towards her.

And saw that he had Jack's eyes.

Seventeen

Gabriel heard the booming retort of the forty-four and slid to a halt, pressing back against the wall as he stared up at the dark stairwell.

After a few seconds, there was a muffled retort, then silence. High up he could see a shaft of light, starlike in the distance.

"Still can't contact the State boys in the control center," Stephan said into his ear.

"Got shooters on the roof?"

"Yep. The first stage launch screen is up. It's difficult to see anyone inside. No one's responding to calls."

"What about Sam?"

"She's not responding, either."

Sam was a by-the-numbers cop. If she didn't answer, she was either injured or dead. Anger slithered through him. She might not be a friend, and she certainly wasn't his partner, but she was someone he certainly wouldn't mind getting to know better. If she was dead, if he'd lost that chance, Jack would pay. "What about Kazdan?"

"No sign of him."

He had to be here, somewhere. He wouldn't be careless enough to arrive at the last minute and hope to get inside.

"The PM?"

"Two minutes away."

They didn't have much time left. Nor could they delay the Prime Minister's arrival much longer without the press figuring out that something was wrong.

"I'm heading up."

"Be careful."

That was one warning his brother didn't need to give. He switched off the audio again. Then, keeping his back to the wall, he carefully eased up the stairs. From above came the brief mutter of conversation and the light winked out. He halted, listening.

Someone was walking down. He hunkered down in the corner of a landing, and waited. The soft steps came closer. Whoever it was, they were making no effort to conceal their presence. Feet came into view—joggers so white they practically glowed in the darkness.

It was a teenager who barely looked old enough to be out of grade school. He wasn't one of the security staff, nor was he one of the regular port staff, despite the fact he was wearing an ID tag. Given the total lock down, he had to be one of Kazdan's men—though the term "man" was something of a misnomer in this case.

He was also apparently night blind, walking right past without so much as twitching. Gabriel rose swiftly and moved up behind the skinny youngster. Still no sign of awareness. Shaking his head at Kazdan's stupidity for employing people like this, he clamped one hand over the kid's mouth and grabbed the gun with his other.

"Move and you die," he whispered into one diamond-studded ear.

The youngster froze, yet his entire body trembled. Where in hell had Kazdan got this one from—kindergarten? "Is the lady police officer upstairs? Nod if the answer is yes."

The teenager swallowed convulsively and nodded.

"Is Kazdan upstairs?"

Another nod.

"How many other people? One nod per person."

Five nods. Not good odds. He was fast, but he wasn't a fool. He pressed the audio switch back on. "Byrne, the PM arrived yet?"

"Just now."

"Herd him into the Security Center. I don't care how or why, but get everyone else out. I'm coming in with a prisoner."

"Sounds like a plan."

"Maybe." And maybe it was just plain suicide. Still, if Kazdan was already in the control tower, they had no other choice. He was obviously disguised, if the sharpshooters on the roof couldn't see him. Someone had to go in. "I'll explain when I get there. We'll need some duct tape, knives, a few Kevlar suits, a Holcroft laser or two, and a few packets of blood."

"Nice shopping list. I'll see what I can do."

Gabriel nudged the teenager. "I'm about to take my hand from your mouth. Make any sort of noise and you're dead. Okay?"

The kid nodded again. Gabriel pushed him down the rest of the stairs, and then he urged him into a run at the bottom. He had a horrible feeling time was running out. He had to get upstairs, before it was too late—for Sam, more than anyone else.

***

Sam came to slowly. Something warm and sticky pasted her shirt to her chest, pulling at her skin when she shifted. Her shoulder burned, a deep-set ache that pounded through her body, churning her stomach into knots.

"Shame to waste all that blood," Jack commented, amusement evident in his soft tone. "But I really haven't the time for a snack right now."

She opened her eyes. She was lying on her side on the control tower floor, her back resting against a metal panel. Jack stood to her right, arms crossed, leaning casually against a well-lit radar screen. Two men stood near the elevator, and another two guarded either end of the half-circle window. All five were wearing State ID's. Courtesy of the soon to be dead Wetherton, or some other high placed clone, no doubt.

The real tower staff lay in a heap near the bathroom door. Her gaze skated over them quickly, and she grimaced. By the look of the woman lying nearest to her, Jack had already indulged in a little snack or two.

She eased upright. The fire in her shoulder became a pyre, and she hissed. Sweat broke out across her brow, and warm moisture began to trickle down the inside of her shirt. Gingerly, she cradled her right arm in her left and glared up at her partner.

Jack laughed softly. "You should have joined me, Sam. It would have been a whole lot easier."

She snorted softly. "I'd rather mate with a crocodile."

"Now that conjures up some interesting images." He studied her for a moment, eyes dilated and blood hungry. "How did you escape the cell?"

She smiled sweetly. "I opened the door."

His gaze narrowed. "How? I removed the key-coder from your boot."

"So you did. Maybe I'm magic."

He snorted softly. "Not yet, you're not."

And what was that supposed to mean? Just what had those tests revealed about her?

Jack glanced at his watch, then at the two men at either end of the windows. As one, they made their way across to the stairwell doorway. His gaze returned to her. "Where's Stern?"

"Around." Where, she had no idea. Hopefully, he or someone else had realized she was in trouble by now and was doing something about it. "You'll never succeed, Jack. The whole place is under tight security."

His smile was almost serene. "Of which we're a part."

As if to confirm his claim, a voice broke into the brief silence.

"Flint's just left the Security Center. Heads up, everyone. Kazdan's around somewhere."

The voice, she realized, was Gabriel's, and it was coming from both her wristcom, which was sitting on the sat-link desk next to her gun, and Jack's.

"Indeed he is," Jack said, pushing away from the radar terminal. "Two minutes, boys."

The two men near the door raised their weapons. They were more robots than men, she thought.

The wristcom buzzed again. "Redfern, you there?"

Jack smiled as he glanced at Sam. "Indeed I am," he said, voice several shades deeper than normal.

"Flint's on his way. I'm heading up the stairs."

She opened her mouth to scream a warning and found the gleaming barrel of a pistol laser staring her right between the eyes.

"One word and you die. I swear it," Jack said

She had no doubt that he meant it. There was something very cold, something less than human, in his eyes. The vampire half of his nature was beginning to override his human sensibilities.

He kept the laser cocked and ready. Sweat trickled down her nose as she stared at the stairway door. The heavy sound of footsteps became clearer. Then the door was flung open, and Gabriel stepped into the room.

To be greeted by two rifles and a smiling Jack.

Gabriel ignored them, his gaze searching the room. Relief ran through his eyes when he saw her. She realized that he'd known about the trap and had willingly walked into it to see if she was safe.

Warmth ran through her, momentarily wiping away her pain.

"And the whole family's together again," Jack said sardonically. "Stern, release the weapon and wristcom."

Gabriel dangled the laser on one finger and allowed the man on his left to take the wristcom. "Nice disguise, Kazdan. Wouldn't have known you."

"Obviously not. I'm here, and you're my prisoner. Check him."

Gabriel kept his arms raised as one of the men patted down his sides and legs.

"Nothing."

Jack pointed his weapon toward her. "Sit next to our bleeder,

Stern, and don't try to warn anyone. Mike, watch them."

Jack walked to the elevator, followed by the two men who'd been stationed near the door. Gabriel sat down beside Sam, close enough that his shoulder brushed hers. His gaze was both calculating and concerned when it met hers. "How's the shoulder?"

"Sore."

"Lost a little blood."

He was making small talk, she realized, probably trying to put their guard at ease. If he'd willingly walked into a trap, he obviously had a plan to get them out. She hoped. "But a hell of a lot less than the tower folk."

His gaze went to the pile of bodies. His fingers clenched and unclenched. "We've got a hungry vampire in our midst."

"So it would seem."

He nudged her shoulder, catching her attention again. He looked over his shoulder, down towards his back, then back to her. She nodded minutely.

Keeping a careful eye on both Jack and their guard, she slipped her hand behind his back, stopping only when the guard glanced at her. She feigned interest in what Jack was doing. A soft hum came from the elevator shaft—Flint was on his way up. The guard looked away.

Wriggling her fingers under Gabriel's shirt, she slipped her palm across the smooth warmth of his skin until she touched something cold and metallic.

Her gaze met his, and his smile was grim. Slowly, carefully, she pulled the duct tape away and slid the parcel down to the floor. Holcroft lasers, loosely joined by tape.

His hand joined hers behind his back. His fingers ran warmth across her skin, briefly caressing, then he grasped one of the lasers. His gaze met hers, and then it flickered to the guard. She wrapped her hand around the second laser and carefully pulled. The tape tore loose, and she coughed to cover the sound. But the cough became a groan of pain as fire burned down her right side. For an instant, the whole room spun. She leaned her head back against the panel and took several deep breaths.

Gabriel's hand touched hers again. She released the laser, wrapping her fingers in his, drawing strength from the comfort of his touch. It was odd, really, that a man she barely knew could offer her such solace. Especially when she'd never found *that* sort of comfort in a man's touch.

When the pain began to ebb again, she squeezed his hand lightly and let go. "I'm okay," she said, opening her eyes.

His hazel eyes were full of concern. "You need a doctor."

"I need an ending."

Understanding flickered through his eyes. "Wait," he said softly, holding up four fingers.

"We wait and the PM dies."

"No." There was certainty in his voice.

She glanced at the clock. Six minutes to four. She clenched the Holcroft laser and waited. A minute later, an explosion ripped across the silence.

"About time," Jack muttered. "Battle stations, boys."

The wristcoms buzzed to life. "Stern, Redfern, there's been an explosion in the kitchen. Batten down the tower and keep the PM under wraps until we give the okay."

Jack picked up the wristcom. "Bringing up the second launch screen."

He pressed a button. Motors hummed and a metal screen began to ease upwards, covering the windows. Light flared overhead as the room became darker.

"Let the game begin." Jack's voice was flat and cold. "Positions, boys."

The two men stepped back, weapons raised and ready. Jack stood in the middle of the room, facing the elevator, gun armed and held by his side.

"Your plan won't work," Gabriel said into the silence. "No bomb ever destroys all the evidence. They'll run autopsies on the remains, cell tests. They'll discover the truth."

Despite the casualness of his voice, Sam sensed an underlying urgency in his words. He didn't want the PM shot any more than she did, so why was he talking rather than acting?

Jack's smile was almost bitter. "I'm not a fool, Stern. There won't be anything left for them to autopsy."

"All it'll take is one piece of skull showing a laser burn, and your plan will come undone."

"Tell me Stern, have they found any pieces of Hanrahan for you to identify? No? How tragic." Jack's voice was cold, mocking. "The bomb we're using is bigger than the car bomb that destroyed the SIU. Even so, we're not taking chances. They won't find any skull fragments bearing laser burns, believe me."

Sam raised an eyebrow. The car bomb hadn't destroyed the SIU—even she knew that. Had Jack failed to keep updated on current events? Would that help them, somehow? She glanced at Gabriel. His eyes were calm, despite the tension and anger she felt in him.

"We have to stop them," she said.

"Move and you both die," Jack said, not looking at them.

They were going to die anyway, so why not die trying to stop a fiend? As if reading her thoughts, Gabriel squeezed her hand. Patience, his eyes seemed to say. She frowned and bit her lip. The elevator chimed softly, and the doors slid open. Five men were inside. The PM, David Flint, stood at the rear of the elevator, his body shielded by the four Fed boys.

She clenched the laser. They were dead meat if someone didn't *do* something. Gabriel wrapped his fingers round her arm, holding her hand down and preventing her from moving. She glared at him.

"Wait," he repeated. "Just wait."

Wait for Jack's plan to succeed? What sort of game was he playing now?

"Welcome, Prime Minister," Jack said, then raised his gun and fired.

The men in the lift didn't have a chance. Blood sprayed against the elevator walls as the five of them went down.

"Mike," Jack said, then turned and fired at the guard near them. The bullet took him in the shoulder and flung him back. He fell to the floor. Jack rounded his gun immediately on them. "Don't even think about moving."

She stared at him. "Have you gone totally mad?"

Jack snorted softly. "Far from it. Mike, you okay?"

The big man made a series of low curses as he pulled himself off the floor.

"I'll take that as a yes." Jack walked over and picked up a wristcom. "Control, Redfern here. We're under attack. I repeat, we're under attack. Flint's been hit. Stairs are occupied. We're taking the elevator."

"Sending teams one and five to help."

Jack smiled and clicked off the wristcom. "Transformation time, Mike."

The big man raised his fingers to his face and slowly dug in. With an odd sucking sound, his mouth, nose, everything, began to peel away. David Flint lay underneath the mask.

"A clone," she murmured.

"A clone," Jack said, tone smug. "Eddie, time for your

magic."

The skinny man near the elevator door pulled a small box from his pocket and walked to the control panel. Jack squatted down next her. Slowly, carefully, she eased the laser into her pocket. Gabriel's was long gone—she hadn't even seen him move it.

"Time to get out of here, my friend."

"Thanks, but I think I'd rather remain here with the dead."

"Sorry, that wish has already been granted to Stern."

He grabbed her shoulder, callously digging his fingers into her wound. Through a haze of pain, she heard Gabriel swear. Almost in slow motion, she saw Jack raise his gun, saw the flash as the bullet was fired. She felt Gabriel's shudder as if it were her own. Screamed when his blood splashed across her face.

Jack laughed. Then fire leapt into her skull, and for an instant, everything went black.

"Bastard," she heard Gabriel mutter, voice taut with pain.

He was alive. Relief swam through her, dissolving some of the pain. Shuddering, she took a deep breath, trying to control the churning in her stomach. Then she opened her eyes.

Gabriel's face was white, his forehead beaded with sweat. His hands were clenched around his thigh, and blood seeped slowly between his fingers.

The best way to stop a shapechanger was to wing him, Jack had once told her. Then they were useless in either form.

"I've decided I don't need the disks enough to cart you around with me, Stern. You're a little too dangerous to warrant the effort." There was no humanity left in Jack's eyes now. The vampire had risen fully to the surface. "I'd love to stay and watch you bleed to death, but time is against me. Up, Sam."

He pulled her roughly to her feet. "Terry, get those bodies out of the elevator. Eddie, you ready?"

Acid burned up Sam's throat. Sweat trickled down her forehead, dripping into her eyes, stinging. She blinked and met Gabriel's gaze. His eyes were intense, full of anger, and yet she sensed that even now, he was holding himself in check, waiting. For what? His gaze went to the clock then back to her. Frowning, she looked at the clock. One minute to four. It would take less than a minute to go down in the elevator. He'd asked her to wait until four before she moved. He was asking her to hold back again.

Against all reason, something deep within her trusted Gabriel.

For the moment, she'd do as he asked.

Jack jerked her forward. Pain leapt like fire through her muscles, making her knees go weak. She staggered at little, trying to keep her balance.

"You're dead meat, Kazdan." Gabriel's voice was flat, holding no emotion, no anger, and was all the more frightening because of it.

Jack laughed harshly. "No. You're the meat. See that bomb? It's primed and counting down. You have less than two minutes to say your prayers."

Jack thrust her into the lift. She hit the wall and slid down, struggling to breathe as the bright lights danced before her eyes.

But her gaze caught Gabriel's as the elevator doors closed, and she knew she was not alone. Somehow, he would come after her.

***

The doors were barely closed when the dead came to life. The four Federal Police rose, three moving across to the stairwell door and the fourth to the bomb. Flint rolled to one side, his shape shifting, reforming, as he moved. Stephan, in his Byrne identity, got to his feet.

"I thought he was going to shoot your fucking head off," Stephan said as he knelt beside Gabriel and dug a medi-kit out of his pocket. "You don't know how close I came to shooting the bastard right there and then."

"Glad you didn't," he said between clenched teeth. "Sethanon will be around here somewhere. We might just catch him if we let this whole thing play out."

Stephan's blue gaze was dubious. "And he might just let Kazdan kill Ryan."

He shook his head. "Kazdan needs her."

"You'd better hope so." Stephan tore the dressing open and placed it on the lid, ready to use. Then he dug the knife out of the kit and glanced up. "This will hurt."

"Having a bullet stuck in my leg is not exactly pleasant, believe me." Why the fucker hadn't blasted right through, given the close range, was beyond him. Maybe his shapechanging bones were tougher than he thought. "As the ad says, just do it."

Stephan nodded. Gabriel moved his hands from his leg. Blood pulsed from the wound and ran freely down his thigh. Stephan cursed, and slashed Gabriel trousers open. Then he did same to Gabriel's leg.

Gabriel hissed as the knife plunged into his flesh, gritting his teeth against the bellow that tore up his throat. Sweat beaded his brow and ran down his back, and yet, his skin suddenly felt as cold as the arctic.

He slammed his head back and closed his eyes, trying to think of something, anything, other than the feel of the blade digging into his flesh. He saw Sam's eyes, and the trust so evident in their shadow-ringed blue depths.

He couldn't let her down.

"Got it," Stephan muttered, and then mercifully, the digging stopped. Something metallic clattered across the tiles.

He opened his eyes. With the bullet out of his leg, he could at least shapechange and go after Kazdan. Stephan sprayed on an antiseptic sealer, slapped on the dressing and quickly bandaged the wound.

"This isn't going to hold for long if you insist on running around on it."

He ignored the concern in his brother's eyes. "Help me up."

Stephan grabbed his arm and held him steady as he clambered upright. "At least wear one of the vests. It saved our lives. It might save yours."

"Haven't got the time to climb into one. Besides, you may yet need it. Stopping the clone won't be easy." He glanced across the room. "That bomb safe yet?"

"Safe as houses," the Fed said with a smile, and tossed it into the air.

"Then it's time for me to go."

"Try to make sure you come back alive," Stephan said softly.

His smile was grim. "I can't exactly come back dead, can I?" He squeezed his brother's shoulder and headed for the stairs.

***

"See, everything is going to plan," Jack whispered, his breath brushing warmth past her ear.

She shuddered and blinked away the sweat rolling into her eyes. The elevator jerked to a halt, and the doors opened. A dozen armed State Police Officers were waiting for them.

"One move, one wrong word, and they all die," Jack murmured. "Eddie has another shiny toy in his pocket."

"Then we'll all die. Your precious clone included."

Jack's smile sent shivers through her soul. "See that man to the right? His name's Barter. His wife has just had a little boy. Should we make her a widow right here and now?"

"You're a bastard," she muttered. He knew her too well. Knew she wouldn't take the risk.

"And a good one at that." He jerked her forward. "Barter, take the PM to the car and get him out of here. I'm taking Ryan to the medics."

"The attackers?"

"Upstairs, but be careful. They're well armed."

Barter and several Feds whisked the clone away. The rest of security headed for the stairs. Jack and his remaining three men walked back into the shuttle port. They were stopped several times, and each time they were allowed to move on. They had the right uniforms and the right ID. No one bothered to look any closer.

She tried to study where they were going, but he was pushing her so fast she was almost running. Everything was blurred—or was it her eyes? It very quickly became obvious they were not headed for the medical center, but rather outside. A clock chimed into the silence. Four o'clock.

Time to move. She clenched her fingers round the laser in her pocket. Jack pushed her on. They approached the shuttle port's main entrance. The doors slid open. Outside, there was little activity. The shuttle port had been closed down tight, a fact that was now working in Jack's favor. He marched her through the doors, and then stopped, cursing fluently.

"Where the hell is Suzy?"

"Maybe she gained some sense and ran like mad," she muttered.

Jack growled and threw her against the wall. "You stay! Eddie, go get us some transportation."

She slid down the wall, battling for breath as a red haze danced before her eyes. Overhead, she saw a brown hawk wheel and dive for the rooftop. It land awkwardly, as if it were injured.

Relief coursed through her. Gabriel. It had to be. She slipped her hand from her pocket. Her fingers were still wrapped round the laser, concealing it. Timing was everything, Jack had once told her. She waited patiently, watching him pace, her shoulder almost as numb as her mind.

A red Ford sedan roared up. Eddie climbed out. *Time*, a warm voice whispered into her mind. Gabriel, she thought again, and wondered if his voice were real, or simply her imagination.

She raised the laser and fired at the rear of the car. The gas tank exploded, tearing the car, and Eddie, to pieces. At the same time, two more red-blue flashes lit the air, and Jack's other men were little more than headless corpses lying prone on the concrete.

"What the fuck?" Panic filled Jack's voice as he swung around. His gaze widened as it settled on the weapon in her hand. "Where the hell did that come from?"

"Magic," she said softly. "Hand's up, Jack."

He slowly raised his hands. But however much his human half might fear, his vampire half still had control. It was evident in the calculating coldness of his eyes. "It's against the law to kill me. You know the rules. You've lived with them all your life, and you can't abandon them now."

She smiled sadly. She *had* lived within the rules all her life. She might not have always followed orders, but she had stayed within the letter of the law, even when Jack had tried to convince her to do otherwise.

Look what it had gained her—a phony friendship, a shattered apartment and goddamn loneliness.

"What was that phrase you always used to say?"

A frown flitted across his features. She saw him tense, knew he was ready to leap.

"Oh yeah," she said softly. "Fuck the damn rules."

He sprang. She fired. Once. Twice. The laser caught him in the head and the chest and disintegrated both. She closed her eyes and heard the soft thump as his remains hit the concrete. She had her ending. It was over.

So why did she feel so empty, so cold?

She dropped the laser, closed her eyes, and let her head rest against the wall. After several seconds, she heard the soft flutter of wings, then hesitant footsteps.

Gabriel, she knew, without looking. She could smell his aftershave, a warm woody scent that tingled through her nostrils. She could somehow feel him in her mind, a wall of heat she could see but not yet touch.

His arms went around her, pulling her into the warmth of his embrace. She bit her lip, then buried her face against his shoulder and let the tears flow.

Epilogue

"What do you mean suspended until further notice?" Sam stared at the captain, a weird sense of déjà vu running through her. Though it was an entirely different office in which the two of them now sat, the events seemed to be rolling out just the same.

He sighed heavily. "It means that, until further notice, you're suspended from active service with the State Police."

"Did some form of evidence come to light when I was in the hospital?"

"No. You're cleared of all charges relating to the death of Detective Jack Kazdan."

The clone's rapidly disintegrating body, and the subsequent discovery of the massive doses of growth accelerant in his body, had proven true her statement that it wasn't the real Jack she'd shot the first time. And Gabriel had testified that when she'd shot him the second time, it was in self defense.

Granted, she shouldn't have killed him the second time, either, if only because they might have been able to coerce information about Sethanon out of him. But, as Gabriel had pointed out, if she hadn't have shot him, *he* would have been forced to, if only to save her life. Besides, if this Sethanon was the force of evil everyone was saying, would he leave a general alive to shoot his mouth off? Unlikely.

"Then why am I being suspended?"

The captain rubbed his forehead wearily. "Look, I'm just the middle man around here. I do what I'm told. And right now, my orders are to get your skinny ass down to the SIU."

She blinked in surprise. "The SIU? What the hell do they want to see me for?" Gabriel had promised no more tests. Surely he wouldn't go back on his word.

But then, Gabriel didn't run the SIU. Byrne did. Stephan had arranged a smooth takeover for Hanrahan's successor, and the transition had gone as planned. As Byrne, Stephan still ran the SIU, still ran the Federation. Or so she figured, given that Gabriel's reaction to the man was a little too similar to his reaction to Hanrahan. He certainly didn't treat Byrne as a superior.

"Maybe they want to give you a commendation for your help in rescuing the PM."

The captain's dry tone told her it was highly unlikely. "Come on, Cap, you must have heard something."

He smiled, brown eyes amused. "As I said, I'm just a middle man. Go. The SIU do not like to be kept waiting."

"Yeah, so you said the last time." She rose, knowing she would get nothing more from him. "See you around, Cap."

"I doubt it," he said, and went back to his paperwork.

Dismissed yet again. She walked out of his office and past the office she and Jack had shared, not even bothering to stop. There was nothing left for her in there. Nothing more than memories she no longer trusted.

She pressed the elevator button and impatiently tapped her foot. After several seconds the door opened. She swiped her pass through it and pressed the button for the SIU. The doors closed, and the elevators whisked her downwards.

Gabriel was waiting in the foyer. He'd come to visit her in the hospital, but she hadn't seen him since she'd gotten out, just over a week ago.

"What the hell is going on?" she said.

"Your guess is as good as mine."

He made little effort to conceal his annoyance, and she raised her eyebrows in surprise. "I thought assistant directors were told what was going on."

"Not this one—not on this occasion, anyway."

He led her down a long corridor and past several well-secured entrances. The furniture became plush and rich in color, contrasting oddly against the harsh white walls. They were in the director's suite, she realized.

Gabriel approached a desk and stopped. The blonde behind it looked up and smiled. "Assistant Director Stern, the Director is expecting you. Please, go on in."

He glanced at Sam. There was wariness in his gaze, tension in the set of his shoulders. He obviously knew his twin was up to something, but he wasn't sure what.

"Ladies first," he said, ushering her through the open doorway.

"Gee thanks," she muttered, feeling like a lamb about to enter the hungry lion's den.

Jonathan Byrne looked up as they entered. The impact of his gaze stopped her so suddenly Gabriel had to do a quick step around her. In the intense depths of Byrne's blue eyes, well beneath the sharp amusement, there was a calculating iciness that boded them no good. But she sensed Gabriel, more than she, wasn't going to like whatever it was his twin had to say.

The door slammed shut behind them, and a faint buzzing ran across the silence. Voice scramblers, she thought, surprised.

"What the hell are you up to?" Gabriel stalked to the desk and stared at his brother. His voice held no respect. No wonder Byrne had the scramblers up.

"I told you a while ago that I wanted you to have a partner, that these missions of ours, both here and with the Federation, were far too dangerous to continue with alone." Byrne's gaze went from Gabriel to her then back again, and a smile touched his thin lips. "And now, I believe I have found you the perfect partner."

"I work alone. Always have, always will." Gabriel hesitated and glanced around at her. "No offense."

"None taken." She stepped up beside him. "I have absolutely no desire to join the ranks of the Spook Squad, so you can transfer me right back upstairs."

"Gabriel, you have no choice. And you didn't volunteer, my dear, you were drafted. We will begin your training straight away."

"No you won't, because I'll quit if you don't transfer me back."

"We both know that'll never happen, because you have no life beyond your job, so let's not pretend."

Damned if he wasn't right. She was stuck, and they both knew it. And in some ways, being here was better than being up in State. She might have been cleared of Jack's murder, but people hadn't forgiven her. Whether or not she was in the right, she'd still shot the man she'd thought was her partner. She'd stepped over that line, and there was no going back now.

Byrne leaned forward, crossing his arms on the desk. "You worked too well together. I saw it, Gabriel—at the house, and at the shuttle port. There's an instant understanding between you, something rare and precious. Sam obviously has talents that are still developing, and she will need monitoring, while you, my brother, have talents you refuse to explore. Together, I think you will make quite a lethal combination."

They stared at him in silence. There was little else they could do.

He smiled again. "I'll take your silence as acceptance. Now, get the hell out of my office, and go do some work."

Gabriel glanced down at her, his hazel eyes as cold as the antarctic, then turned and walked from the room. She had no choice but to follow. She'd lost one job and gained another—and a new partner in the process. Some days, you just couldn't win.

"This is great," Gabriel muttered as he strode along the hall. He ran a hand through his hair and glanced back at her. "Nothing personal, of course. I just prefer working alone."

"Which is not a current option."

"There's always another option," he shot back, "and always a way around orders."

"He won't send me back upstairs. You heard him say that."

"And *I* won't work with a partner." His gaze was almost challenging, like she was somehow a threat to him.

She raised an eyebrow and wondered what the hell she was missing. "It's not like either of us has much of a choice. Why not accept it gracefully and just get on with whatever it is we're supposed to do?"

"What I'm supposed to do now is take you downstairs and register you for training, which I will do. But nothing more. You and I will never work together."

"Why not? I mean, we did work well together, didn't we?"

He didn't even bother glancing at her. "Yes, but that doesn't alter my decision."

He strode off. She had no choice but to follow "What the hell have you got against having a partner?"

He didn't answer. But it really didn't matter, because they were both stuck with the situation, and there was nothing they could do but put up with it the best they could. He would see sense, sooner or later.

Besides, unwanted or not, there was one good thing about her being drafted into the ranks of the SIU. Their computers had a far greater access to secure records than the state police computers did. Maybe here she could uncover the truth about her being dumped at the orphanage. Maybe here she could finally uncover the truth about the past she couldn't remember.

And she wouldn't let one stubborn assistant director, intent on *not* having her as a partner, stop her journey of self-discovery.

Printed in the United States
216960BV00001B/50/A

9 781893 896352